Scattered Thoughts

Betrayed by Love, Book 1

HD KELLEY

Green Way
PUBLISHING

ISBN: 0-9974335-5-8
ISBN-13: 978-0-9974335-5-5

PUBLISHED BY GREEN WAY PUBLISHING
www.greenwaypublishing.com

Disclaimer:
This book is not suitable for younger readers. There is strong language, adult situations, and some violence.

Dedication

A special thank you goes out to my family for their patience during this journey, and to my best friend, Christine, for her encouragement in the early stages, without which I may not have finished. And a very special thank you to God for giving me the courage to follow my dreams.

Scattered Thoughts

Chapter One

My eyelids were heavy and I struggled to hold them open. Something was covering my face. I pulled my arms toward it but they wouldn't move. I pulled again, even harder this time, still nothing. My arms were tied. My heart started to race and my breathing quickened. I twisted and turned, tugging against the restraints, trying to get free.

"Welcome back," a raspy voice whispered breathlessly against my ear. My body stiffened when I smelled it, alcohol and tobacco plus something else; a familiar sweet smell.

"Who are you?" I opened my mouth to ask but no sound came out. I couldn't speak. Everything was moving in slow motion.

There was a faint noise in the background. I concentrated hard on the sound, blocking out everything else around me. Violins and flutes were flirtatiously moving through the melody. I'd heard it before but couldn't place it now. My head was too foggy. The music was too low.

He ran his mouth down my cheek, stopping at my chin, biting it softly. His hand was in my hair. He pulled hard, jerking my head back, exposing my neck. His mouth was on mine. My jaw tightened as I pressed my lips together, trying my hardest to resist his efforts. He pulled my hair harder. When I cried out he won, pushing his tongue deep inside my mouth in a hardened kiss. His taste was even worse than his smell.

"Stop!" I pleaded when he finally pulled away, but my voice was barely audible. He released my hair and the music suddenly got louder. I recognized the eerie sound of the church bells; *Dreams of a Witches' Sabbath*. My body tensed once more as the bassoons and tubas barked out the haunting chant for the dead. My heart was beating so fast it left me breathless.

"Beg me," he whispered, his mouth against my ear once again.

Tears rolled down my cheeks. "Please," I begged.

A sudden pain in my ribs made me lose my breath. "Please what?" he shouted. I opened my mouth to answer but was still to breathless to make a sound. "Please what?" he screamed. The pain came again before I could answer that had me gasping for air that time.

"Stop! Please stop!" I said with panted breaths.

"Not until it's gone, Bella. All of it." He turned my head to the side and I felt a sharp pinch on my neck. My eyelids closed. I wanted to open them again but they were too heavy.

"What's gone…?" I asked, my voice fading fast.

• • • • •

I jolted upright in bed. Sweat covered my body, my face was flush, my breathing ragged. "It was only a nightmare, Izzy," I said out loud trying to reassure myself of that now. I took a few deep breaths in an attempt to slow my breathing and calm my racing heart. In through my nose and out through my mouth, focusing on each breath as it passed my lips.

It was still dark outside, too early to be up really, but I knew I'd never go back to sleep now. Not with the memory of that nightmare still fresh in my mind. My head felt foggy, a side effect of waking up breathless I suppose, but I did my best to shake it off as I crawled slowly out of bed.

My whole body objected as I stood. I grabbed the half empty bottle of Advil off the nightstand and popped two   pills into my mouth, swallowing them without water.

A sharp pain pierced my side when I pulled my nightshirt over my head but I ignored it like I had all the rest. They were only dreams after all; the pain couldn't possibly be real. I continued to dress for my morning workout then headed downstairs to the kitchen to start a pot of coffee.

The moon was reflecting off the surface of the water through the bay window in the breakfast nook. I stared out into the darkness, quickly getting lost in the peacefulness of the predawn hours, something I'd been doing a lot of these past four months. Sleep had quickly become a fading memory since that package arrived.

I'd thought it was a birthday present when the courier handed it to me. It had been my birthday after all and the box was wrapped in beautiful pink and silver paper. Only it wasn't a gift at all. No, it was my worst nightmare coming true; a box full of pictures of naked women and a letter claiming my husband of nineteen years was a sexual sadist.

There were dozens of photographs. Women

trussed up in a myriad of sexual positions, suspended from the ceiling by chains and leather cuffs, tied to a bed, to a wooden cross. Red marks and bruises all over their bodies, masks covering their faces effectively hiding their identities.

Tears pricked my eyes as I recalled the moment I'd confronted Spencer with the contents of that package. His eyes turned to stone when he saw them. A cold look I'd never seen there before. He'd insisted he didn't know those women. He'd demanded I believe it wasn't him positioned just far enough out of frame that his face was never completely visible.

"Damn it, Bella. You have to believe me. That isn't me," he'd said.

"If it isn't you then why were they hand delivered to me?" I'd shouted, unable to hide the disgust, the hurt, the anger I was feeling. "Why the hell would someone send me this trash then?" I'd demanded to know.

"To hurt us," he'd said simply, his icy stare still etched in my memory. He'd begged me to believe him but I'd filed for divorce instead.

"What if it *wasn't* him in those pictures?" I thought now. Tears rolled slowly down my cheeks as I mourned the loss of our nineteen year marriage.

The coffee pot beeped, bringing me back to the here and now. I wiped the tears from my face, poured myself a cup of the hot liquid and carried it outside into the cool morning air.

A strong sea breeze pushed the waves onshore. I closed my eyes and let my mind get lost in the sound but it quickly drifted back to Spencer. How could he do that to me, to us? We'd been so happy together, so in love, at least that's what I'd thought.

Tears rolled down my cheeks again, but this time I let them fall. I needed to let my pain out so I could finally move on. And I was more than ready to move on.

A strong gust of wind rushed over me, leaving me feeling cold. I shook my head, wishing I could shake it hard enough to erase the images of those women from my mind. Setting my now cold coffee aside I pulled a bottle of water out of the mini fridge on the patio and headed out for my morning run.

I jogged slowly onto Beachview Drive, picking up speed with every step as I wondered if I'd ever be able pick up the pieces of my broken heart. Faster and faster I pushed, trying to outrun the pain I was feeling, until my lungs were screaming for air. I inhaled deeply, but a sharp pain in my ribs stole my breath bringing me to a sudden stop.

I coughed as I struggled to catch my breath, instinctively reaching for my side but unable to still the pain. For a moment I thought it was my heart ripping in two from the pain of losing someone else I loved so completely. I was five when my mom left us but I still remember the pain of knowing she was really gone like it was yesterday. I'd thought I'd never experience pain that bad again, but I was wrong. Losing Spencer, having my family ripped apart, hurt so much worse.

When the coughing finally stopped I turned back around and jogged slowly toward home, doing my best to maintain even breaths while I pushed through the pain. As bad as my side hurt I was happy to have something to focus on other than my failed marriage.

The sun had just started to rise when I made it back to the house. I went straight upstairs to shower.

The pain in my ribs reminded me of that terrible dream that woke me as I pulled my t-shirt over my head. I stepped out of my shorts and panties and climbed into the shower, hoping the warm water would soothe my aching body.

After I dried off I slipped into a pair of linen pants and a long sleeve tee, my favorite work-from-home outfit. It was an arrangement I'd recently negotiated, but one my boss wasn't thrilled with. "A small concession, I suppose," he'd finally agreed when I refused to let it go. In return for his generosity I agreed to *try* to be at the office one day a week, although I hadn't made it in at all during the past three weeks with my new self-imposed travel schedule.

Spencer and I decided to hold off telling the kids about the divorce until after graduation, but with the words *sexual sadist* still fresh in my mind I hadn't been at all thrilled about sleeping under the same roof as him so I had volunteered for nearly every out of town project in the past four months.

Shaking all thoughts of Spencer and our pending divorce from my mind, I headed downstairs to start work.

Anna was in the kitchen making breakfast when I popped in for a second cup of coffee. "Good morning, sweetie," I said.

"Good morning, Mom. I'm making chocolate chip pancakes. You want some?"

Food had been the farthest thing from my mind recently, yet another side effect of all the stress I'd been under. "Thanks, but I'm not hungry."

Anna tilted her head to one side. "Your loss," she said with a crooked smile that reminded me of

Spencer. Tears pricked my eyes and I knew I had to get out of there before she started asking questions.

I poured myself a cup of coffee and hurried to the sanctity of my home office. With its large picture window overlooking the Choctawhatchee Bay and sunbeam colored walls the room felt vibrant and alive. It used to be my favorite room in the house with its grand view of the sunset, but lately it had become my escape, my safe place to hide from all the hurt I so desperately wanted to escape from.

My desk was littered with papers, another reminder of the funk I'd been in. Stacks of unopened mail, contracts I still needed to review, notes I'd scribbled on scraps of paper haphazardly strewn across my desk like snowflakes, each one its own unique shape and size. Pretending to still be madly in love with Spencer, when the mere sight of him made my skin crawl, was definitely taking its toll.

Graduation was less than two months away now. All I had to do was hold on for a few more weeks and Spencer would be out of my life. I'd never have to think about those awful pictures again. I would finally be free.

I'd been so lost in thought I hadn't realized my phone was ringing until it vibrated, notifying me of a new voicemail. I looked at the caller ID. Shit, Tim Howard, VP of Reputation and Issues Management at Dimarco, also known as my boss. *The one who isn't thrilled about the idea of you working from home*, my inner voice snapped.

I took a few deep breaths to clear my head then dialed Tim's number. "You *are* Izzy James," I said out loud as I dialed the number, my own private pep-talk to myself. "You're confident and in control," I added trying to convince myself of that now. Four months ago there wouldn't have been even the slightest doubt, but opening that package changed things.

Tim answered on the first ring. "Izzy, where were you? Did you get my voicemail?" he fired in rapid succession.

"I haven't listened to your voicemail yet," I said in a low tone, doing my best not to sound annoyed that it wasn't even eight o'clock yet and Tim was already breathing down my neck. I took another deep breath. "What's up?"

"I really like your approach to Ultimate Cruise's issue. I think the client will too."

"Thanks," I said cautiously, knowing full well that couldn't possibly be the only reason he'd called. I closed my eyes and braced for the bad news.

"I'm afraid something came up and I can't make the trip to Tampa with you today."

Tampa? Double shit! *The Ultimate meeting…* I'd forgotten all about it.

"What time's your flight?" Tim asked jolting me back to the conversation.

I opened my mouth to answer but then closed it again as I desperately searched my memory for the details of the itinerary Jonathan emailed me. "Noon," I finally answered, relieved I managed to remember. My voice was shaky and sounded almost panicked now; not at all the confident Izzy James Dimarco hired to do this job.

"Call me after the meeting and let me know how it went."

I blew out the breath I hadn't realized I was holding, relieved now that Tim hadn't noticed the shakiness in my voice. "Sure thing," I managed before he disconnected the call.

"Get it together, Izzy!" I admonished, disappointed I'd forgotten about the meeting.

Immediately, I tossed my phone to the side. There was no time to spare. It was almost eight and I needed to be in Pensacola for a twelve o'clock flight. It'd take at least an hour to drive to the airport with the spring break traffic *and* I still had to finish the timeline. I opened the Ultimate folder in the client directory on my hard drive and got right to work.

When I was satisfied with the work I'd done I packed up my laptop and hard copy notes then ran upstairs to change. With no time to obsess over wardrobe I went with a basic black pencil skirt, a pink multicolored sleeveless scoop neck blouse, and my favorite pink blazer. The outfit didn't exactly scream business professional but it was one I loved and I'd need all the comfort I could get now that Tim had left me hanging.

As I stripped out of my clothes I caught a glimpse of myself in the bathroom mirror. I'd lost weight these past few months, not surprising given the stress of the divorce and the nightmares, but still. My face was thin, too thin really, and pale. Definitely not the first impression I'd hoped for with this high profile new client but there was nothing I could do about that now. I took a deep breath and dressed as fast as I could.

I'd hoped to leave by ten so I could swing by the office to pick up the mockups I needed for the meeting but it was almost eleven by the time I pulled out of the driveway. Now I'd have to go with Plan B.

I hit the Bluetooth button on my steering wheel and dialed my office.

Jonathan answered on the second ring. "Izzy James' office."

"Hey, I'm running late," I said getting straight to the point. "Print copies of the timeline I just emailed you for the Ultimate project, then pack up the marketing pieces that arrived yesterday and meet me at the airport."

"Sure thing, Izzy. Oh, before I forget, Mr. Payne will be joining the meeting today—"

"Alec Payne, as in the CEO of Payne Enterprises?" I asked, unable to mask the confusion in my voice.

"That's the one…" I could hear Jonathan saying something else but his words weren't registering. I was still trying to digest what he'd just said.

Alec Payne is coming to the meeting. Surely the CEO of Ultimate's parent company had more important issues to handle than deflecting negative press about onboard illnesses and mechanical failures. It wasn't like *Ultimate's* ships had experienced any actual problems yet.

"Earth to Izzy," Jonathan laughed.

"I'm sorry… what were you saying?"

"Do you need me to print another copy of your action plan?"

"Actually, I'm good. I printed a couple spares already but I will need you to email me a copy of Mr. Payne's bio from the master file."

"Sure thing. Anything else?"

"After you confirm my return flight and schedule a car to pick me up at TIA, that'll be all."

"Already done. I'll see you at the airport."

"Thanks," I said with a loud exhale as I disconnected the call. I was nervous enough about the meeting without the added pressure of Alec Payne.

• • • • •

When the flight attendant announced it was safe to use electronic devices I powered my phone back on and got busy reading the bio Jonathan sent. I already knew Alec Payne was beyond wealthy and owned more companies than I had clients, but I was hoping the report would help me uncover who he really was, what made him tick. None of my previous research had uncovered much about him personally, other than he had a reputation of being a royal pain in the ass. There was plenty of information on his wealth, what properties he owned, how the stock prices had risen in every single company he'd ever bought. But who was he really? That's what I needed to know before the meeting.

Unfortunately, Dimarco's bio didn't tell me much more than I'd already known. The only new piece of information I uncovered was that he wasn't married, which surprised me given the fact he's forty five and has more money than many small countries. "Something must be wrong with him," I thought, even though nothing in the reports I'd read so far suggested it.

When I finished reading his bio for the second time, just to make sure I hadn't missed anything, I powered off my phone and tucked it safely inside my bag. I ran through my meeting notes one last time then allowed myself to relax for the first time in days. I closed my eyes and blocked out the chaos around me.

Spencer is yelling but I can't hear what he is saying. His voice is muffled. Who is he yelling at? Is it me? He moves closer, his eyes cold and dark. My head is spinning.

I jerked forward in my seat, my eyes wide open, my heart racing. Around me passengers were gathering their bags. We'd landed. I must've dozed off and was having another bad dream. I took a deep breath to steady my nerves then began gathering up my things, waiting to exit the plane.

Chapter Two

I followed the line of passengers off the tram and into the main airport terminal. After a quick scan of the area I spotted a tall, muscular man dressed professionally in a black suit with a white shirt and thin black tie. He was holding a sign that read "Ms. James", and I knew he must be the driver Jonathan hired. I walked toward him, flashing a welcoming smile as I approached.

"Hi, I'm Izzy James," I said, extending my hand for a handshake.

"Hello, Ms. James," he said, taking my hand in his. "I'm Preston. Mr. Payne's driver."

"Mr. Payne's driver?" The words were out of my mouth before I could stop them. I was expecting a car service to pick me up *not* Alec Payne's driver. Preston's lips curled as he tried to hide the smile that threatened. "Sorry, it's just I was expecting a car service."

"Mr. Payne wouldn't hear of it, ma'am."

The muscles in my jaw began to clench. I hadn't even met the man and he was already getting on my nerves. Did he really think I wasn't capable of getting myself from the airport to his office? "Thanks," I said, finally recovering my professionalism.

Preston nodded and reached for my bags, which I gladly handed over as my shoulder was aching under their weight.

Following Preston, he led me down the escalator, through the crowded baggage claim area, and outside to the waiting jet black BMW X6. He opened the rear passenger side door and motioned for me to get in. "Ms. James," he said simply.

"Thank you," I replied as I climbed into the car. When I looked up at Preston I couldn't help but notice how handsome he was; his freshly shaven head, his dark brown eyes, his caramel skin. He flashed a small smile and I quickly looked away, embarrassed I'd been caught staring. Preston closed the door without saying a word, but he didn't have too. I was already embarrassed by my reaction to him picking me up today and now I'd been caught gawking at him. This was not how I'd envisioned my trip to Tampa starting.

It was a short ride to Ultimate's office at 100 North Tampa. Preston pulled into the garage and parked in a space labeled *Ultimate Cruises*. He collected my bags and led me to the elevator. After pressing a code into the keypad, the doors promptly closed and the elevator started to move. The sudden jolt knocked me off balance. Preston grabbed my elbow, stopping me from falling backward into the elevator wall.

"Thanks," I muttered, embarrassed now by my clumsiness too. A small smile crossed his face for the second time but again he didn't say a word.

As we ascended toward the 42nd floor, I began to think about Alec Payne. I was still bothered by my lack of knowledge surrounding his reason for being at the meeting today. I'd spent hours discussing their issue and the desired outcome with Lily Roberts, Ultimate's CEO, plus several other department heads at Ultimate during the identification phase of this process. Any change at this point would jeopardize the timeline and could derail the entire project.

By the time the elevator stopped, my nerves were on edge. This was it. I was out of time. Taking a deep breath to steady my nerves I let Preston lead me out of the elevator and into the modestly decorated lobby of Ultimate Cruises.

The room was empty with the exception of a rather small seating area in the far corner, a long reception desk in the center, and a few potted plants scattered about. The space wasn't exactly what I'd expected given the address. 100 North Tampa had long been considered the premier address among Tampa businesses, so I was expecting something a little more grand.

A professionally dressed young woman with short, jet black hair stood to greet us. "Preston, Ms. James," she said coolly as we approached the desk. She scowled at me, her icy stare making me shiver. "I'll show you to the conference room," she said with the same cool tone. Without waiting for me to respond, she rounded the desk and began walking down the long hallway.

"Thank you," I replied as I rushed after her.

The grandness of the conference room certainly made up for the subtleness of the lobby. The view of the city below and the ocean beyond extended farther than the naked eye could see. Mesmerized by the beauty, I walked toward the floor-to-ceiling glass wall, momentarily forgetting all about Miss Jet Black and my fear of heights. I was reminded of both when my knees started to buckle.

"And there's a bathroom over there," I heard her say right before the door closed.

"Wait, where?" I asked when I'd recovered my equilibrium, but it was too late. She'd already gone.

It didn't take long to set up the few presentation materials I brought. All I had left to do was connect my laptop to their overhead projector and I'd be ready for the meeting. I attached the cable to my laptop first and was just about to connect the other end to the projector when the conference room door swung open.

"Ms. James," the young man at the door called out. I stopped what I was doing and looked over. "My name is Raul," he explained. "Mr. Payne has asked me to set the projector up for you."

"Thanks, Raul, but I can manage." I'd done this many times before and had the utmost confidence I could handle the job now.

"Mr. Payne insisted I take care of it, ma'am," he said as he gently took the cables out of my hand.

Control freak! My inner voice snapped. I wanted to slap her down but she was right, the meeting, his driver, Raul. The fact that Alec wasn't married suddenly made sense. He's a control freak. Who could possible put up with that long term?

"She's all yours," I said, stepping out of Raul's way. I'd dealt with the control freak type many times and one thing I'd learned was you have to pick your battles wisely if you've any hope of keeping up. I wasn't about to waste energy on something as trivial as this. If Alec was going to get all controlling over something as simple as setting up a projector I could be in for a long afternoon.

Raul finished in record time and left me alone once again. I glanced at the clock on the wall. Luckily, there were a few minutes before the meeting was supposed to start because I really needed to pee. I walked to the other end of the room where Miss Jet Black had pointed earlier and tried the first door I came to, praying it was a bathroom. It was locked. I tried another door but it was locked too. I moved to the opposite corner of the room and tried the only remaining door. I was relieved when it opened and moved quickly inside to take care of a pressing need.

My reflection in the mirror startled me as I washed my hands. "No wonder Miss Jet Black was scowling," I said out loud. Mascara was smeared all over my eyes, and my hair was a frizzy mess thanks to the Tampa humidity.

With a wet paper towel I wiped the mascara off gently, doing my best not to make it any worse. I dug a brush out of my bag and gathered my hair into a bunch before securing it with the clip I'd packed just in case I needed it. I freshened up my makeup then took one final look in the mirror before I headed back into the conference room.

When I opened the bathroom door, I was immediately frozen in place by the sight of what could arguably be the most beautiful man I'd ever seen. He was standing at the other end of the conference room, all tall and slender with a muscular build, his chocolate brown hair tousled in a way that seemed just perfect. Maybe it was just my libido talking but *damn* was he hot.

The mystery man wore dark gray slacks and a crisp white dress shirt that he had open to the second button. His sleeves were rolled halfway up to his elbow and completed his semi-casual look just perfectly. He stood with one hand in his pocket and tugged on his bottom lip with the other. I licked my own lips as I imagined what it would be like to have his sexy lips on me.

He looked up and for the second time today I was caught staring. I blushed and looked away, too distracted to even move. I took a deep breath to steady my nerves and when I looked up again he was standing in front of me. His bright green eyes staring back at me. I bit my lip and let out an unintentional gasp.

He broke out in a full mouth smile. "Ms. James?" he asked holding out his hand. I accepted it with a firm grip. "I'm Alec Payne."

My heart skipped a beat. I had to look away to hide the guilty look on my face. Alec Payne. This beautiful man I was just fantasizing about was *Alec Payne*, as in my new client? I squeezed his hand tighter. "It's a pleasure to meet you, sir," I said when I finally recovered my voice.

Alec pulled his hand back, shaking it in the process as if protesting the strength of my grip. "The pleasure is all mine, Ms. James," he said with a grin on his face, a crooked, wicked sort of grin that made me squirm.

I looked away again to hide my now flaming red cheeks. *Does he have this effect on all women?*

Only the sex crazed ones, my inner voice chimed in. I shook her off. This was no time for her sarcasm.

"Please, call me Izzy," I finally managed to say.

"Isabella."

I had to bite my cheek to keep from rolling my eyes. My inner voice was right. Alec Payne *is* a control freak.

"Mr. Payne, Ms. James," Lily Roberts said as she bounced through the door, quickly closing the distance between us. I opened my mouth to speak but she pulled me into a hug before I could say anything. "It's so good to finally meet you in person."

"It's nice to meet you too," I said when she released me.

"Did you have a chance to look over the email I sent," Lily asked, turning her attention to Alec.

"Yes. But I take it you haven't read my reply."

"Not yet, I've been in meetings all afternoon…" her voice trailed off as the two of them walked back to the opposite end of the room, leaving me to collect my thoughts and pull my head out of the gutter.

By four o'clock the eight invited executives, and the uninvited control freak, were all seated and waiting for me to start. I took a deep breath to steady my nerves then began. "Good afternoon," I said in my best Izzy James presentation voice. "For those of you I haven't met, I'm Izzy James. I'm the lead Issues and Reputation Manager at Dimarco."

"Oh, I like a woman on top," Alec whispered.

I resisted the urge to scowl at him, knowing my cheeks were undoubtedly red. *Is he intentionally trying to throw me off my game?*

Shaking him off, I continued. "I've been assigned to combat the negative effects the recent mechanical failures and illnesses onboard your competitor's ships are having on your business." I smiled at myself, happy my professionalism had returned. "Let me start by saying thank you for the opportunity to help you solve this problem. Ms. Roberts and I have discussed the issue at length and I've already prepared a full analysis."

I walked to the edge of the table and hit enter on my keypad. The presentation illuminated on the projector screen. "This first slide, ladies and gentlemen, shows the financial impact this problem has had on your bottom line this calendar year alone." I paused to give everyone an opportunity to absorb the figure on the screen before advancing to the next slide.

"There's no denying the problem, so it's really how we handle it that's going to make a difference," I continued. I pulled the copies of the action plan from my folder and passed them around the table.

"Does your plan include changes to our shipboard processes?" The director of operations asked without even looking at the document I'd just handed him.

"Actually, I'm proposing several changes to your current processes." I glanced around the table to gauge the reactions and was relieved when no one flinched. "All of the changes I'm recommending are designed not only to prevent the spread of illness but also to put your passengers at ease." I advanced to the next slide that highlighted the changes I was recommending.

"Are all these changes really necessary? We haven't had any problems with illness using the processes we already have in place."

"Just because you haven't experienced an outbreak of illness doesn't mean you've been problem free, Mr. Payne." I took a deep breath, doing my best not to sound annoyed. "Your current processes don't take into consideration public perception, and in many cases perception of a potential issue can be more harmful than the issue itself, sir." I turned back to the slide that showed the impact on Ultimate's bottom line. "I'll admit the cost of resolution is high, but as you can see the cost of not resolving this issue is even higher."

A wicked grin crossed Alec's face. "Fair point, Ms. James."

I flashed my professional smile, but on the inside I was screaming. Did he honestly think I'd waste my time suggesting changes that weren't necessary? Clearly Alec had no idea how busy I was.

After answering a multitude of questions surrounding the process changes, I handed out copies of the implementation plan and timeline. "I recommend implementing the changes one ship at a time," I said as everyone looked over the documents.

"Why not just rip the Band-Aid off?" Alec asked. I clenched my jaw, my nostrils flaring as I resisted the urge to roll my eyes. "It's a figure of speech, Ms. James. I mean why wouldn't we implement the changes all at once and just get it over with?"

"No shit!" I wanted to shout but I opted for deep breathing instead.

Alec tilted his head, his eyes never leaving mine.

"Sure, we could do that," I finally answered. "Of course, we'll have to decommission your entire fleet to make it happen."

"Let's not get ahead of ourselves," Lily interjected. "I want to go over this with our Shipboard Directors before we finalize the details, but I think the timeline will work just fine. Wouldn't you agree, Mr. Payne?"

I tilted my head to the side then too, a satisfying smile crossing my face as I secretly celebrated another win. Lily was on my side and, luckily, my contract was with her. Alec's jaw visibly clenched but he didn't disagree.

With that settled I went over the logistics of implementation, answering question after question as we went along. When we reached the last page of the report I invited everyone up to get a closer look at the mockups I brought. Alec stood, whispered something to Lily, and left the room. My body immediately relaxed the second he left. I hadn't expected the meeting to go off without a hitch, but I also hadn't expected a battle with an arrogant control freak.

"I love your approach, Izzy," Lily said, bringing me back to the here and now. "I'll review the timeline with our directors this week so we can get started."

After everyone had returned to their seats, I thanked everyone for their time and concluded the meeting. I smiled a satisfied smile, relieved the presentation was over.

Raul returned to disconnect his equipment from my laptop as I gathered up the rest of the materials I'd brought. I set the mockups on the table first then started breaking down the travel tripods.

A noise behind me caught my attention. I spun around to see what it was. My heart jumped into my throat when I saw him. Alec Payne was standing in the doorway.

"Did you have another question, sir?"

Alec strolled through the door, not saying a word, quickly closing the gap between us. My body tensed; my feet fused firmly to the floor. He reached around me and lifted the mockups off the table, gently brushing my hand as he did. My insides started to tingle. Damn my body.

Alec held up the prints. "I'd like to keep these," he said. "I might have more questions later."

"Sure," I answered, my voice barely above a whisper. I pulled a business card out of my jacket pocket and handed it to him. "You can call me if you think of any more questions." He took the card slowly from my hand, brushing my fingers once again. My insides were on fire. I looked down and zipped my bag, doing my best to hide my crimson cheeks.

"I can think of a few questions already."

"I'm sorry, Mr. Payne, I thought I'd answered all the questions." I took a deep breath and said a silent prayer that my color had returned to normal before looking up at him again. "Where would you like to start?"

Alec's head tilted to one side, a smile spread across his face. "What time is your flight?"

"It's not until ten o'clock, so I have plenty of time to go over your questions now."

His smile broadened. "Soon," he said looking right into my eyes. He reached up and pressed the button on the Bluetooth earpiece I hadn't noticed before. "Five minutes," he said before pressing the button again.

Bringing his attention back to me, he continued. "I'll meet you in the lobby in five minutes, Isabella." With that he sauntered out of the room, leaving me standing alone and confused, by both my reaction to him and what he had planned. I'd made plans to meet up with another client for drinks while I was in town and now I was left hoping this wouldn't take too long.

Preston appeared out of nowhere and grabbed my bags. "This way, Ms. James," he said.

I followed him down the hall and back to the lobby where Miss Jet Black was waiting. "You can wait over there," she said motioning to the only seating area in the room.

Not bothering to respond, I walked over to the white leather loveseat and sat down. Preston put my bags down next to me before disappearing once again.

I fished my phone out of my bag and typed out a quick text to my client, letting her know my meeting was running late, and then did a quick check of voicemail. Tim had already called looking for an update on the meeting I'd just finished. I laughed quietly at his impatience and deleted the message.

Spencer had left a message too. He called to tell me he wouldn't be home tonight after all. Something about an emergency he had to deal with in Chicago, but he hadn't elaborated on the details, not that he needed to. I was just relieved I wouldn't have to deal with him tonight.

"Ready, Isabella?"

The sound of Alec's voice made me jump and I almost dropped my phone. "Yeah," I said quickly, disconnecting from voicemail before tossing my phone inside my bag.

I hopped up off the couch and reached for my bags, only Alec beat me to them. "Allow me," he said, motioning toward the elevator where Preston was already waiting.

Deciding not to battle over who carried my bags, I headed toward Preston. "Where are we going?" I asked when the elevator started its descent.

"Do you like sushi?"

I nodded cautiously, unsure where he was going with his question.

Alec flashed a broad smile. "I thought we'd eat before we go over my questions," he said. I opened my mouth to object but my stomach stopped me with a loud rumble, a reminder that I hadn't eaten all day. "I really don't think I could concentrate over the rumbling in your stomach."

"Sorry, I… um, I skipped lunch today," I offered as an explanation, embarrassed by the sound my stomach was making.

"Good thing Oishi is close then," Alec said with a raised eyebrow that gave the distinct impression he was scolding me somehow. "Especially since you can't seem to remember to feed yourself," he added.

I gritted my teeth to still the snarky comment that desperately wanted to escape. When I eat, or don't eat for that matter, was none of his business.

We inched along in silence through the heavy downtown traffic before finally coming to a stop outside the Channelside Bay Plaza. "We're here," Alec said before hoping out of the car.

Distracted by the enormous ship anchored a few yards away, I didn't move, not until Alec opened my door. I accepted his outstretched hand and climbed out, my eyes moving to the ship's logo. It was one of Ultimate's.

"That's the Ultimate Fantasy, the newest in our fleet," Alec said, following my gaze to the massive vessel. "Her maiden voyage is Friday."

"She's beautiful."

Alec leaned closer. "Yes, she is," he whispered. His warm breath on my ear sent goosebumps down my side and I had to bite my lip to keep from moaning. It'd been months since a man had been that close to me and my body wanted more. Only Alec Payne wasn't just any man. He was a client. I pulled my hand back, but he tightened his grip.

"This way," he said, tugging me gently toward the

courtyard of the Plaza.

We walked past the fountain and the palm trees in the middle of the outdoor shopping center then up a steep staircase to the second floor where there were noticeably fewer people. Many of the storefront windows were empty and everywhere I looked I saw signs that read "space available."

"Where are all the stores?"

"Some closed, some relocated."

"Why? This place seems pretty cool."

"It *was*." Alec closed his eyes and smiled. "It will be again," he said when he reopened them.

"You sound certain."

"That's because I am, Isabella."

Controlling and clandestine! My inner self chimed in and I rolled my eyes at them both.

"Did you roll your eyes at me?"

My face turned bright red as I realized I'd been caught. I opened my mouth to speak but closed it again, not sure what to say at the moment.

"Well?"

Something about the way Alec asked made me squirm. My breathing increased and a nervous grin crossed my face. I broke away from his stare before my heart beat out of my chest. "Yes!" I said, much louder than I'd expected.

Alec squeezed my hand tighter and pulled me inside the restaurant without saying another word. He led me through the large dining room, past the Hibachi stations, finally stopping at a quaint booth in the far corner. I slid around the table far enough to ensure a clear look at the inside of the dining room full of tropical plants, Japanese antiques, and the most beautiful hand carved wooden tables I'd ever seen.

The deep rich colors of the décor and soft lighting offered a romantic feel that made me wonder why he brought me here.

"Can I bring you a drink, Mr. Payne?" our waitress asked.

"Bring us a bottle of the 2009 Wehlener Sonnenuhr Auslese and two glasses of water," he ordered without so much as consulting me. She nodded and walked away.

"It's a Riesling," he said, finally looking in my direction.

"What if I don't like Riesling?"

"Do you?"

"Well, yes," I answered honestly. "But that wasn't my question."

"You're the issues manager, Isabella. I'm sure you'd figure something out."

I shook my head, my level of annoyance climbing another notch.

The waitress was back in no time with our drinks. She opened the wine and poured us each a glass before placing the bottle in the center of the table. I picked up my glass and eagerly took a sip. "Oh, this is amazing," I admitted after I tasted it.

"I'm glad you like it. It's one of my favorites." Alec picked up his glass and took a slow drink, his eyes never leaving mine.

The intensity of his stare made my heart race again and I had to look away. "Do you know what you're having?" I asked, reaching for the menu.

"I do."

Alec motioned for the waitress before I'd even gotten the menu open, and she quickly returned. I looked up, ready to tell her I still needed a minute, but

Alec spoke first. "We'll have the Sex on the Moon and a Pink Lady," he said, flashing me that wicked grin of his.

A rush of heat coursed through me and I felt compelled to tell Alec about Spencer. "It's probably just the wine," I said silently, trying to convince myself he had no effect on me. But the words were out of my mouth before I could stop them. "Alec, I'm married," I blurted out.

He titled his head. "You're not wearing a ring."

"We're um… we're getting divorced."

Damn it Izzy! my inner voice admonished. I hadn't told anyone but Dr. Leonard and my attorney about my failed marriage. And this was hardly the time or place to start, either. I took another drink of the wine to strengthen my resolve. When I looked up again Alec was staring at me. "I'm sorry. I'm not sure why I brought that up. Can we just change the subject?" This was not a conversation I should be having with a client, especially one that made me wet just by looking at me. I took a long drink, then another, not stopping until the glass was empty this time.

Alec lifted the bottle and poured me a second glass. I took the opportunity to steer the subject of the conversation back to him. "Do you always order for your dinner guests?"

"I want what I want, Isabella." He lifted his glass of wine, his eyes still fixed on mine. "And right now I want to talk more about this issue you couldn't manage."

"I am managing the issue!" I snapped, my brain-to-mouth filter temporarily rendered useless by the effects of the alcohol. "You know, Mr. Payne, not all solutions include a happily ever after."

"Or maybe you just haven't found the right solution."

My mouth dropped open. Was he seriously going to try and tell me I hadn't worked hard enough to save my marriage? Oh, he wasn't just a control freak. No, he was an arrogant ass! He didn't know me, and he certainly didn't know the circumstances that led to my divorce.

Right when I was prepared to tell him what I thought of his assumptions and his opinions, the waitress returned with our food.

Seemingly unaware of my pending rage, Alec placed a couple pieces of each sushi roll on my plate. "I hope you like spicy," he said.

He lifted a piece from his plate in the air with his chopsticks. "To your new found freedom, Isabella." When I realized he was going to hold the food in the air until I said something, I lifted one of the pieces he put on my plate but immediately dropped it. We both laughed as I struggled to pick it up again with the chopsticks.

"You can use a fork, you know."

"No. I'll get it."

"Stubborn, I see."

"I'm not stubborn," I snapped. Alec raised his eyebrows. "Well, maybe a little."

"A little?" he laughed.

"Well, what about you?"

"What about me? I know how to use chopsticks."

I rolled my eyes and exhaled loudly, completely exasperated by this man.

"Didn't your parents ever teach you it's rude to roll your eyes at people?" he asked.

I rolled them again in an exaggerated fashion

then took a long drink from my wine glass, strengthening my nerve even more. "Apparently not."

"It's never too late to be taught, Isabella." Alec pressed his lips in a thin, hard line making me squirm. I tried to ignore his stare and the tingling between my legs but failed miserably. My insides were on fire.

Surprised by my reaction, I looked down at my plate and did my best to focus on the food before I said something I might regret tomorrow. I jabbed the chopsticks into the piece of sushi and somehow managed to get it into my mouth without dropping it this time. Alec poured us each another glass of wine and we sat in silence while we ate.

"How long have you worked at Dimarco?" Alec asked when I finally looked up from my plate.

"Long enough…" I lifted my wine glass and took a long drink. "You have nothing to worry about, Mr. Payne. We're the most requested team in Issues Management because we're good at what we do."

"I'm sure you are, Isabella." With a raised eyebrow Alec took the wine glass from my hand, replacing it with the glass of water he'd ordered me. His fingers brushed against mine and it was all I could do to sit still. "Drink this," he ordered. My sex tingled and I bit my bottom lip to suppress a moan. "Drink," he said again.

Without a word, I lifted the glass to my lips and took a long, slow drink, my eyes fixed on his now.

Stop this, Izzy! I shouted silently, willing myself to look away. I closed my eyes and took a deep breath, hoping to regain some resemblance of professionalism.

"Do you have any other questions, Mr. Payne?"

"Several," he said, that wicked grin returning. "How long ago did you file for divorce?"

"Four months." I quickly set the glass of water down on the table. "Alec, I haven't told anyone about the divorce yet. And I know I'm the one who brought it up, but could we please not talk about it?" I dropped my head, praying he'd let it go.

"How about a tour of the ship before your flight?" Alec asked after a long and uncomfortable silence.

"I'd love that," I answered honestly. I knew it probably wasn't a great idea, given all the wine I'd had to drink, but I didn't care. I was just thankful we were moving on.

Chapter Three

The sun had already set by the time we left the restaurant, and the air had begun to cool. Luckily it was a short walk to the ship anchored just behind the plaza. I grabbed hold of the rail and stepped onto the gangway, doing my best not to look down. The heel of my shoe caught on the metal surface of the passageway, and I stumbled. Alec reached down and grabbed my arm a mere second before my knee hit the ground. He pulled me into him, his arm gripped tightly around my waist. The warmth of our bodies touching had my insides tingling once again. This was so wrong. He was my client, and I was still married.

"Thanks. I've got it now," I said trying to pull away. Alec held on to me tight as he stared deep into my eyes. At that moment I wanted nothing more than to reach up and kiss him, to taste the saltiness on his lips. It took every ounce of strength I had not to. I knew I had to break the connection between us before it was too late.

With both hands on his chest, I pushed away from him. Alec let go of my arm, but wrapped his hand around my wrist and continued up the ramp.

"Welcome aboard, Mr. Payne," the security guard

called out as we boarded. Alec nodded but kept walking, not stopping until we reached the ship's main lobby.

An enormous stained glass chandelier with rich gold tones caught my eye. The dim lighting reflected of the marble floors, the deep red, blue, and green accents highlighted by the lighting two floors up. I could've stood there longer and watched the lights move, but Alec tugged on my arm.

Alec led me under the chandelier, past the grand staircase, toward a glass elevator in the atrium lobby. My eyes followed the lights on the elevator shaft, toward the ceiling some seven floors up. "Stunning," I said breathlessly.

"Isn't she?" Alec whispered, pausing momentarily to take a look around.

"Come with me. There's something I want to show you." Alec stepped inside the elevator, taking me with him. He pressed the number eighteen on the operating panel and the doors quickly closed.

The glass walls of the elevator offered an incredible view of the atrium as we ascended to the top deck. I moved closer for a better look but stopped when I felt my knees starting to buckle. Before Alec could notice, I stepped back to a safe distance so I could enjoy the view without the fear of falling or fighting the tingles that ran through me every time Alec touched me.

When the elevator stopped Alec led me out onto the open deck. My eyes darted from left to right, trying to soak it all in. "This way," he said as he gently tugged on my hand.

"Is that a track?" I asked when I spotted the smooth surface circling the deck.

"It is. Would you like to try it out?"

I did love to run but I wasn't so sure about running that close to the edge, especially this high up. "Aren't you afraid someone will fall overboard?"

"No," Alec laughed. "That's what the guardrail is for."

"Yeah, well, I tripped walking up the gangway, remember?"

Alec laughed harder. "Another good point, Isabella. Maybe you should stick to the track inside the fitness center."

I crossed my arms, feigning injury to my ego. Alec pulled me into his chest, my back to his front, and wrapped his arms tightly around me. "Pouting makes me crazy, Isabella," he whispered into my hair.

The energy between us was dangerously electric. I wanted to give in but I couldn't. I took a deep breath and wriggled free.

"Feisty," Alec breathed with a huskiness in his voice that had my insides tingling all over again. "Oh, I like feisty."

"Then you're gonna love me," I blurted out without thinking.

"Are you trying to tempt me?"

I tilted my head to one side. "Whatever do you mean, Mr. Payne?"

Alec shook his head. "Isabella, you're playing a dangerous game." I nervously bit my thumbnail to hide the guilty look on my face. He was right; flirting with a client was very dangerous, but certainly not a game.

"Wasn't there something you wanted to show me?" I asked, quickly changing the subject, my distraction technique hard at work.

"I know what you're doing, Isabella." Narrowing his eyes, he continued. "Luckily for you there *is* something I want to show you." He took my hand once more and moved gracefully toward the stern.

Alec pointed over the guardrail. "Down there," he said.

I took a step closer, willing myself to look. My legs began to tremble, but I grabbed on to the guardrail and peeked over the edge anyway. *Big mistake.* My knees buckled and I lost my balance.

"Whoa!" Alec reached out and grabbed me around the waist with both hands to steady me. His touch was like a jolt of electricity straight through my body and I quickly pulled away. "Are you okay?"

"Yes, um… thanks. I'm fine," I muttered as I stepped farther away from the edge and out of Alec's reach where I could regain my balance, a fact that didn't go unnoticed by Alec.

He inched toward me until I could feel the heat radiating off his body. "Is it heights you're afraid of? Or is it me?" I heard the question but for the life of me I couldn't make sense of the words. My mind was spinning. My legs were giving out. I reached out and grabbed Alec's arm. The corners of his mouth curled into a smile. Damn it. He was enjoying this. "So I guess its heights then."

My hand quickly retreated. "I'll never tell."

Alec took another step forward. Less than an inch separated us now. "Don't tempt me, Isabella, because I have ways of making you tell." His eyes narrowed and I wondered if that was a promise or a threat. My insides began to tingle once again. This was so wrong. He was a client, and I was still married. That couldn't happen, no matter how much I wanted him to make me talk.

"Is that a waterfall?" I asked by means of distraction, more for me than him this time.

"It is," he relented. "Here, take another look."

I took a deep breath to steady my nerves before accepting his outstretched hand. Anxiously, I walked back to the edge, doing my best to hide my mounting fear. With a firm grip of the rail I peeked over the edge once more.

The water flowed into a large, oval shaped pool that was surrounded by a garden of tropical plants several decks below us. I focused on the sound of the falling water and soon forgot all about my wobbly legs.

"Alec, it's amazing."

"It is," he said with a satisfied look that made me smile. He moved closer, wrapping his arms around me now.

Instinctively I leaned into him. *Stop this. Stop this now!* my inner voice shouted. I stood up straight but Alec didn't let go. And honestly, I didn't want him to.

"I could stand here with you all night, Isabella," Alec whispered in my ear, "but you have a plane to catch."

No, I wasn't ready to go. I wanted to stay in this moment, wrapped in his arms, warmed by the heat of his hard body, no matter how wrong it was.

Alec released me then tugged my arm, forcing me to let go of the rail. As we walked back toward the elevator I spotted a miniature golf course that I hadn't noticed earlier and was suddenly curious about the ship. "An outdoor track, a waterfall, a garden, mini-golf, what else do you have onboard?"

Alec pressed number fourteen on the control panel of the elevator. "I guess we have time for a quick tour," he said.

We stepped out onto the promenade deck. "There's a theater that way," Alec said, pointing toward the bow. He tugged on my hand, leading me in the opposite direction. "There's a video arcade for kids here and a casino for parents over there." He paused briefly, allowing me a chance to look around. "The bar behind me is alcohol free for our younger guests, but we can get a drink in the lounge."

Alec led me through the spacious lounge to a barstool in front of the sleek black bar and motioned for me to sit. He stepped behind the bar and pulled two wine glasses off the shelf, placing them both on the counter in front of me. When he leaned down I heard the cooler door slide open, and when he stood up again he was holding a bottle of Riesling. The same wine we'd had with dinner.

Alec moved with ease behind the bar and it made me wonder how much time he's spent here. *He probably brings women here every night*, my inner voice offered. I shook her off. She was probably right but I didn't want to think about that right now. It had been so long since I'd enjoyed a man's attention. And I was definitely enjoying Alec's. He filled both glasses and returned the bottle to the cooler before handing me a glass.

"Let's go. We don't have a lot of time." Alec extended his hand and I accepted it willingly.

We walked past a multitude of restaurants and shops, an art gallery, and several night clubs before coming to a stop outside the garden we'd viewed from the top deck. A sign outside the entrance read *adults only*. I looked at Alec, wide eyed, curious as to what I was getting myself in to.

"It's a place where adults can relax without the chaos of kids," he said as if reading my mind. I nodded, completely understanding the need for an escape, and not just from kids.

Beyond the entrance was a lush garden of tropical plants. There were several species of palms, plus an array of calla lilies, orchids, and the greenest big leaf philodendron I'd ever seen. Alec motioned for me to sit in one of the many lounge chairs that circled the pool.

I walked to the row of chairs and cautiously took a seat, taking extra care not to trip. I'd expected Alec to follow me, but when I turned around he wasn't there. Before I had a chance to look to see where he'd gone, the light inside the pool caught my eye. Quickly, the colors changed, fading from blue to purple to red before jumping out of the pool in a fabulous display of light and water mixed with sound.

"What do you think?" Alec's voice was a whisper behind me that made me jump.

"There you are," I exhaled, quickly turning to face him.

Alec broke out in a full mouth smile. "Are you always this jumpy?"

You'd be jumpy too if you were having nightmares almost every night, my inner voice snapped. I crossed my arms, feigning insult.

"Are you deliberately trying to drive me crazy, Isabella?"

The temperature of my face rose and I immediately looked away to hide my crimson cheeks. "Am I?" I wondered. He'd told me earlier pouting made him crazy and here I sit, arms crossed, bottom lip protruding.

Before I could answer, Alec grabbed my chin between his thumb and forefinger, slowly lifting my head until my eyes met his. "Don't say I didn't warn you."

I pulled away. "I have no idea what you're talking about."

Alec shook his head. "Rolling your eyes, pouting, and now *lying*." He inhaled sharply, closing his eyes as he did. The muscles in his jaw tightened when he said, "Someone needs to teach you some manners."

A nervous grin crossed my face. My insides were on fire. My heart beat faster and faster still. I hadn't even realized I was biting my lip until I tasted the blood. *Damn it, Izzy!* I admonished. *This is so wrong.* I took a deep breath, inhaling slowly through my nose and out through my mouth, over and over again until the tingling between my legs stopped.

I raised the wine glass to my lips and took a long, slow drink. "The lights and fountain are a nice touch," I said finally.

That wicked grin crossed Alec's face. "Dangerous, dangerous game, Isabella." He took a seat behind me. Heat radiated from his body and before I knew it my heart was racing all over again.

Breathe, Izzy, I chanted to myself. I took another long drink, nearly draining the glass this time. I was walking a fine line and I needed to get out of here before I completely crossed it.

Quickly, I stood. "We should go."

Alec looked up at me, his wicked grin replaced with a blank stare. "Okay." He stood, his eyes fixed on mine. "This way," he said walking past me.

I emptied my glass and put it down on the table

before following him out of the garden, neither of us saying a word until we were back inside the elevator.

"Thank you," I said finally. Alec's eyebrow raised, unsure what I was thanking him for. "Dinner. The tour of the ship. The ride to the airport."

"Anytime."

I smiled, a genuinely appreciative smile. In all honesty I hadn't had this much fun since that awful package arrived, confusion and all. I just wished it didn't have to end. But it did.

I stepped out of the elevator and began retracing the steps we took earlier. Alec quickly caught up to me. His hand brushed up against mine, sending sparks all the way through my body. I inhaled sharply and looked away, embarrassed by both my reaction and my behavior this evening. I did my best to steady my breathing as I picked up speed. Suddenly afraid of what might happen if I didn't get away from this man. "Dangerous, dangerous game," he'd said and I wondered now what he meant.

"Isabella, what's wrong?"

"Nothing," I answered quickly.

Alec grabbed my hand and stopped, forcing me to stop too. "Tell me. And I want the truth."

His sharp tone caught me off guard and had me spilling my guts. "Alec, I'm sorry." I looked down at the marble floor, shaking my head in disappointment of my indiscretions this evening. "You're a client and I've behaved unprofessionally tonight. I should go." I pulled my hand free from his grip and started toward the exit once more.

Alec's footsteps echoed behind me.

"Goodnight," the security guard called out as I walked quickly past him. I waved goodbye without slowing down, desperately needing to get off this ship. I moved carefully down the gangway, keeping a firm grasp on the rail in case I tripped. Every step had my breathing quickening and by the time my feet reached the concrete I was completely out of breath.

I walked back toward Channelside Bay Plaza, doing my best to regain my composure. I couldn't believe how I'd behaved. I was still married for God's sake. What the hell was I doing here with Alec?

"This way, Ms. James," Alec called out from behind me. I glanced over my shoulder to see which direction he was headed then changed course toward the car that was parked on the street nearby.

Preston opened my door when I approached. "Thanks," I said as I got in. He nodded and closed the door behind me. I took a deep breath, relieved to be alone, even if it was only for a minute. "Pull it together, Izzy," I whispered out loud.

Moments later the door opened and both Alec and Preston climbed in. "TIA," he said coolly.

Alec turned toward me, every muscle in his jaw clenched. I looked away, rolling my eyes as I did. I had my own issues right now. I certainly wasn't in the mood to deal with his.

"Just so I'm clear, Isabella, tours are off limits but you consider eye rolling professional behavior?"

I whipped my head back around, my look mirroring his. "As a matter of fact, I do."

Alec narrowed his eyes and I nervously bit my lip again. He reached over and tugged at my chin, freeing the trapped piece of flesh from my teeth. "Dangerous.

Dangerous game," he said once more.

Alec's touch was so electric it jolted me back in my seat. I had to stop this. Now. I pulled out of his grip and crossed my arms. "I wasn't playing a game, Mr. Payne. You asked me a question and I answered it. It's not my fault you can't accept the answer I gave."

Alec's jaw dropped. He closed his eyes, his jaw tightening once again and I got the feeling Alec Payne wasn't used to being challenged. "You're right, Isabella, you should go now."

Now you've done it, my inner voice chimed in. *You've pissed him off. This is why you don't get involved with clients!* I sat back in the cool leather seat and stared out the window, praying my unprofessional behavior tonight wouldn't jeopardize my business relationship with Ultimate Cruises.

We rode in silence the rest of the way to the airport. Preston pulled the car next to the curb in the passenger loading and unloading area and promptly hopped out. "Alec," I said, turning so I was facing him. "Thank you again and—"

"It was my pleasure, Isabella," Alec interrupted. He lifted my hand to his lips and kissed it gently. Instantly my insides began to tingle and I couldn't stop the sigh that escaped. Alec's grin returned. "Well, maybe not *all* mine."

Preston opened my door, pulling me away from that tantalizing moment. I hopped out of the car and looked back at Alec one final time. "You have my card, sir." With that I closed the door, relieved I'd managed to get out of there before things got any more out of hand. With a final wave goodbye I walked through the automatic doors toward the self-check kiosk.

When I got to my gate I sat down in one of the chairs and pulled out my phone. I needed a distraction before I started to panic about all that'd happened today. My reaction to Alec had me on edge. I'd never imagined meeting someone like him, let alone being remotely attracted to him. I wasn't sure what surprised me more, the fact that he was drawn to me, or that I could be drawn to someone as controlling as him.

My phone rang. Excitedly I looked at the screen, a pang of disappointment shooting through me when I saw it was only Tim. I should've answered but I wasn't sure what I'd say. *You played a dangerous game and lost!* my inner voice snapped. *You could tell him that.* I tried to shake her off but I couldn't because, once again, she was right.

"What have you done, Izzy?" I admonished. Dimarco had strict guidelines on professional conduct and they definitely wouldn't approve of my behavior tonight. "You've worked too hard to throw it all away," I scolded.

Even for the sexiest man alive? my inner voice chimed in again, in full temptress mode now. I closed my eyes to fully consider the question but was interrupted before I could come up with an answer.

"Flight 452 traveling to Pensacola now boarding at gate A15," the agent announced. I pulled out my boarding pass and photo ID, gathered my bags, and got in line, more than thankful for the distraction this time.

• • • • •

It was nearly midnight when we landed in Pensacola and I still had a forty-five minute drive to Ft. Walton beach ahead of me. I meant to have Jonathan book me a room since I had to be back here tomorrow morning for a mandatory staff meeting, but in my recent absentmindedness I'd completely forgotten.

There was very little traffic this time of night, so the trip home was quick. Even still it was well after midnight when I finally got there. The house was dark when I entered, with the exception of the light in the foyer that turned on automatically when it got dark.

Drew and Anna were fast asleep and the house was quiet. I sighed with relief when I remembered Spencer's trip had been extended. I was much too tired to deal with him tonight. I pulled a bottle of water from the refrigerator and headed upstairs to get ready for bed.

I'd finally managed to get Alec out of my mind and was ready for sleep to find me. Out of habit I picked up my phone to do a final check of email before turning off the light. Much to my surprise, there was a message from Alec.

Date: April 14, 2015 10:10 PM
To: Isabella James
From: Alec Payne
Subject: Your visit to Tampa

Ms. James,

Please let me know you've made it home safely. I look forward to discussing what else you consider professional behavior.

Until then,
Alec Payne
CEO, Payne Enterprises

I smiled as I read his email a second time, his words from earlier still ringing loudly in my ear. "Dangerous. Dangerous game," he'd warned over and over again. While I had no idea what he meant, my heart skipped a beat just thinking about him. These feelings I was having for this man were too conflicting. Part of me wanted to run away screaming, but the other part was begging to play. I decided to email him back tonight so he wouldn't worry, being Mr. Control Freak and all.

Date: April 15, 2015 12:51 AM
To: Alec Payne
From: Isabella (Izzy) James
Subject: Safe at home

Mr. Payne,

I made it home safely. Thank you again for dinner and for your concern regarding my safety.

Maybe we should discuss what you believe to be professional behavior. As you may recall, you didn't much care for my earlier consideration on the subject.

Izzy James
Issues & Reputation Management
Dimarco

I leaned back against the headboard, a satisfied smile on my face. When my phone vibrated with Alec's quick response my smile broadened.

Date: April 15, 2015 12:52 AM
To: Isabella James
From: Alec Payne
Subject: Your consideration on the subject

Ms. James,

Your earlier consideration was unreasonable. We can start there.

Get some sleep.

Alec Payne
CEO, Payne Enterprises

"What are you doing to me Alec Payne?" I asked out loud, even more confused now. I closed the email app and put my phone back on the nightstand before switching off the light. I pulled the covers over my head and squeezed my eyes tightly. Thoughts of Alec filled my mind as I drifted off to sleep.

• • • • •

It was cold and dark. I felt someone standing over me. I turned so I could get a better look but I couldn't move. My arms were tied above my head. I felt his hand on my face. I tried to pull away but he squeezed my checks, preventing me from moving. My heart was racing so fast I couldn't breathe. I didn't want him to touch me. I wanted to scream and run away, but I couldn't.

"Feel me, Bella," he moaned; his mouth on mine once again.

No, no, no! I opened my mouth to scream but no sound would come out. He claimed my mouth, plunging his tongue to the back of my throat. He smelled of liquor and cigarettes and something sweet. It was an awful combination that sent a shiver down my spine.

"No!" I finally managed to shout when he pulled away. I twisted and kicked my legs, trying to get away.

"Fight me, Bella. I like it when you fight me." The voice was so familiar.

"Get off me," I screamed as loud as I could, relieved my voice had returned. "HELP ME! PLEASE, SOMEBODY HELP ME!" I felt a sharp pinch on my neck. My eyes were too heavy to hold open.

Chapter Four

I jolted upright in bed and pulled my hands toward my face. Relief washed over me when they moved. Beads of sweat covered my forehead. My face was wet with tears and my heart was still racing. I took a deep breath, in through my nose, out through my mouth; first one breath then another until my heart rate slowed.

With moonlight shining through the window, I glanced around the room, stopping when I reached the doorway. My door was open. I was certain I'd closed it when I came to bed last night. I froze, my whole body tensing all at once. A shadow in the corner of my room moved. Heat filled my body as panic started to set in.

"Spencer!" I screamed instinctively, momentarily forgetting he wasn't here, and about our pending divorce. I switched on the lamp, but when I looked back at the corner where I'd seen the shadow, there was no one there.

"It was just a bad dream," I said out loud, hoping to calm my shaky nerves. "Just a stupid dream."

I lifted my phone off the bedside table; 5:11

flashed on the screen. "Not again," I sighed. "Not another sleepless night." My nightmares had been sporadic at first but that was the third one I'd had in the past week. Dr. Leonard said the dreams were most likely being manifested by stress and had suggested I take a few days off to unwind.

"If you want to get rid of your nightmares you need to find the stressor," she'd said. I knew she was right but with all the new clients I'd taken on this year, time off just wasn't a possibility, which left me with Plan B. It wasn't my ideal solution, as it required me to actually try to remember the dreams, but it was the only other suggestion she'd offered. I removed the spiral bound notebook from the bedside table drawer, flipped to the first blank page and started to write. All I'd managed to remember so far were a bunch of scattered thoughts but I kept doing it anyway.

Dr. Leonard's instructions echoed in my mind. "You're not writing sentences here, Izzy, just words," she'd said. "Consider all your senses." Dark. Cold. Pain. My body tensed as I remembered the pain and I dropped the pen.

"Breathe, Izzy," I said out loud. Knowing I had to get through this, I took a deep breath and closed my eyes. The chanting of the bassoons and the barking of the tubas rang in my ears and I recognized it immediately. It was the first symphony I'd ever heard, *Dreams of a Witches' Sabbath*. Spencer had taken me and my best friend, Valerie, to hear the Miami Symphony Orchestra not long after we met. Val had never shown much of an interest in classical music but she'd really wanted to come with us, and I hadn't objected. She'd always been like a sister to me. We'd grown up in the same tiny town, attended the same high school and even the same college. It felt natural that she'd want to experience this with me too. And, boy, was it an experience. That night I felt music in a whole new way, far beyond the isolated upbringing of a rancher's daughter. I was forever changed by the power, the emotion, the drama, the story without words.

Before going away to college my cultural experiences had been shaped solely by the events I'd managed to convince Jack Jones, my overprotective father, to let me attend while he worked the livestock auction at the Colorado State Fair. Most kids couldn't wait for the annual event, but I hated the fair. It was a constant reminder that a cattle ranch was merely a business, and the cows I'd helped care for since their birth were our product, a product that would end up on dinner tables everywhere. The only thing that made it bearable was the hope of seeing a concert, a rodeo, an art show, or some hot new product exhibit. It had been my only window to the world for years.

That trip to Miami was full of firsts for me. My first symphony, the first time I'd had sushi, the first time I'd ever been drunk. Not to mention the first and only time I ever kissed a girl. The three of us never talked about that night again. The details of the whole crazy weekend were still a blur really, except for that amazing concert that reached all the way to my soul.

I shook my head. "Focus, Izzy," I said out loud. I took a deep breath, closing my eyes once more, concentrating on smell this time. A shiver ran down my spine as I recalled the smell: cigarettes, alcohol, and something else, a familiar sweet smell. I opened my eyes and scribbled down what I'd managed to remember then quickly stuffed the notebook back in the drawer, relieved to be done with that brutal exercise.

Every sore, aching muscle in my body objected as I climbed out of bed. I picked up the bottle of Advil and shook four pills into my palm this time. I popped them all in my mouth at the same time then took a long drink from the water bottle I'd brought upstairs with me last night.

Gingerly, I made my way to the bathroom to take care of a pressing need. After my hands were dried, I brushed my teeth, pulled my hair into a ponytail, all the while doing my best to ignore the dark circles that had formed under my eyes from the severe lack of sleep.

My body was too sore for a run this morning so I slipped on my robe and headed downstairs for some much needed coffee. Voices caught my attention as I neared the bottom of the stairs. Nervously, I wondered who it could be. Drew and Anna weren't usually up this early and Spencer was in Chicago, wasn't he? As I got closer to the kitchen I could clearly make out Anna's voice, but the other one was still too faint. It sounded heavy, like a man's voice.

As soon I stepped into the kitchen I froze. *Spencer.* He wasn't in Chicago. He was here. My body tensed as images from last night's dream flashed through my mind.

"It was just a bad dream," I whispered, praying I was right. I wanted to ask Spencer when he'd gotten home but I was afraid I'd make a scene with the amount of adrenaline coursing through my veins.

"Look who's home," Anna said, bringing my attention back to her. "He made my favorite breakfast too."

Anna threw her arms around Spencer's neck and began a barrage of kisses on his cheek. He tickled her until she finally stopped. The two of them laughed hysterically as if sharing in some private joke, typical for them really. Anna and Spencer had shared a special connection from the moment he first held her. She'd always been daddy's little princess, and he treated her like one too.

I forced a smile in Anna's direction as I tightened the sash on my robe, suddenly feeling underdressed in Spencer's presence. When I looked up, I was relieved to find the two of them had returned to their conversation. I poured myself a cup of coffee and took a seat at the end of the breakfast bar, doing my best to hide my growing anxiety, desperately wanting to know when he'd gotten home.

"Mom!" Anna shouted. I looked up from my coffee. "I asked if you could drive me to school this morning."

"Sure. But I'll need to drop you off before eight."

"I better hurry then. Thanks for breakfast, Dad," Anna called out as she ran out of the kitchen.

I glanced at the clock on the stove. It wasn't even six yet. Anna may have been in a hurry, but it wouldn't take me near as long to get ready. There was plenty of time for me to get the answers I needed. "When did you get home?" I asked when I was certain Anna was out of ear shot.

"I've been home for hours, Bella," Spencer said. He leaned toward me, his face inches from mine. "That was some dream you were having." The smell of cigarettes and bourbon poured out of his mouth. The tiny hairs on the back of my neck stood on end and a shiver ran down my spine.

The room started to spin, my nightmare suddenly feeling all too real. My stomach somersaulted and I sprinted down the hall toward the bathroom, barely making it before the contents of my stomach were violently expelled into the toilet. The pictures, *those pictures*, flashed through my mind like a twisted silent movie. Deep down I knew Spencer would never hurt me, but even still, I couldn't shake the feeling of just how real my nightmare had been.

"You okay, Bella?"

"I'm fine," I snapped. "And stop calling me, Bella." The mere mention of that nickname made my stomach queasy recently, although I wasn't entirely sure why. I pushed my way past him and sprinted up the stairs, not stopping until I reached the master bathroom.

Locking the door behind me, I buried my face in my hands and I collapsed on the floor. "Please, Lord, let it be a dream," I cried. "They couldn't be real. How could they be real?" I cried harder. Spencer wouldn't hurt me. Not sweet, loving Spencer. Not the man who volunteered his time fundraising for Drew's soccer club and Anna's volleyball team, or donated his time to rebuild the no-kill animal shelter that hurricane Ivan destroyed, or spearheaded the holiday canned food drive every year.

No, but Spencer the sexual sadist might, my inner voice chimed in.

No, it couldn't be him. Not the man who thwarted every attempt for playfully rough sex. "I don't want to hurt you," he'd always say. Spencer never made me feel unsafe, not once in our nineteen year marriage. He wouldn't. He couldn't.

"Why is this happening?" I cried. "Why didn't I believe him?" He'd insisted it wasn't him in those pictures. He was so desperate for me to believe him but I'd filed for divorce instead. Maybe my nightmares weren't dreams at all. Maybe the stress was too much for Spencer to handle and he snapped.

An overwhelming urge to get out of the house came over me. I pulled myself off the floor and into the shower. The hot water was soothing to my aching muscles, but there was no time for that now. All I could think about was getting as far away from Spencer as I could possibly get.

• • • • •

I grabbed my phone and purse off the bedside table then headed downstairs to collect the materials I needed for today's team meeting. When I reached the bottom of the stairs I took my shoes off and slipped silently across the tile floor to my office. If Spencer was still in the kitchen, I certainly didn't want him to hear me. After I'd collected what I needed, I sent Anna a quick text, telling her to meet me in the car. The sooner I could get out of the house the better. I reached for the knob leading to the garage, but it turned before I even touched it. I jumped backward and tripped over my own two feet, landing hard on my backside.

"Mom, are you okay?" Drew asked as he reached down to help me up.

I accepted his hand with both of mine and he pulled me to my feet. "Thanks," I laughed, trying to play it off. "I'm fine."

"Where ya headed so early?"

"I'm taking Anna to school then I have a meeting."

"Anna can ride with me. You just worry about getting to your meeting in one piece." He laughed now too. Drew enjoyed poking fun at me and my clumsiness, in a kind-hearted, with all the love in the world kind of way. Fortunately, neither of my kids inherited my propensity for accidents but rather Spencer's athletic prowess.

"I have plenty of time. Plus, I already told Anna I'd drive her." "Well un-tell her." His smile faded. "If she'd get her license already she could drive herself. Now seriously, I'll take her."

"Alright, alright," I said, holding my hands up in mock protest. "You can take her." Really, there was no point arguing with him. They were headed to the same school, after all.

"Good. Now drive safe." He wrapped me up in a tight hug, kissing my cheek before letting me go.

"Have a good day, Drew. I love you."

"I love you too, Mom."

As soon as I got in the car I locked the doors, just in case Spencer was lurking around the garage, and then called Anna to tell her about the change in plans.

"I'm trying to hurry," she said as she answered the phone.

"Honey, Drew is going to take you. I hope that's okay."

"Actually, that works better. It'll give me more time to get ready."

I smiled as I imagined the stack of clothes Anna had already changed out of this morning piled high on her bed. "Have a great day, sweetie. I love you."

"I love you too, Mom."

When the security gate opened wide enough for my car to squeeze through, I hit the pedal, beyond thankful I'd managed to get out of the house without seeing Spencer again.

The drive to Pensacola gave me time to think, too much time really. Drew and Anna were graduating in June and Spencer would be moving out soon after. In less than two months my life would be forever changed, again. I'd been a wife and a mother for almost half my life and I wondered what I'd do now without either around to need me. It had been so long since I put myself first that I didn't even know where I'd start.

Valerie would know where to start. She had always been the queen of "me," refusing to be put second, no matter how many husbands it took to get what she wanted. The last time I talked to her she seemed happier than she'd been in a long time. Her new husband, Cody, also known as husband number four, was a successful finance manager and made a ton of money. Plus, he treated Val like a queen. That was all she'd ever really wanted, a man with more money than sense who would put her first no matter the cost.

Maybe we'd be able to squeeze in a girls' weekend while she was in town for graduation. It'd give us a chance to catch up and I could finally tell her about the divorce. She would be mad I hadn't told her sooner, but hopefully she'd understand why I couldn't. It wasn't like I got married without telling her, like she'd done to me, twice. Val had divorced her third husband before I even knew she had gotten remarried. To this day Val hasn't spoken his name to me, referring to him simply as "husband number three."

Traffic was heavy as I neared Palafox Street. A glance at the clock revealed it was twenty after eight and I was only five minutes from the office. The extra time would go a long way in helping me clear my growing to-do list. All the traveling I'd been doing lately had left me less time for paperwork and I was falling way behind.

My cell phone rang as I pulled into the parking garage. "Izzy James," I answered in my professional office voice.

"Good…good morning, Mrs. James," a shy voice I didn't recognize came across the speakers. "This is Haley, ma'am, Mr. Howard's new intern," she said, saving me the trouble of asking.

"Welcome to Dimarco, Haley. What can I do for you?"

"Well, Mrs. James," she fumbled the phone, "Jonathan isn't here and your eight o'clock appointment is wondering when you'll be in."

"Eight o'clock appointment," I thought to myself, searching my memory for details, coming up empty this time.

"I'm parking the car now, Haley."

"Um…okay. Is that what you want me to tell Mr. Payne?"

"Alec Payne?"

"Yes, that's him."

I exhaled loudly, not even trying to mask my frustration. "Show him to the conference room and tell him I'll be with him shortly." I disconnected the call without waiting for her response. Banging my palms on the steering wheel, I screamed as loud as I could. As if my earlier nightmare and dealing with

Spencer weren't enough, this was exactly what I needed today. There went my plan of getting caught up on my growing pile of work. Now I had to deal with Mr. Control Freak.

A hot control freak, my inner voice added. He was wonderfully good looking, but that certainly wasn't helping my mood at the moment.

I took the back stairs up to my office, hoping the exercise would cool my raging nerves. Unfortunately, my plan backfired as I grew more annoyed with each flight I climbed. The nerve of that jerk, he'd showed up without an appointment, and then told my bosses new intern I was late, for an appointment we didn't have! By the time I opened the stairway door on the fifth floor my blood was boiling.

Jonathan handed me a caramel macchiato as I stormed past his desk. I accepted it with a forced smile even though I really did appreciate that he'd gotten it for me. "He said he made the appointment directly with you," Jonathan said by means of an explanation for my early morning visitor, knowing all too well that I didn't like to schedule meetings before nine.

"That's right." I took a slow sip of the coffee, not offering any further explanation. "Thanks for the coffee, Jonathan. Please tell Mr. Payne I'll be five more minutes." I walked into my office and collapsed on the sofa, slowly sipping the sweet concoction, taking deep, deliberate breaths between sips. I needed to regain my composure before even attempting to deal with Mr. Control Freak, no matter how long it was going to take for that to happen.

Fifteen minutes turned out to be the magic amount of time it took before I could force myself off the sofa. Flipping through the files on my desk, I pulled out Ultimate's. With a final deep breath I tucked the file under my arm, pulled my shoulders back and glided down the hall to the conference room, ready now to take on the control freak that was waiting inside.

Chapter Five

I walked into the conference room where Alec had been waiting for the last hour. "Good morning, Mr. Payne."

Looking up at me, he said, "Good morning, Ms. James." That wicked grin crossed his face, making me blush. I looked at the floor, out the window, everywhere but at him until he stood and extended his hand.

Placing my hand in his, I expected a handshake but he lifted it to his mouth and kissed my knuckles instead. "It's a pleasure to see you again, Isabella."

My insides quickened. I pulled my hand from his grip and walked swiftly around the table, intentionally taking a seat on the opposite side, safely out of his reach. I needed to squash whatever ideas he had gotten from our dinner and tour yesterday. Dimarco had strict guidelines on client relationships and I wasn't about to break them to become Alec Payne's latest conquest.

"Did we have an appointment, sir?" I asked, doing my best to maintain a sense of professionalism despite my overwhelming annoyance.

"Don't you check your email?"

Seriously? my inner voice snapped and I couldn't help but roll my eyes. When exactly was I supposed to check email? He knew how late it was when I got in last night, and he was here before I even made it to the office.

Alec's jaw tightened. "So, you did read it?" His harsh tone told me instantly what email he was talking about.

"Please don't tell me you came all this way to discuss my views on the necessity of eye rolling." I laughed at the ridiculousness of it all.

"That, plus any other unreasonable considerations of professionalism you may have."

"You think *I'm* unreasonable?" I snapped, annoyed that he was wasting my time. "I'm not the one who boarded a plane and flew almost two hours to discuss whether or not eye rolling is an appropriate response to the ramblings of a control freak," I shouted, surprising even myself with my boldness in front of a client.

Alec leaned back in the chair, folding his arms across his chest, the muscles in his jaw clinching. I maintained eye contact, unwilling to concede defeat this time. "Control freak?" he said, finally putting an end to the awkward silence.

"Control freak," I repeated. "And now that we're both up to speed, Mr. Payne, I have a lot of work to do today." Alec's mouth dropped open but I didn't care. He was toying with me and I was in no mood to play. Not now, and especially not at my office. I might have crossed the line last night but I sure as hell wasn't about to let that happen again. I had to put a stop to this.

Gathering the file I needlessly brought with me I stood to leave, pausing to add, "The next time you're in need of self-discovery, please, make an appointment." I moved quickly toward the door before he had a chance to gather his thoughts. "Enjoy your day, sir." I called over my shoulder as I exited the room.

"I bet he wouldn't like it if someone wasted *his* time like that," I mumbled as I stormed off in the direction of my office. Alec Payne might have been accustomed to getting his way, but not this time. Not with me. I wasn't about to jeopardize my career to become his latest fling.

"Move my nine o'clock meeting to ten and hold all my calls," I said as I passed Jonathan's desk on the way to my office. Closing the door, I plopped down in my leather desk chair. "Control freak!" I said out loud, tossing the file I'd needlessly taken with me on top of the credenza.

I leaned back in my chair and stared at the stack of files still awaiting my attention. Exhaling slowly, puffing out my cheeks out as I did, I picked up the top file and started reading.

An hour later there was a knock on my door. "Excuse me, Izzy," Jonathan said poking his head into the room. "Your next meeting starts in five minutes."

"Thanks, Jonathan. Can you print five copies of the Sandestin action plan and the Ultimate timeline I just emailed you?"

"Sure thing." He pulled his head back out and closed the door.

Gathering the files I'd been reading into a neat stack, I placed the list of hand written notes I'd just compiled on the top. I took a deep, calming breath as I prepared to leave the safety of my office, not realizing until that moment I was about to return to the very room where I left Alec, mouth wide open, undoubtedly stunned by my outburst.

"He's gone, Izzy," I reassured myself. Alec Payne was not the kind of man who was going to sit around and wait for anything, well, except maybe an unscheduled meeting with me. The thought made me smile for the first time today and with a renewed sense of confidence I opened my office door and strolled down the hall to the conference room.

My team was already assembled when I arrived. I did a quick scan of the room and, just as I'd thought, there was no sign of Alec. A sigh of relief escaped me. "Good morning," I said in full business mode now. "We implement at the Sandestin next week, so let's start there." I passed around the reports Jonathan printed for me then took my seat at the table.

• • • • •

My list of notes was long and it took over three hours to get through them all. I assigned the necessary action items and was confident the work would be handled. I walked back to my office, exhausted from the marathon problem solving session, and more than ready for lunch. I'd skipped breakfast again this morning, a fact my stomach was refusing to let me forget.

"I'm going to Hopjacks," I announced as I passed Jonathan's desk. I needed food, and I needed to get out of here, even if it was only for an hour. Hoping to avoid Tim, I hurried down the hall to the stairs. If he saw me I knew I could forget about lunch. I ducked inside the stairwell and moved quickly down the five flights of stairs, pausing only to straighten my skirt once I reached the bottom floor. I needed time. Time to breathe, time to process all that had happened since yesterday and, more importantly, time to figure out how to get Alec Payne out of my head because no matter how hard I tried, or how much I wanted to, I hadn't been able to make that happen.

The cool, salty, air invigorated me and I strolled down the sidewalk toward Hopjacks Pizza. There was already a line of people at the door: business professionals, families, locals, tourists, all waiting for a table. But not me, no, I moved past the mob and headed straight for the bar.

"What'll it be?" the bartender asked after I'd settled into one of the high back stools.

"Caprese salad and a glass of water, please."

And a glass of that Riesling you like so much, my inner voice coaxed. "I'll have a glass of Chateau St. Michele too," I added, quickly surrendering to her temptation.

"Coming right up." The bartender poured the wine and set the glass down on a cardboard coaster in front of me. I wasted no time in tasting it. It wasn't as good as the wine I'd had last night with Alec, but it was still one of my favorites.

Blocking out the chaos around me, I sat in silence, sipping the glass of wine as I waited for my lunch to arrive. Without permission, thoughts of Alec kept popping into my head: his beautiful body, his smile, that wicked grin. His words, "Dangerous, dangerous game," rang in my ears again and I couldn't help but wonder what he'd meant.

The bartender set my lunch on the counter in

front of me. "Can I get you another?" he asked, pointing to the nearly empty glass of wine in my hand.

As much as wanted another glass I still had work to do today. "I better stick to water."

He smiled and walked away, leaving me alone to eat my lunch. One bite of tomato drizzled with the balsamic vinegar glaze, and food was all I could think about. My stomach growled, encouraging me to eat faster. The fresh mozzarella practically melted in my mouth, and that was all the encouragement I needed. Bite after bite I powered through the food on my plate.

When I'd finished eating the bartender returned with a fresh glass of wine. "Compliments of that gentleman over there," he said, motioning to the end of the bar. I closed my eyes, secretly hoping it was Alec but afraid to look.

"Thanks," I said when I opened my eyes again. I lifted the glass and took a long drink, deliberately looking in the opposite direction of where he'd pointed. If it wasn't Alec, I didn't care who'd sent it, and if it was him, well, that was a whole different problem.

The mystery was quickly solved when Alec took the seat next to me. "Drinking on the job, I see," he teased.

"It's from a client," I snapped, conflicted by the feelings he elicited and my responsibility of professional conduct. "What are you doing here?"

"Ironing out the details of my latest contract."

Shit. Now I'd have to apologize. I'd accused him of flying here to see me when really he had business to take care of. Before I could formulate a complete sentence that resembled an apology, I heard my name being called.

"Izzy." I heard again, only this time I knew who it was. I turned just in time to see Tim approach, waving a file in his hand.

"Hey, Tim, what's that?"

"Our newest contract."

"Ultimate's contract?" I asked cautiously. Tim nodded and I slowly started to put the pieces together. Alec wasn't meeting about some other contract. He'd gone over my head and finalized the Ultimate contract with my boss. Turning back to the bar, I took a long drink of the wine Alec had ordered for me, trying not to think about what all the control freak managed to change without my knowledge.

"Wait until you hear the good news, Izzy," Tim said, barely able to contain his excitement. "We're going on a cruise."

"Who's going?"

"You and Tim," Alec chimed in. "You're coming on the maiden voyage of Ultimate's newest ship."

"The Ultimate Fantasy," I muttered, unable to believe what I was hearing. I'd declined the trip two weeks ago when Lily invited me. Going away would involve rescheduling dozens of meetings and that would put me even further behind than I already was.

"Yes, that's the one," Tim said.

"But that cruise departs Friday, as in two days from today."

"Actually, you're flying over tomorrow," he said. "It'll give you an opportunity to observe the crew's processes before the passengers arrive." It didn't take a genius to figure out who came up with that bright idea. *Control freak!*

"Mr. Payne is sending his corporate jet to pick you up tomorrow night."

I shook my head. "Of course he is," I snapped, my nerve strengthened once again by the wine.

"That isn't a problem for you, is it?" Alec asked.

Of course it's a problem you control freak! I wanted to scream and yell and maybe even throw things, but I doubted Tim would appreciate any of those things so I opted for deep breathing instead.

"Izzy, this isn't a problem, is it?" Tim asked in that 'you better not ruin this for me' kind of tone.

"Not at all," I said finally. When I looked over at Alec, that wicked grin crossed his face and I blushed. *Damn it.*

"It's settled then," Tim said. "Alec, I'm sorry about how things went with your morning meeting but I'm glad it gave us the opportunity to finalize your contract with Dimarco."

Alec shook his hand. "I'm happy we got that finalized too. It's nice to meet someone who appreciates client expectations as much as I do." Alec looked right at me. "And strives to meet them."

"I'm afraid I have to get back to the office, but Izzy will email you the finalized contract later today." Tim nodded at me then walked away, leaving us alone.

I took another drink from the wine glass I was now clutching. "I should go too. Apparently I have a contract that needs to be edited and emailed to a client today, along with all the other shit on my to-do list."

"Maybe your client will give you until morning."

"Doubtful. He's a real control freak."

"Maybe he just knows what he wants."

I took another drink. "Maybe he needs to realize he can't always get what he wants."

"Says who?"

"The Rolling Stones for starters. They have a whole song about it."

Alec laughed. "Fair point, Isabella, but I'm afraid I don't subscribe to every belief someone has written a song about."

I rolled my eyes. "So, what, you just expect people to give you what you want simply because you want it?"

"I expect a lot of things, but I never expect them to be *given* to me."

"Then you don't expect to always get what you want?"

"That's not what I said. I work very hard to secure the things I want, Isabella." Alec leaned toward me and pushed my hair off my shoulder. Goosebumps covered my neck then ran down my arm. "And what I want right now is for you to stop rolling your eyes at me."

My insides quickened. I took another drink to strength my nerve. "Well, you're going to have to work extra hard to make that one happen." I bit my bottom lip to keep from rolling my eyes at him now.

He reached over and pulled on my chin, simultaneously freeing my trapped lip and making me squirm. "I guess I could learn to live with that," he whispered.

I lifted the wine for another drink, but Alec took the glass out of my hand. "I'd say you've had enough wine for a workday lunch. Let's go. I'll walk you back to your office."

I sighed, unable to mask my irritation at his

controlling tendencies any longer. "You go ahead. I need to settle my tab."

Alec pulled a fifty from the money clip in his front pocket and tossed it on the bar next to my glass. "Now can we go?"

I opened my mouth to object but closed it again. There was no point in arguing with him. Besides, he owed me lunch after going over my head to get what he wanted. Alec put his arm around my shoulder when I stood to leave and escorted me through the crowd to the sidewalk.

"Thank you for lunch, Alec," I said after we left.

"You're quite welcome. I would have preferred if we'd eaten lunch together though."

"And I would've preferred it if you hadn't gone over my head to get your way."

"Fair enough."

Alec and I walked in silence the remaining distance to the lobby door of the Theisen building. He released my arm and turned to face me.

"I'll email you the new contract documents as soon as they're finished," I said nervously.

He held open the door. "Until then," he whispered, dangerously close to my mouth. It was more than enough to make me blush. Damn him. Clearly he could see the effect he had on me and it made me wonder why he was purposely trying to get a rise out of me.

I walked to the bank of elevators and waited. Normally I'd take the stairs so I didn't have to wait, but today it sounded like a good idea. I was still irritated that Tim had committed me to this cruise without talking to me about it first, so I wasn't in a hurry to get back to the office.

As I waited for the elevator I replayed Alec's words again and again in my mind. "I work hard to secure the things I want," he'd said. I couldn't help but wonder what it was he really wanted. Sex? Control? To annoy the hell out of me?

Jonathan wasn't at his desk when I got back to the office, so I was able to slip by without being noticed. Tim had left a copy of his notes on my desk chair, ensuring I'd see them I guessed. I picked up the stack of papers and began scanning for changes.

Everything seemed reasonable until I reached the page that covered reporting. The new contract called for a weekly in-person status update. I skipped ahead to the budget to see if Tim left any money at all in the contingency account. My mouth dropped open when I saw the changes they'd made there. All travel related expenses were being funded separately by Payne Enterprises with an indeterminate dollar amount.

"Control freak," I growled.

After I'd regained my composure, I turned back to the page that committed me to a weekly trip to Tampa for the next several months and started editing. I did a final run-through to make sure I caught all the changes. When I was satisfied I'd found them all, I hit save then emailed it to Alec and Lily, copying Tim on the email so he'd know it'd been done.

I shut down my computer and packed up the files that still needed my attention. Since I was leaving town tomorrow I was left with no choice but to take them with me. Stuffing the files in my laptop bag, I turned off the light and made my way to the parking garage and the sanctity of my car.

Chapter Six

I pulled out of the parking garage and drove slowly toward home. I hadn't heard from Spencer all day, so I had no idea if he'd be at home tonight or not. With my anxiety building I gripped the steering wheel tight. I didn't want to stay at the house with him there, not after that dream last night, or after finding him there this morning.

Just call Anna, my inner voice coaxed. If anyone had heard from Spencer it'd be Anna.

She answered on the first ring. "Hey, Mom."

"Hey, sweetie, how was school?"

"It was amazing. I had meetings all morning so I got out of most of my classes. Prom committee, senior activities committee, French club, there's so much going on." That's my Anna, Ms. Social. She spent the next several minutes filling me in on the details of prom and the upcoming panoramic picture of the senior class they were trying to schedule. Focusing on the road, I did my best to keep up with what she was saying.

"Oh, before I forget, dad left a little while ago. He said he'd be gone until Saturday. You'll be here though, right?" Anna didn't like it when Spencer and I traveled at the same time and had only recently come to accept it as a reality for our family. It wasn't that Anna was afraid to stay home alone, well, with Drew. But what she *was* afraid of was having some place she needed to be and no ride to get there. Drew would let her tagalong with him most of the time, but only if they were going to the same place. It drove Drew nuts that Anna refused to get her license.

"Actually, I have a trip too. I'm leaving tomorrow night, but I'll call Sara to see if she can stay at the house until dad gets back." Sara Pike, our part-time housekeeper, also doubled as Anna's own personal taxi service from time to time. Anna adored Sara and was always excited when she stayed over. They were almost like sisters really. Sara had lived with us while she was in college and the two of them became pretty close.

I hung up the phone, relieved I wouldn't have to see Spencer again until after my trip but worried Sara wouldn't be able to stay. I crossed my fingers and dialed her number.

"Hi, Izzy."

"Hey, Sara, I need a favor," I said, getting straight to the point.

"Sure, what's up?"

"Spencer and I are both traveling, and I'm hoping you can stay at the house with the kids for a few days."

"Of course. I'd love to stay. Brandon is away for some training thing and it's been so lonely around here."

"Oh, Sara, thank you. You really are the best."

"You know I love staying with them, Izzy. How

about I come tonight?"

"Sure. Come anytime." I couldn't help but think how blessed we were to have someone like Sara in our lives.

When I walked inside the house an hour later I could hear Anna and Drew laughing. The smell of shrimp flowed from the kitchen, pasta and garlic too. Putting my bag down on the entryway table I walked toward the sound.

"Mom," Anna squealed when she saw me.

"Look, Sara made dinner, angel hair pasta with shrimp and a white wine garlic sauce," Drew said.

"Wow, thanks, Sara. It smells delicious."

Sara poured a glass of wine and handed it to me. "I hope it tastes okay. I'm still getting a grip on the whole cooking thing."

"I'm sure it'll be amazing," Drew said.

"I'm so grateful you could come on short notice. I don't know what we'd do without you, Sara."

"Don't be silly, I'm glad you called. I was going out of my mind in that house all alone."

The timer buzzed. Drew pulled a tray of garlic bread out of the oven. Sara drained the pasta. Anna began setting the table. All three moving in synchronized rhythm. A smile crossed my face as I soaked in the moment, doing my best not to think about how much I was going to miss this when they left for college in a couple of months.

When the dinner mess was all cleaned up, I kissed the kids goodnight, thanked Sara again, with a big hug this time, and headed upstairs to get ready for bed, more than exhausted now.

I picked up my phone to do a final check of email but thought better of it and dropped it on the side table. Turning off the light, I laid my head on the pillow. The moonlight flooded my room, enveloping me like a blanket, soft and comforting with a gentle ease. I closed my eyes and drifted off to sleep.

• • • • •

The next morning I woke up early, relieved I hadn't had another nightmare. After washing up I pulled on my running clothes then headed downstairs for a cup of coffee. Sara was already up and had the coffee brewed. We made small talk while I drank my standard morning cup before I headed out for a run.

Faint shades of orange and blue slowly chased the night away as I ran along Beachview Drive. The pain in my ribs was all but gone now, so I pushed myself harder than I had in days. It felt good to work this hard. The sound of my feet hitting the pavement soothed me like nothing else could. The faster I ran, the harder I worked, the more relaxed I became.

I sprinted up the stairs to shower as soon as I got back. There were several things left for me to do before my trip and I didn't have all that much time. Grabbing my phone from the bedside table I glanced down at the screen to see exactly how much time I had.

Shit. I'd already missed three calls. Quickly, I ran through caller ID: Tim, Tim, Jonathan. Given it was barely after seven o'clock in the morning I decided whatever it was they needed could wait until after my shower.

I dried off then slipped on a pair of linen pants and a long sleeve t-shirt. I'd change for my flight later but there was no reason I couldn't be comfortable now. Pulling my hair into a loose ponytail I headed downstairs to my office.

My phone rang again before I could even sit down at my desk. "Good morning, Jonathan. What's up?"

"Have you talked to Tim today?"

"Not yet. What's going on?"

"There's a picture of you and Mr. Payne on the home page of the Daily News and he's on the warpath about it." We all knew the risks of taking on such a high profile client, so I couldn't imagine what the big deal was all about, not to mention the Daily News was nothing more than a glorified gossip rag, with reporters following around high profile business professionals and local celebrities to garner higher advertising dollars. Tim should be more embarrassed to admit he actually read the trash they call news.

"What is it, exactly, that he's mad about?"

"A picture is worth a thousand words, Izzy."

"Alright, give me a second. Let me pull it up." I fired up my laptop and pulled up the webpage. *Shit.* Sure enough, right on the home page, there was a picture from Hopjacks. Alec was whispering in my ear. I was biting my lip, a wine glass in hand.

"It's not what it looks like."

"You don't have to convince me. I know you'd never cross the line. Tim's the one who's freaking out."

"Thanks," I said, feeling more than a little guilty, knowing how dangerously close to the line I'd been with this client. "I better give him a call."

I hung up the phone and stared at the picture that was splashed across the page as I waited for the article to print. *Now you've done it*, my inner voice snarled.

"Alec Payne, billionaire entrepreneur, reportedly in town to finalize the purchase of the Bayfront Stadium, spotted having a romantic lunch at a local restaurant yesterday with an unnamed

female companion," the headline read. Good, they hadn't mentioned my name. I quickly scanned the article. *"The two were later seen in what could be described as an intimate embrace outside the Theisen building,"* the article said. Double Shit!

My phone rang again. I took a deep breath then answered it. "Good morning, Tim."

"Have you seen the picture on the Daily News?"

"I'm reading the article now."

"What the hell happened after I left you two yesterday?"

"Nothing. I finished the glass of wine Mr. Payne ordered for me and then he walked me back to the office. End of story."

"Yeah, well, this picture tells a much different story."

"I can see that," I snapped, annoyed by his assumptions. "Fortunately, my name isn't mentioned and neither is Dimarco's. And now we know to watch out for reporters when Mr. Payne is around," I added, doing my best to minimize the issue.

"I'm having second thoughts about you taking this trip now, Izzy. Maybe you should have Steve run point on this project." Triple shit. He wasn't just mad, he was pissed. Tim had never pulled me off of a project before.

"Are you serious?" When Tim didn't answer I took a deep breath to calm my nerves. "If that's what you really want I'll email Ms. Roberts and Mr. Payne today to notify them of the change."

"Let me know when it's done." He slammed the phone down in my ear and I had my answer. I ran my hands through my hair, unable to believe this was happening. I'd told Alec I was only interested in a professional relationship. I told him there were strict guidelines at Dimarco. I even tried to ward him off but

I'm the one in trouble?

"It's so unfair!"

"What's not fair?"

I looked up from the article only to find Drew standing in front of my desk. "It's nothing, just work."

"That doesn't look like nothing," he said pointing at the picture of me and Alec. I rubbed my forehead, not him too.

"Pictures can be deceiving, Drew."

"So you're telling me you're not having a glass of wine and biting your lip as that man," he leaned over my desk a little farther, "that billionaire, pushes a strand of hair off your shoulder?"

"Drew, please—"

"Answer me, Mom. Were you on a date with that man? Are you cheating on dad?"

"Of course not!" I stood in protest. "I was at lunch. Alone. I had no idea Mr. Payne was even there."

"So you admit you know him."

"Yes. He's a new client. He was having lunch with my boss when he saw me eating alone and he stopped to say hello."

"Has dad seen this?"

"There's nothing to see, Drew. Now I just told you what happened and I'm not going to discuss it anymore." I sat back down, staring down at my desk. "Why aren't you in school anyway?" I asked, desperately wanting to change the subject.

"Ya know, I'm not as blind as you think I am." Drew stormed out of my office, slamming the door behind him.

"This is so unfair!" I screamed at the top of my lungs. Drew was mad at me and my boss had asked me to step down, all because of one stupid picture. We weren't even having lunch together. And I certainly wouldn't call it romantic.

Leaning back in my chair I took a deep breath, and typed out the message. This was out of my hands and I was just ready to get this over with.

Date: April 16, 2015 07:45 AM
To: Alec Payne; Lily Roberts
Cc: Tim Howard; Steve Lange
From: Isabella (Izzy) James
Subject: Personnel Change

Mr. Payne and Ms. Roberts,

Effective immediately Steve Lange will be running point on your project. Steve has been involved with the project from inception and I expect a seamless transition.

Sincerely, Izzy James
Issues & Reputation Management
Dimarco

Maybe this was best. My life had gone from bad to worse since meeting Alec Payne. His words rang in my ear again. "Dangerous, dangerous game," he'd said. I wondered now if this was what he'd meant.

That familiar tone announced a new email. Great, it's from Tim. I'd already done what he asked. What could he possibly want now? I double-clicked on the message and braced for the worst.

Date: April 16, 2015 07:50 AM
To: Isabella (Izzy) James

From: Tim Howard
Subject: Ultimate

Izzy,
Perhaps I overreacted. You're still running point.

Use caution.

Tim Howard
VP Issues & Reputation Management
Dimarco

Just when I'd convinced myself this change was for the best. Silently I wondered if Alec had anything to do with Tim's sudden epiphany, until the tone sounded again.

Date: April 16, 2015 07:52 AM
To: Isabella James
From: Alec Payne
Subject: Personnel change

Isabella,

In case you haven't already heard, your request is denied.

I'm sorry about the picture. Preston will pick you up at seven thirty.

Until then,
Alec Payne
CEO, Payne Enterprises

"He's sorry about the picture?" I said out loud. My boss was furious. My son thought I'd betrayed his father. And Alec was sorry? I shook my head, unable to believe this was happening.

I should've known Mr. Control Freak would object to the change. After all, he did revise the contract so I'd be forced to come to Tampa every week for a status update, a task that could easily be accomplished with a phone call. I tossed the newspaper into the trash, hoping for an out-of-sight out-of-mind kind of thing.

Pulling myself to my feet I headed into the kitchen for another cup of coffee. It wasn't even eight o'clock and I was already exhausted. All these ups and downs, I was ready to get off this rollercoaster ride.

After the fresh pot of coffee had finished brewing I poured myself a cup then went straight back to my office. I buried myself in work, not emerging from behind my locked door until I heard Anna and Sara in the kitchen several hours later.

I walked out of my office, doing my best not to think about that unfortunate photo op, praying Anna hadn't seen it too. "Hey," I said as I entered the kitchen.

"How was work, Mom?" I couldn't help but notice the clipped tone in her voice but didn't call her on it.

"It's work. I'd rather hear about your day."

Anna tossed a copy of the picture from the article on the counter in front of me. "Well, I want to hear about this!"

Shit. I closed my eyes and took a steadying breath. "Anna, it's not what you think."

"Then what is it?"

"He's a client. I ran into him at Hopjacks yesterday when I was having lunch. That's it. There's nothing else to tell."

"The article says you were having a romantic lunch."

"Anna, I have no control over what's published on that site, but I'm telling you, he's just a client."

"Mom, look at this." She poked the picture with her index finger. "Look at the way he's touching you. Look at your face. Don't sit there and tell me he's just a client!" she screamed.

I'd never seen Anna this angry before. I opened my mouth to speak, but closed it, afraid anything I said now would only make matters worse. She stormed out of the kitchen. I called after her, but she didn't stop. Sinking down onto the stool at the breakfast bar I buried my face in my hands.

"She'll be okay, Izzy," Sara said, handing me a glass of wine. "Drew's mad at me too." I took a long drink from the glass Sara gave me. Both of my kids thought *I* betrayed Spencer.

"It's so unfair."

Chapter Seven

The rest of the afternoon was a disaster. Drew refused to look at me and Anna couldn't look away. Her stare so intense, I thought her eyes would burn a hole right through my heart. They barely spoke to me either, and what they did say was so painful I didn't want to hear it. Drew and Anna were convinced I was having an affair and there was nothing I could say that was going to change that. I wanted to tell them the truth about the divorce, to tell them this wasn't my fault, that I hadn't done anything wrong. But I couldn't. Not now, not right before I left on business, not with Spencer out of town too. It wouldn't be fair to them.

I'd decided to take an earlier flight to Tampa. Drew and Anna needed time to process what they were feeling, plus, I really didn't want to risk another picture of me and Alec. Especially not one of me boarding his private jet. I shuddered as I considered the headlines of that article.

"Maybe this trip will do you some good, Izzy," I said out loud. Dr. Leonard had suggested I take some time off. While this wasn't exactly time off it was time away from the chaos in my life. For three whole days I'd be able to pretend my life wasn't unraveling at the seams. I could at least pretend I was still in control.

When I'd finished packing everything I couldn't live without the rest of the week, I headed downstairs where the car service was already waiting. Tears pricked the corners of my eyes as I took one final look around. The house that was once filled with life and love had been forever changed.

Passengers were just starting to board when I arrived at the gate. With this new contract Payne Enterprises was paying for all my travel expenses, so I booked a first class ticket, considering it combat pay for what I was going through because of that picture.

Settling into the roomy seat, I closed my eyes, ready to get this flight over with. My peacefulness was disrupted when my phone rang. After silencing the ringer I caught a quick glance of the screen. *Spencer.* I wasn't about to risk a dramatic event now, not with a plane full of people. I sent Alec a quick message so he'd know not to pick me up then powered down my phone and dropped it into my travel bag.

· · · · ·

The car service dropped me off outside the Port of Tampa just before seven. Passengers weren't arriving until tomorrow so the check-in process was quick. The porter took my suitcase and escorted me to my suite, an oversized room with a sitting area, a queen size bed, and a large en suite bathroom with a garden tub and separate shower. And the floor-to-ceiling glass doors leading to the balcony made the room seem even bigger than it was.

I thought about calling Alec to tell him I'd arrived, but I wasn't in the mood to deal with him yet. I needed a little time to get past the fact that he was the reason I was in this mess. Instead, I unpacked my suitcase then headed off to explore the ship on my own.

There was a deck map mounted on the wall near the elevator and I took a few minutes to study it. The ship had nineteen decks and I could easily get lost. "This is gonna take more than a weekend," I said out loud.

"How long is it going to take then?" I spun around and was immediately frozen in my tracks at the sight of Alec standing in front of me. The porter must've told him I'd boarded, but how did he know where to find me?

"Mr. Payne," I finally managed to say.

"Welcome aboard, Ms. James," he said with a smile that exposed his perfect white teeth. "Is there a problem with the schedule already?"

"I wasn't talking about the schedule."

He tilted his head as if waiting for me to continue.

"I was just thinking out loud about how many things there are to see onboard."

"This is the *Ultimate Fantasy*, Ms. James." He took hold of my hand. "Come with me, we have a tour to finish."

I pulled out of his grip. "Alec, stop." He turned to look at me. "This, whatever *this* is, it can't happen. You're a client. Please try to understand that."

"Are you objecting to a tour of the ship?"

"No."

"Then what exactly is the problem, Isabella?"

"Alec, that picture, you have no idea the trouble it's caused."

He moved closer, taking my hand in his once

more. "I'm sorry, Isabella. I should've warned you about the press. I feel terrible. Let me make it up to you."

My luxurious trip to Tampa flashed through my mind making me blush. "Actually, you already did," I confessed. "You bought me a first class ticket to Tampa."

A broad smile crossed his face. "Oh, Isabella, I can do much better than that."

Nervously, I bit my lip. *Stop this! Stop this now!* my inner voice shouted but I felt almost powerless near him. "Alec, please," I breathed. "That picture almost cost me my job. And now my kids think I'm having an affair." I shook my head, wanting to rid that awful memory.

"I'm sorry that your kids got the wrong impression, really. If there's anything I can do to make that situation better just say the word and I'll do it." If only it were that easy. I wish someone else could handle the chaos in my life, but that wasn't a real possibility and I knew it.

"But Tim—"

"You let me worry about Tim Howard," Alec interrupted.

"That's easier said than done, Alec. He's really mad at *me* and *I'm* the one who works for him."

"Fair point, Isabella, but you don't need to worry about any of that now. You're kids aren't here. Tim's not here. And more importantly, the press isn't here." He moved closer placing his hands on my hips, pulling me closer to him. "Right now nothing else matters but you." My knees buckled, and at that moment I knew I couldn't resist him.

"Fine, but just a tour," I finally agreed.

· · · · ·

We spent the next couple of hours exploring the ship. I got to see first-hand the work that went on behind the scenes as Alec escorted me through the staff only areas. Crew members were busily moving about, making final preparations before guests arrived. Alec was surprisingly relaxed and carefree as we strolled from deck to deck, exploring the ship. Not at all the control freak I'd expected.

He pulled his hand to his ear and pressed the Bluetooth button. "What is it, Tina?" Alec said sharply. "Was anyone hurt?" He turned his back to me as he listened. "Thank God. Get Marcus on the phone. I want a full report." He pressed the button once again then turned back toward me.

"I'm sorry, Isabella. I have to deal with an emergency." He took my hand and we walked toward the elevator.

"Is everything okay?"

"Yes," he said as we stepped inside. He pressed a button on the control panel then stepped back out. "This will take you to the Lido deck. Your cabin is near the bow."

"What about the meeting with the crew?"

"It's been cancelled. I'll pick you up at ten for a late dinner." And just like that Mr. Control Freak was back.

My nerves were frayed by the time I found my way back to my cabin. I'd been wrestling with thoughts of Alec and professionalism and my job all day, our earlier interaction only making it worse. I opened the mini bar in search of something that might calm me down. When I saw the small bottles of Chateau Ste. Michelle inside, I couldn't help but smile. I pulled a bottle off the shelf and poured myself a glass, beyond ready to leave the stresses of my life behind.

After finishing the tiny bottle I still had some time to kill so I decided to check voicemail. The automated voice announced I had two new messages. I skipped over the first message when I heard Spencer's voice. He was the last person I wanted in my head right now. The second message started to play. "You're officially single," the caller said. "Your divorce was finalized earlier today," he continued and I finally put the pieces together, Mark, my divorce attorney. I listened to the message again to make sure I'd heard him correctly. Divorced. It was over, done, finished. Nineteen years of marriage, gone, just like that. Tears filled my eyes and I couldn't stop them, not this time. I collapsed on the bed and cried myself to sleep.

A knock on the door woke me. Shit. Alec. Our dinner plans. I scrambled out of bed and headed to the bathroom to wash away the evidence of my tears. A more insistent knock sounded through the cabin and I hurried to open the door.

"Isabella, what's wrong?" Alec asked as soon he saw me. He stepped into the room, forcing me to take a step back.

I shook my head, not wanting to get into it, knowing I wouldn't be able to hold the tears back if I did. "It's nothing."

He held my head between his hands and stared into my eyes. "I don't like half-truths, Isabella. Now tell me what's wrong."

Alec's words were my undoing. I buried my face

into his chest, unable to stop the tears now. He wrapped his arms around me and held me close.

"Tell me what's wrong?" Alec said. "And I want the truth this time."

I closed my eyes tight. I didn't want to talk about my divorce with him, not now, maybe not ever. But I already knew he wouldn't let it go. "My divorce was finalized today," I blurted out.

Alec held me at arm's length, looking right into my eyes. "And you're having second thoughts?"

"Yes, no, I don't know." I pulled my hands through my hair. "Don't get me wrong. I'm glad the divorce is over. It's just, well, nineteen years is a long time. It feels weird to know my marriage is really over." Alec wrapped his arms around me and pressed a kiss to the top of my head before pulling away. "No, please don't go," I whispered as he moved toward the door, all concerns of professionalism forgotten, at least for the moment.

Alec opened the door and picked up a large gold box that was resting against the door jamb inside the hall. "Get dressed," he said, handing me the package. "I'm taking you to dinner."

Grabbing a tissue from the nightstand, I dried my tears. "What is this?" I asked hesitantly, remembering the last time I opened a package.

"It's an apology, for the picture."

"But you already bought me an apology gift."

"No, you bought yourself a gift that I paid for. There's a big difference." The sharpness in his tone made me blush. "Now, open the box."

Damn, he's demanding. I lifted the lid, gasping when I saw the metallic gold Oscar de la Renta that was inside. I pulled the dress from the box. "Alec, it's beautiful," I gasped.

You can't keep that! my inner voice snapped. I knew she was right but I at least wanted to touch it. I'd never held a dress that expensive before, let alone worn one.

"Get dressed, Isabella. I'm hungry."

"Alec, this dress is too much. I can't accept it."

He put his arm around my waist and pulled me into his chest, his eyes piercing through all the pain and confusion I'd been feeling. "I want you to wear this to dinner, Isabella. And I want you to hurry."

I bit my lip, an enormous grin on my face. "Control freak!" I laughed, but took the dress into the bathroom to change anyway.

After fixing my makeup and twisting my unruly hair into a bun, I finally emerged from the bathroom. I'd tried to hurry given how hungry Alec said he was. So when I found him lounging on the bed, watching highlights from the earlier hockey games on his phone, it surprised me.

Alec must've felt me staring because he looked up, and his mouth dropped open. "Stunning," he said simply. I was sure he was talking about the dress but the compliment made me blush anyway, or maybe it was the guilty feeling of accepting such an expensive gift from a man I barely knew.

I pulled my strappy heels from the wardrobe and slid them on. Alec bent down and fastened the strap around my ankle. My insides quickened when he touched me and an involuntary gasp escaped. Looking up at me, he smiled, clearly enjoying the effect he had on me.

"Let's go," he said after he finished buckling the second shoe. I didn't argue. My stomach was growling now too.

He led me to the Da Vinci dining room, a large, open space on the sixth deck. Di Vinci's art adorned the walls; *Virgin of the Rocks*, *Madonna of Carnation*, *The Last Supper*. I looked around the room as Alec led me to a small booth near the window. The passengers hadn't boarded yet so the dining room was empty. We were completely alone with the bottle of wine chilling tableside. My heart beat faster, butterflies fluttered.

I slid behind the table at the circular booth and Alec sat on the other side. He filled the two wine glasses that were on the table, handing one to me, lifting the other. He took a long drink, his eyes never leaving mine.

With a nervous smile on my face I lifted my glass and took a long drink. "Thank you for this amazing dress," I said finally.

Alec lifted my hand in his. "It's only a dress, Isabella. You make it amazing." His words made me blush again and I looked away. "Don't do that," Alec scolded, tugging on my chin until I was facing him again. His touch made my heart skip a beat and my breathing quicken. Without warning Alec leaned in and kissed me, a soft, sweet kiss, right on the lips sending a tingle through my body. I tried to pull away but he held my face in both hands and kissed me harder, sliding his tongue past my lips this time.

My body was on fire, my panties soaked by the effects of that one kiss. I pulled away again and this time he let me go. "Alec," I said breathlessly. I wanted him to keep kissing me but I knew if I didn't stop him now it would be too late. "We can't do this."

The waiter arrived with our dinner before either of us could say anything further. Alec sat back in his chair, that wicked grin of his spreading across his handsome face. I wondered what he was thinking but I didn't dare ask. We were treading in shark infested waters and I needed to steer the conversation to a safer place.

"How's the emergency?"

Alec's expression hardened and he pulled his hand through his hair. "It's being handled," he said coolly. He refilled his wine glass and took another drink.

Great, I'd touched a nerve. I changed tacks again. "So, what made you start a cruise line?"

He pulled both hands through his hair this time. I'd expected that to be an easy question, but apparently I'd touched another nerve. "It was a wedding gift for my ex-wife."

His confession surprised me. None of the research I'd done said anything about a wife.

Shaking his head as if clearing some awful memory, he continued, "But she ran off with my finance manager after they embezzled millions of dollars from me."

"Why did you keep it? Why not just sell?"

"Believe it or not, cruise lines aren't exactly in high demand." He took another drink. "Plus, selling would put the jobs we created at risk. Some of our staff members left other jobs for this opportunity, others relocated, uprooted their lives, their families' lives, all to work for Ultimate. I owe it to them to see this through."

"I wouldn't have guessed you to be the humanitarian type, you know, being Mr. Control Freak and all."

"Oh, Isabella, you have no idea."

I wondered silently what he meant, but I didn't

ask. I wasn't exactly having good luck with conversation tonight. "What made you want to buy all these companies, anyway?"

"I'm an investment banker. That's kind of what we do."

He really was clandestine. Maybe that was why I hadn't been able to find out anything about his motivations already. But I'm Izzy James. Digging into issues, discovering the unknown, that was what *I did*. "How'd you get started in investment banking then?"

Alec took a long drink from his wine glass, stalling maybe. I kept my eyes fixed on him, preparing myself to wait him out, no matter how long it took.

"I was a real handful growing up," he said finally. "My parents died when I was young, so I moved to New York to live with my aunt." He paused and took another drink. I raised my eyebrows, urging him to continue. "As if losing my parents and little sister wasn't bad enough, I had to leave my friends behind too. I felt completely lost and started rebelling, vandalizing street signs, breaking into cars, stupid stuff really.

"Well, one day I got caught smashing the window of a pretty expensive sports car. The police officer had me cuffed and in the back of his cruiser before I even heard him coming." He shook his head, a small smile on his face. "Boy, was my aunt pissed," he laughed.

Intrigued by his reaction, I tilted my head, ready to hear more. "Turns out, the owner of the car was a high-profile investment banker. And when my aunt told him about my parents he took pity on me, agreeing not to press charges in exchange for a little hard labor. Needless to say I spent the next three months mowing his lawn, pulling weeds, trimming trees, anything he could find to keep me busy. I guess he got used to having me around because when he ran out of yardwork for me to do he started teaching me about investment banking. Eventually, he helped me get into Bendheim then gave me my first real job after I graduated."

"So, in a way, breaking into cars saved your life?"

His smile grew. "I guess you could say that."

"What happened to your parents?" As soon as the words were out of my mouth I wished I could take them back. Alec's smile faded instantly. His whole body tensed and the grip on his wine glass tightened to the point I was worried he might actually snap the stem.

"There was a home invasion," he sighed. "I was the only one who survived."

"Oh, Alec, I'm so sorry. I didn't mean to pry."

He took a deep breath. "It's okay. It's just not something I typically talk about."

I reached across the table and covered his hand with mine, the enormity of what he'd just said really sinking in. Not just about his parents death, but that he'd shared this intimate detail of his life with me. "Thank you for trusting me with that, Alec."

When he looked up at me there was sadness in his eyes that tugged at my heartstrings. I didn't know what else to say. Luckily, Alec came up with the answer for me. "I'm done talking about me. I want to talk about you now," he said, and I didn't argue, even though there were so many questions I wanted to ask. They'd have to wait for another time. "Did you always want to be in public relations?"

"All I really knew when I left for college was I

didn't want to be a rancher," I said honestly. "I changed my major dozens of times those first two years. By the beginning of my junior year, I was getting pressured to declare a major I would stick to. My dad had always told me I was a natural problem solver so I picked PR and went with it."

"Do you like what you do?"

"Actually, I do. I love my job, or maybe I just love working, but whatever it is I've been happy at Dimarco."

"Have you ever thought about doing anything else?"

"Not really, but after that picture maybe I should start considering a new career," I teased.

Alec shook his head. "I really am sorry about that."

I wanted to tell him it was okay, that this dress, this night, more than made up for it. But that would've been a lie. He'd almost cost me my job, and I had no idea if my kids would ever forgive me.

"What were you like when you were a little girl?" Alec asked, changing the subject.

Good, another easy question. "I was never much of a 'girl' growing up. I was raised by a single father and we owned a cattle ranch. I worked hard every day."

"That helps explain your feistiness, but certainly not your lack of discipline."

"Lack of discipline," I snapped, unable to stop the words from spewing out of my mouth. "I happen to have an abundance of self-discipline, I'll have you know."

"I'll try and remember that," Alec laughed.

I rolled my eyes, momentarily forgetting he wasn't

a fan of that, but we were so far over the line of professionalism I didn't really care at that moment. He refilled both our glasses, that wicked grin settling on his face. "Although, your refusal to stop rolling your eyes at me suggests the exact opposite of what you're saying."

"Yeah, well, that's a lack of tolerance. It has nothing to do with discipline." I picked up my glass and took a long drink.

Alec laughed even louder but thankfully changed the subject. "Were you able to see your mom often?"

A deep sigh escaped, involuntarily. My pathetic excuse for a mother was the last thing I wanted to talk about. "Judy walked out on us when I was five and I haven't heard from her since."

Alec lifted my hand to his lips. "I'm sorry, Isabella," he whispered, his breath warm against my skin.

I jerked my hand back. "Don't feel sorry for me," I snapped, his pity an unwelcome intruder. "I survived just fine without her."

Alec grabbed my hand again and held it tight. "Isabella—" he breathed. His eyes closed and by the time he opened them again he was pulling me to my feet. "Let's dance."

Before I could object we were walking arm-in-arm toward the dance club at the ship's stern. We spent the next three hours dancing, talking, and getting to know each other better. He told me about his ex-wife, "Charlee loved my money. She never loved me," he said. I told him about Spencer's affair, leaving out the part about the pictures. We talked about the twins' plans after graduation and about how much my life was changing. We laughed, I cried, he teased. And by the time he walked me back to my cabin I felt as though I'd known him for years.

"I had a great time, Alec."

He moved closer. Instinctively, I stepped back until I was pressed against the door of my cabin. "Me too," he whispered, his lips inches from mine. I closed my eyes, waiting, wanting him to kiss me again even though I knew it was wrong. My divorce may have been finalized but that didn't change the fact that he was still my client.

Before I could object, Alec lifted my arms over my head and kissed me. Softly at first, his tongue circling mine. I knew I should push him away, but I couldn't. It'd been so long since I'd been touched like that. Passion burned deep inside me. He pinned my wrists against the door with one hand, his other hand trailed down my side, and I didn't object then either. I wanted him, right there, right then.

Without warning, he released my arms and pulled away. "Isabella, I'm sorry," he said, unable to look at me now.

No, please, don't stop, I wanted to say but his kiss had left me breathless.

Alec opened my door, the door I'd been leaning against, and I had to step back to keep my balance. Pressing a soft kiss on my lips, he whispered, "Goodnight, Isabella."

My eyes found his and were begging him to stay. But he closed the door instead, leaving me standing alone, wondering what just happened, wanting more.

I stepped out of my new dress and hung it in the wardrobe before getting in the shower. Thoughts of Alec were still fresh in my mind. His gorgeous green eyes, his grin, that kiss...my insides tingled just thinking about him. Maybe I was just lonely, but that night I felt things I hadn't felt in such a long time.

Maybe you just need sex, my inner voice chimed in, getting straight to the point. I tried to shake her off but she made a good point. It'd been over four months since I'd had sex, no wonder this control freak had me practically begging.

Chapter Eight

When I woke the next morning I felt refreshed after a full night's sleep. I started a pot of coffee in the tiny coffee maker and fired up my laptop. I wanted to run through the boarding process checklist one more time before Tim arrived so it was fresh in my mind. If he even thought I'd been doing anything other than working last night it'd make for one rough weekend. It didn't take me long to get dressed and by the time the coffee was finished I was able to get right to work.

I'd gone over the process several times and was just about to shut my laptop down when a knock at the door caught my attention. Tim wasn't expected until later, so I knew it had to be Alec. An involuntary smile crossed my face and I had to remind myself again that he was a client. Even still I couldn't shake the smile.

A quick look through the peep hole revealed it wasn't Alec, but rather the porter who'd helped me to my room yesterday. I opened the door with a cheerful, "Good morning."

"Good morning, ma'am," he said with a smile of his own. Handing over a black hinged box and an envelope, he added, "These are for you."

"Thanks," I said hesitantly, wondering what this was all about. The porter offered no clues either, simply nodding and walking away after transferring the items to my hand. There was only one way to find out now, open the box.

I opened the card first. *My apologies for last night. Alec,"* it read. My insides quickened as thoughts of his kiss flooded my mind, that passionate kiss that made me want him, the kiss I haven't been able to stop thinking about.

My mouth dropped open the second I lifted the lid on the hinged box and saw the round cut diamond tennis bracelet inside. But before I could fully process the completely-over-the-top gift Alec had sent, the second such gift in two days, the alarm went off on my phone, reminding me that boarding was about to begin.

Reminding myself this was a business trip, I set the box on top of the wardrobe to deal with later, grabbed my binder off the table, and went to find Todd, the Shipboard Director, and our guide during the boarding process.

• • • • •

Passenger boarding didn't take as long as I'd expected. Turns out Ultimate had limited the amount of tickets available for their maiden voyage. "Plus, we never book rooms on the same floor as Mr. Payne," Todd explained when he escorted me back to my cabin. He reminded me about the launch ceremony then disappeared down the hall.

Figuring there would be plenty of press on hand, I

ducked inside my room to change into a more professional outfit, just in case I got caught in another unfortunate photo op.

I hadn't heard from Tim all day. I called him to see if he'd boarded but his voicemail picked up. After leaving a quick message about the launch ceremony, I dialed my voicemail to see if he'd called me back. There was one new message, only it wasn't from Tim. "I can't stop thinking about you. I'll pick you up at one." I broke out in a full mouth smile as I listened to Alec's message again. The truth was, I hadn't been able to stop thinking about him either. With a smile still on my face, I hung up the phone. When I glanced at the clock that smile quickly vanished. Shit, it was almost one. I scrambled to my feet to find a change of clothes.

Before I could finish getting ready, Alec was knocking at the door. I hurried to put on my shirt while I peeked through the peep hole, just in case it wasn't him. When I saw it was in fact Alec, I opened the door. "I'm almost ready."

Alec tapped his watch. "It's one o'clock, Isabella."

"Yeah, well, some of us had work to do this morning," I called over my shoulder as I headed back into the bathroom to freshen up my makeup.

"Are you suggesting I didn't?" Alec called after me.

"If the shoe fits," I said, laughing while I pulled a handful of mousse through my hair to calm the frizzy curls the humidity was causing.

"I'm not sure what shoe you're talking about," Alec said from the doorway of the bathroom. "Because I got up extra early this morning so I'd be ready in time for the launch. Now hurry up. The ceremony will be starting soon."

Five minutes later Alec was pulling me toward the pilot house. "Why are we watching it from up here?"

"Did you see all the press down there?" Alec paused for a second to point over the railing. "If they get wind I'm aboard I'll never get you alone."

Wait. What? "Is that why Tim hasn't arrived, because you want to get me alone?"

"I'll never tell," he whispered, a wicked grin on his face that said it all. At that moment I realized this wasn't a business trip at all.

• • • • •

"Stay with me tonight," Alec said as I packed up my suitcase to leave. I really wanted to stay. The last three days spent with him were the happiest I'd had in months, maybe even years. We'd walked through the garden, had drinks by the pool, and even watched a movie under the stars. Alec took me on a helicopter tour of the islands and snorkeling in Green Turtle Cay. He'd held me in his arms as we watched the sunrise over the Atlantic from the panoramic view of the Star deck, and later that night he held me even tighter as we watched the sun set over the Sea of Abaco from a beach in Marsh Harbour. It was a whirlwind of experiences packed into one unbelievable weekend.

All thoughts of work had been pushed far from my mind. Not one nightmare, not one worry of home. It was exactly what I'd needed. I didn't want it to end, but deep down I knew it had to. We were back in the real world now, a world with guidelines on client relationships, and travel schedules, and two kids who were mad at me, who would surely blame *me* for the divorce.

Alec pulled me into his arms, his lips brushing up against mine like he'd done so many times this weekend. As I melted into his arms I knew I wouldn't be able to resist.

"Alec Payne, what are you doing to me?"

"I told you I was dangerous, baby." He kissed me hard and swatted me playfully on the backside. "Now let's go. Preston will see to your bags."

Alec led me down the elevator to the staff only gangway. He stopped at the top of the stairs and looked around, checking for photographers and overly zealous reporters, I presumed. He announced the all clear then tugged my arm, moving me quickly down the stairs to the waiting limo. "Where are we going?" I asked when we were both inside the car.

"My condo," he replied with that wicked grin I'd come to enjoy so much.

My insides quickened as I considered the possibilities a night in his private space might bring. *Finally! Sex!*

"For dinner," he said, as if he'd heard my private thoughts. He kissed me on the hand, his grin bigger now. I sat back in the cool leather seat, silently wondering what I was getting myself into.

We stepped out of the elevator and into the large foyer of Alec's condo. I was instantly struck by the breathtaking view of Tampa Bay from the floor-to-ceiling glass wall in the great room. I stared out over the water as thoughts of the first day Alec and I spent at sea flooded my mind. We'd stood on his private balcony, his arms wrapped tightly around me, watching the sea pass by. "I could stand here with you forever," he'd said. And I'd secretly wished we could.

"Amazing view, isn't it?" Alec said, pulling me into his arms. He kissed me gently then released me, leaving me wanting him that much more.

Without another word, he tugged at my arm and I followed him into the kitchen. "Sit," he commanded, pointing to a stool by the breakfast bar. The tone in his voice was stern and it made me think about that swat from earlier. I couldn't help but smile.

"What are you smiling about?"

"Just thinking about the weekend," I answered truthfully. "I had an amazing time, Alec. I can't thank you enough." Although I was already thinking of a few ways I'd like to try.

Alec smiled silently as he opened the refrigerator and began pulling out ingredients.

"What are you doing?"

"Cooking you dinner."

"Can I help?"

He poured two glasses of wine then handed me one. "You can tell me about that dream of yours," he said causally as he began rinsing the vegetables he just pulled out of the refrigerator.

My body tensed, how could he possibly know about my dreams? My heart began to beat faster and a lump formed in my throat. I took a long drink from the glass he'd handed me.

Alec looked up from the cutting board where he was now busy chopping; his eyes finding mine, silently demanding an answer.

"What dream?"

Alec stopped chopping and leaned in until his lips were touching mine, then bit my bottom lip. Hard.

"Ow," I protested.

He went back to chopping vegetables. "I told you, Isabella. I don't like half-truths." My sex tingled and I squirmed on the stool. "Now, are you going to tell me about that dream?" He leaned forward again. "Because I have ways of making you talk." I bit my own lip this time, my insides quickening.

All this sexual tension had me ready to explode. I took a long drink, adding just the right amount of courage I needed. "Well, I'm not telling," I said, practically begging him to make me talk. I'd wanted him since that first kiss and right then I didn't care that he was a client. I hadn't had sex in months and I was beyond ready.

Alec set the knife down and slowly wiped his hands on the kitchen towel. I took another drink of wine as he drew near. Without words, he removed the glass from my hand and set it down next to the knife. My eyes widened with anticipation. "You have no idea what you're getting yourself into, Isabella. I'm very dangerous." At that moment I didn't care how dangerous he was. He'd had my nerves on end all weekend, kissing me, exciting me, leaving me wanting. It was time for him to put an end to this misery.

He pulled me into him, my back to his front, snaking one arm around my waist and moving my hair to the side with the other. Trailing a line of kisses down my exposed neck, Alec's hands roamed my midsection, down to my thigh, under my dress, trailing his finger along the waistband of my panties. His erection pressed against my back and I moaned softly. "Is this what you want?"

"Yes," I gasped. He pulled his hand back to my waist and turned me around. "Yes, Alec, yes," I moaned again.

"Not until you tell me about that dream."

"Alec! That's not fair."

He smiled and kissed me on the nose. "I told you, I have ways of making you talk."

"Taking advantage of a sex starved woman is hardly something to brag about, Mr. Payne." I reached past him and picked up my wine glass, draining it quickly this time.

Alec's eyebrows shot up. "Sex starved, huh? You better start talking then." He started a pot of water then added the vegetables he'd been chopping to a sauté pan.

"What are you making?"

"Pasta, now stop stalling or I'll be forced to try harder." Alec unwrapped the ball of dough he'd pulled out of the refrigerator earlier and began kneading it.

I helped myself to another glass of wine. It'd been such a great weekend. I hated to ruin it by even thinking about my nightmares, but what choice did I have? After another long drink I said, "There isn't much to tell, really." Alec looked up from the dough he was kneading, his eyes narrowed. "How do you even know about my dreams anyway?" I asked, praying a distraction would do the trick.

"Dreams? As in more than one?" *Shit. Shit. Shit.* Had he been talking about something else? "How often do you have these dreams?"

"I haven't had one in days. Now tell me how you know about them."

"You dozed off when we were waiting for the sun to rise. You were talking in your sleep."

Dammit! My heart began to race. "What did I

say?"

"Not until you tell me about that dream."

Alec began rolling the dough through the pasta press, but his eyes stayed fixed on me. I didn't want to talk about this but I knew he wasn't going to let it go. "They started a few months ago. My doctor says they're caused by stress. End of story."

"What are they about?"

Dropping my head, I whispered, "Just a bunch of scattered thoughts. None of it makes sense."

Alec stopped rolling the dough and looked deep into my eyes. "You sounded really scared, Isabella."

"Alec, please. I haven't had to relive those stupid dreams since before we left. I don't want to think about them now."

He leaned in and kissed me softly on the lips. "Fair point, baby."

"It's your turn," I said, more than ready to take the spotlight off me for a while. "Tell me more about your marriage."

Alec dropped the pasta in the boiling water and stirred the vegetables. "I wouldn't call it a marriage, really. We met. We got married. We got an annulment. Our entire relationship lasted six weeks."

"Six weeks." The words were out of my mouth before I could stop them.

"Six weeks," he repeated. He emptied the wine in his glass now too, and I knew I'd touched a nerve.

"Oh, speaking of money," I said, hoping to lighten the mood once again. I opened my purse and pulled out the outrageously expensive bracelet he'd sent to my cabin the first day of the cruise. "I can't accept this." The dress was one thing, but diamonds? That seemed way too much too soon.

Alec tilted his head to one side. "Well, I can't take it back. It was an apology."

I moved the box closer to him. "What? No cruise line?"

He pushed the box back toward me, his mouth pressed in a thin, hard line. "If you're going to intentionally push my buttons, Isabella, you're going to need your strength." Shit. My plans to lighten the mood fell flat. Alec tossed the pasta and vegetables together then mixed in the white wine sauce he'd made.

Carrying the two plates to the table, he pointed to the dining table. "Sit," he commanded.

"Control Freak," I whispered but sat down anyway.

The vegetable capellini he made was delicious, but I wasn't in the mood to eat. Half an hour ago I was ready to rip Alec's clothes off and devour every inch of his body, but talking about my dreams had reminded me just how messed up my life had become since that package arrived.

"Don't you like it," Alec asked as I moved the pasta around the plate with my fork.

"Actually, it's delicious. I'm just too distracted to eat."

His wicked grin returned. "Distracted by what?"

"By you, by this, by what happens next."

Alec stood up and pulled me into his chest. "What happens next is entirely up to you. But you should know it's all or nothing with me. I don't do half way."

Alec kissed me, softly at first, then deep and hard, dissolving all my doubts. My heart beat so hard I could feel it in my toes. "Can you handle that, Isabella? Can you handle all of me?"

I wondered what he meant but right then I didn't care. "Yes," I said breathlessly. Yes, I wanted all of him, inside me, here, now. I greedily ran my hands over his chest, his back, around his waist. I ran my thumb along the waistband of his pants.

He grabbed my wrists and pulled my hands to his mouth, kissing each one gently before wrapping my arms around his neck. "Hold on," he commanded. I immediately did as he asked. "Good girl," he whispered after he scooped me into his arms. "I'm taking you to bed now, baby."

Alec carried me out of the kitchen then up the stairs, not stopping until he was standing outside his bedroom door. "We don't have to do this if you don't want to. You can still say no."

Oh no, he was not backing out this time. I kissed him, hard. "I've wanted this since the first time you kissed me."

Without another word he carried me inside his room and set my feet down on the ground. His eyes were fixed on mine as he slowly lifted the hem of my dress over my head. I squirmed with anticipation. *This is really happening.* Alec dropped my dress to the floor then held me at arm's length, staring, soaking me in. "You are so beautiful, Isabella." His words made me blush and I looked away, suddenly feeling naked and exposed. Spencer was the only man who'd ever seen me naked and I felt self-conscious with Alec's eyes on my bare flesh.

Sensing my discomfort, Alec lifted my chin until my eyes found his. "Beautiful," he whispered.

With a trail of warm kisses Alec slowly moved from my lips, to my chin, and down my neck while his hands roamed my body. He reached behind me and unfastened my bra, sliding the straps over my shoulders, letting it fall to the ground. Alec ran a finger along my side from my waist all the way to my breasts then wrapped a hand around each one, gently caressing. I squirmed again. "Patience, Isabella," he warned.

Alec unbuttoned his shirt, exposing his tan, chiseled muscles. I reached up and touched his chest, his hard body only making me want him more. I pushed his shirt over his shoulders letting it fall to the floor then reached for the buckle on his belt, but in one swift move Alec scooped me up and deposited me on the bed.

Crawling on top of the bed, he kneeled between my legs then leaned down and kissed the top of my panties. Trailing a line of kisses up my body, to my breasts, my neck, my mouth, then back again, Alec devoured my naked form. I squirmed beneath him, my body begging him to take me, each kiss bringing me that much closer to the edge of ecstasy.

"Patience, Isabella. I want to savor you. Lifting my foot he added, "Every inch of you." Not waiting for me to respond, he began his barrage of kisses once more, my toe, my instep, my ankle, slowly moving up my leg until he reached my sex. I bucked my hips, wanting, needing, ready to burst. "Be still, Isabella," he warned before starting the process over with my other leg.

I tried not to move but my body was on fire, all sensation and carnal desire. Before I knew it I was squirming beneath him. "You're so impatient, Isabella." His wicked grin returned. "I'm going to enjoy fixing that." Alec climbed on top of me, pinning me under his weight, his erection pressing into me.

He kissed me again.

"Alec, please," I begged when he finally broke the kiss.

Tantalizingly slow he slid my panties over my hips. I lifted off the bed to aid the process but he wasn't in any hurry as his hands explored my body. My breath hitched as he skimmed the edge of my folds. He alternated kisses and nips on my inner thigh until I thought I'd explode.

"Please, Alec," I begged again. "I want you. I need to feel you inside me."

He ran his tongue over my folds. "Every inch of you," he said again. I bucked my hips, looking for friction, anything to help me find the release I so desperately craved, but he pulled back. A moment later all I could feel was the wet heat of his tongue circling my clitoris.

My body began to unravel. "Oh, God, Alec," I panted. I fisted my fingers through his hair as I climbed closer and closer to the edge, the sensation almost too much for me to handle. When he slid a finger inside me, expertly moving it around, all my built up tension had me ready to explode. "Alec," I cried out, unable to contain the pleasure any longer.

"That's it, baby. Come for me." His words were my undoing. My body stiffened, my muscles contracting as I fell over the edge of my release. Alec kissed me on the mouth, my salty pleasure still on his lips, leaving me with an overwhelming urge to taste him too.

I pushed him off me until he was flat on his back, then straddled him as I ran my hands over his chest, teasing him as he'd done to me. I kissed my way down his chest as my hands busily worked to undo his jeans.

His erection strained the bounds of the fabric of his boxer briefs as I rubbed him through the thin fabric. I pulled the waist band down freeing his hardened length, the sight of which beckoned an involuntary gasp.

A moan escaped me as my tongue circled the head of his penis, the musky scent of his arousal sending waves of pleasure through my body again. I brought him all the way into my mouth, sucking and circling as my hands greedily roamed his torso.

His cock twitched on my tongue and he quickly sat up, pulling me into his arms. "If you keep doing that I'm going to come before I even get inside you," he said, grasping at the edges of restraint.

Without another word he flipped me onto my back and was once again between my legs, kneeling as he rolled a condom over his erection. Ever so slowly he pushed past my opening until his erection was deep inside me, filling me completely. I wiggled beneath him as I adjusted to the exquisite sensation. When I finally stilled he slowly began to move.

"Jesus, Isabella, you're so tight," he moaned as he thrust deeper inside me. I raised my hips to meet his; in, out, in a tantalizing rhythm. It had been so long since I'd had a man inside me that the feeling was almost too much to take.

My insides began to quicken as another orgasm started to build. I dug my nails into the flesh of his toned back. "Oh…Alec…feels...so good..."

He tilted my hips and pushed himself deeper inside me. "I'm close, Isabella. Come for me again," he whispered breathlessly in my ear. His words were my undoing and I exploded around him. My insides continued to spasm as my orgasm ripped through me for a second time. That's when he really started to move, not stopping until he found his own release. Once his body relaxed, he kissed me softly on the lips then collapsed on top of me, both of us spent.

Chapter Nine

Sun flooded the room through the floor-to-ceiling glass wall. I sat up and looked around the room. "Alec's room," I said out loud, regaining my bearings. Only Alec wasn't anywhere to be found so I climbed out of bed to find him.

My suitcase was as the foot of the bed. I fished around the bag until I found my toothbrush and a hair tie then went into the bathroom to clean up. I slipped on the shirt Alec was wearing last night, his scent still covering the fabric. Burying my face in the collar, I breathed him in. The events from last night replayed in my mind and I wrapped myself in a hug, but it was his arms I wanted around me. I hurried downstairs to find him.

Alec was pacing back and forth in front of the glass wall in the great room when I found him. "How'd they get in? Damn it, Marcus. Figure it out," he shouted into the Bluetooth earpiece he wore before ripping it out of his ear and throwing it against the wall.

Startled by his angry outburst, I gasped involuntarily. Alec looked up when he heard. Pulling his hands through his hair, he paced toward me. "Isabella," he said, quickly closing the gap between us. His brows were furrowed and there was no sign of humor on his face now. He reached up and touched my cheek softly. "Get dressed, baby. We need to go."

Just like that, he pulled his hand away and disappeared into the kitchen. Not exactly the good morning I was hoping for.

I headed up the stairs, wasting no time getting ready. I wasn't sure what was bothering Alec but I definitely wasn't a fan of his mood.

Alec was waiting by the front door when I made my way back down, my bags in tow.

"Are you ready to go?" he asked. I nodded but didn't say a word, letting him take my bags as he led me to the elevator.

We rode in silence all the way to the airport. Alec hadn't offered any clues to what was bothering him, and I hadn't pushed for answers. His earlier outburst and subsequent cold reception still had me a little shaken. Alec may have been used to one-night stands, but I sure wasn't, and I refused to let him see how much his silence was bothering me.

"What's wrong, Isabella?" Alec asked when we were safely in the air.

I whipped my head around, a stunned look on my face. "Me? I could ask you the same thing."

He opened his mouth then closed it again. I continued to stare, waiting him out. "It's nothing," he finally said.

"Yeah, what was that you were saying about half-truths?"

Pulling his hand through his hair, he exhaled. "There was an emergency at my office, but it's nothing for you to worry about." He leaned over to my seat and kissed me on the mouth. "Plus, I'm not looking forward to being away from you."

A smile crossed my face for only the second time that day. "Really? Because I was starting to wonder."

"Wonder what?"

Shit. Why had I opened my mouth? The last thing I wanted was to sound needy.

"Wonder what, Isabella?"

"You were so cold this morning," I blurted out. "I thought maybe you'd gotten what you wanted and were done with me now."

Alec squeezed my hand. "All or nothing, remember?" His words from last night rolled around in my mind now, and I couldn't help but wonder what I'd gotten myself into.

• • • • •

Alec excused himself to the rear of the plane to take a phone call some time ago and had yet to return. I stared out the window, wondering who he was talking to and what the emergency at his office was all about.

"Are you going to the office today?"

Surprised by Alec's voice I jerked my head toward him. "And risk an interrogation from Tim? Not a chance." The mere thought of having to explain to Tim why I hadn't flown back yesterday gave me chills. "Actually, I think I'll skip the office altogether this week."

He tilted his head to one side. "Is that something you do often, Ms. James?"

"Maybe I do. Is that a problem for you, *Mr.*

Payne?"

Rubbing his chin between his thumb and forefinger as if seriously considering my question, Alec said, "It sounds more like an advantage than a problem to me." I bit the nail on my index finger as I considered a few advantages of my own. "Come with me to New York. You can skip work there."

"I'm skipping the office, Alec, not work."

He leaned over and bit my lip. "You can skip the office in New York then."

I wanted to go with him, to spend another night wrapped in his arms, but no matter how much I wanted to I knew I couldn't. Not when Drew and Anna were at home, probably still mad at me over that picture. "I can't. I have to go home."

He pulled his hands through his hair, something I noticed he did a lot when things weren't going the way he wanted them to. "Will Spencer be there?"

Pausing to search my memory for the answer, I came up empty. "I don't know."

"How can you not know, Isabella?"

I laughed nervously, his reaction from earlier this morning still fresh in my mind. "Don't get your panties in a bunch. I haven't exactly been thinking about Spencer these last few days."

"I'm not thinking about Spencer either," he snapped. "I'm thinking about you."

Shit. My distraction failed and now he was mad again. *Seriously?* my inner voice snapped, and I couldn't help the eye roll that followed.

Reaching over me, Alec unbuckled my seatbelt and pulled me into his lap surprising me once more. "If you have something to say, Isabella, then say it, but stop rolling your eyes at me."

My heart beat faster, adrenalin coursing through my veins. "Control freak!" I teased, not sure what to make of this sudden attitude he'd developed.

Alec leaned forward until his mouth was next to my ear. "All of me," he whispered. I laid my head on his chest, half excited the other half afraid of what I'd started with this man.

• • • • •

"Thank you for everything, Alec. I had a great time."

"Anything for you, Isabella." He kissed me on the lips. "Don't forget to call me when you get home so I'm not worried."

I waved goodbye. "I won't forget, but don't worry anyway." He closed the car door and walked back to the plane. Watching his retreating form, I leaned back against the seat and while the car service Alec hired to drive me home pulled away from the jet.

Traffic out of the airport was heavy so I took the time to get caught up on emails. The tiny envelope on the home screen of my Windows phone indicated several new messages, the majority of which were from Jonathan. I read through them all, mostly updates on what I'd missed while I was gone and the reports I'd asked for before I left.

One message grabbed my attention though. Jonathan scheduled a new client meeting in New York on Friday but hadn't said who the client was. Payne Enterprises is in New York, but surely that couldn't be it. I'd just spent the last four days with Alec and he didn't mention anything about giving Dimarco that contract. I made a mental note to ask

Jonathan about it later then opened the last message, the only one from Tim.

After Tim missed the cruise he'd been so excited to take I hadn't expected good news, but I hadn't expected this either. He was demanding we revisit my working arrangement, again. And just like that I was back to the real world, thoughts of the weekend slipping away, only to be replaced by the stresses in my life.

The house was quiet when I walked through the door. I did a quick check of the garage, looking for Spencer's car, and was relieved to find it wasn't there. I carried my suitcase upstairs to unpack before starting my work day. The Oscar da la Renta gown Alec bought me had already been cleaned, courtesy of Preston sometime last night or early this morning. I tucked it in the back of my closet, knowing the kids would never believe nothing was going on between me and Alec if they saw that dress.

I listened to my voice messages as I unpacked. Spencer's voicemail from last Thursday played first. "Great picture, Bella. Couldn't even wait until the ink was dry?" he'd said. I hit delete without listening to the rest of the message. He had no room to talk. After all *he* was the reason we'd gotten divorced in the first place.

Tim's message played next. "Call me," he said simply. No welcome back, no how was your trip, no thanks for giving up your entire weekend, just "call me." Exhaling loudly, I deleted his message too.

I walked downstairs to my office, unpacked my laptop, and decided to call Tim back while I waited for it to boot. I said a silent prayer he'd forgotten about his email from Friday, and his list of demands.

"Mr. Howard's office. Haley speaking."

"Hi, Haley, it's Izzy. Is Tim available?"

"Yes, he's waiting for your call, Mrs. James." The hold music began to play.

The hold music ended abruptly and Tim's voice filled the air. "Izzy, great job, I've been trying to close that account for months."

"Um, thanks," I said, clueless to what he was talking about.

"Of course, you'll be running point."

I may not have known what account he was talking about but I did know my schedule wouldn't allow me to run point on any more projects, especially for a new client. "I was thinking we'd let Steve handle this one."

"Very funny, considering how well that suggestion went last time. Plus, Mr. Payne insisted."

Annoyed by this new development, I exhaled loudly. "I'm already spread pretty thin. Payne Enterprises will need a full time IR Manager and I just don't have that kind of time right now."

"That's what I wanted to talk to you about, Izzy. I know how devoted you are to your clients, but the Payne Enterprises contract is contingent on you running point. We'll need to divide your current projects among your team to clear your schedule."

"But—"

"No buts Izzy. This contract will bring in more revenue than all our other contracts combined. We need you on this." Tim's tone said it all. There was no getting out of this.

"When do we start?" I asked finally.

"You have a meeting Friday at Payne Enterprises. I'll leave it up to you to work out the details from there."

My head started to spin. Jonathan emailed my itinerary for Friday before I made it home from the airport. When did Alec send over the contract? And more importantly, why hadn't he told me about it?

"I better get busy then," I said, doing my best to hide my mounting frustration. Ending the call, I tossed my phone on the desk. I couldn't believe this was happening. It was bad enough that I had to give up the clients I'd worked so hard to win over, but knowing Alec did this without so much as even a hint had me ready to scream.

I went upstairs and changed into my running clothes. I was too mad now to even think about work. I'd call Alec to yell at him for screwing with my job, but it wouldn't do any good. Plus, I'd had just about all of Mr. Control Freak I could handle for one day. I laced up my shoes, grabbed my iPod off the dresser, and set off for a run.

"All or nothing," Alec had said last night before taking me upstairs. If I'd known that meant he'd be interfering with my job I might have made a different choice. Although it was hard to imagine turning him down after the unbelievable sex we had. I was still sore from having him inside me, his large cock stretching me farther than I'd ever been stretched. When I closed my eyes I could still feel him, even smell him. But none of that was helping with the frustration I felt over him messing with the job I loved.

An hour later I walked through the back door, sweat dripping down my face, a sure sign of a good workout. I could hear my phone ringing but I decided to ignore it until after I cleaned up.

Considering I was in no hurry to start the process of transitioning my clients, I took my time in the shower. They'd be in good hands with my team, but that was hardly the point. They were *my* clients. Contracts *I'd* closed. Relationships *I'd* fostered. Plus, the mere thought of working for Alec full time had me beyond worried. Would I be able to handle dealing with him day in and day out?

By the time I made it back to my office I had four missed calls: one from Steve, one from Kari, and two from Alec. Surprisingly, there was only one voicemail. "I thought you were going to call me when you got home," Alec's message said. Still irritated about being pulled from my other projects thanks to him, I deleted it without listening to the rest.

"Oh, you're lucky I haven't called you," I said out loud, certain he wouldn't like anything I had to say to him at the moment.

I printed the summary report Jonathan created and ran through each client, one by one, trying to figure out just who to hand each one over to. It was a long, tedious process as I considered personalities, client issues, and their past histories, all while weighing in the current stage of each project and the timelines too. By six o'clock I was satisfied with the choices I'd made, or was forced to make anyway.

Anna's laugh echoed past my office door. I pushed my notes aside and followed the laughter into the kitchen just in time to hear Sara telling Anna about a mishap at the grocery store that sent a display of cereal boxes crashing down on top of her. Anna was laughing so hard she was struggling to catch her breath. Until she saw me, that is.

"Mom," she said softly. I smiled, relieved she

wasn't still mad. "What are *you* doing here?" No, I was wrong, she was still mad.

I pulled my hands through my hair, a habit I seemed to have picked up from Alec this past weekend. "Anna, please."

"Please what, Mom. You should have told us."

"Anna, I did tell you. It was only a picture."

She jumped to her feet, the stool she was sitting on falling to the floor. "Don't play dumb with me! Dad told us everything. Did you honestly think you could get a divorce without telling us?" She stormed out of the kitchen before I could say anything, all evidence of her good mood long gone. I couldn't believe Spencer told them about the divorce. We'd agreed to wait until after graduation. If he'd wanted to tell them sooner he could have at least waited for me to get home so we could do it together.

That asshole! my inner voice snapped. He'd managed to make *this* my fault too. Nothing I said to Anna would matter now. Spencer screwed this up and he was going to have to make it right.

Sara stood at the stove, her back turned, undoubtedly uncomfortable after another episode of the James' family drama. "Do you know where Spencer is?" I asked.

"He flew to Atlanta this morning. He'll be back on Wednesday." I exhaled slowly. On one hand I was happy to have a couple more days to figure out what to say to Spencer, but on the other I was irritated I'd have to wait until Wednesday for him to fix the mess he created.

I poured myself a glass of wine and headed back into my office to drink, alone. After clearing the papers from my desk I made a to-do list for the following day, anything to keep my mind off of everything that had happened since I got home.

That familiar tone chimed alerting me to a new email. Reluctantly I opened it.

Date: April 20, 2015 06:27 PM
To: Isabella James
From: Alec Payne
Subject: Waiting for your call

Isabella,

Should I be worried or mad? Call me.

Alec Payne
CEO, Payne Enterprises

I closed my email program without responding. "Let him worry, or be mad, or whatever he wants to be," I shouted. He was on my shit list too for forcing me to hand over my clients. After powering down my laptop I headed back to the kitchen for another glass of wine but froze when I saw Drew.

"Welcome home," he said when he saw me.

Cautiously I smiled, trying to gauge his mood. "Thanks."

Drew moved closer, pulling me into a hug, and I hoped I was forgiven. "Drew, I'm really sorry we didn't tell you guys sooner."

"Look, this sucks, but knowing sooner wouldn't make it suck any less. Plus, I kinda see why you wanted to wait."

I took his hand in mine "Your maturity never fails to surprise me. You're growing up so fast."

He pulled his hand back. "What I don't understand is why you wanted a divorce in the first place." Maybe I'd spoken too soon.

"Anna said Dad told you everything."

"Dad told us you guys had a fight and then you filed for divorce."

Can this get any worse? Dropping my head, I whispered, "More or less."

"Mom, I know there's something you're not saying. I wish you'd trust me enough to tell me the truth."

Tears filled my eyes. I'd never be able to tell Drew what really happened. Not because I didn't trust him, but because it wasn't something any child should know about their parent. "Some things are just better left unsaid. I hope you can understand that."

Refilling my glass of wine, Drew said, "I think I do." He kissed me on the cheek then hopped up to help Sara finish dinner leaving me to my own thoughts.

When we sat down for dinner, the tension was so thick it was palpable. Drew and Sara made small talk, doing their best to lighten Anna's mood. Drew gave me the prom update, looking over at Anna from time to time, trying but failing to coax her into conversation. He shared details about the upcoming senior picnic and the Grad Bash too, nothing worked.

"I need to get back to my homework," Anna said finally. Setting her plate in the sink she disappeared from the kitchen without a second glance or another word.

"We all need time to adjust," Drew offered. Even though I knew he was right it hadn't made it any easier.

After the dinner dishes were all cleaned, I said goodnight to Sara and Drew then headed upstairs to bed. It had been a long first day back, and I was beyond ready to get some sleep.

· · · · ·

"You're such a bad girl, Bella." His voice was gruff. I couldn't see. Something was covering my eyes. I wanted to move it but I couldn't. My arms were tied. Pain radiated all the way to my fingers as I tried to free my arms.

"Why must you defy me?" I know that voice, but who? "Answer me!" he screamed. My ribs hurt now too. I couldn't breathe.

His mouth was on mine, his breathing ragged. He smelled of alcohol and cigarettes, and something sweet, familiar even. Pain shot through my side again. Tears rolled in steady streams down my cheeks. "Cry, Bella. I like it when you cry."

"Why are you doing this?" I asked, finally able to speak.

"What's mine is mine, Bella." His voice was harsh. The pain came again and again, harder with each blow, making it almost impossible to breathe. I closed my eyes, trying to absorb the pain as the hits continued.

"Please, stop," I begged.

"You can't have what's mine!" The pain came again completely taking my breath that time. I felt a sharp pinch on my neck. My head started to spin. My eyelids closed and this time they wouldn't reopen.

Chapter Ten

I jolted upright in bed, breathless, my heart racing. Tears covered my face, my silk nightshirt wet and clinging to my body. I looked around. There was no one here. "It was only a nightmare," I said out loud, dismayed by their return.

It was still dark outside. Picking up my phone to check the time, a sharp pain radiated from my wrist all the way to my elbow and I dropped it quickly. Lifting it up with my other hand, I unlocked the screen; 3:13 a.m. flashed. It was way too early to get up. My body needed sleep. Doing my best to give my body what it desperately needed, I laid my head on the pillow and closed my eyes, but images, those images, filled my mind.

"Not one nightmare the entire time I was gone," I said out loud. Maybe it was the house, just being here; the stress of all the memories we'd shared over the years too great. Maybe *I* should move out instead of Spencer. But could I handle losing my husband and the security of my home all at once? I lay awake in bed, watching the shadows from the moonlight dance on the ceiling, knowing sleep wouldn't find me now.

Every muscle in my body screamed as I climbed out of bed. Pain radiated through my arm when I gripped my toothbrush but I pushed past it. "It can only hurt if you let it, Izzy," my dad's words rang in my ears now. I washed away the evidence of last night's dream then slipped into my running clothes.

My heart was still in hyper drive as I made my way to the kitchen so I decided to skip the coffee for now, instead opting for a bottle of water before heading out into the darkness of the predawn hour for my morning run. Jogging slowly at first I quickly picked up speed. Taking the route I'd used hundreds of times made up for my lack of sight. I'd memorized every turn, every crack in the sidewalk, every imperfection in the pavement.

By the time I got up to full speed the pain in my ribs had come back with a vengeance, stopping me dead in my tracks. A sharp stabbing pain had me doubling over, my lungs screaming for air that wouldn't come. In through my nose, out through my mouth, tiny breaths were all I could manage. I limped my way back home doing my best to ignore the pain but by the time I made it home I was beginning to wonder if I really had hurt myself somehow.

As I dried off from my shower, I stared at myself in the mirror with disbelief of the reflection staring back at me. Dark circles had formed around my eyes as if I hadn't slept in days and my side was shadowed by what appeared to be the formation of a bruise. Yesterday morning I'd looked so rested, so relaxed. Today I looked like I'd been run over by a truck. What a difference one day home had made.

After pulling on my favorite linen pants and a long sleeve t-shirt I headed downstairs to make some coffee. Faint voices coming from the kitchen caught my attention as I came down the stairs. Drew and Anna weren't usually up this early and it sent my defenses up.

Taking as deep a breath as I could manage, I braced for what was sure to be an early morning battle.

"Good morning, Izzy," Sara said when I walked into the kitchen. "Look who I found when I went out for the paper."

My eyes shifted to where she was pointing. My mouth dropped open the second I saw him, my feet suddenly frozen in place.

"Isabella, I'm glad to see you're in once piece."

"What are you doing here?"

"You didn't call. You didn't answer my email. I went with worried, but I see I've made the wrong choice."

Shit. I couldn't do this. Not at my house, in my kitchen, and certainly not this early. Drew and Anna would be down for breakfast soon. They couldn't find Alec here. "My office is right this way, Mr. Payne." I walked out of the kitchen leaving Sara by herself, wide eyed, no doubt wondering what this was all about.

"Why are you here?" I asked when we're safely behind the closed door of my office. "You know how mad my kids were when they saw that picture of us. How mad do you think they'll be if they find you here, especially this early?"

Alec stepped toward me. "We just went through this, Isabella. You didn't call. You didn't answer my email. I was worried."

"Did you stop to think maybe there was a reason I didn't call you back? Like maybe I was too mad to even think about talking to you."

"Mad?" He tilted his head to one side.

"Yes, Alec. Mad. Regular people have feelings too, ya know, and right now I'm feeling mad, at you!"

Taking a step back, he said, "Okay, let's have it. Why are you mad?"

I crossed my arms. "My job, Alec. I worked hard to get where I am in my career and just like that it's changing, all because some control freak with more money than sense said so."

Alec pulled his hand through his hair. "Change is inevitable, Isabella. And I thought you'd be happy to spend more time with me, or at least be excited about the opportunity to advance your career."

I opened my mouth to speak but closed it. I was so mad at Alec I hadn't even considered what having Payne Enterprises in my portfolio could do for my career. "Well, you could've at least told me."

Alec rubbed his chin between his thumb and forefinger. "And deny myself the opportunity for make-up sex, not a chance," he said smiling, my words from yesterday amusing him now.

"Who said anything about sex?" I snapped, unable to hide my annoyance.

He pulled me into his arms. "Ow," I cried, reflexively pulling my arm back.

Alec's forehead wrinkled. "Baby, what is it?"

"It's nothing." His jaw tightened, clearly not buying my story. "My arm hurts but it's no big deal."

"You were fine yesterday. What happened?"

I rubbed my forehead wishing I knew myself. "I had another nightmare. My arm hurts. End of story."

"Dreams can't hurt you, Isabella. Now what's really going on?"

"Seriously, Alec, it's nothing. I probably hit my arm on the bedside table or something. Now please, just drop it." I looked up at the ceiling, praying he'd let it go.

Alec kissed me on the forehead. "Okay. I'll drop it. But only if you promise me you'll get it looked at."

A sigh escaped me. I didn't want to argue with him, especially knowing Drew and Anna would be down for breakfast soon. I needed to get him out of my house. They were mad enough at me as it was and Alec being here before breakfast was the last thing I wanted to have to explain. "Fine. I'll get it looked at."

Wrapping his arm around my waist Alec pulled me into him, his mouth inches from mine. "That's not the answer I was looking for, Isabella."

"I said I'd get it looked at." Alec narrowed his eyes, still not happy with my answer. "I'll call the doctor," I added, but his expression still didn't change. "I promise."

Alec cupped my face between both his hands and brushed his lips against mine, his tongue urging me to open. His hands slid to my neck, tilting my head up toward him. My lips parted and he claimed my mouth with his tongue, his hands fisting in my hair. I ran my hands up his back, the shooting pain in my arm temporarily numbed by my throbbing sex.

When he pulled away I had to hold on to his shirt to keep from falling. "I have to get back to New York. Come with me."

The effects of that kiss lingered and I paused to consider his offer, but only for a moment. "I'd love to, Alec, but thanks to this incredibly demanding new client of mine I'm overloaded with work this week," I said, finally recovering my equilibrium.

"Demanding, huh?" That wicked grin crossed his face. "Baby, I'll show you demanding," he whispered in my ear. His words made me blush. Damn my body for betraying me whenever he was around. "Thursday night. You and me. Tampa."

•   •   •   •   •

Dr. Leonard sent me for x-rays to rule out any broken bones. She said it was unlikely but wanted to be certain. I'd tried to object but she wouldn't hear it, not even when I told her I was swamped.

The imaging center agreed to squeeze me in so I couldn't really complain about the long wait either. I had back-to-back meetings scheduled for tomorrow, one of them in Tampa, so waiting was my only real choice. Luckily they had Wi-Fi so at least I was able to get some work done while I waited.

By the time they called my name I'd gotten through all the client notification emails on my list except one, Chris Matthews, the General Manager of the Sandestin Beach Resort. I had the email prepared to send but decided at the last minute a phone call would be better. Two weeks earlier Chris had been the client I dropped everything for, now he was being dropped. Breaking the news by email seemed cruel somehow.

In a matter of minutes the x-rays were done and I was on my way home. I still had to finish the client reports I'd been working on for my meetings with Kari and Steve in the morning so I decided to call Chris on the drive home to maximize my time.

"Sandestin Beach Resort," the tiny voice answered. "Hi. It's Izzy James. Chris Matthews, please."

"He's been trying to reach you, Ms. James, please hold."

"Izzy, hi, I just got off the phone with the photographer. Everything is set for Saturday." *Saturday? Photographer?* Then it hit me; the photo shoot Anna asked me to help her arrange for the senior class. Dozens of students gathered on the beach in their formal attire taking advantage of the picturesque backdrop the Gulf provides.

"You're awesome. These are going to be the best prom pictures ever." I took a deep breath. "Chris, I'm afraid I didn't call about the photo shoot. I called to let you know Kari will be handling your account for the next few months."

"Why? What's going on?"

I didn't want to lie to him but I wasn't sure how to tell him the truth either. "I just have a lot on my plate with my new travel schedule and I feel the Sandestin's needs will be better served this way." It wasn't the full truth but it wasn't a lie either.

"Izzy, I don't think I like this."

"You love Kari," I said. Distraction deployed. "She'll do a great job for you. And it's not like I'm leaving the team. I'll be around if there's a problem she can't handle."

"So this is a done deal then?"

"I'm afraid so."

"Well, thanks for the call, I guess," he said, his bubbly demeanor gone.

"Call me if you need me, okay."

"Sure, fine." Just like that the line went dead. I exhaled loudly. At least he took it better than I'd expected; no yelling or whining or sarcasm. He wasn't happy but I hadn't expected him to be. I'd been by his side since he first took the job at the Sandestin almost ten years ago. He trusted me, but he'd learn to trust Kari too.

I spent the rest of the afternoon jotting down notes my team would need when they took over my accounts. It felt wrong as I put pen to paper, writing detail after detail, so many secrets I'd kept stored, in my mind only, not daring to risk client confidentiality by adding them to some file that had the potential to be hacked.

With the day coming to an end, and several details I still needed pulled together before I left town in the morning, I knew I'd never get them done on my own. I shot a quick email to Jonathan for the help I needed and was about to close my email program when a new message arrived.

Date: April 22, 2015 05:37 PM
To: Isabella James
From: Alec Payne
Subject: Lunch tomorrow

Ms. James,

Lunch. Tomorrow. I'll pick you up at 1:30. It's not a request.

Alec Payne,
Incredibly Demanding CEO, Payne Enterprises

His signature made me laugh but that didn't mean I could have lunch with him tomorrow. Thanks to him I was going to be buried in meetings all day. I typed a quick response.

Date: April 22, 2015 05:38 PM
To: Alec Payne
From: Isabella (Izzy) James
Subject: Lunch tomorrow

Incredibly Demanding Control Freak,

I'm booked solid tomorrow. Aren't you in New York anyway?

Izzy James
Issues & Reputation Manager
Dimarco

I waited a few minutes for a response but when it didn't come I shut down my computer and headed into the kitchen for dinner.

Anna had a Prom Committee meeting and Drew had made plans to eat with his friends so it was just Sara and I, and the bottle of White Zinfandel she brought over. We made small talk while we ate. I asked about her husband, their new house, her plans for graduate school, anything to keep the conversation off my divorce, and Alec's early morning visit.

After the dinner dishes had been cleaned I headed upstairs to pack before calling it a night. I'd hoped to smooth things over with Anna before heading out of town again but it wasn't looking like that would happen now, not this trip anyway.

When my suitcase was all packed I climbed into the shower, excited to call it a night. Another early morning had left me more than exhausted. As I slid into bed I picked up my phone to do a final check of email and found one missed call. I scrolled through the call log and discovered it was from Alec. I was way too tired to risk any more surprises today so I decided to send him an email instead.

When I opened my email app I broke out in a full mouth smile.

Date: April 22, 2015 9:07 PM
To: Isabella James
From: Alec Payne
Subject: Lunch tomorrow

Ms. James,
Lunch. Tomorrow.

IT'S NOT A REQUEST.

Alec Payne,
Incredibly Demanding Control Freak & CEO, Payne Enterprises

Control freak, my inner voice snapped. I typed out a quick message.

Date: April 22, 2015 9:39 PM
To: Alec Payne
From: Isabella (Izzy) James
Subject: Lunch tomorrow

IDCF,

Fine. But you're clearing it with my boss.

Sorry I missed your call.

Izzy James,
Overworked & Totally Exhausted IR Manager
Dimarco

I hit send and before I could close out of my email I heard that familiar tone.

Date: April 22, 2015 9:39 PM
To: Isabella James
From: Alec Payne
Subject: Lunch tomorrow

Overworked & Totally Exhausted,

Let me remind you. YOU work for ME. Get some sleep. I'll see you tomorrow.

Alec Payne,
CEO, Payne Enterprises

Tossing my phone on the table, I switched off the light, a smile on my face. Alec's demanding ways were starting to grow on me. I pulled the covers around me and closed my eyes, waiting for sleep to find me.

Chapter Eleven

I was up before the sun again the next morning but I didn't care. I was just relieved I hadn't had another nightmare. After dressing in my office clothes, I headed downstairs to make a pot of coffee, taking my suitcase with me. I still had a lot to do before my flight and since I was up anyway I figured I might as well get to the office early.

The house was dark with the exception of the dim light in the foyer. My body tensed as I moved further into the darkness. Even though last night had been nightmare free that uneasy feeling of the darkness still lingered. Walking as fast as I could to the kitchen, I hit the switch in there. When I saw the room was empty I let out the breath I didn't know I'd been holding.

After the coffee finished brewing I poured the hot liquid into a travel mug and headed to my office to pack what I'd need for the day then, with my bags in tow, I headed for the car.

Traffic was light in the early morning hour and I made it to the office in well under an hour. Jonathan wasn't in when I arrived so I was able to slip into my office without delay, where I wasted no time getting down to business. I couldn't afford even one setback if there'd be any hope of having lunch with Alec later.

The morning flew by with the back to back meetings I had scheduled. Jonathan hadn't been around all day so when I heard his voice it surprised me. "Izzy," he called out from the doorway.

"Jonathan. Hey. What's up?"

"The car service is here to take you to your next appointment."

An unintentional smile crossed my face. "Thanks." Jonathan was gone as quickly as he'd appeared. After checking myself in the mirror, I rushed out the door, doing my best to contain my growing excitement. I'd somehow managed to avoid delays all morning but I wasn't about to take any chances now, not with Alec waiting downstairs, so I slipped out using the back stairs.

Preston was standing next to the car when I pushed open the heavy metal door from the stairwell. "Good afternoon, Ms. James."

"Hey, Preston." He opened the door and I slid in.

Alec looked at his watch. "You're late."

The smile on my face got even bigger. I slid over and kissed him on the lips. "Just be happy I made time for you at all." My teasing brought out his smile and I kissed him again before moving over to my seat. "Oh, speaking of time, I'm afraid I don't have a lot of it."

"Forget about your seatbelt, Preston, Ms. James is in a hurry."

I rolled my eyes in mock protest of his teasing. Alec unbuckled my seatbelt and pulled me onto his lap. "And you should be happy we're not alone right now," he whispered in my ear.

"Why is that?"

"Because I'd show you what I *really* think about your eye rolling." Nervously I bit my lip, silently wondering what he meant.

Alec nibbled on my earlobe, sending goose bumps all the way to my toes, before releasing me. Quickly, I moved back to my seat, struggling with the seatbelt this time, momentarily forgetting my arm still hurt like hell when I used it.

"Did you call the doctor?" Alec asked when he saw the pained expression on my face.

"I promised, didn't I?"

"That's not an answer, Isabella."

"Oh, but it is, Mr. Payne," I teased. Every muscle in Alec's face tightened and I couldn't help the smile that formed. "Okay, okay, I called. I even went for x-rays." The words were out of my mouth before I could stop them.

"X-rays?" *Shit*. That was a detail I hadn't wanted to share until I knew for certain they were negative.

When my phone vibrated in my hand, I answered without looking to see who was calling, relieved to have any distraction I could get at that moment. "Izzy James."

"Mrs. James this is Dr. Leonard's office. We got your x-rays back. I'm afraid you have two broken ribs and a fracture in your left forearm."

"What? Broken? How's that even possible?"

"I'm not sure, but Dr. Leonard wants you to see an orthopedist as soon as possible. You'll need a cast for your arm." Double Shit. I wished I'd let voicemail pick up this call. "Dr. Choi is right down the street from your office. I'll call and see if they can squeeze you in this afternoon."

"I can't today. I'm leaving for Tampa in a couple of hours."

"You really should have that break casted before you leave town."

I looked out the window, horrified by what she was saying. "Fine. Let me know what they say."

Disconnecting the call I nervously glanced over at Alec. The look on his face said it all. He was going to want an explanation I didn't have.

"Are you going to tell me what happened to your arm now, Isabella?"

I wasn't sure what to say. I'd already told him what I thought had happened but he didn't believe me. Dropping my head in my hands again, I sighed.

"Baby, please tell me."

"I don't know what to say."

"Just tell me what happened."

"I already did, Alec. It was a nightmare. Somehow I managed to fracture two ribs and my arm. That's all I know." I could hear how ridiculous the explanation sounded but it was the only one I had.

Tears filled my eyes as realization hit. My dreams were no longer nightmares, they were injuries, and the injuries were real.

• • • • •

"Thanks for lunch, Alec, and for understanding why I had to cancel my trip to Tampa today."

He pulled me into him for one last kiss. "Anything for you, baby."

"Seriously though, it's just a fracture. I can drive myself."

"We went through this at lunch, Isabella. Preston will drive you. End of story." Damn it, he was using my own words against me again. I'd need to learn how to be more careful of what I said around him.

"Control freak," I mouthed the words.

"Don't forget incredibly demanding," he said with his wicked grin that instantly had my sex tingling.

Preston opened my door and I reluctantly slid out of the car. "I'll see ya tomorrow for our first official client meeting."

"Until then, baby."

After talking things over with Alec during lunch I was excited about working on the Payne Enterprises account. I'd worried this contract was Alec's way of keeping me close, being Mr. Control Freak and all, but as it turned out there was a lot for me to do.

"Izzy!" Jonathan said from behind an oversized bouquet of white lilies. "Look what came for you."

My smile grew wider. "I wonder who these are from," I said although I was pretty sure I already knew the answer. I opened the card, *Congratulations on your new job*, it read.

"Well, who sent them?"

"It doesn't say."

"You want me to call the florist to find out who they're from?"

I hesitated for a minute to consider his question. I was sure they were from Alec. He probably just didn't want to get me in any more trouble with Tim, but the card seemed so impersonal, not at all like the Alec Payne I'd come to know. "Yeah, maybe you should," I said finally.

Knowing Alec I was sure Lily already knew I wasn't coming for the meeting but I didn't like to assume, especially when clients were involved. I sent her a quick email and attached the latest status report while I was at it.

No matter how hard I tried I couldn't get Alec out of my mind, and the flowers certainly weren't helping. The florist wasn't able to give Jonathan much information about who'd ordered them, only that a blonde woman came in yesterday and paid for them in cash. Distracted by the mystery I finally decided to email Alec to put a stop to all the wonder.

Date: April 23, 2015 2:55 PM
To: Alec Payne
From: Isabella (Izzy) James
Subject: Flowers

Mr. Payne,

Thank you for the flowers. Lilies are one of my favorites.

Izzy James,
Issues & Reputation Manager
Dimarco

I sat back in my chair and waited for Alec's reply. It wasn't like I was getting much work done anyway. I'd been looking forward to spending another night with Alec, but thanks to my broken arm that wasn't going to happen.

My cell phone rang bringing me back to where I was. "Izzy James," I answered.

"Hi, Mrs. James, this is Dawn from Dr. Leonard's office. I have good news. Dr. Choi had a cancellation and he can see you today."

While I wasn't looking forward to the appointment at least it'd be over and I'd be able to make the trip to New York tomorrow for the Payne meeting. Alec was going to introduce me to his executive team so I could get started on my first assignment, and I was really looking forward to that.

"Great. What time?"

"That's the thing. It was a last minute cancellation so you'll need to go right away."

Shit. I was expecting some sort of notice. I certainly wasn't prepared to drop everything and run to an appointment. "Alright," I sighed. "I'm on my way."

I grabbed my purse and keys and walked out into the hall. "I need to go out, Jonathan. Reschedule my last two meetings for early tomorrow morning." I hurried down the hall not waiting for a response. Alec was going to freak when he found out I drove myself to the appointment but it was the only choice I had. Preston wasn't back from taking Alec to the airport yet and there was no time to wait for a cab.

• • • • •

When I walked out of the orthopedists office sporting a short arm cast I was horrified. There was no hiding the injury now. Luckily Dr. Choi said my ribs would heal without intervention, as long as I adhered to the long list he gave me of things to avoid, but the cast was hideous.

Not surprisingly, Dr. Choi hadn't believed me when I told him how I got hurt. "You have a spiral fracture in your forearm, Ms. James, and the only way to get that type of injury is by literally twisting your arm," he'd said. I shuddered as I considered his words. Someone did this. There was no way I'd broken it in my sleep.

What I didn't know was who it could be, or how they'd gotten inside the house. Spencer installed a top-of-the-line security system a few years back, including door and window alarms. If anyone so much as cracked open a door or window without entering the alarm code the entire neighborhood would know about it. So if someone *had* gotten in, did that mean they had the code? My head was spinning with possibilities. Then I remembered the shadow. Spencer. No, it couldn't be him. He wouldn't hurt me. Would he?

When I got back to the office I decided to use the stairs, hoping to avoid being seen. My plan was to grab what I needed and sneak back out before anyone even knew I was there. The fewer people who saw me in this stupid cast the better.

Jonathan was barely visible behind the huge vase of flowers so I was able to duck into my office unnoticed. The cast slowed my progress but I finally managed to get my laptop and the files I needed into my bag.

Opening the door, I peeked out. "Hey, Izzy, Jonathan said you weren't here."

Shit. Busted. "Hey, Kari. I just got back, come on in."

Kari's mouth dropped open when she saw the cast. "Oh my God, Izzy, what happened?" Great, she was making a scene. As fast as I could, I pulled her into my office and shut the door before anyone else could see me.

"Oh, you know me," I said with a fake laugh. There was no reason to tell her the truth, well, the only truth I knew. No one seemed to believe it, including me. Distraction was my only hope of avoiding a long explanation. "Have you emailed Chris yet?"

"Yeah, we're having lunch tomorrow. I'll be on site overseeing his remodel anyway."

"Perfect. I think this change will be good for both of you."

"You'll still be around for our weekly team meetings, right?"

"I'm still working out the details with Payne Enterprises but that's the plan." I glanced down at my vibrating phone. It was from a private number so I let voicemail pick it up. When I looked up again I noticed the frown on Kari's face. "You'll be fine, Kari. You're great at what you do. And you can always call if you need me."

"Thanks, Izzy. I needed to hear that." My phone vibrated again. I glanced down, it was Preston this time. Kari stood to leave. "I can see you're busy. I'll let you get back to work. Try to have some fun while you're in New York."

Thoughts of Alec raced through my mind at the mere mention of New York and an involuntary smile crossed my face. "I'll do my best."

Kari closed the door behind her as I dialed voicemail to retrieve the two messages. I was happy to hear Preston made it back from the airport so I could get out of the office. I deleted his message and the next one started to play automatically, the message from the private caller. I recognized her voice immediately.

"Hey, Bella," Valerie said. "I want to see you. Call me." I'd been meaning to call her but with all the traveling I'd been doing I kept forgetting. I scribbled a note to remind myself to call her and dropped it into my purse. That familiar tone signaling a new email chimed. I just wanted to get out of the office.

Date: April 23, 2015 4:55 PM
To: Isabella James
From: Alec Payne
Subject: Unclear

Ms. James,

Apparently my instructions were unclear. PRESTON WILL DRIVE YOU. Is that clear enough for you now?

And I didn't send you flowers.

Alec Payne
Incredibly Demanding & *Now Irritated* Control Freak, Payne Enterprises

How did he possibly know I'd left the office, much less driven myself. But more importantly, he didn't send the flowers. *Congratulations on your new job*, the card read. There were only a handful of people who knew about my new job and most of them were in this building. Chris must've sent them, that was the only explanation that made sense.

Chapter Twelve

Preston was waiting for me in the parking garage when I finally managed to get out of the office. He transferred my bags from my car to the trunk of his then drove me to the hotel I'd booked after having to cancel my flight. My trip to New York for the Payne Enterprises meeting was still on for tomorrow so there was no reason to make the hour long drive back to Ft. Walton Beach. Especially considering Spencer was supposed to be back tonight. Until I figured out exactly how I managed to break my arm there was no way I was sleeping in the same house as him.

Neither of us said much during the ten minute drive from my office to the Crowne Plaza. Alec was pretty mad at me for driving to the appointment by myself and I could only imagine what he'd said to Preston. Plus, I couldn't stop thinking about the flowers. My favorite flowers. *The flowers Alec didn't send.*

• • • • •

After I settled into my room I ordered a mixed green salad with coconut crusted chicken and a mango salsa from room service before getting into the shower. Dr. Choi used a waterproof cast material but he said it would take an hour or so to dry. Jonathan rescheduled the two meetings I'd had to miss thanks to the ridiculous cast I was wearing for early tomorrow morning and I didn't want to be up all night waiting for the damn thing to dry.

Alec said he'd call later but I was much too tired to deal with him or his demands, and especially his irritations, so I powered down my cell phone and ordered a wakeup call from the front desk. There would be plenty of time for Alec to freak out about me driving myself to the doctor on the plane ride to New York tomorrow, assuming we were still flying out together.

The next morning I woke feeling refreshed and thankfully nightmare free. I'd left the drapes partially opened last night and could see the sun was just starting to rise. The sky was filled with shades of red and orange and blue as the sun slowly chased away the night. It was a wonderful time of day, watching, patiently waiting for the sun to rise.

Considering I'd woken up early I cancelled the wakeup call then went down to the hotel lobby for a cup of coffee. Business travelers were rushing about gathering their breakfast before heading out to wherever it was they were going. I grabbed an apple then poured myself a cup of coffee before going back to the peacefulness of my room.

After I'd dressed I ran a straightener through my hair then pulled it back into a ponytail. The cast made the process more challenging but I finally managed to get it done. When I'd finished, I sped through my makeup routine, gathered up my luggage, and headed downstairs to find Preston.

The elevator door opened in the lobby where I saw Preston waiting for me. "Good morning, Preston."

"Good morning, Ms. James." He reached for my bags. "Here, let me get those."

I didn't object as my cast was making almost every task a challenge. "Thanks." He nodded but didn't say anything. "I'm sorry about yesterday. I hope you didn't get into too much trouble."

"It was nothing, ma'am. But I do hope you'll let me drive you next time." He smiled as he said it and I knew I was forgiven.

Preston dropped me at the office with the promise of being back at ten thirty to drive me to the airport. I had to get through the last two meetings held over from yesterday before I could leave though, and the more people who saw me wearing a cast the greater the odds I wouldn't be ready to go when he got back. I slipped quietly into my office to grab what I needed for both meetings before hurrying down the hall to the conference room.

• • • • •

By the time my last meeting ending I was ahead of schedule. All I had to do now was lay low until Preston came to pick me up. I'd just about made it back to the safety of my office when Jonathan spotted me. "Ohmygosh, Izzy! What happened?"

"It's nothing. It's just a small fracture," I offered.

"So that's where you ran off to yesterday. You should have told me!" Shit. He was almost shouting. I had to get away from him before everyone in the office took notice.

Holding up the file folder in my hand, I moved past Jonathan in the direction of my office. "I have to get this report finished before I fly out." Redirection deployed.

Preston wouldn't be here for another ten minutes so I opened my email to do a quick check before leaving. There were several emails from clients extending their well wishes, but nothing from Alec. He couldn't still be mad about me driving. Could he?

My phone rang and I answered it quickly. "Izzy James."

"Bella, hey, I've been trying to get ahold of you."

You have caller ID ya know, my inner voice chimed in. I shook her off. Preston would be here any minute so I didn't have a lot of time. "Hey, Val. Sorry I haven't called. I've been traveling a lot lately."

"I miss you, Izzy. I want to see you."

I wanted to see her too. I missed my friend. There was so much for us to catch up on, especially now that Spencer told the kids about the divorce. "We're doing a photo shoot at the Sandestin tomorrow night for prom, you should come."

There was a knock on my door but it opened before I even had time to answer. "I just heard about your arm. Are you okay?" Shit. Tim. Now I'd never get out of here on time. I held up a finger indicating I'd need a minute.

"Val, I'm so sorry but I'm going to have to call you back."

She sighed loudly. "Fine! But you better call me back this time."

"The Sandestin Beach Resort. Tomorrow," I said before I disconnected the call and turned my attention to Tim. "Hey, Tim, what's up?"

"Jonathan told me about your arm. What happened?"

"It was just a bad dream." I shook my head slowly. "I hit it on the bedside table or something."

"Oh Izzy, only you could break an arm in your sleep," Tim laughed, and I laughed too. He believed me, thank the Lord for that.

There was another knock. Damn it. I just wanted to hide out in here alone until Preston got back and my office was turning into Grand Central Station. "Excuse me, Izzy, there's a delivery for you." Jonathan stood in the doorway holding a vase of tulips, another one of my favorites. My heart started to race as I thought back to the lilies, still unsure who sent them.

Tim stood to leave. "I'm glad you're okay, Izzy. Call me Monday to let me know how it went with Payne Enterprises."

"Sure thing."

Jonathan set the vase on my desk and handed me the card. I opened it quickly. *I hope these make you smile. IDCF,* it read.

"Who are they from?"

"IDCF, IDCF," I said over and over again in my mind.

"Earth to Izzy," Jonathan said bringing me back to the here and now. "Who are they from?"

A smile crossed my face as I remembered Alec's email from yesterday. *Incredibly Demanding Control Freak.*

"Oh, sorry, they're from a client."

"The same client who sent those gorgeous lilies?" Thankfully Jonathan's phone rang before I had to answer his question and he rushed out to grab it, leaving me to read the card again. *I hope these make you smile. IDCF.* I sat back in my chair, an ear-to-ear smile on my face.

"Your ride's here," Jonathan called from his desk.

"Thanks." Sighing with relief, I packed up and headed out the door, the smile still on my face.

Butterflies filled my stomach as we got closer to the airport. While I was excited to see Alec I was nervous at the same time. I hadn't heard from him since his angry email yesterday afternoon, with the exception of the flowers, and I hoped he wasn't still mad.

Preston collected my bags then escorted me up the steps to the waiting jet. "Ms. James, Preston," Alec said coolly when we boarded.

Preston nodded then stowed my bags.

"Hi," I said enthusiastically but Alec didn't say anything more. Shit, he was still mad but I pretended not to notice. "Thank you for the flowers. Tulips are another one of my favorites." I bit my lip. "But I'm sure you already knew that, IDCF and all."

Alec's expression softened. He pulled me onto his lap and kissed me on the lips. I kissed him back, all the excitement to see him exploding in that one kiss that made my sex tingle. I wanted to rip his clothes off and devour him right there.

He pulled back, *No!* my inner voice shouted.

"Sit," he said, pointing to the seat next to him. Disappointed, I slid over and buckled my seatbelt. Alec flashed his wicked grin and I knew he wanted me too.

Pointing to my cast, Alec said, "Pink, huh?"

"Yep," I laughed, still recovering from that kiss.

· · · · ·

"Are we in Tampa?" I asked as Alec led me down the jet stairway, confused by why we weren't in New York.

"Yes. There was another break-in." He held the car door open so I could get in then slid in next to me. I couldn't help but notice he'd said another break-in, yet this was the first time he'd mentioned anything about it.

"Another one? Where?"

"Payne Enterprises. This is the second time they've gotten past security."

"What did they take?"

He pulled his hand through his hair. "Information."

"What kind of information?"

Alec shook his head. "Okay, that's enough questions."

"But—"

"No buts about it. This isn't your problem to solve, Isabella." Alec kissed my hand softly. "I don't want you at the office until we figure out how that son-of-a-bitch got in." He pulled both hands through his hair this time. "You're used to working from home so plan on doing that for now."

Trying to hide my disappointment, I looked away. Spending time with Alec was the best part about this new job.

"Don't pout, Isabella. You know how crazy that makes me." He leaned over and bit my lip before kissing me, neither of which made the new arrangement any easier to take.

We ate lunch at the Élevage in the newly opened Epicurean Hotel. "You'll stay here tonight," Alec said, rubbing his forehead. "I have to go back to New York but Frank will be here to take you anywhere you want to go."

"Who's Frank?"

"He'll be your driver until your ribs heal."

Wait, did he say until my ribs heal? "Alec I told you, I don't need a driver."

His jaw tightened and he pulled both hands through his hair. "We're not discussing this again, Isabella." I decided to let it go, for now anyway. The break-in had him pretty shaken and I didn't want to be the one who pushed him over the edge.

Alec stood to leave and I followed. "I have to go now, baby."

"Thank you for lunch."

"Anything for you, Isabella," he whispered in my ear. "I'll see you soon." Pulling me into his arms he kissed me one final time before heading out of the hotel, leaving me standing in the lobby, disappointed that another night alone with him had been foiled.

The bellman appeared out of nowhere and carried my luggage to my room. I thought about flying back to Pensacola but Alec had already paid for the room, and it was a great hotel. Not to mention Spencer was supposed to be home.

Flowers filled the room as I walked inside the spacious suite. Everywhere I looked; vase after vase, tulips, lilies, orchids, all my favorite flowers in all my favorite colors. When I spotted the card with my name on it, I couldn't wait to read it. I tipped the bellman and as soon as he disappeared I opened the cared. *Do I make you smile? IDCF*, the card read. And it did.

I pulled a bottle of water from the mini bar and walked out onto the balcony to get a closer look at the view of the Hillsborough Bay. Thoughts of Alec occupied my mind, the conference room where we'd first met, dinner at Oishi, sunset in Marsh Harbour, snorkeling in Turtle Cay, the night we spent together at his condo, the break-ins that were keeping us apart.

My phone rang and I ran inside to answer it, hoping it was Alec but when I glanced at the caller ID my heart sank.

It wasn't Alec but I answered the call anyway, happy at least for the distraction. "Hey, Val."

"I thought you were going to call me back," she snapped.

"I planned on calling you after my meeting. So are you coming this weekend?" I asked hoping to redirect the conversation.

"Oh, Bella, I can't this weekend. But I do want to see you."

"You're still coming for graduation though, right?"

"I wouldn't miss it," Valerie said. "Will you be able to do a girl's weekend then?"

"I'll have family in town but I'm sure we can find some time to catch up. What's going on with you anyway?" Valerie never called just to say hi, there was always another reason.

"What's your problem, Izzy? Can't I just call to tell you I miss you?"

That certainly would be a first but anything was possible. "I just meant what's new. We haven't talked in so long."

"And whose fault is that?" Valerie could be so

temperamental when she didn't get her way, like when Spencer proposed without telling her about it first. She freaked out that day and drove her car right through his garage door. Usually I let her tantrums roll off my back but I just wasn't in the mood for any of that right now. I'd planned on spending the night with Alec, naked, not getting reprimanded for being busy. I seriously started to rethink answering her call. "Val, that's my boss calling. I need to go."

"Again… Geez, Izzy, I remember when you'd make time for your best friend."

"I'm sorry. I'll take a few days off after graduation and we'll hang out, just the two of us."

"What about Spencer?" Shit. I still hadn't told her about the divorce but I wasn't about to get into that on the phone, not with her pissy attitude that was for sure. I couldn't bear the wrath of Val for keeping that news from her.

"Just us, no men allowed. Call me when you book your flight. I've gotta go."

"Fine," she snapped before slamming the phone down in my ear. I felt bad for lying to her but I wasn't in the right frame of mind to deal with her attitude. She was clearly upset about something but she would've made me drag it out of her. It was the attention she really wanted. It wouldn't matter that my life was spinning out of control. I powered off my phone, all hopes of a relaxing evening far out of reach.

The hotel was less than a mile from the scenic Bayshore Boulevard and a walk sounded pretty good after that call. Dr. Choi suggested I wait a couple weeks before resuming my normal workout routine but luckily walking was on the recommended activities list. I changed into my running shoes and headed down to the lobby.

A tall man in a black suit and tie that looked remarkably similar to the one Preston wore approached me as soon as I got off the elevator. "Ms. James?" he asked.

"Yes. I'm Izzy James. Who are you?"

"I'm Frank, ma'am. I'm your new driver."

Great, just what I needed right now. "It's nice to meet you, Frank."

He handed me a business card. "This is my cell phone number. I'm available any time day or night."

"Thanks." I put the card in my pocket. "I'm just going for a walk tonight but I'll call you in the morning when I'm ready to go."

"I'll come with you."

I held up my hand. "No thanks. I'd like to be alone."

"Mr. Payne insisted I escort you if you left the hotel, ma'am."

I rolled my eyes. I was starting to get really annoyed with this overprotective nonsense. I'd agreed to let Frank drive me, not babysit me. "Well, what Mr. Payne doesn't know won't kill him, Frank." I walked past him through the automatic doors. When Frank followed me outside I knew that was one battle I wasn't going to win.

Storming back inside the hotel, I headed straight to the bar where I ordered a bottle of wine to take to my room where I could sit on the balcony and watch the sunset, by myself!

• • • • •

The flight back to Pensacola seemed longer somehow. Probably because my head had been pounding since I woke up and the noisy plane was only making it worse. Alec called before I left the hotel but I'd been in the shower and missed his call. His message said he'd be tied up until after lunch. I'd been looking forward to hearing from him but all I could do now was wait.

Yesterday I left my car in the parking garage at my office and I planned to drive it home. I didn't like the idea of being dependent on someone else. Alec wasn't going to be thrilled about me driving but it was my car I didn't like the idea of leaving it at the office all weekend. Besides, my ribs felt fine, as long as I didn't run, or lift, or twist too fast. "I need to go to my office, Frank," I said when he pulled away from the airport.

"Sure thing, Ms. James," he answered, without question.

I offered him the address to my office but he already had it. I should've known. He probably had the address to my house already too.

"Pull the car in that open space near the elevator."

"That's a loading zone, Ms. James."

"You're just dropping me off. You can move the car into a space after I get out."

He did as I asked. "Call me when you're ready to go."

"Okay." I looked out the window, unable to look him in the face knowing that what I was about to do would likely get him in hot water with his boss.

Frank moved the car in search of an open parking space and as soon as he was out of sight I made a mad dash to my car and took off toward home. In no time I merged onto the highway and mashed down on the accelerator.

On the drive home I called Sara to find out if Spencer was in town. I was relieved to hear he'd left again and wouldn't be back until the following night. I planned to move to a hotel in the morning but I was thankful to be in my own house for the night. All I wanted to do was crawl into bed, my own bed, and sleep this off.

Spencer and I would need to work out a schedule for staying at the house the next couple of months but I was still too mad to talk to him. He cheated on me and I was the one taking all the blame, and this blaring pink cast served as a constant reminder of the nightmares I'd been having as a result, the nightmares that resulted in two cracked ribs and a fractured forearm.

Drew and Anna were in the kitchen when I got home. Drew's mouth dropped open when he saw the hot pink cast I was sporting. "Mom! What happened?"

Closing my eyes, I said a silent prayer he'd believe me. "I had a bad dream and must've bumped it on the nightstand or something." Even though I knew that couldn't be true it was the only explanation I could offer because there was no way I was going to suggest that someone actually did this.

Anna pulled me into a tight hug. I winced as she squeezed my arm but didn't say anything. I was just happy she wasn't still mad at me anymore. "Careful, Anna," Drew admonished.

"It's not a big deal guys. I just have to wear this hideous thing on my arm for a few weeks." I held the cast up. Distraction deployed.

Drew kissed me on the cheek. "Well, I'm glad you're okay."

"Me too," Anna said, "but hot pink?" She threw her arms in the air making us all laugh, the way we used to laugh before all this craziness started.

"What time are you leaving for the photo shoot?" I asked, taking the spotlight off of me.

"The limo isn't coming until four o'clock. I wanted to leave earlier so I could get ready at the hotel, but Drew won't drive me."

"You really need to get your license, Anna. What are you going to do when you leave for college and I'm not around?"

"Leave me alone, Drew. You know I don't like to drive."

"Too bad because I'm not taking you."

Anna folded her arms across her chest, her bottom lip protruding. "Please, Drew."

"I'll take you, Sweetie." Drew rolled his eyes but I didn't care. Anna was talking to me again and that's what really mattered.

She threw her arms around me again. "Thank you!" she screamed in my ear. "I'm gonna take a shower. Let's leave at noon, okay?" I nodded my agreement and she ran off upstairs.

"You know you're only enabling her."

"Maybe," I laughed, and Drew laughed too.

"I guess I better get ready, too. I still have to pick up Chelsea's corsage." He kissed me on the cheek and disappeared up the stairs.

It was only ten o'clock so I headed upstairs to lie down for a while, hoping to get rid of this awful headache. Every step I took was just another reminder of how much I drank last night. Sprawling out across my king sized bed, I closed my eyes. Thoughts of Alec raced through my mind. His email from a couple days ago, "PRESTON WILL DRIVE YOU," he'd written. He was so controlling, too controlling. Mr. Control Freak, IDCF. The flowers, all the flowers, *"Do I make you smile?"*

And he does.

Chapter Thirteen

"Mom, wake up, we're gonna be late."

The sun shone brightly through the window when I opened my eyes. "What time is it?"

"It's noon already. Get up!"

Twelve o'clock. Shit. I sat up in bed, my head still throbbing. "I'm up, Anna. I'm up."

"Good, now hurry." She stormed out of my room.

I swallowed two Advil then moved slowly out of bed and into the bathroom to wash my face, hoping the cool water might help rid my headache.

Despite my efforts to hurry it was almost twelve thirty by the time I made into the kitchen where Anna was waiting. She handed me a travel mug. "Here, drink this. It's the ultimate hangover cure," she said. She tugged at the elbow of my good arm and I followed her to the car, silently wondering what was in the cup, and more importantly, how she knew it cured hangovers.

It was a quick drive to the hotel. Chris was so excited to see me, despite me transferring his account to Kari, that he upgraded Anna and her friends to a suite, free of charge. His easy going nature was one of the things I'd really enjoyed about working with him.

In my haste to get Anna to the hotel on time I'd left without my purse. Fortunately there was plenty of time before the shoot to drive home and get it. If only I could get rid of my screaming headache. Reluctantly I took a long drink from the concoction Anna gave me. I swallowed quickly, not exactly sure what was in the cup. It tasted surprisingly familiar. I took another drink. "Orange juice," I laughed out loud then drained the mug.

I reached up to activate the gate remote when I turned into my driveway and almost rear ended the car that was parked in front of the gate. *Shit.* I slammed on the brakes barely avoiding the collision. The driver door opened and a man stepped out. *Double shit.* Preston. His narrowed eyes didn't exactly say 'happy to see you' either. I climbed out of the car to see what was going on, my heart beating in my throat. But when he reached for the back door I thought for certain I was going to faint.

"*Alec,*" I gasped.

He glared at me with an intensity I hadn't seen in his eyes before. He opened his mouth to speak but closed it again. I stood still, frozen in front of him, not sure of the best way to proceed. I knew he wouldn't be happy that I ditched Frank and drove myself home, but the thought of him showing up at my house to confront me about it had never crossed my mind.

Alec stepped closer. "Do you know what a driver does, Isabella?" Without waiting for me to answer, he continued. "He drives! I told you I didn't want you driving yourself until your ribs healed, yet here you are." He threw his hands up in the air. "The doctor said you should avoid driving and I expect you to follow his orders."

Seriously? I took a step back and folded my arms across my chest. I'd had just about enough of this third degree shit. "First of all he said driving wasn't recommended, he never said I *couldn't* do it. And second, I'll drive *my* car whenever *I* feel like it."

He pulled his hand through his hair. "I only want you safe, Isabella. Can't you see that?"

"And I appreciate that, Alec. But I'm more than capable of taking care of myself." He rubbed his forehead again. His angst couldn't only be about me driving. There had to be something else going on. It made me wonder if there was more to those break-ins than he was telling me. Cupping his cheek in my good hand, I said, "I'm fine, okay?"

Alec pulled me into a hug and held me close, until my stomach growled. "Have you eaten today, Isabella?" Great, just what I needed, something else for him to freak out about. I shook my head and hoped for the best.

To my surprise, Alec took the keys out of my hand. "Lunch it is then, but I'm driving." He walked around the car to the passenger side and held the door open. I climbed in without argument, glad he'd stopped yelling at me, beyond happy he was here. Alec slid in behind the wheel and backed out onto the street.

"I have to be in Destin by four fifteen."

"For the photo shoot?"

"Yes," I said hesitantly. "How do you know about that?"

"Drew invited me."

My head started to spin. "You talked to Drew? When? Why?" I fired the questions in rapid succession.

"Don't get your panties in a bunch, Isabella." Shit. I really needed to stop giving him ammunition to use against me. "Drew called my office this morning. He's worried about you."

"What's he worried about?"

Alec looked over at me. "Let's see, could it be that hot pink cast you're wearing, maybe?"

"But why would he call you?"

"You'll have to ask him that."

Anxiously, I asked, "You didn't tell him about my ribs, did you?"

Alec shook his head. "That isn't my story to tell, Isabella."

"Well what did you tell him?"

He looked over at me and smiled. "That's between me and Drew." *Seriously?* My son called him and he's not even going to tell me what they talked about. Control freak!

• • • • •

"Baby, what's wrong?"

"What if Spencer decides to show up?"

"So what if he does?"

"It's just," I put down my fork and looked into his eyes. "Anna is so protective of him." The memory of her anger when she saw the picture of me and Alec still haunted me. "Alec, she was so mad at me and—"

"Isabella, lots of people will be at the shoot. Anna will be too busy to notice who's there and who isn't. And besides, Spencer won't be there anyway so stop worrying about it."

"What, did he call you too?"

Alec's jaw tightened. "Don't be ridiculous, Isabella. Drew told me."

I shook my head, still trying to wrap my mind around why Drew felt the need to call Alec. It wasn't like we were even an item, not really anyway. We'd spent very little time together outside of the cruise, and that one night in his condo. But Drew couldn't possibly know that, could he? "What else did you and Drew talk about?"

"I told you, that's between the two of us, but I will tell you he's not buying your 'I broke my arm in my sleep' story."

Great. I'd really hoped I wouldn't have to try and explain my injuries again because the only other explanation I had was the one the doctor offered, and I certainly wasn't going to tell Drew that. Not until I was absolutely sure he was right. I mean, come on, someone broke into my house, without setting off the alarm, without waking me up, now *that* was crazy. "Do you believe me?"

Alec put his hand over mine. "No," he said simply. I pulled my hand back but he caught it and held me in place. The lines on his forehead deepened. "I want to believe you, Isabella, because the alternative scares the hell out of me." The look on his face said it all; Mr. Control Freak had found something he couldn't control.

• • • • •

The Sandestin did an amazing job putting together the Paris inspired theme for the photo shoot. Dozens of teenagers dressed to the nines in designer gowns and tuxes ready to have the time of their lives. Anna in the Tony Bowls mermaid gown Spencer bought her, Drew in his custom tailored Vera Wang tux. Nearly every senior at Ft. Walton Beach High was there to preserve the memory of their special day.

Luckily, Spencer hadn't shown up at the shoot. Drew assured Alec that Spencer wouldn't be there but I had still worried about him showing up to surprise Anna. And just like Alec had said, there were so many people there I barely had a minute to talk to either of my kids.

Alec and I stayed long after the last limo left, walking along the shoreline watching the breathtaking sunset the clear night offered. We shared an order of lobster ravioli at The Funky Blues Shack while enjoying the sounds of a local blues band. Alec tried to convince me to spend the weekend at the hotel but I was really looking forward to sleeping in my bed, even if it was only for one night. And besides, I didn't even have my purse with me, or a change of clothes. Fortunately, he hadn't pushed too hard.

A cool breeze picked up that had me shivering. "Let's get you home," Alec said. "I need to get back anyway."

"You're flying out tonight?"

Alec pulled me into his chest and kissed me softly on the lips. "I wish I could stay, baby, but I have to get back." My lower lip protruded protesting the news. He bit my lip. "Don't pout. I'll be back on Monday."

I wrapped my arms around him and buried my face against his chest. I didn't want him to go. I wanted to stay there all night, wrapped in his arms.

What are you doing to me, Alec Payne? I asked myself, surprised by my overwhelming desire to be near him.

When we pulled into the garage at my house I was relieved to find Spencer's space empty. He wasn't expected back until morning but that wouldn't have been the first time he'd come home earlier than expected. I wasn't sure if it was the wine, or the walk on the beach, or the drive home, but I was spent and couldn't wait to get into bed.

"I'll see you Monday," Alec whispered before kissing me on the mouth, a kiss so full of promise it had my knees buckling.

Preston drove through the open gate and Alec took a step toward the car. "Travel safe," I called after him, my equilibrium finally returning.

"No driving, Isabella. Don't make me tell you again."

A mischievous grin crossed my face. "And what if I do?"

Alec's jaw tightened. "No. Driving," he said again in a tone that made my insides tingle. "Are we clear on that?"

"Yes," I breathed, my insides still tingling from the effects of that kiss. I would've agreed to almost anything at that moment. Alec closed the gap between us and sealed it with one last kiss before walking toward the car, leaving me wanting, again.

He climbed into the car and just like that he was gone. I reached in my jacket pocket for my house keys only they weren't there. I checked the other pocket, no keys. *Control Freak!* my inner voice snapped. No, surely he hadn't taken them. I fished out my phone and dialed his number.

"Payne," he answered.

"Did you take my keys?"

"So what if I did?" he asked, using my words against me once more.

I closed my eyes and exhaled loudly into the phone. "How am I supposed to get inside the house, Alec?"

"Check the door, Isabella. It's unlocked."

"Seriously," I snapped. "What if there's an emergency? What if I *need* my car?"

"Frank will be arriving soon. He'll take you anywhere you want to go, day or night."

"What do you mean, Frank will be arriving?"

"Since you refused to stay at the hotel you left me no choice but to have Frank stay there with you."

Had he honestly expected me to just accept that he'd made such a big decision about my life without talking to me about it? Who the hell did he think he was? "Yeah, I don't think so, Alec. You can't just decide who stays at my house and who doesn't." The idea of having some stranger staying with me was absurd. *I'm Izzy James, damn it. I'm a strong, independent woman.* And I sure as hell didn't need someone looking after me. And I most definitely didn't need a driver!

"Baby—"

"Don't 'baby' me, Alec Payne! I can't believe you decided this without so much as talking to me about it. I'm an adult, damn it."

Alec sighed heavily into the phone. "I told you, Isabella. I just want you safe."

"Whatever!" I screamed into the phone. "But don't expect me to be happy about it." Disconnecting the call, I stormed up the stairs, my head spinning. I wasn't sure how I felt about this, whatever *this* was.

Sand clung to my ankles from our walk on the beach so I got in the shower to wash it off, still fuming about Alec's lack of boundaries. And I was even more worked up after my shower when I came downstairs to find Frank sitting at the breakfast bar. This wasn't his fault. He was just following orders, undoubtedly what Alec expected me to do as well.

I directed Frank to the spare room down the hall from Sara's, then went back to the kitchen for a glass of wine. One glass quickly turned into two, my courage strengthening with every drink. Who did this control freak think he was? I poured a third glass and stormed upstairs to find my phone, determined to tell Alec Payne exactly how I felt about all his nonsense.

Damn it! The call went straight to voicemail. "You can't control me ya know. I'm Izzy James. I don't need a damn babysitter!" I disconnected the call and fell face down on the bed, disappointed I didn't get to yell at him.

· · · · ·

It was dark and I couldn't see. Something was covering my eyes. I tried to move it but my arms were tied. That smell, not that smell; alcohol, cigarettes, and gardenias? My head was so heavy.

A harsh tone filled my ears. "Who sent you flowers?"

I felt a sharp pain in my side. "No, please, stop," I opened my mouth to speak but my voice failed me.

Symphonie Fantaqstique blared all around. "Who!" he shouted. The pain came again, and again.

"No," I tried to scream but I couldn't. The pain in my ribs was too great and I struggled to breathe.

"Who makes you smile?" He was yelling at me now. I knew that voice. But who? That smell, that terrible smell. "Answer me!" The pain came again. I tried to answer but words failed me. Pain, there was so much pain. "Why do you insist on defying me, Bella?" he shouted, louder still. My head was groggy. His hand fisted in my hair, pulling my head back and exposing my neck. It was so hard to breathe.

"It's just another dream," I told myself. I wanted to wake up now. "Wake up," I pleaded with myself. "Wake up damn it." I twisted and turned, pulling on my restraints. *Wake up! Wake up! Wake up!*

Tears fell down my face in a steady stream. "Please," I finally managed to say.

"I like it when you beg, Bella. I'm gonna make you beg." His voice was in my ear. My body tensed. He pulled my hair harder and when I cried out he claimed my mouth with his tongue. He tasted of whisky and cigarettes. I turned my head trying to resist him but it was no use.

The music blared around me, louder and louder still. "Who are you?" I asked.

"Don't you know me, Bella? Can't you taste me?" The pain came again making me cough this time. There was a sharp pain on the back of my neck. My head was foggy. My eyes were too heavy to hold open.

• • • • •

I jolted upright in bed. Tears were falling in a steady stream down my face. My heart was racing so fast I could barely breathe. I pulled my arms down, instantly relieved when they moved. "It was just a dream," I said out loud. "Just another stupid nightmare."

My body ached as I climbed out of bed. A sharp pain pierced my side when I tried to take a deep breath. It felt so real. *The pain is real*, my inner voice snapped. My body tensed as I considered the reality of it. My fractured ribs. This hot pink cast. But Frank was downstairs. It had to have been a dream.

After pulling on my robe I headed downstairs for a bottle of water. The house was dark, the only light coming from the foyer. I'd almost gotten to the bottom of the stairs when a shadow in the doorway caught my eye. I stood still, frozen in my tracks, my whole body trembling.

The shadow moved and I knew it was real. Someone was here. "Frank?" I called out, but there was no answer. The shadowy figure moved again. I screamed and turned to run back upstairs but my foot got tangled in my robe sending me toppling head over heels down the stairs, onto the marble floor. My head was fuzzy but I could see someone standing next to me. Those eyes, I recognized those eyes.

"Mom! Wake up. Wake up mom." I heard voices in the distance. Anna, Drew, lots of voices all around me.

"Stay with us, Mrs. James." His voice was unfamiliar. "We're almost to the hospital, ma'am." Did he say hospital? There were more voices, and lights, lights everywhere. I closed my eyes and shadows surrounded me. Those eyes. I remembered his eyes.

It was dark. My head was foggy. There was so much pain. "No," I shouted, "no, no, no!"

"Mrs. James, are you okay?" a voice asked, a soft, sweet voice I didn't recognize. "You're in the hospital, Ms. James. You had an accident." She shined a light in my eyes making me flinch. "Are you having any pain?" Pain, yes. There was pain.

"Yes," I breathed, my voice barely a whisper.

"Okay, we can take care of that." She left. No, don't leave me. I didn't want to be here alone. My eyes were too heavy and they closed.

When I opened my eyes again the woman was back. She injected something into the plastic tube coming out of my arm. "This will help with the pain," she said softly. "It will help you sleep too." *No. Please. I don't want to sleep. Dreams. Nightmares.*

· · · · ·

My eyes flew open. My head felt funny. Tubes were coming out of both arms. My cast was gone. I reached up and touched my face only to find a tube coming out of my nose too. For a minute I wondered if I was still dreaming. I sat up and looked around. A faint light peeked under the oversized door providing the only light in the room. "Where am I?" I asked out loud but no one answered.

There were voices on the other side of the door and I strained to hear what they were saying. "She's my wife. You can't keep me from her." Spencer? No. Those eyes. I didn't want to see him. My body tensed and my heart began to race. A loud beeping noise sounded all around me. The door swung open and a team of people rushed in. Spencer followed.

"Do you know where you are, Mrs. James?" one of the women asked. I shook my head. "You're in the hospital." She checked the wires that were attached to me. "I'm Nina. I'm a nurse here." Another nurse checked my blood pressure while a third one shined a light in my eyes.

"Blood pressure is normal."

"Pupils are reactive."

"Here's the problem," Nina said holding up a wire. "It's just a loose wire." She connected it to the round sticker on my ankle then pressed a button on the monitor.

"Thank you, Nina," I said, relieved that awful noise had finally stopped.

"Welcome back, Mrs. James, how are you feeling?"

"Groggy," I whispered. "Where am I?"

"You're at the Ft. Walton Beach Medical Center. You had an accident and were unconscious when they brought you in last night."

"I'm so thirsty."

"I'll get you some ice water. Do you want to try to eat something?" I shook my head. Food was the furthest thing from my mind right now. "Okay. I'll be right back with that water."

She turned toward Spencer. "You can visit now, Mr. James, but keep it short."

Spencer moved closer to the bed. "Izzy, we were so worried." His voice was raspy and sounded strained. He smelled of cigarettes and bourbon.

The tiny hairs on the back of my neck stood on end. "Why are you here? How did you even know?"

"Anna called me." Spencer scrubbed his hands over his face. "Just because we're divorced doesn't mean I don't still care about you, that I don't still love you."

"Stop, Spencer, just stop."

"I'm so sorry, Izzy." He dropped his head into his hands. "I'm sorry about the pictures. I'm sorry for lying to you." He looked at me, tears rolling down his cheeks. "I do know the woman in those pictures."

The blood rushed to my face. "Who are they?"

"It's only one woman, and who she is isn't

important. It should've never happened. It was a mistake. I hurt you. I hurt us." He sat on the edge of the bed, his head in his hands once more. "I tried to end it but then she sent you those pictures. I'm sorry, Izzy. I'm so sorry."

He'd had months to tell me about the pictures and the woman he'd been sleeping around with, but he'd chosen this moment? My heart beat faster. "Why are you telling me this? Why now?" The monitor sounded again sending Nina running back in.

"Your heart rate is dangerously high, Mrs. James." I looked away to hide the tears that had started to fall. "Your wife needs to rest, Mr. James, you can visit her again later."

"Okay," Spencer agreed all too quickly. Part of me wanted an answer but I was happy to see him go. "I'll check on you later, Izzy." He left before I could tell him not to bother.

Nina handed me a glass of ice water then injected something into my IV before turning off the room light. "Try to get some sleep, Mrs. James. Dr. Leonard will be by to check on you later." She walked out into the hall, the door closing behind her.

I laid my head against the pillow, tears falling in a steady stream now. "Why did he have to come here?" I cried. "Why did he need to tell me that now?" I was so drowsy. My eyes closed.

The sound of the door opening woke me and I opened my eyes in time to see two women wearing white coats come into the room. I recognized Dr. Leonard but I'd never seen the other woman before. "Welcome back," Dr. Leonard said. "This is Dr. Jensen from toxicology. She's here to talk to you about your lab results."

Toxicology? I sat up in bed. "What about 'em?"

Dr. Jensen moved closer. "To put it simply, Ms. James, you were drugged. We found evidence of more than one drug in your system so we'll need to run a few more tests to determine exactly what combination was used." *Drugged*. Did I hear her right? My head started spinning. My nightmares…My arm…My ribs… "Dreams don't break bones, Isabella…" Suddenly I felt sick.

"You'll need to stay in the hospital for a day or two. We'll keep you on IV fluids to flush out of your system."

"Okay," I whispered; my voice barely audible. Drugged? I couldn't believe what I was hearing.

"Have your nurse call me if you need anything, Izzy." Dr. Leonard added before the two women left. Drugged? I buried my face in my hands, stunned by what I'd just been told.

It wasn't long before the door opened again. Nina. And she was carrying a syringe. "Dr. Leonard wants you to sleep," she said as she injected the medicine into the IV. I didn't object this time. I wanted to sleep. This was too much to deal with. I closed my eyes and gladly drifted off.

Chapter Fourteen

My head still felt a little groggy when I woke from the medicine induced slumber but thankfully it had stopped throbbing. Light seeped through the edges of the blinds and I wondered what time it was, or what day it was for that matter. I swung my legs over the edge of the bed, my whole body objecting as I sat up. My legs wobbled as I struggled to get to my feet, and I had to grab onto the IV pole to avoid falling. I pushed the pole into the bathroom to take care of a pressing need.

My reflection frightened me when I moved to the sink to wash up. Dark circles had formed under my eyes and a purple and blue bruise stretched across my face. My hair was matted to my forehead with blood but I couldn't tell where it was coming from.

The cool water from the dampened washcloth was invigorating and instantly improved my mood. Gently I ran the washcloth over the matted mess in my hair freeing the strands so I could rinse the blood out.

The unopened toothbrush and small tube of toothpaste next to the sink grabbed my attention. I opened them both and squeezed a small amount of the white paste onto the bristles. The minty flavor was refreshing and when I'd finished brushing I felt almost normal again.

When I pushed the bathroom door open I was immediately frozen in my tracks. "Alec," I gasped, wondering what he was doing here, and how he even knew I was here. I opened my mouth to ask but words failed me. "What? How?" was all I could manage.

Alec closed the gap between us and pulled me gently into his arms. "Oh, Isabella, I'm so sorry. I came as soon as I heard."

He held me at arms-length, his eyes scanning my body, before helping me back to bed. "I was so scared," he whispered, pulling me gently into his arms, enveloping me in the safety of his grasp. I could feel the tension leaving his body as he held me close. "I'm sorry, baby. Sorry this happened, sorry I wasn't there to protect you." He kissed my forehead. "Sorry he got away." There was no denying it anymore. Someone had done this. "Tell me what happened?"

I shrugged my shoulders. "All I remember is falling and then those eerie eyes glaring down at me." I shook my head. "The doctor said I was drugged."

"Drugged?"

Just then the door opened and a man I'd never seen before entered the room. And just like that the tension I'd felt earlier in Alec arms was back. "Hello, Mrs. James, I'm Detective Rux with the Ft. Walton Beach police department," he said. He turned toward Alec and extended his hand. "Mr. James."

Alec accepted his hand. "Detective Rux," he said. "I'm Alec Payne."

"My apologies, Mr. Payne." The detective turned back toward me. "I'm investigating your attack and need to ask you a few questions."

"Can't this wait, Detective?"

"I only have a few questions. It won't take long, sir."

Every muscle in Alec's face tightened. He opened his mouth to speak but I reached over and touched his hand. "It's okay, Alec. I'll just do it now."

"Are you sure you're up to it?" I nodded and forced a smile. I didn't want to talk about last night at all but I figured it was inevitable given the circumstances and just wanted it over with. Alec sat back down next to me.

"I need to speak to Mrs. James alone, sir."

No! my inner voice screamed. That wasn't part of my plan. I didn't want to do this at all, much less alone. "Can't he stay?"

"It's important I speak to you alone, Ms. James. We won't be long and Mr. Payne can wait right outside the door." He moved closer to the bed and the look on his face said he wasn't going to budge.

"Okay," I sighed. "Let's just get this over with."

Alec squeezed my hand. "I'll be right outside, Isabella." And with that he was gone.

Detective Rux pulled a chair next to the bed and sat down. "What can you tell me about the attack?"

"Not much I'm afraid. I've been having nightmares, or at least I thought they were nightmares." I looked over at the monitors. "But after this I don't know what to think anymore."

"How long have you been having these nightmares?"

"They started right after..." I closed my eyes and dropped my head in my hands, knowing if I told him about the package I'd have to tell him about the affair too and I didn't want to go into any of that. Not like this anyway, and especially not with Alec right outside the door. "Right after I filed for divorce."

He opened his small notebook and wrote something

down. "Tell me what you can remember about them."

"There's not much to tell, I'm afraid, just a bunch of scattered thoughts."

"Take your time, Ms. James, any detail you remember could be important."

I closed my eyes, doing my best to focus. Images flashed through my mind. "Cigarettes," I blurted out, "he smelled like cigarettes and alcohol. Whisky I think." My heart started to race. I was wrong. I couldn't do this now, or maybe I just didn't want to. "My journal," I sighed, relieved I'd remembered it. "It's in my bedside table. It has everything I've managed to remember about the dreams."

He wrote in his book again. "Were you home alone last night, Ms. James?"

"No. Frank was there. Sara could've been there too."

"Sara who?"

"Sara Pike, she works for us."

"Is it usual for Ms. Pike to stay over?"

"Yes. No. Well sometimes."

His brow furrowed. "Which is it, Ms. James, yes, no, or sometimes?"

"She stays over from time to time, usually when Spencer and I are both traveling, but her husband is out of town so she's been staying with us more often. I'm just not sure if she was there last night."

He wrote in his notebook again. "How long has Mr. Reynolds worked for you?"

"Who?"

"Frank Reynolds, the man who called in the attack." Perfect. I didn't even know the last name of the man who'd slept in my house.

"Actually, he doesn't work for me. He works for Mr. Payne."

Detective Rux tilted his head to side. "And what's the nature of your relationship with Mr. Payne?"

My heart beat faster. "Relationship," I thought to myself, the word rolling around like a lost marble in my mind. "He's a client. We have a professional relationship," I said finally. But my cheeks flushed as I considered how far past the boundaries of a typical professional relationship we'd gone.

"Are the two of you romantically involved?"

My jaw dropped. "Where are you going with this, Detective?"

Looking up from his notebook, he said, "The two of you seemed fairly, shall we say, intimate, when I got here."

The detective wrote in his book once more. "Who all has keys to your house?"

Adrenalin coursed through my veins and I was beyond ready for this to be over. "All of us, Spencer, Drew, Anna, Sara, me. We all have keys."

"Who knows the alarm code?"

"Why does that matter?" I snapped, my patience with his questions wearing dangerously thin.

"Well, Ms. James, there was no sign of forced entry and your alarm was turned off." What was he saying? "Was the alarm active when you got home last night?"

I'd been so mad at Alec for taking my keys that activating the alarm never even crossed my mind. My head started to spin. "Ms. James, did you turn on the alarm last night or not?"

"No," I whispered.

Again, he wrote in his book. "My team is searching for evidence. We'll need fingerprints of everyone who has been in your house recently."

"Fine. Are we almost done?"

He looked up from his notebook, his eyes finding mine once more. "Do you know who did this, Ms. James? Did Mr. James do this?"

Those eyes, my inner voice reminded me, *those familiar eyes*. Tears rolled down my cheeks. My heart beat faster still. "It couldn't be Spencer," I cried, desperately wanting that to be true. The mere thought that he could do this was a pain too great to bear.

The door flew open as the alarm on the monitor started beeping again. Alec rushed into the room, Nina close behind him. "Your heart rate is very high, Ms. James," Nina said as he injected something into my IV.

"We're done here, Detective," Alec snapped.

"There's just one more thing, sir. We weren't able to find Mrs. James' car keys. Do either of you know where they are?"

"I have them," Alec answered quickly.

Detective Rux opened his notebook once again. "And where were you Saturday night during the attack?"

Alec squeezed my hand. "New York. I'll have my office send over my flight plan if you want confirmation."

"Perfect." The detective handed Alec a business card then stood to leave. "You can fax it to that number there," Detective Rux said, pointing at the number he wanted Alec to use.

He handed me a card too. "Call me if you remember anything else, Ms. James, anything at all." With that he showed himself out.

"You've had enough excitement for one day," Nina said. "You need to get some rest."

Alec sat on the bed beside me and pulled me close him. "You're safe now, Isabella. You're safe with me." I closed my eyes and melted into his arms as the medicine

Nina injected took effect.

When I opened my eyes again it was dark. I must've dozed off. The street lights were visible through the partially open blinds. Alec was curled up in the room's only cushioned chair and it made me wonder how long he'd been there. I swung my legs over the edge of the bed and slowly stood. My legs wobbled under my own weight and I fell back onto the bed, gasping as a sharp pain radiated through my side.

Alec rushed to my side. "Here, let me help you," he said lifting me to my feet. My knees buckled once more and he wrapped his arm around my waist pulling me into his hard body. "You're weak, Isabella, you need to get back in bed."

"Bathroom," I muttered, my bladder urging me to hurry. Helping me to the in room bath, Alec opened the door and pushed the IV pole inside. I removed his hand from my waist. "I've got this now."

"No, let me help you."

"Alec, you're not coming into the bathroom with me."

"Fine, stay right there. I'll get the nurse."

"I don't need a nurse. I need to pee. Now move." I pushed my way past him, shutting the door behind me.

The bruise on my face was even bigger than it had been this morning. A shiver ran down my spine as I started to remember tiny details of the attack. I was walking down the stairs. Something stopped me; those eyes. I turned to run. Oh, God, I'm falling. My heart started racing. "NO!" I screamed.

The door swung open. "Isabella, what's wrong?" Alec grabbed my waist and turned me toward him. "Baby, are you okay?"

I fell into his chest, throwing my arms around him,

my whole body shaking now. "His eyes," I cried. "He was in the foyer. I saw him."

"It's okay, baby. You're safe. He can't hurt you now." Tears rolled down my cheeks. Those eyes were so familiar. I wished I could remember more.

Alec scooped me up in his arms and I was too emotionally drained to object. Setting me gently on the bed, he sat down beside me. "The nurse said you haven't eaten since you got here." He slid the hospital tray table under the bed and I noticed a tray of food that hadn't been there before. He lifted the plastic dome exposing a bowl of chicken noodle soup.

My stomach turned at the mere sight of food. "Alec, I'm not hungry."

"You haven't eaten in two days, Isabella. You're weak. You need to eat." He lifted the spoon to my mouth. Reluctantly I took a bite. "Good girl," Alec said, his wicked grin making a brief appearance. It was enough to make me blush and I had to look away to hide my crimson cheeks. "All of it," he said lifting the spoon to my mouth again.

I took another bite. "Control Freak," I whispered.

Alec lifted my chin until my eyes met his. "That's right. I am a control freak. And you'd be doing yourself a favor to remember that." He leaned in and kissed me hard on the lips. When he pulled away I was left wanting yet again. "Now eat."

"Okay, okay. Relax." I slurped a noodle slowly off the spoon.

Alec shook his head. "Dangerous, dangerous game, Isabella."

The door opened. "It's good to see you eating," Dr. Leonard said as she approached the bed. "How are you feeling?"

I put the spoon down. "Much better. I think I could manage at home."

"You are not going home," Alec snapped, every muscle in his face clenched tight. "Someone got into your house, drugged you, and attacked you. And this isn't even the first time. You are not going back to that house."

My mouth dropped open. "Locks can be changed, Alec. And I'm not staying in the hospital forever," I snapped back. This was not his decision to make, even though he did have a point.

"You've got some time to figure it out. I want to keep you here tonight to monitor your vitals and we'll talk about discharge tomorrow." Dr. Leonard removed the stethoscope from around her neck and listened to my heart. "Get some rest, Izzy. I'll be back in the morning and we'll go from there."

"You can't go back to that house, Isabella," Alec repeated as soon as she'd left.

Tears filled my eyes as I considered the gravity of the situation. Alec pulled me into his arms. "Don't cry, baby. We'll figure it out."

Wrapping my arms around him, I buried my face in his chest, all my built up emotion exploding in the form of a steady stream of tears. "What about Drew and Anna?" I cried. "What if this psycho tries to hurt one of them?"

"Drew and Anna are safe. They're staying at the Wyndham Garden. Frank is with them." His reassurance didn't make me feel that much better. Frank had been at my house when I'd been attacked. How could I be sure he could protect them?

I squeezed him tighter. "Why are you doing this?" I cried.

"Shhh," Alec whispered in my ear. "Don't cry, baby. I don't like it when you cry." He kissed me softly on the forehead. "I've told you, Isabella. I just want you to be safe. And when you're with me I know you're safe."

What was he saying? Was he planning on staying at the hotel too? Was he going to finally let me travel with him for work like he'd said when I started this contract?

Drugs from the attack still lingered in my system. Add that to the emotional breakdown I'd just had and I was more than exhausted. "It's late. You should go."

"I'm not leaving you, Isabella."

"Alec, please. We both need sleep." I reached up and touched his cheek. "I'll be okay here."

Reluctantly, he finally agreed. "Okay, I'll go but I'm coming back first thing in the morning."

"I'll see ya in the morning then." Truthfully, I didn't really want him to go but it wasn't fair of me to ask him to stay. We weren't even seriously involved and already Alec had done more for me than I would've expected even if we had been.

He kissed me goodnight then turned out the light on his way out the door. I turned on the hospital's ambient relaxation channel, and closed my eyes, letting the soft sounds of the ocean lull me to sleep.

Chapter Fifteen

Light flooded the room when I woke the next morning. The air was filled with the sweet smell of flowers. Everywhere I looked there were flowers, vase after vase overflowing with tulips, and orchids, and lilies, all in an array of amazing colors. My drab hospital room had been transformed into a beautiful garden. A smile crossed my face. "Alec," I whispered, knowing it could only be him.

My legs were stronger this morning and I made my way to the bathroom with ease. The shower was calling my name but I wasn't sure how I'd manage with an IV in each arm so I settled on washing up in the sink again. The bruise on the side of my face had spread even bigger but at least it'd started to heal, the dark shades of purple fading to hideous shades of blue and yellow, and the scab wasn't nearly as big as I'd thought it be given the amount of blood. "It'll heal," I said out loud, doing my best to reassure myself that it was only temporary.

I brushed my teeth then hurried out of the bathroom and away from the mirror. As I stepped back into my room, my own private garden, I was reminded of the garden Alec and I toured onboard the Fantasy the day we met. Closing my eyes, I thought back to that day. The electricity between us so strong neither had been able to stay away.

The door swung open and my smile quickly disappeared. "Who sent you these?" Spencer snapped, his voice dripping with disdain as he motioned around the room.

"Does it matter?" I snapped back, my icy tone mirroring his. "Izzy, wait. I didn't come here to fight."

"Then why are you here, Spencer?"

He moved to the edge of the bed, lifting my hand in his. "I came to check on you, to make sure you're okay." I pulled my hand away. "I know you're mad at me, and you may never forgive me, but I still love you. I'll always love you." I looked away. I wasn't ready to talk about this with him. "Izzy, please, look at me, talk to me."

"Seriously, Spencer? I was drugged, and attacked. And to top that off you decided the best time to tell me about your affair was while I was lying in a hospital bed." Adrenaline rushed through my veins. "It was bad enough knowing you cheated on me. But you didn't just cheat, Spencer. You had an ongoing, intimate relationship with another woman. And I don't want to talk about this with you right now."

"Damn it, Bella, I said I was sorry."

"Sorry!" I shouted, my emotions boiling over. "Sorry doesn't begin to cut it, Spencer. I said I don't want to talk about this. Now please, just go."

"Izzy," he said; the tone in his voice desperate now. "Please, I need you to forgive me."

"She said not now, Mr. James."

Spencer spun around. "Well, well, well, if it isn't Alec Payne." He turned back toward me. "Now it makes perfect sense; that picture, the cruise, Drew and Anna's security detail. And you're mad at me? Isn't that the pot calling the kettle black, Bella?"

"Not even close," I screamed, all my anger exploding. How dare he accuse me of adultery? "I NEVER cheated on you, Spencer!"

Alec stepped between us, effectively blocking my view of Spencer. "It's time for you to go, Mr. James."

Spencer stormed toward the door, throwing his arms in the air. "Fine." He turned to look at me once more. "But at least I'm honest about what I've done, Izzy." With that he slammed the door behind him.

I covered my face with my hands, embarrassed by what just happened; even more embarrassed that Alec was there to witness it. "Alec, I'm sorry."

He pulled my hands away from my face. "You don't need to apologize for him. He's an asshole for putting you through that." He stroked my cheek. "Besides, I'm the one who's sorry. I knew I shouldn't have left you here alone." Leaning closer to me, Alec kissed me gently on the lips.

"Good morning, Ms. James, Mr. Payne," Detective Rux called out as he strolled through the door.

"Detective," Alec sighed. "Do you have any news?"

"We pulled a partial print from the alarm keypad. We're running it through our database now." He opened his notebook and looked right at me. "It says in my notes that you kept a journal."

"That's right."

"We've searched your house from top to bottom but I'm afraid we didn't find it."

"What do you mean? It's right next to my bed."

"We searched everywhere, ma'am," he said, his tone all business. "It's possible your attacker took it. I'll need you to go through the house to see if anything else is missing." The realization that some creep could be reading my private thoughts, even if they were all scattered, made me feel sick. I nodded my head, afraid I might throw up if I tried to speak now. "We've finished collecting evidence so you're free to return home anytime. I recommend rekeying all the locks and changing the alarm code though." I nodded once more.

"The department has also increased patrols in your neighborhood and I want you to call if you see anything suspicious." He closed his notebook. "I don't want to scare you, Ms. James, but you need to accept that this wasn't a random act. This perp chose to come after you and there's a real possibility he'll come back."

"Thank you, Detective," Alec said, looking right at me, a smirk on his face. "I was just telling Ms. James last night how unsafe it was to stay at that house until you figured out who was behind the attacks."

"I'm not telling you what to do, Ms. James, but if you have another place to stay I'd seriously consider it." He made a move toward the door. "I'll be in touch when we get results back from the crime lab. In the meantime let me know if you notice anything missing."

"Okay," I managed to say, my voice a whisper. The door closed and just like that he was gone. I pulled a pillow over my face and screamed. My life was spinning out of control and I felt completely powerless to stop it. Alec sat down beside me and pulled me into his arms, neither of us saying anything.

When the door opened again it was Nina who walked in. This time she was carrying a stack of papers. "Are you ready to get out of here?"

"Dr. Leonard is releasing her already?"

"Her labs look good today. Both Dr. Leonard and Dr. Jensen think she'll be okay at home." Alec's jaw tightened but he didn't say anything else. Nina handed me the stack of papers she was holding. "These are your discharge instructions. You'll need to limit your activity and get plenty of rest for the next couple of weeks. Dr. Leonard is also recommending you to take at least two weeks off work, preferably three."

"Yeah right," I laughed. "I've already taken too much time off."

"You hit your head so hard you blacked out, Ms. James. Your brain is bruised. It's important for you to get plenty of rest and limit stress so your body can heal."

"Are you sure it's safe for her to leave?"

"She'll be fine," Nina said, "as long as she follows doctor's orders that is." I rolled my eyes at the tone in her voice. And when I turned my attention back to the two of them Alec was staring at me, his head tilted to one side, every muscle in his jaw tightened. I wondered what is was about him and eye rolling but this certainly wasn't the time to ask. Nervously I bit my bottom lip and his expression softened.

"I'll see that she does," Alec said without taking his eyes off me. Great, that's just what I needed, Mr. Control Freak watching my every move, armed with a whole new list of things I shouldn't be doing.

Nina removed my IVs and put my fractured arm in a removable splint. I'd started to object but decided it was better than that ridiculous cast I'd been wearing. She went through the rest of the instructions then left me to get changed. Carrying the bag Anna packed for me into the bathroom, I hopped into the shower.

Alec took the bag from my hand when I emerged from the bathroom and escorted me into the hall where the hospital transporter was waiting with a wheelchair.

"I can walk," I protested.

"Hospital policy, ma'am."

I opened my mouth to object but Alec stepped in front of me. "Sit down, Isabella," he said. I groaned in protest but did as he'd ordered knowing that arguing with him would only slow the process.

When we made it outside, Alec helped me into the car then slid in next to me. "The Wyndham, Preston," he said. I leaned back against the cool leather seat, thankful to be leaving the hospital, even if it meant staying at a hotel.

Chapter Sixteen

The suite at the Wyndam Garden was bigger than I had expected. Complete with a large sitting area and a balcony that overlooked the Gulf, plus three bedrooms, each with its own bathroom, and a master suite almost as big as my room at home, but after two weeks it felt as though the walls were closing in around me.

Spencer went back to the house as soon as he heard it had been cleared. He said he couldn't handle sleeping in the same hotel where Alec and I were staying. And honestly, I was glad he'd left. Dealing with him was the last thing I needed.

Drew and Anna stayed with me at the hotel for the first week but had gone home now too. Spencer changed the locks, and the security code, and managed to convince them both they'd be safe, that it was me who was in danger and not them. The novelty of the hotel had worn off fairly quickly for them and they were both set on going home. I couldn't blame them. Hell, I'd have gone home if I'd thought I'd be safe.

Only four miles separated me from my kids but it might as well have been a thousand. I'd barely seen them this past week, and when I was fortunate enough to spend time with them it was only one at a time. It felt like ages since we'd hung out as a family. I missed our time together; all those simple moments I'd taken for granted, breakfast, dinner, bedtime. I knew the day would come when they'd be living away from me, but I wasn't ready for it so soon.

Alec left for Houston yesterday. I'd begged him to let me come. "Please, Alec, I need to work," I'd said. "I'm going crazy here doing nothing." He wasn't having it though. Nothing I said was going to change his mind. Damn Dr. Leonard and her overly cautious discharge instructions. If she hadn't recommended I take a few weeks off work then I'd be in Houston too instead of being stuck inside a hotel. "You *are* doing something, Isabella," Alec had said. "You're resting so your body can heal. And I expect you to continuing resting while I'm gone." What he hadn't understood was I was too restless to actually rest.

Unfortunately, Alec had repeated his orders to Frank before he left for Houston and Frank followed me wherever I went. I couldn't even open the door without him knowing about it. I needed a break from him, a break from all of this.

"Ahhhh!" I shouted at the top of my lungs.

Almost instantly there was a knock at the door. I jumped up off the couch and stormed to the door. "I'm fine, Frank," I shouted through the thick wooden barrier.

Another knock followed. "Mom, it's me," a muffled voice said.

I swung open the door. "Anna!"

"Mom," she said, wrapping her arms around me. "Are you okay? I heard you yelling."

Frank poked his head around the corner. "Nice to

see you again, Miss Anna."

Anna let go of me. "Hi Frank," she said with a big wave. Grabbing her hand, I pulled her inside my room. It had been two days since I'd seen my daughter and I had no plans of sharing our time with Frank.

"I'm glad you're here. I've missed you so much."

"I've missed you too, mom."

"Is Drew with you?" Anna shook her head. "Dad?" She shook her head again. "Then how'd you get here?"

Anna opened her purse and pulled out her wallet. "I drove," she said flashing her new driver's license in front of my face.

"You got your license! Oh, Anna, I'm so proud of you." I pulled her into a tight hug. "When did you get it?"

"Today. I drove straight here to tell you about it."

"Whose car are you driving?" I asked cautiously, hoping she wasn't driving my E350. Surely, Spencer wouldn't let her drive my car, at least not the first day she got her license, would he?

"Mine!" she squealed.

I tilted my head to one side, surprised by her answer. "Yours?"

"Oh, mom, stop acting like you don't know Alec bought me a car."

"What do you mean Alec bought you a car? When?"

"It came today. Did you really not know about it?" I shook my head, not trusting myself to speak. "I'm sorry. I assumed you knew. Are you mad? Please don't be mad. Please say I can keep it."

Control freak, my inner voice snapped. There was no way she could accept a gift like that from him. She was *my* daughter. It wasn't right for Alec to buy her a car. But how was I supposed to say no after he'd already given it to her?

Spencer couldn't be happy about this either. Maybe he'd be the one to tell her we had to give it back. "Did dad say you could keep the car?"

"Yeah, he helped me pick it out."

That was a surprise. I certainly hadn't expected the two of them to become chummy, not with the way Spencer had reacted when he saw Alec in my hospital room. "You guys went car shopping together?"

"No," Anna laughed. "Alec had some brochures sent over and told me to pick the one I wanted, and I asked dad to help."

Was I the only one who thought this was a bad idea? I took a deep breath to calm my nerves, not wanting to put a damper on her excitement.

"What kind of car did you get?" I finally asked, doing my best to hide my frustration with Mr. Control Freak.

Her face lit up. "I don't know, a Volvo something." She waved her hands in the air. "It's the coolest blue. You have to come see it." Before I could object Anna grabbed my hand and pulled me into the hall.

We made it all the way to the elevator before Frank caught up to us. Damn Frank. I'd swear he had supersonic hearing. Every time I opened my door he seemed to know it. Despite my objections he followed us into the elevator. Anna could hardly stand still she was so excited. And when the elevator doors opened she grabbed my hand once again, pulling me toward a row of cars, stopping in front of a brand new Caspian blue Volvo S60.

"Isn't the color amazing?"

"It's awesome, sweetie," I said with a forced smile. All the while wondering who in their right mind would buy a teenager a *brand new* car. It was bad enough knowing Alec had gone behind my back and gotten her one, but finding out the car was brand new made it that much worse.

"Get in. I'll take you for a drive."

"I don't think Mr. Payne would like that, ma'am," Frank offered.

Well, too bad! If he hadn't wanted me to take a ride with her then he shouldn't have bought her the damn car. I opened the passenger door. "I'd love to go for a ride, Anna."

"Ms. James—"

"Frank," I interrupted before he could say anything more. "I appreciate your concern here, but I'm going for a ride with my daughter, alone. Now, if you'll excuse me." I pulled on the door, encouraging him to move out of the way.

Reluctantly, Frank stepped aside. "Please drive careful, Miss Anna," he said nervously.

Anna climbed in behind the wheel then shifted into reverse. "Don't worry, Frank. I will."

She drove east on Santa Rosa Boulevard then sped off in the direction of the Miracle Strip Highway. "You have to see how this thing handles," she said excitedly. "With these sport seats you won't even know we're going sixty."

Nervously, I bit my lip. Suddenly the thought of barreling down the highway at sixty miles per hour didn't seem like the smartest thing for me to be doing. It wasn't like Anna didn't know how to drive, I mean, she'd gotten her permit when she was fifteen and she had logged hundreds of hours behind the wheel these past three years, but Dr. Leonard warned even the smallest head injury could cause permanent damage until the bruise on my brain had completely healed.

Anna merged into traffic then mashed down on the accelerator, propelling me back against the seat. It was too late for second thoughts now. Gripping the door handle, I squeezed my eyes tightly shut.

Within minutes of our drive my phone started to ring. I fished it out of my pocket to silence the ringer, and to see who was calling. "Alec," I sighed when I saw the screen. I wanted to answer the call; to tell him exactly how I felt about the gift he'd bought Anna, but it wasn't the right time for that. I sent the call to voicemail instead.

"Mom! Why'd you do that?"

"I didn't want to distract you while you're driving," I said quickly, her question surprising me. It wasn't that long ago that she'd gotten so mad she stopped talking to me, all because of a completely innocent lunch where Alec just happened to show up. And now she was scolding me for not answering his call?

"You could have at least answered and told him that," she snapped. "You know how much he worries about you." I shook my head, unsure of what was happening.

Anna's phone rang before I could answer her. "Hi, Alec, you're on speaker."

"Anna, where are you? Is everything okay?"

"Everything's fine," I said, doing my best to hide the irritation in my voice. "We're just taking a drive in Anna's new car." *The car he bought without your knowledge or permission*, my inner voice snapped.

"Why isn't Frank with you?"

"We're just taking a short drive, Alec. There was no reason for him to come."

"We can debate that later." Yeah, he had one thing

right, we would definitely be debating later, just not about whether Frank needed to ride with us. I wanted to lash out at Alec, to tell him exactly how I felt about him buying the car in the first place, but that was a conversation I'd have with him later, when Anna wasn't in ear shot.

"Alec, Anna's a new driver. Can we talk later?"

"Fair point as usual, baby. Call me when you get to wherever it is you're going. We'll talk then."

"She will," Anna said, jumping into the conversation.

"Drive safe, Anna. You call me later too."

"Yes, sir. I will." With that she disconnected the call.

My mouth dropped open. Had she just called him 'sir'? "That's quite a turn-around in your attitude toward Alec. I hope it doesn't have anything to do with your new car."

"Of course it doesn't," Anna snapped. "I can't believe you'd even say that." She glanced over at me, her eyes narrowed. "I mean, sure, I didn't like him at first but that was only because I thought the two of you were having an affair. When I found out that wasn't true, I stopped being mad at him. And when I stopped being mad I realized he's a pretty great guy."

"I told you from the beginning we weren't having an affair."

"I know but, no offense, I didn't believe you. Not until Drew pointed out you didn't even meet Alec until after you and dad filed for divorce." I wondered how Drew knew when Alec and I met, and what else he knew for that matter. I said a silent prayer that he didn't know about Spencer's affair, and especially not about the pictures.

"Well, what makes him so great?" I asked. Distraction deployed. Anna rolled her eyes as she looked over at me. "Are you blind, Mom? There's nothing that man wouldn't do for you. He's gone out of his way to keep you safe, to keep us all safe. Can't you see he's completely fallen for you?"

"He hasn't fallen for me, Anna."

"Keep telling yourself that," she laughed. "But it won't make it true."

Sitting back in the seat, I stared silently out the window, wondering. Had Alec fallen for me? Was it even me he wanted or was it control he was after? I hadn't hopped into bed with him on our first date, willingly given him whatever he'd wanted like so many women had probably done. Was he out to prove he could have whatever, and whoever, he wanted?

Anna moved from lane to lane on the scenic highway, showing off her new found skill. "Driving is a lot more fun than I thought it'd be," she said, finally breaking the awkward silence that had fallen between us. "Don't tell Drew, but he was right. I should've gotten my license sooner."

We both laughed at the thought of her keeping a secret from her brother. It was something she'd never been able to do for very long. And she was right too. Drew would never let her live this down. He'd told her hundreds of times how much fun driving was.

Anna pulled into the parking lot of the Sandestin and turned the car around. "We better head back. The Senior Activities Committee is meeting tonight to finalize the plans for our class trip."

Great, something else I'd missed. "Class trip?"

Anna reached over and squeezed my hand. "I'm sorry, mom. With all the chaos lately I forgot to tell you. We're going to the Bahamas! And it's going to be amazing; no parents, no school, no responsibilities, just five straight days of all-inclusive fun."

"Who's going? When do you leave?"

"We leave the day after graduation. Final reservations are due tonight. That's what the meeting is for."

"How much is this going to cost?"

"Nothing, it's completely free."

"Free?"

"Yeah, it was a gift to the senior class."

"Who's the benefactor?"

"Seriously, do you really not know the answer to that question?"

Closing my eyes, I gritted my teeth. *Alec!* I screamed to myself, my patience with him wearing dangerously thin. First the car. Now a trip for the entire senior class. Did he not understand boundaries?

Anna pulled under the portico at the main entrance to the Wyndam Garden and I hopped out. "Thanks for the ride, sweetie. I love your new car."

"You're welcome," she said with a smile that reached all the way to her eyes. "Don't forget to call Alec," she added before pulling away.

Biting my tongue to keep from telling Anna how I felt about calling Alec, I waved goodbye and watched her until the car was out of sight.

Chapter Seventeen

I'd decided to stop at Manatee's bar in the hotel lobby for a drink before heading upstairs to my room to deal with Alec. I was still fuming about him buying Anna a car without at least talking to me about it first. And this whole senior class trip thing was way over the top. He needed to be stopped, and by the time I'd finish my second drink I'd garnered all the strength I needed for the job. After settling my tab I strolled confidently to the bank of elevators, determined to put an end to Alec's meddling once and for all.

My phone rang before I made it back to my room. I glanced down at the screen. Anna. "Hey, sweetie."

"Have you called Alec?"

I sighed heavily into the phone. "Not yet."

"Mom, I promised him you'd call."

"Okay, okay, already, I'll call him as soon as we get off the phone."

"You better. I'm going to call you after my meeting to make sure you did."

Oh yes, Alec definitely needed to be stopped. As soon as Anna hung up I dialed Alec's number. He answered on the first ring. "Isabella, where are you?"

"Alec, this has to stop. You can't keep doing this."

"Have you been drinking?"

No, no, no, that wasn't going to work this time. He was not using redirection to get out of this mess. Not with the level of irritation I felt, or with the amount of alcohol running through my veins. "Did you even consider asking me first? Did you stop to think for one second that maybe I didn't want her to have a new car?"

"Where are you, Isabella?" he asked again, completely ignoring what I'd just said.

I exhaled loudly into the phone. "Seriously, Alec. This has to stop!"

"I agree. This does have to stop, Isabella. Frank is there for your protection and I expect you to let him do his job. Now tell me where you are!"

My mouth dropped open. *Really, he's mad at me?* There was no way I was going to let him make this mess my fault. "Alec, I'm serious!" I stomped my foot, my free hand fisted at my side. "I can't believe you bought Anna a car. And then there's this whole senior trip you're paying for."

"Isabella, I'll be happy to talk about the car and anything else you want to pitch a fit about after you've sobered up. Now tell me where the hell you are!"

"I'm at the hotel," I shouted. "And I've only had two drinks I'll have you know."

"From the sound of your voice, I'd say that was one drink too many. Stay put and we'll talk about this in the morning."

"But—"

"But nothing," he snapped. "I'm in the middle of a meeting. Eat. Sleep. We'll talk about it tomorrow." Just like that the phone went dead.

I swung my room door open and tossed my phone

on the sofa. "Ahhhh," I screamed as loud as I could. I wanted to talk about it now.

There was a knock at the door. "Ms. James," Frank called out. "Is everything okay?"

"No! Everything is not okay," I shouted, throwing my hands in the air. "I'm surrounded by control freaks!"

The door opened. "What is it, Ms. James? What's wrong?"

"Frank! What the hell are you doing? You can't just come into my room."

"I'm sorry, ma'am, but I heard you screaming. I was worried."

"Well, as you can see, I'm fine," I said through gritted teeth. This was too much. The walls were closing in. I was suffocating and had to get out of there. Storming past him, I headed for the stairs.

"Ms. James, wait," he called after me.

"I'm going for a walk, Frank. And I want to be alone!" I called over my shoulder. Swinging open the door to the stairwell, I hurried down the stairs, taking them two at a time, desperate now to escape the madness that was consuming my life.

By the time I made it outside, the sun had already started to set, turning the sky brilliant shades of blue and orange underneath the dark gray storm clouds. A strong sea breeze slammed waves against the beach. Sheets of rain fell from the clouds on the edge of the horizon and were moving rapidly toward the shore. Thunder rolled, and lightning flashed in the distance. The force of Mother Nature surrounded me. The beauty of the storm had me captivated.

The tide rose higher and higher until water rushed over my feet, my sandals becoming emerged in the smooth wet sand. When the water retreated, the soft ground under my toes went with it. Shuffling my feet and waving my arms, I tried to maintain my balance, but my efforts were fruitless and I fell backward, landing hard on the sand. A sharp pain pierced my side and I instinctively reached for it.

An unfamiliar voice startled me. "Are you okay?"

"Yeah, I'm fine," I said quickly, embarrassed by my clumsiness, but even more embarrassed this blonde haired stranger had been there to see me fall. "The sand moved and I lost my balance."

He extended both hands toward me. "Here, let me help you up."

I grabbed hold and allowed him to pull me to my feet, his piercing blue eyes staring down at me. "Thanks."

"No problem. Are you sure you're okay?"

"Yeah, just embarrassed is all."

A smile crossed his face, exposing his perfectly straight teeth. "Don't be embarrassed. The ocean is a powerful force. It takes some getting used to."

I burst out laughing. "I live on the beach."

The stranger laughed too. "Then you should be embarrassed." Smiling, he continued, "I'm Nathan by the way."

I opened my mouth to speak but pain pierced my side and took my breath. I pulled my arm into my ribs, looking for any relief I could find.

"Are you hurt?"

"It's nothing, just an old injury."

He tilted his head the side. "Broken ribs?"

My body tensed, the tiny hairs on the back of my neck suddenly standing on end. *How did he know about my ribs? Could he be my attacker?* My heart racing, I made a move toward the hotel. "That storm is moving in pretty quick. I better get inside."

"Wait. What's your name?"

"I'm Izzy," I called over my shoulder, not stopping for even a second.

The sky turned bright white, thunder crashed around me. I picked up speed and ran as fast as I could to the safety of the building. The pain in my side worsened with every step, making it almost impossible to breathe. By the time I reached the lobby I could barely stand.

Frank gasped when he saw me. "Ms. James. What happened? Are you okay?"

Before I could answer Frank was at my side, his arm around my waist, helping me stand. "I'm fine," I finally managed, doing my best to hide the pain on my face. "The storm just scared me."

"Yeah, that's some storm rolling in."

Frank helped me into the elevator. "Who was that you were talking to on the beach?"

Turning in his arm so I was facing him, I asked, "Were you watching me?"

"My job is to keep you safe, Ms. James, and I'd appreciate it if you'd allow me to do that. We both know Mr. Payne isn't going to like that you were out alone, so please, who was that you were you talking to?"

"Who cares if he likes it? It's none of his damn business," I said, pulling out of his grip.

"He only wants you safe. Now, do you know that man or not?"

Throwing my hands in the air, I shouted, "No!" Frank's eyes closed, his jaw tightening. "I fell and he helped me up. He said his name was Nathan." There was no way I was going to tell Frank that Nathan spooked me, that it was him I was running from and not the storm. One control freak was more than enough for me to handle.

My clothes were dripping with sand and salt water, so I headed straight for the shower when I got back to my room. I stripped down and stepped in, closing my eyes, letting the warm water run over my face. Thoughts of the day floated through my mind: Anna's car, the class trip, Alec, and Nathan, the stranger with steel blue eyes, shoulder length blonde hair, and creamy skin. I wondered if he was staying at the hotel, if I'd see him again, if he could be the man who broke into my house and attacked me. A shiver ran up my spine as I considered that possibility.

A loud knock at the door brought me back to the here and now. I turned off the shower. "Just a minute, Frank," I called out quickly before he decided to burst into my room again. I pulled on the fluffy white robe the hotel provided and headed to the door.

"Everything's fine, Frank, I was in the shower," I called through the door as I wrapped my hair in a towel.

"Uh, its room service, ma'am." My whole body tensed. That voice; I know that voice. "I have your dinner, Mrs. James."

"I didn't order dinner," I said quickly, wondering how he knew my name. Alec had insisted on booking the room in his name so the psycho who was after me wouldn't be able to track me as easily.

When I looked through the peephole all I could see was a man in a hotel uniform leaning over a service cart, his face not visible. Cautiously, I opened the door and he looked up. "*Nathan.*"

"Izzy, hey."

My body tensed once more. *It's just a coincidence*, I told myself, doing my best to slow my breathing. "What are you doing here?"

Nathan pushed the cart forward, nudging me a little. "Bringing you dinner," he said.

"But I didn't order dinner."

"Maybe I have the wrong room. Let me check." He pulled a slip of paper from under the tray and looked it over. "Are you Isabella James?"

I nodded slowly.

"I've got the right room then."

Alec must've ordered it. Control freak! Reluctantly I held the door open, allowing Nathan to push the cart inside.

"Do you want this on the table?"

"Yeah, sure," I said, cautiously watching Nathan's every move. From my place in front of the door I had a clear view of him inside the suite.

He transferred the tray of food to the small table then pushed the cart back into the hall.

"Thanks," I said, when he was standing in the hall too.

"Just doing my job," he said with a crooked smiled. "How long are you staying at the hotel?"

I shrugged my shoulders. That was a question I'd been asking myself lately, but one I hadn't found the answer to just yet.

"Is Mr. James staying with you?"

"We're divorced," I blurted out, caught off guard by his question.

Nathan looked up from the cart. "Oh yeah?" he asked, seemingly intrigued by the news.

He stepped in front of me, effectively blocking my escape. The tiny hairs on the back of my neck stood on end again. *Where's Frank when you need him?* my inner voice snapped. My legs began to tremble. *Could he be the one? My attacker?* I stood frozen, unable to move, not wanting to look up. I wanted to scream, to push him out of the way and lock myself in my room, but I couldn't. My legs wouldn't move, and when I opened my mouth no sound came out. A startled squeal escaped me when Nathan leaned closer. I squeezed my eyes shut, saying a silent prayer Frank heard me. "Who's Frank?" he asked, his mouth only inches from mine then.

"Who the hell are you is a better question."

My eyes flew open. "Frank," I shouted, more than happy to see him this time.

Nathan spun around and the two men were face to face. "Dude, relax. I'm from room service, and I was just leaving."

"That sounds like a good idea," Frank barked, as he snatched the ID badge off Nathan's maroon colored server jacket. "And if you value your job you'll stay the hell away from this room. Are we clear on that?"

"Yes. Of course, sir." Nathan turned toward me and nodded. "Ms. James." With that he pushed the cart quickly down the hall in the direction of the elevator.

Frank kept his eyes glued to Nathan until the elevator doors closed, with Nathan inside. Only then did he turn back toward me. "Are you okay, Ms. James?"

My knees were still trembling when Frank spoke, stunned by what just happened. I nodded. "Thank you, Frank," I whispered, with a whole new appreciation of him. God. What would I have done if Frank hadn't shown up when he did?

"If he comes back I want you to call me. And whatever you do, don't answer the door." I didn't argue. How could I after he'd rescued me from that frightening encounter with Nathan.

Frank started to walk away then abruptly stopped and turned to look at me again. "You know, Ms. James, we could have avoided this whole situation if you'd let me know you were ordering room service."

I raised my hand, palm out. "Hold it right there. You need to discuss that with the control freak you call a boss, because I didn't order room service, he did."

A smile crossed his face and for a fleeting moment there was gentleness in his eyes I hadn't known existed. "My apologies, Ms. James, I'll be sure to do that."

It was just a coincidence, I told myself over and over again after Frank left, doing my best to calm my racing heart. Nathan must've been on his way to work earlier when he'd seen me fall. I gave him my name but there was no other way he could've known which room I was in. *Plus, he did bring you food*, my inner voice chimed in.

I lifted the metal dome off the tray. The aroma made my mouth water: roasted rosemary potatoes, steamed green beans, grilled chicken. My stomach rumbled, reminding me I hadn't eaten all day. I picked up the fork and dug in, happy now for the distraction of food. The food Alec ordered.

My cell phone rang but I ignored it and kept eating. The food was delicious and I wasn't about to risk ruining my appetite. Bite after bite, I stuffed my face, until I couldn't possibly eat any more.

Feeling full and satisfied I moved to the couch to lie down, switching on the television. Getting lost in the mindless activity, before I knew it, I started to doze.

Startled by the ringing of the hotel phone, I jumped up off the couch. Pain pierced my side, a reminder of my earlier fall. Still groggy I picked up the receiver. "Hello," I answered quietly.

"I've been trying to call you."

"Val? Is that you?"

"Of course it's me, why haven't you called me

back?"

That was Valerie alright, self-centered, always-about-me, my best friend in the whole world. "I'm sorry. Things have been so crazy around here lately." It wasn't a total lie. Things *had* been crazy: the divorce, the attack, Alec. But I couldn't tell her any of that, not over the phone, not without hurting her feelings that I hadn't trusted her enough to keep my secrets. And hurting her wasn't something I ever wanted to do again. No, I'd done that once and the pain she felt nearly killed us both.

"Crazy. Let me tell you about crazy," she said. "He left me, Izzy. Cody left me."

"What?" I couldn't have heard her right. She left him, definitely. But he left her? Not likely.

"Yes," Val cried into the receiver. "He left me, Izzy."

"Oh Val, I'm so sorry. Tell me, what happened?"

She cried louder. "It wasn't my fault, Izzy. Well, not really. He's been so distant, and he was never home. I was just lonely."

My head started to spin in anticipation of what she was about to say. "What are you saying, Val?"

"I cheated on him." The wound in my heart split open as her words sunk in. "It was a stupid thing to do," she continued. A queasy feeling started to take over. That was what Spencer had said, as if those words would magically take away the feelings of betrayal. I mean, no shit! Of course it was a stupid thing to do. Spencer hadn't understood that no words would ever erase the memory of knowing he'd been with another woman. Valerie wouldn't either.

Would it matter if whoever she cheated with meant something to her? Spencer had said his affair meant nothing. Maybe that was what really bothered me, knowing he'd thrown away the sanctity of our marriage for *nothing*. "Is it serious? The affair I mean?"

"I love him, if that's what you're asking, but he's married too."

No. It hadn't helped. Knowing she'd cheated with a married man was way worse. Why did I have to ask? My stomach contracted and I had to swallow hard to keep the food I'd just eaten down. "Val, I don't know what to say." There was more than enough drama in my own life. Dealing with her affair was more than I could take. And she certainly wasn't going to like anything I had to say about what she'd done to Cody.

I did my best to listen, but I couldn't really make out what she was saying between the tears. Not to mention the pounding of my heart. I didn't bother to ask who the new guy was because truthfully, at that moment, I didn't really care. She'd cheated on Cody, the man she'd sworn her love to.

We talked for a while longer before she finally calmed down. With a promise to call her in a few days I got off the phone. Not even bothering to change out of the robe I was wearing, I crawled into bed and wrapped my arms around one of the spare pillows, closing my eyes, focusing on the sound of the waves coming in from the open window. The storm had long since passed and the ocean was once again calm and peaceful. Slowly but surely, my breathing slowed and my body began to relax.

Chapter Eighteen

My eyelids were heavy. I pried them open and looked around. It was so dark. All I could see was night. Waves were crashing violently against the shore, and I could hear the faint sound of thunder in the distance. A cold wind blew through the opened balcony door, making me shiver. I reached for the blanket, but my arm wouldn't move. I tried the other arm. Nothing. My heart started to race. "Please, let it be a dream," I whispered over and over again, praying that's all it was, the stress of last night sneaking up on me while I slept.

A familiar voice stole my breath. "Welcome back, Bella." My heart beat even faster.

I turned toward the sound but it was too dark, and I still couldn't see anything. "Who's there?" I asked frantically.

"Don't you know who I am?" The voice was so familiar, but I couldn't place it. My mind was too fuzzy.

"Who are you? Why are you here?" My voice echoed in my ear. Pain. There was so much pain.

"Ask yourself that question, Bella. You brought me here." A sharp pain pierced my neck. My eyes were so heavy.

• • • • •

I jolted upright in bed. I pulled my arms toward my face, relieved when they moved. Beads of sweat covered my forehead. The sun peeked through the drapes, so it was easy to see. My eyes darted around the room. The lock on the sliding glass door was firmly in place. "It was just a stupid dream," I said out loud. Pain pierced my side as I inhaled deeply, a reminder of my fall on the beach last night, of Nathan. A chill ran down my spine. "It was only dream," I said again, but with certainty that time.

My mind lacked the mental sharpness a good night's rest usually provided, which was odd, considering I'd gone to bed pretty early and had managed to sleep in until after sunrise. The stress of everything that had happened in the past few months was playing tricks on me. I needed to clear my mind and rid myself of the horrible feeling that was stirring inside. A run, that's what I needed.

Alec was coming back this afternoon and I knew opportunities to run would be limited, so I changed into my running clothes, pulled a bottle of water from the mini fridge, and quietly opened the door so Frank wouldn't hear me leave. Looking to the right, then to the left, he was nowhere to be seen. Gently, I closed the door behind me and hurried to the stairs, hustling to the lobby, knowing that if Frank figured out I'd left he'd surely come looking for me. And I really needed some time alone.

The morning sky was a brilliant blue, all evidence of last night's storm long gone. A gentle sea breeze blew off the water, cooling the air, perfect weather for a run. I jogged down the beach toward John Beasley Park, slowly at first but quickly picking up speed. Faster and faster I ran until the stabbing pain in my side become impossible to ignore. I slowed my pace but kept moving. I'd had enough of that taking it easy crap. I was ready to get my life back to normal; whatever that was now.

My lungs were screaming for air by the time I made it to the park, the pain in my side serving as a constant reminder of all the chaos in my life lately. I spotted an empty park bench near the water. There was so much for me to sort out and, since I wasn't in any hurry to get back to the hotel, right now seemed like a good time to start.

I'd been trapped inside that suite for too long. What I really needed was to get out of there. I made a mental note to add moving out of the hotel to the ever growing list of things to discuss with Alec when he got back.

Where are you gonna go, Izzy? my inner voice chimed in. I closed my eyes to consider the question, seriously this time. Spencer and I each owned half the house so I could live there. The house was big enough for us both, especially with our travel schedules. The downstairs bedroom Sara used when she stayed over had its own bathroom. Surely, it would be better than a hotel. And it was closer to my home office than my old bedroom, the bedroom Spencer and I once shared.

Goosebumps covered my body as I thought back to our lives together which made me think maybe sharing a house wasn't the best idea I'd ever had. The last thing I needed was to complicate my life any more than it already was. *This is ridiculous, Izzy, just buy a new house*, my inner voice offered.

"That's it," I shouted. That was the answer I'd been looking for. I'd buy a new house, a house of my very own. Of course, I'd need to get back to work so I didn't lose my job. It'd be impossible for me to buy a house without an income.

I was more than ready to get back to work and I planned to add that to the growing list of things to get straight with the control freak later, too. And if he wasn't going to let me do my job, then I resolved to find a client that would. Dimarco had plenty of clients that would love to have me on their team, clients who'd actually want me to do my job, and who wouldn't feel the need to give me or my kids inappropriately extravagant gifts.

Satisfied I'd come up with a solid plan, I jogged back to the hotel.

Frank was pacing up and down the beach when I got back. I spotted him long before he saw me. When he finally figured out it was me jogging alone on the beach he started toward me at a rapid pace. "Damn it, Izzy," he snapped when he was close enough to ensure I'd hear him. "We talked about this. You've got to let me do my job."

"Well, good morning to you too, Frank."

"Mr. Payne is not at all happy right now."

I walked past him without stopping. "Exercising is a great way to improve your mood. Maybe you and Mr. Payne both need to go for a run." Frank exhaled loudly, obviously not any happier with my suggestion than with me going out alone, but I didn't care. I was an adult and if I wanted to go for a run, then that was exactly what I would do.

I got straight in the shower as soon as I made it back to my suite. Frank said Alec wasn't happy, but I had a few complaints of my own that I couldn't wait to discuss. I wasted no time washing up either. Alec must already be back if he knew I was out alone. Surely, Frank wouldn't have volunteered that information and gotten himself in hot water for letting me out of his sight, would he?

I'd just finished dressing when the bedroom door swung open. My whole body tensed. All the talk about my safety had me so paranoid, I couldn't stand it. I opened my mouth to scream but nothing came out. Then I saw him. "Damn it, Alec," I shouted. "You scared the hell out of me."

He closed the gap between us, pulling me into his body. "Good, because you scared the hell out of me."

I put both hands on his chest and pushed, simultaneously loosening his grip and giving me the space I needed to get through the conversation I had planned. "Seriously?" I snapped. "You need to get a grip, Alec. I needed some time alone, so I went for run, on a public beach, in broad daylight."

Alec's jaw tightened. "You went for run? Alone?"

Shit. I thought that was what he was talking about. "If that's not your problem, then what is?"

He pulled me back into his body, wrapping his arms tightly around me. "Someone broke into your house. Your office was destroyed."

"Drew, Anna, Spencer, is everyone okay?"

"Yes, yes, Isabella. Everyone is fine." He squeezed his eyes tightly closed. "You weren't answering your phone and when Frank came to check on you, you were gone." He stared me in the eyes. "The police haven't figured out what this psycho wants or how far he's willing to go to get it. You have to be more careful."

Tears filled my eyes. *More careful?* I was already suffocating. How could I possibly handle more?

Alec kissed me on the forehead. "Frank is there for

your protection. You have to let him do his job, baby."

Tears rolled down my cheek. "Alec—"

"Promise me, Isabella. I want you to promise you'll stop ditching your security."

No, no, no. This was not the plan. There was no way I could promise him that, not if I planned on being honest. But I also knew he wouldn't just let it go either. Distraction was my only hope. "We've been through this already, Alec. You can't always get what you want. Now, tell me about the break-in."

Every muscle in Alec's face tightened. He latched on to my arm. "Come with me," he said, pulling me toward the door.

"Where are we going?"

Alec didn't say a word, but rather opened the door and pulled me down the hall. "Wait," I pleaded, "I need to get my purse."

"You won't need it," he said over his shoulder. He dragged me inside the elevator, his hand still tightly gripped around my arm.

"Alec, stop. Where are you taking me?"

He looked deep into my eyes. "I want you to see the damage for yourself, Isabella. Then maybe you'll finally understand the danger you're in."

I opened my mouth to object but closed it again. A big part of me wanted to see what all the fuss was about. For all I knew Alec was blowing everything way out of proportion and going could prove to be the evidence I needed to set him straight.

Preston was waiting at the car when we got there. He opened my door. "Ms. James," he said with an icy tone.

Great, he was mad at me too. Rolling my eyes I slid into the back seat without saying a word. Alec climbed in beside me and Preston took his place behind the wheel. In no time at all we were speeding off toward my house.

The five mile drive seemed endless as my anticipation built. It had been almost a month since I'd been home, since I'd walked on *my* beach, slept in *my* bed, worked in *my* office. I wondered if the house would look the same, if my new Lionheart Tango lilies had bloomed and if they were as blue as the salesman had described.

Staring nervously out the window, I wondered if Spencer would be there. That was a possibility I hadn't even considered until that moment. Was I ready to see him? What would I even say? The thoughts spun around and around in my mind until I was dizzy.

We pulled up to the gate and were stopped by a uniformed officer. "This area is closed," the officer said.

"Mr. Payne and Ms. James to see Detective Rux."

"Oh yes, Detective Rux is expecting you." The officer pressed the code into the keypad and the gate opened.

"A guest at my own house," I whispered, the whole situation becoming harder and harder to believe.

Spencer's car wasn't in the garage when we pulled up and I was beyond relieved. On the drive over I decided I wasn't ready to face Spencer yet, especially not with Mr. Control Freak glued to my side. The last time the three of us were in the same room together, it ended with some pretty harsh accusations from Spencer.

Alec squeezed my hand. "Are you ready?"

Taking a deep breath to steady my nerves I said, "Let's do this."

Anxious to see the damage, I headed straight to my office. *How bad could it be?* my inner voice said, coaxing me to open the door. Quickly, I turned the knob and stepped inside before I had the chance to change my mind.

My heart dropped when I saw all the destruction. It was much worse than I'd imagined it'd be. My office had been completely destroyed; papers were strewn all over the room, desk drawers tossed onto the floor, every bookshelf emptied. "What's mine is mine," was spray painted in large red letters covering every wall. The glass had been broken out of the pictures that once hung neatly on the walls. All my paintings had been sliced to pieces, the cushions on the sofa torn to shreds, the lamp smashed into a thousand pieces all over the floor.

A flicker of light near the bay window caught my eye and drew me toward it. Broken glass crunched beneath my feet, making it impossible to get all the way to the window. I squinted, trying to get a better look. Something had been etched in the glass. I gasped when I finally made out the words. "DIE BELLA."

"Do you understand the danger now, Isabella?" Alec asked. He'd moved in behind me and was wrapping his arm around my shoulders. "Promise me you'll let Frank do his job, baby."

Seeing the destruction with my own eyes brought a whole new perspective to the need for security. Whoever was after me was deadly serious. There was no denying that now. I closed my eyes and melted into Alec's arms where I felt safe. "I promise."

Alec turned away from the etching, taking me with him. To my surprise, Detective Rux was standing in the doorway. His hair was ruffled and the stubble on his face was far beyond a five o'clock shadow. He looked as though he hadn't slept in days.

"Detective," Alec greeted him. "Did you figure out how he got in?"

"I'm afraid not, Mr. Payne. The alarm was active when we arrived on the scene and, just like last time, there was no sign of forced entry."

"Did you check the security video?"

"Someone hacked into the wireless network and wiped the hard drive."

"Damn it. I knew I should've handled the security."

"Our computer crimes division is checking to see if anything can be recovered."

"How long, Detective? It's been over a month since the first attack. How long is it going to take to get some fucking answers?"

"We're working as fast as we can, Mr. Payne."

"Thank you, Detective," I said by means of rescue. I wanted answers as much as Alec, maybe even more, but berating the man in charge of the investigation certainly wasn't going to get them any faster.

Spencer burst into the room, making my whole body tense. He was the last person I wanted to deal with at the moment. Given the fact that Alec's arm was draped over my shoulders he surely wasn't going to help ease the tension in the room.

"What the hell are you doing here, Izzy?" Spencer barked. "You have no right to be here."

The venom dripping from his words made my blood boil. All the calm I felt just a few minutes early was suddenly nonexistent. "This is my house too, Spencer. I have every right to be here."

"Yeah, well, I'm the one who lives here. And you left us, or don't you remember that now that you're shacked up with Mr. Money Bags over there?"

I moved quickly toward him, wagging my finger inches from his face. "Seriously!" I screamed at the top of my lungs, ready to finally give him a piece of my mind. He was the one who'd cheated, and he had the nerve to blame me for leaving. "Did you honestly expect me to stay after you cheated on me?"

Spencer grabbed my shoulders with both hands. "Damn it, Bella. When are you going to let that go?"

Alec stepped between us, pushing Spencer backward. "Take your fucking hands off her."

Spencer staggered into the door jamb, barely able to maintain his balance. "This has nothing to do with you, Payne. This is between me and my wife."

"She isn't your wife anymore."

Spencer lunged toward Alec, his fist drawn. "Get the hell out of my house!" He took a swing.

"Spencer. No!" Damn him. What was he doing?

Alec caught Spencer's fist in his hand and with one quick motion he pinned Spencer's arm behind his back and took him to the ground. "I'm willing to let this slide, considering all that's happened here today, but put your hands on her again and we're going to have a real problem. Are we clear about that?"

Spencer wriggled on the floor, trying to free himself from Alec's unrelenting grip. "Get the fuck off me," he shouted.

"Okay, okay, let's break it up," Detective Rux chimed in, finally putting a stop to the madness before it got completely out of hand. "It's natural for tempers to flare in situations like this but it's important that we all keep a level head, especially in the middle of the crime scene."

Alec released Spencer and stood back up. He straightened his shirt then turned his attention to me. Tears were rolling slowly down my cheeks. Seeing the destruction was bad enough by itself, but the two of them fighting was more than I could handle. Alec moved to my side. "Are you okay?" I nodded silently, too stunned to speak. Alec pulled me into his arms and kissed me on the top of the head. "Baby, don't cry. Everything's going to be okay. You're safe with me."

Spencer pushed himself back up to his feet. "GET OUT," he shouted, pointing toward the door before lunging at Alec again. "Get the hell out of my house."

Detective Rux stepped between them. "Mr. James, control yourself. This is still an active crime scene."

Spencer threw his hands in the air. "Whatever. But I want them out of here. And I mean now!"

Alec had made his point by showing me the damage so didn't hesitate to escort me out of the house and into the waiting car, his arm gripped firmly around my shoulders. Detective Rux suggested Drew and Anna stay away from the house until they could figure out who was behind the break-ins. But, unfortunately, Drew was just as stubborn as his father. Spencer kept insisting I was the only one in danger and given the fact that they'd all been home during the last break-in and none of them were injured, I knew I'd have a battle on my hands trying to convince Drew to leave.

"What's wrong, Isabella?"

I shook my head, not wanting to talk about it.

Alec lowered his eyebrows. "You know how I feel about half-truths."

A sigh escaped me. "What if Drew won't leave? Or Anna? Oh Alec, I don't know what I'd do if anything happened to them."

Unbuckling his seatbelt, Alec slid over next to me on the seat, wrapping his arm around my shoulders. "Everything is going to be okay, baby. I won't let anything happen to them."

I burst into tears. "How can you keep them safe?" I

cried. "They're leaving for college soon and it's not like you can keep them trapped inside a hotel room too."

He lifted my chin until he was staring right into my eyes. "Trapped? Is that how you feel?"

"Yes," I whispered.

Alec pulled his hands through his hair. "You're free to come and go as you please, Isabella. Frank is there for that very reason."

"Yes, Frank. Everywhere I go he's there. I'm suffocating, Alec. I miss my privacy. I miss my home and my job." That confession had the tears coming even faster.

"Please don't cry," Alec whispered in my ear. "Frank is there to keep you safe, not suffocate you."

"I'm not some weakling that needs protection, Alec. I'm Izzy James. I can take care of myself."

Alec put his arm around me again, tucking me into his side. "I'm sure you can, baby." He kissed me on the forehead. "I'm sure you can."

His condescending tone grated on my nerves, giving me just the push I needed to set the record straight. "I'm serious, Alec. I don't need a damn keeper. And I want to go back to work. If you aren't going to let me do my job I'll find another client who will."

"Feisty." He chuckled. "I like it when you're feisty."

"Alec, this isn't funny."

"You're right. There's nothing funny about your safety."

I rolled my eyes. "Distraction isn't going to work this time. I'm going back to work and that's final."

Alec moved back to his seat and fastened his seatbelt. "That's a dangerous game you're playing, Isabella. All of me, remember?" I wasn't sure what he was talking about but right then I didn't really care. I was going back to work and there was nothing he could say or do to stop me.

Preston pulled under the portico at the hotel entrance. I hopped out of the car as soon as we stopped, slamming the door behind me. "You've lost your mind if you think I'm going to sit by and let you control my life," I mumbled as I stomped inside the hotel. Alec called after me but I kept walking, too angry to talk to him, not stopping until I reached the bank of elevators.

Nathan stepped out of the elevator as soon as the doors opened. He wasn't wearing his uniform and he looked as though he'd just gotten out of the shower causing the hairs on my neck to stand on end. "Hey, Izzy."

I stepped back. "Nathan," I said.

"Did you enjoy dinner last night?"

"Yes," I said hesitantly.

"I'm glad you liked it." He glanced over my shoulder. "Good morning, Mr. Payne."

Alec took my arm and practically shoved me into the elevator. "Good morning," he said through gritted teeth.

"What was that all about?" Alec asked when the elevator doors closed.

"It's nothing."

His eyes narrowed. "You know how I feel about half-truths, Isabella."

I sighed. "He works here, Alec. He delivered dinner to my room last night. The dinner you ordered."

Without another word, Alec reached up and activated his Bluetooth device. "Pull the hotel security video from the elevators. The man in blue jeans and a t-shirt who just rode down to the lobby. I want to know who he is and where he's been."

"Alec, I told you. He works here. And his name is

Nathan."

Alec pulled both hands through his hair. "Baby, I didn't order dinner for you last night."

Everything went dark. The only sound audible was the pounding of my heart. If it wasn't Alec or ordered me dinner, then who could it have been? Thoughts whirled through my mind like a spinning top. Had my attacker tracked me to the hotel? How? Alec had been so careful. But Val knew where I was too. And if he knew where I was, why did he break into my house? Alec didn't order me dinner.

Chapter Nineteen

Tomorrow was the day; the day I'd been simultaneously dreading and looking forward to all year. In less than twenty four hours Drew and Anna would walk across that stage and receive their high school diploma, officially bringing another chapter of their lives to an end. My dad was flying in for the big event and I'd been a nervous wreck all morning. I still hadn't told anyone about my divorce and the one person I dreaded telling most of all was Jack Jones. I'd hoped to keep the news of our divorce under wraps as not to cast a shadow on graduation, but there was no way I'd be able to hide it from my dad. As soon as he laid eyes on me, he'd know. Especially considering Alec hadn't left my side since learning Nathan didn't work at the hotel, if Nathan was even his real name.

Alec wanted to move me to a different hotel but I refused to leave the Garden until after graduation. Five miles was as far away from my kids as I was willing to go at this point. As it was I hated not being under the same roof as them. Moving twenty minutes further away, the distance to the closest hotel, was out of the question. A fact Alec wasn't exactly happy about.

He brought in a second security team to ensure there were no more unauthorized visits to my room, though, and I hadn't even told him about the nightmare I had that night. I couldn't imagine how he might've reacted if he thought for even a second someone had been in my room while I was sleeping.

"Are you ready to go?"

I spun around, Alec's voice startling me. "Almost."

"We need to leave soon if you want to be there when your dad's plane arrives."

"Give me five minutes, okay?"

Alec looked at his watch. "You've got exactly five minutes." I rolled my eyes. Quickly, Alec closed the gap between us, pulling me into his arms. He kissed me hard on the mouth then pulled away, leaving me tingling inside. "The next time you roll your eyes at me, Isabella, I'm going to show you exactly how I feel about it." He swatted me playfully on the butt. "Now get ready."

I opened my mouth to object, but Alec disappeared before I could find the words. *Damn it, Alec Payne*, my inner voice snapped. The effect he had on my body was so unfair.

• • • • •

We arrived at the Northwest Florida Regional Airport with plenty of time to spare. Butterflies danced around in my stomach, making it impossible for me to stand still. I paced back-and-forth, anxiously awaiting my dad's arrival.

Alec put his arm around my shoulder, forcing me to stop moving. "Are you okay, baby?"

I held on to his waist. "I should've told him about the divorce. He's going to be mad that I kept it from him and I hate it when he's mad."

"Isabella, I'm sure your dad will understand."

"Understand what?"

I spun around. "Daddy!"

Jack lifted me up in a bear hug. Luckily, my ribs had healed or that would have really hurt. "I've missed you." He put me down and held me at arm's length. "Look at you, Iz. You're too thin. Are you sure you're eating enough."

"Dad," I objected. I certainly didn't need him giving Alec something else to fixate on. He still had his hands full making sure I followed Dr. Leonard's discharge orders, even though it'd been almost six weeks since I was released from the hospital. My dad picked me up again and kissed me on the cheek.

"I'm so glad you came."

"I wouldn't have missed this for anything." A sigh of relief escaped, distraction scored again. "Now, what is it you needed to tell me, Isabella?"

Shit. I was wrong. My distraction had failed but this wasn't a conversation to have at the airport, especially with Alec glued to my side. Redirection was my only hope of avoiding the awkward situation that was about to occur. "We'll talk about that later. Right now I'd like to introduce you to Alec Payne. Alec, this is my father, Jack Jones."

Alec extended his hand. "It's nice to meet you, Mr. Jones."

"Please, call me Jack." The two men shook hands. "How do you know Izzy?"

"Alec's a friend, daddy," I answered quickly.

"Well it's nice to meet you, Alec Payne, friend of Izzy." The look on his face said it all. He knew there was more to the story, but I was relieved he was letting it go, for now anyway.

"You must be hungry after that long flight. How about we go to the Brick and Spoon before heading to the hotel?" Food was the last thing I wanted, but they made an amazing mango mimosa and that sounded pretty good at the moment. I wouldn't be able to keep the news of my divorce a secret much longer, and I was going to need some liquid courage to help me get through that conversation.

"I could eat."

"Brick and Spoon it is then," Alec said.

We collected my dad's suitcase then walked out to the car where Preston was waiting. Alec hopped in the front seat, leaving the back seat for the two of us. Preston typed the address I gave him into the GPS then started off in the direction of the restaurant. With traffic it would be a thirty minute drive, but I didn't mind. My dad wasn't much of a phone talker, and I hadn't seen him since Christmas so we had a lot to catch up on.

"Izzy, I have something to tell you." He took a deep breath. "I'm selling the ranch."

We'd barely left the airport and my dad had already dropped a bomb. "What do you mean, you're selling the ranch?" I asked, surprised by the news. He'd gotten several offers over the years, but I never thought he'd actually sell it.

"I'm getting too old to be a rancher, Iz, and the offer was just too good to pass up this time."

"Was too good? That sounds like you've already accepted it."

"I did. We close as soon as I get back."

"Why didn't you tell me?"

He cupped my face in his hand. "Because I knew you'd worry about me."

"Well, you still should've told me," I said, folding my arms across my chest.

"Don't pout, Isabella. Maybe I should've told you sooner, but it wouldn't have changed anything. My mind was made up."

"What are you going to do now? Where will you live?"

"That's the other thing I wanted to talk to you about. I've met someone."

I rolled my eyes. "Oh, now it makes perfect sense."

"Isabella, I may be too old to take you over my knee but I'm sure your *friend* up there wouldn't mind doing an old man a favor."

"I'd be more than happy to oblige, sir," Alec said all too quickly.

My face turned fire engine red, the space inside the car suddenly feeling too small for all four of us.

"See, he's more than happy to help out. Now, do you have anything else to say about this or can we move on?"

I stared out the window, trying to figure out what surprised me more, dad selling the ranch or him finding a girlfriend. He'd been single for so long. I kind of thought he'd stay that way forever.

"Who is she?" I asked, finally putting an end to the awkward silence.

"Her name is Francine Walker. We met at church."

"And what, you're gonna live with her now?"

"Don't be ridiculous, Isabella. I bought a condo at One Ski Hill. Francine owns the property and she gave me a great deal on the place."

"A condo? Seriously, Dad? You sold your ranch and bought a condo?"

"Izzy, please don't be upset. She makes me happy.

Don't you want me to be happy?"

"Of course I want you to be happy. It's just…" I exhaled loudly. "I just don't want you to get hurt."

"There are never any guarantees in life, Iz. We both know that all too well." He dropped his head, shaking it gently. "I loved your mother with all my heart and soul. But she's been gone for a long time now. It's time for me to move on."

I reached for his hand and squeezed it softly. "You're right. I'm sorry. You deserve to be happy." He'd worked hard his whole life. And when my mom left he'd gone out of his way to make sure I felt loved, even sacrificing his own happiness to give me the best life he knew how.

My dad looked up at me; his eyes filled with tears. "Thank you, sweetheart," he whispered. "You have no idea what it means to hear you say that."

"I just don't understand why you didn't tell me sooner."

"For the same reason you didn't tell me about you and Spencer I reckon."

My mouth dropped open. "You know about me and Spencer?" He nodded but didn't say a word. "How?"

"Oh, Izzy." He laughed. "You've never been good at hiding things from me."

"Did one of the kids tell you?"

"No one *told* me, but it isn't exactly rocket science, young lady." I tilted my head to one side, waiting for an explanation. "You're not wearing your wedding ring, and the lack of a tan line on your finger says you haven't had it on in quite some time. Add that to you showing up to fetch me with your new *friend* up there, the one who can't seem to take his eyes off you, and that's all the evidence a father needs."

• • • • •

Jack and Alec chatted like old friends over brunch while I quietly sipped mimosas in the corner of the booth. By the time I'd finished my third one the shock of my dad selling the ranch had finally worn off. I'd even managed to warm to the idea of him and Francine, but only a little. He hadn't been this happy in a long time, plus I learned they had a lot in common, including the loss of a spouse. Granted Judy hadn't died, but she might as well have. We hadn't heard from her since the day she left. "It's a pain you have to experience to fully understand," my dad had said. How could I stay mad after hearing that? He'd been through so much over the years, raising a daughter on his own and always putting me first no matter what the cost. He'd dated a few times when I was younger, but he walked away every time, for me.

"So, Dad, who's buying the ranch? Anyone I know?"

"Doubt it, not unless you've taken up the pot since you left home."

I tilted my head to one side. "The pot?"

"You know, *marijuana*," he whispered. A smile crossed my face as I processed what he was saying. "I sold the ranch to a couple who want to be pot farmers," he said, laughing. "Isn't that just about the craziest thing you've ever heard before, pot farmers." He took a sip of his coffee. "They've been smoking a little too much of that if you ask me." I glanced at Alec, who was doing his best to hide the growing smile on his face.

The waiter approached the table. "Would you like another drink, ma'am?"

"Absolutely," I said, more than thankful for the

relief today.

"And for you, sirs?" The waiter looked from Jack to Alec then back again.

"You better bring us all another round. And bring me the check," my dad said.

The waiter cleared a couple of dishes from the table. "Sorry, sir, the check has already been taken care of, but I'll be right back with those drinks."

"Now, Alec, you came all the way to the airport to get me, and I'd planned on treating you."

"Habit, sir."

"Well, you might just go broke with a habit like that," Jack warned, oblivious who Alec was. The socks Alec was wearing probably cost more than our lunch.

The smile on Alec's face grew larger. "I'll do my best to remember that."

Jack got in the front seat with Preston when we left the restaurant. "I don't much like the back seat," he said. "Can't see where you're going."

Alec opened my door and I climbed in. He slid in next to me and I leaned against his chest. My dad clearly knew there was something going on between us, so there was no reason to pretend anymore.

Frank was waiting in the parking garage when we got back to the hotel, a worried look plastered across his face. Alec hopped out of the car as soon as we stopped. "Stay in the car," he snapped, looking right at me.

"What's that about?" my dad asked.

I shrugged my shoulders. "I'm not sure," I whispered, all the while praying it had nothing to do with the attacks. Alec pulled his hand through his hair then stormed back toward the car. My heart skipped a beat. *Please be nothing*, I pleaded silently.

Alec jerked open my car door. "Nathan was in your

room?"

Shit. It wasn't a dream after all. I had been so sure. I hopped out of the car. "Alec, please, can we talk about this later?" My divorce wasn't the only thing I'd been keeping from my dad. I hadn't wanted to worry him, so I never told him about the break-ins, and especially not about the attacks. Too bad I forgot to share that bit of information with Mr. Control Freak.

"Answer the damn question, Isabella."

Double shit. He was pissed. "I was certain it was a dream this time," I whispered.

"Well, it wasn't a dream. His fingerprints are all over the headboard!"

"Whoa there, Alec," Jack said from behind me. "There's no need to shout. I'm sure we can handle this like gentlemen."

Alec looked over my shoulder at him. "I'm sorry, sir, but this is her safety we're talking about here."

My dad spun me around. "What's going on here, Izzy?"

I looked down at the ground, wishing I were somewhere else, anywhere else. "It's nothing."

"Nothing?" Alec snapped. "Some psycho breaks into your house, drugs you, and tries to kill you, and you call that nothing?"

"Isabella Grace what is he talking about?" In a matter of seconds everything I'd hidden from my dad had been exposed. I shook my head. There was no way I was getting into all that, not in the parking garage surrounded by four men who were all glaring down at me.

"You didn't tell your father? Not even when you were in the hospital?"

My dad grabbed my shoulders and pulled me close

to him. "You were attacked and you didn't tell me?" he said, staring right into my eyes. "I'm so disappointed in you, Isabella. How could you keep this from me?" My dad's words were like fire, an incinerator to my heart. No words had ever yielded such power as those. I'd disappointed my father.

Tears filled my eyes. "Daddy, I'm sorry. I just didn't want to worry you."

"I don't want to hear your excuses. You're my only child. Didn't you think I'd want to know that someone was trying to hurt you?"

Stepping away from my dad, I buried my face in my hands, but Alec reached over and lifted my chin until our eyes met. "This isn't a game, baby. You have to stop playing with your safety."

"I know this isn't a game, Alec. It's my life." I pulled out of his grip. "And that's the operative word here, MINE, as in not yours."

"Isabella, that's enough," my dad snapped. "You sound like a spoiled brat right now, and I don't like it one bit." He turned his attention to Alec. "I suggest you take her upstairs and put a stop to all this nonsense."

"Dad!"

"Don't dad me, Izzy. If you're going to act like a child we'll treat you like one." He crossed his arms. "Now, go to your room." Rolling my eyes, I stomped off toward the stairs. Not because he'd told me to, but because I didn't want to hear another word about any of this, from either of them.

I took off my sandals and sprinted up the stairs as fast as I could go. It was bad enough being scolded by my father at my age, but being yelled at in front of Alec was down-right humiliating. I wasn't a child and I'd be damned if I was going to be treated like one. No matter how disappointed my father was.

By the time I reached the seventh floor I was covered in sweat and more than ready for a shower. I inserted my key card in the lock but the door didn't open. I tried it again, still nothing.

"Here, you'll need this." I turned around only to find Frank standing there, holding a new key card. I snatched it out of his hand and unlocked the door without saying a word. I was in no mood for pleasantries.

After downing half a glass of wine, I stripped down and hopped into the shower, anxious to wash away more than just sweat. I closed my eyes and stood under the stream of water, letting it run over my face. The look on my father's face was still fresh in my mind, his words ringing in my ear. "I'm disappointed, Isabella." As if my life hadn't been stressful enough recently, I had to go and disappoint my dad. "It's not fair."

"Stop pouting, Isabella."

My eyes flew open. "Alec," I screamed, surprised to find him here, standing in front of me, inside the shower, completely naked. "What are you doing?"

"Putting a stop to all this nonsense," he said as he took a step closer. And in one swift motion I was pinned against the cold, wet tile, his mouth claiming mine with an urgency that had my sex quivering. I moaned inside his mouth as his tongue greedily claimed mine. His growing erection pressed against my stomach, making my insides quicken, all the drama of the day instantly forgotten.

Alec pulled away, leaving me panting for breath. Without saying a word he dropped to his knees and lifted my leg over his shoulder, opening me up to him. He plunged his tongue inside me as his finger rubbed my clit. I fisted my hands in his hair; biting back the scream as he pleasured me with is mouth.

His tongue flicked against my clit and he inserted two fingers deep inside me. Waves of pleasure threatened. "Oh God, Alec, please take me. I want to feel you inside me." He pushed his fingers in deeper, hitting the spot that instantly had me teetering on the edge. "God, Alec, I'm going to come."

"Yes, baby, come for me. Let me taste your pleasure." His words were my undoing. My orgasm ripped through me, rendering my legs useless. Alec lowered my leg, his hands gripping my hips as he held me up upright. He trailed kisses up my belly, to my nipples, then finally to my mouth where he plunged his tongue inside, letting me taste my arousal.

"Turn around," Alec said when he pulled away. I quickly did as he asked. But at that moment I would have done pretty much anything he'd asked. "Now put your hands on the wall and don't move them until I tell you to," he whispered against my ear. Pressing my hands against the cold tile, I let the warm water run down my back. Alec pushed my hair to one side. "Good girl," he whispered against my ear before kissing his way to my neck.

Arching my back, I tried to absorb the sensation. His finger trailed down my side until I couldn't stand it any longer. I let go of the wall and turned to face him, desperately wanting to touch him.

Alec took a step back and put both hands on my shoulders, turning me back toward the wall. "I told you not to let go," he said in a gruff tone. "We're going to have to work on you doing what you're told." He placed my hands back on the tile then planted a hard swat on my butt cheek, the loud sound of his hand connecting with my wet skin echoing inside the shower. "If you let go again I'm going to punish you." His voice was harsh in my ear and I didn't know if I should be turned on or afraid.

He ran his hands slowly down my side once more. I closed my eyes and bit my lip, every nerve in my body firing simultaneously. He stopped when he reached my waist, pulling me toward him, letting my hands slide down the wet tile. "I'm going to take you now, Isabella. Don't let go of the wall."

In one quick motion he pushed himself inside me. "Alec," I moaned, as I adjusted to the depth of his erection from this position. He shifted his hips as he moved in and out of me, slowly at first.

With his fingers digging into my flesh, he really started to move. "Oh God, Alec," I screamed, the sensation more than I could handle. My sex began to quicken when he found his rhythm. I pushed back against the wall, meeting his thrusts, pushing him even deeper inside me. Alec reached around and circled my clit with one hand, the other hand still on my hip. My sex contracted as another orgasm threatened.

"That's it, baby. Come for me," he groaned. That was all it took. That one little command had my body unraveling around him. He pushed himself deeper inside as he found his own release.

Alec eased his still hard cock out of me. Slowly, I stood up, my hands still on the tile. Alec held onto my wrists and turned me toward him, kissing me softly on the lips. "That was so hot, baby." Not able to speak, I laid my head on his chest, a satisfied smile on my face.

• • • • •

I wrapped the hotel robe around me then climbed

into bed for a much needed nap. The events of the day had left me totally exhausted, not to mention the four mango mimosas with lunch. We were meeting Drew and Anna for a pre-graduation dinner later, and I'd need all the strength I could get. After tomorrow the kids would be off on their own on the class trip, then college. They'd be living their own lives, building their own futures. It was a lot to accept given all the other changes in my life this past year. I closed my eyes and allowed my mind to wander.

It's dark. I can't see.
Why must you defy me?
Who are you?
Don't move.
I'll punish you if you move.
Why are you doing this?
What's mine is mine, Bella.

My heart is racing. I can't breathe.

"Isabella. Isabella, wake up."

I jolted upright in bed, beads of sweat covering my forehead. I glanced around the room. "Alec," I gasped, relieved when I saw him.

He pulled me into his arms. "You were dreaming, baby. Everything is okay. You're safe with me."

"Were you serious?"

Alec tilted his head to one side. "It was just a dream, Isabella."

"No, earlier, in the shower, when you said you were going to punish me. Were you serious?"

A smile crossed his face. "I think you need to be punished. Don't you?" He pulled a tissue from the box and wiped the sweat off my forehead. "After all, you did ditch your security, and you failed to mention Nathan was here."

"I thought it was a dream, Alec. I would've told you if I'd known it was real."

"No excuses, Isabella. You should've told me."

I let it go. Truthfully, part of me suspected it wasn't a dream. I just hadn't wanted to admit it. I was suffocating with the security Alec already had in place, and the thought of more was just too much. "You're right, Alec. I should've told you. Next time—"

"There isn't going to be a next time," he interrupted. "There will be no more secrets, and no more ditching security, for any reason. Are we clear on that?"

I pulled away suddenly. "No, we're not," I objected. "He didn't attack me when I was out. He attacked me here, in this room, with Frank right next door."

Alec pulled me back into his arms, and I could feel a slight tremble. "Please, Isabella. I don't know what I'd do if anything happened to you."

"I wouldn't have to ditch security if you'd let me work. I'm bored, Alec. I miss my job. I'm going crazy here alone."

"Okay," he said finally. "If going back to work is that important to you we'll figure something out."

Chapter Twenty

There was a long line of people waiting for the complimentary muffins and juice the school provided for the mid-morning graduation ceremony, but I managed to push my way past the crowd to the staging area where the graduates were busily readying themselves. I was hoping to steal a minute with the kids before the ceremony. I moved through the crowd, searching for them both, the sea of blue and white gowns making it difficult to pick anyone out of the crowd.

I was just about to give up when I heard Drew laugh. "Drew," I called out, hoping he'd hear me.

"Mom." I heard him call, but I still couldn't see where he was. "Mom." I heard again, behind me this time. Drew lifted me off the ground as he wrapped me into a bear hug. "I wasn't expecting to see you until after the ceremony."

"I wanted to hug you one last time before you graduated," I said, struggling to hold back the tears that were threatening to fall. I didn't want to ruin this day for him with an emotional breakdown. A single tear rolled down my cheek. Drew reached up and wiped it away. Unable to stop myself, I pulled him close, savoring the last hug I'd have before he was officially a high school graduate.

"Mom!" Anna squealed as she ran toward me. Instantly, Drew released me and I wrapped Anna up in a hug next.

"Aunt Val stopped by a little bit ago. Have you seen her?" What? She was already here? Why hadn't she called me? I shook my head.

Someone called from a distance, "Anna, Drew, hurry up, you're holding up the pictures."

Drew kissed me on the cheek. "Mom, we gotta go."

"We'll see you after the ceremony," Anna added, then kissed the other cheek. With that they disappeared back into the crowd.

The auditorium had filled up considerably since I'd first arrived. Scanning the audience, I looked for Alec and Jack. "We're over here, baby," Alec said, sneaking up behind me. I nodded, my heart beating too fast to speak. That whole attacker thing had me on the edge of insanity.

By the time we reached our seats my heart rate had returned to normal. I sat in the empty seat next to my dad. "Have you seen Val?"

"She was having a fairly heated conversation with Spencer when I got here but I haven't seen her since," he said.

I fished my phone out of my purse to call her, wondering where she was, and what the argument was all about. Shit. She'd called me. With all the noise in the auditorium I hadn't heard the ring. I dialed voicemail and listened to the message, shaking my head as it played.

"What's wrong?" Alec asked.

"Val left," I said unable to hide the disappointment in my voice. "There was some sort of emergency she had to deal with," I said, doing my best to hide the disappointment in my voice. Val came all this way and I didn't even get to see her, and now I had her emergency to worry about. It had to be something big for her to miss Drew and Anna's graduation, but she didn't offer any clues about what it could be.

· · · · ·

The ceremony was shorter than I'd expected given the four hundred plus graduates, but by the time we finished taking pictures it was well after two. My dad rode with Drew and Anna back to the house for the party. Spencer invited over a hundred people, so I wasn't in a hurry to get there. I wouldn't be missed, not for a while at least. I'd called Valerie, but her voicemail picked up. I was starting to worry.

"The sooner we get here the sooner we can leave," Alec said, somehow sensing my apprehension. I'd managed to avoid Spencer's parents at the ceremony but I doubted I'd be that lucky at the graduation party. I was sure they'd blame me for the divorce. Nothing was ever Spencer's fault, not in their eyes anyway. Alec was right though. I had to go, and the sooner I got there the sooner I could leave.

"Promise me you'll stay by my side." Surely Gladys, Spencer's mom, would stay clear if Alec was standing next to me.

Alec lifted my hand to his mouth and gently kissed my knuckles. "I promise, Isabella," he whispered. "Now, can we go? Because I'm really looking forward to getting you alone when this is all over."

My cheeks reddened at the possibilities that promise held.

Alec's jaw tightened as Preston drove through the open gate at my house, and I said a silent prayer he wasn't having second thoughts about coming to the party with me. "Does Spencer even care about your safety?" Alec snapped. That was the same tone he'd had when he found out about Nathan, so I didn't dare answer him. The last thing I needed while preparing to face this crowd was a pissed off control freak.

Preston pulled up in front of the house and turned off the engine.

"I want a complete perimeter sweep. And find out where Frank is," Alec ordered, when Preston opened his door.

"Yes, sir," Preston said, his response calm and cool as usual.

Alec walked slowly around the back of the car toward the passenger side where I was sitting. I didn't move, needing every last second to garner the strength it'd take to get through the afternoon. A warm breeze blew over my legs and I realized the door had been opened. Turning to see who it was, I took one last deep breath to calm my nerves, and then stepped out of the car into Alec's waiting arms.

After a lingering hug Alec hooked his arm around mine and escorted me inside, only tensing a little as we passed through the unlocked front door.

The house felt strange somehow, not at all like the home it used to be. Gone were my soft earthy tones and colorful accents. The walls of the foyer had been painted red; a deep, dark red that sent a shiver down my spine, the color of dried blood red.

I stopped outside my office door. Alec tugged on my

arm but I was unable to resist the urge to see what changes Spencer had made in there. My mouth practically hit the floor when I stepped inside the room. The yellow walls that once enveloped the sun had been painted black. My desk that overlooked the Bay had been replaced with a pool table. A bar now stood where the sofa once was. The paintings I'd worked so hard to collect, the books I cherished, all of them gone. There wasn't one thing left in the space that spoke of me.

"Do you like what I've done in here?"

"My office," I gasped. "What have you done to my office?"

"It's not your office anymore, Bella," Spencer chuckled.

"Spencer, how could you? This is still half my house, and you know how much I loved this room."

"I couldn't stand the constant reminder of you. I changed it all, every room, every memory." His words were slurred and I realized he'd already had way too much to drink. Arguing with him would be pointless, so I stormed out of the room instead.

Alec followed me into the kitchen. "I want to go, now," I said when we were far enough away from Spencer I was sure he couldn't hear me. Certainly, he'd have something to say about me leaving so soon, and I was in no mood to hear it, especially not from him.

"Shouldn't you let Drew and Anna know you're here before we leave?"

I rolled my eyes. "Fine, but then we're leaving."

Alec pulled me into his arms. "Considering all you've been through today, Isabella, I'm going to give you a pass this time, but this is the last time. Roll your eyes at me again and I *will* punish you, no matter where we are." My insides tingled and I nervously bit my lip. Damn my body for being so turned on by him when I was busy trying to be mad at Spencer. "Now, let's go find the graduates so we can get you out of here."

He led me through the kitchen and into the back yard where everyone was gathered. Much to my dismay, Gladys spotted me from across the yard the second I stepped out of the lanai and she started in my direction. Snagging a glass of champagne from the tray of a passing waiter, I quickly drank it down. My plan to avoid Gladys had failed and liquid courage was all I had left.

"Izzy, it's so nice to see you," she said, her tone dripping with sarcasm. She moved in for a hug and I didn't fight it. Making a scene wasn't going to make this encounter any easier.

"It's nice to see you too, Gladys."

She released me then turned her attention to Alec. "And you must be Alec Payne." She extended her hand to him. "Spencer has told me a lot about you."

He kissed the back of her hand. "Mrs. James," he said with a look that could melt even the coldest of hearts. "It's nice to meet you too."

Gladys' cheeks glowed red and she quickly withdrew her hand. "Spencer said you were a charmer. In fact, he said you charmed the pants right off Izzy."

I knew her sincerity only seconds ago had been too good to be true. The waiter walked by and I liberated another glass from his tray.

"Mrs. James, it was a pleasure to meet you but I'm afraid Isabella and I have some business to attend to." He flashed a smile then pulled me away from that evil woman.

"Can we please go now?"

"Baby, Drew and Anna are leaving tomorrow morning. Don't you want to see them?"

I exhaled loudly. "Of course I do, but you heard her, Alec. She thinks I cheated on Spencer and I'm sure everyone else here does too."

"Who cares what they think?" He leaned down and kissed me right on the lips. "Now, stop pouting."

"Mom," Anna squealed as she ran toward me. "I was beginning to think you weren't coming."

"And miss the opportunity to see you before your trip, not a chance." Anna threw her arms around me and I squeezed her tight. She smelled familiarly sweet, not at all like the perfume she normally wore. "Are you wearing a new perfume?"

"Yeah, Aunt Val brought it for me. Do you like it?"

"It smells sweet. What is it?"

"Oh, I can't remember right now, white gardenia or something." My body tensed. That smell, alcohol, cigarettes and gardenias?

"Hey, what about me, where's my hug?" Drew asked as he wrapped in his arms me, all thoughts of my nightmares vanishing instantly. Overcome by emotion, I couldn't hold back the tears any longer. My babies were officially grown up.

"Mom," Anna complained. "Stop crying before you make me cry too."

I took a deep breath to steady my nerves. "I'm sorry guys. I'm just so proud of you both."

"As am I," Alec said. "I can't say enough how proud I am of your accomplishment. I can't wait to see what you'll achieve next."

Anna threw her arms around Alec's waist. "Thanks, Alec. That means a lot."

"Yes, thank you, Alec, for everything," Drew added.

We chatted for a few minutes, mostly about the cruise they were leaving for on in the morning. Spencer's dad, Steve, started toward us, and my body tensed again. Alec must have seen my anxiety building because he quickly excused us.

It was hard saying goodbye to the kids, not knowing exactly when I'd see them again, but I'd never been so happy to leave a party in all my life. Most of the guests were from Spencer's side of the family, and it was clear from my conversation with Gladys that Spencer had been less than honest about our divorce. He could've at least said it was an amicable split, but he chose to blame me instead. Maybe in his mind it *was* my fault because I'd been the one who demanded a divorce. Funny how he seemed to gloss right over the reason I'd done it.

Preston was waiting by the car when we approached, an almost expressionless look plastered across his face. He motioned over his shoulder, some sort of unspoken language that Alec seemed to understand perfectly. Alec kissed me on the top of the head then helped me into the car. I watched intently as the two men rounded the back of the car. I couldn't hear what Preston was saying, but from Alec's body language I knew it wasn't good news. One hand fisted in his hair, the other at his side, until finally getting into the car.

"What was that about?"

"There was an explosion in the parking garage of my apartment in Manhattan," he said, his voice barely audible.

"Oh my gosh, Alec! That's terrible. Was anyone hurt?"

"There were a couple of minor injuries. Luckily, everyone is expected to be okay."

My body tensed. "Was it him?" I asked, although I was pretty sure of the answer. Alec nodded slowly. Tears quickly filled my eyes. "I'm sorry, Alec. This is all my fault. It's me he wants to hurt."

"Baby, no. This isn't your fault. We don't know that the bombing is related to the attack on you."

"Yes it is," I cried. "This psycho is after me and now innocent people are hurt. Oh, Alec, what if he hurts you, or one of my kids?"

Alec unbuckled his seatbelt and slid over next to me, snaking his arm around my shoulders. "I won't let anything happen to them, Isabella, or to you. And Preston won't let anything happen to me." I laid my head on his shoulder as I tried to still my tears. "Besides, he's in police custody. He can't hurt anyone now."

"What? They caught who did it? Who is he?"

"That guy you met on the beach, Nathan, although that's not his real name."

"Nathan?" I gasped. "Why is he doing this? I don't even know who he is."

"We'll know more as soon as the police figure out his real identity. The important thing is he's off the streets."

"Are you sure it was him?"

"The police are comparing his fingerprints to the ones they collected to be certain but we have him on video placing the explosives." A shiver ran down my spine as I realized how close to danger I'd really been. Alec had been right all along. The danger *was* real.

• • • • •

Alec was much more relaxed with Nathan, or whatever his name was, in police custody. He'd insisted on moving me to a different hotel just to be safe, but I didn't mind too much. I'd wanted to stay at the Wyndham primarily because of its' proximity to the kids, but considering they were leaving in the morning it didn't really matter where I stayed.

With the recent bombing at his apartment, I'd expected Alec to still be on high alert, but much to my surprise he didn't object when I suggested we take a walk on the beach, or when I asked to have drinks by the pool afterwards.

"What'll it be?" the bartender asked.

I turned toward Alec, deliberately biting my bottom lip, my gaze fixed on his eyes. "I was thinking Sex on the Beach."

"And for you, sir?"

"I'll have a glass of your best Riesling."

"Coming right up."

When the bartender moved away Alec leaned in and whispered in my ear. "Careful what you wish for, Isabella." He kissed me behind my ear, sending goose bumps all the way to my toes. My sex tingled and I nervously bit my lip this time.

The bartender set our drinks down and turned his attention to the group of young women at the end of the bar. I picked up my drink and pulled hard on the straw, my eyes fixed on Alec's wicked grin. "Yes, sex on the beach is definitely what I'm in the mood for."

"Anything for you, Isabella." He moved closer, his lips almost touching mine. "Dangerous, dangerous game," he said. He pressed his lips hard against mine, his tongue begging me to let him in. My lips parted and he claimed my mouth in a passionate kiss that had my whole body on alert.

By the time I finished my second drink I was beginning to feel the effects of the alcohol. It didn't help that I'd barely eaten, but food was the last thing on my mind. My body was on fire and all I could think about was getting Alec alone. "Let's go upstairs," I said, hopping off the stool. My head started to spin and I had to grab on to the bar to keep from falling.

"After you eat."

"But I don't want food. I want you." I folded my arms in protest.

"Pouting isn't going to work, Isabella. You've had three glasses of champagne plus two very strong drinks. You need food."

"I only had two and a half glasses of champagne. Now, take me upstairs and fuck me."

Alec pulled me in to him, cupping my face in his hands, devouring me with a kiss. "As you wish, baby." He tossed a hundred dollar bill on the bar then practically dragged me into the hotel, an ear-to-ear smile on my face celebrating the battle I'd just won.

As soon as the elevator doors closed and I found myself pinned against the wall with my skirt pushed halfway up my thighs. Alec parted my legs with his knee and before I could catch my breath was shoving two fingers inside me. "Alec," I cried out but he swallowed my cries with his kiss as he continued to finger my pussy, his thumb rubbing hard circles over my clit.

I was on the edge of orgasm when the elevator stopped. No! I wanted to finish. I *needed* to finish. Alec scooped me up into a fireman's hold and carried me down the hall to our suite before returning my feet to the ground inside the bedroom. "Clothes. Off. Now," he said firmly. The shock of what just happened in the elevator hadn't quite worn off yet and I was struggling to process what he was saying. Alec ripped open my shirt, sending buttons flying. "Naked, Isabella. Now."

Making quick work of the rest of my clothes, in a matter of seconds I was completely naked. Alec's chest glistened in the moonlight that flooded the room through the sliding glass door. I wanted to touch him, to feel his toned chest against my skin. I reached for him but he caught my wrists in his hands. "On your knees," he said in a clipped tone. A rush of heat washed over me and my heart started to race. Was he mad at me? Had I pushed him too far? Letting go of my wrists he pushed down on my shoulders until I was kneeling in front of him.

He unzipped his pants and freed his growing erection. "You wanted me to fuck you, Isabella, and that's exactly what I'm going to do." He ran his thumb over my bottom lip. "And I think I'll start here." Holding his erection in his hand he rubbed the tip of his penis where his thumb had been. I opened to him and he slid his cock into my mouth. My tongue circled him as I gently sucked him in. He fisted both hands in my hair, effectively holding me in place, and began thrusting his hips. Deeper and deeper he thrust until I could feel him in my throat.

"God, Isabella, I love fucking your mouth." When his thrusts became erratic I knew he was getting close. "I'm going to come," he said with ragged breath. He started to pull away but I grabbed his ass and dug my fingers into his flesh, wanting to finish what I'd started. Relaxing my throat, I sucked him down as the evidence of his arousal hit the back of my throat.

"Fuck, Isabella," he moaned as I continued to suck him all the way through his orgasm.

He pulled out of my mouth and lifted me to my feet. "That was so hot, baby. But I'm not done with you yet."

With a flick of his tongue my nipple hardened, first one, and then the other. Applying just the right amount of pressure he rolled them between his fingers as his tongue roamed down my body. Alec lifted me up and tossed me onto the bed, spreading my legs wide as he pushed my knees apart, plunging his tongue inside me as he found my nipples once more, pinching and releasing, while his tongue explored my pussy. I was dangling on the edge of ecstasy when his tongue began its dance around my clit. "Alec," I panted. "I'm going to come."

"That's right, baby. Give it to me." He pushed two fingers inside my wet canal to finish me. The walls of my vagina clenched around him and my orgasm ripped through my body.

I tasted my arousal when Alec claimed my mouth with his. "I love seeing you come apart for me, baby. Knowing I'm the one giving you pleasure."

"God, Alec. That was amazing."

"Yes, it was," he said as began trailing kisses down neck. "But, baby, I'm just getting warmed up."

Alec leaned against the headboard and pulled me onto his lap, his erection throbbing against my sensitive sex. He covered my nipple with his mouth and he picked up right where he'd left off. I arched my back, pushing my breasts closer to his face as I ran my hands up his thighs, between his legs, my fingers lightly grazing his balls. Wrapping one arm around my waist he lifted me slightly while using his other hand to position his cock at my opening. Steadying myself on his shoulders, I lowered onto his waiting erection.

"Go slow, baby. You're so tight. I don't want to hurt you." I eased myself all the way down his shaft, his penis deep inside me from this position. With his hands around my waist, he lifted me up and down his erection, rotating his hips with each downward motion. The friction on my clit was exquisite. I picked up speed, digging my fingers into his shoulders, rotating my hips now too. I reached behind me, arching my back, getting lost in the pleasure of my building release.

It wasn't long before I was grinding into him, increasing the friction on my clit even more. "Yes, Alec, yes," I screamed.

"That's right, baby. Take me. All of me."

"You feel so good. Oh, God. Don't stop."

Alec reached between my legs and rubbed my clit with his thumb. I climbed higher and higher toward my climax. "Come for me, baby. Let me feel your orgasm."

"Yes, Alec. Yes. Yes. Yes!" I screamed as pleasure erupted.

With a few final thrusts Alec found his release soon after. I collapsed against his chest, too exhausted to move. "That was incredible, baby," Alec whispered. "But I'm still not done with you."

Chapter Twenty One

I winced as I crawled off Alec's lap, my insides sore and swollen from the marathon fuck fest that began last night. Alec's stamina could rival any man, or woman's for that matter. Spencer had been my first and, while we had an active sex life, it was nothing like it was with Alec. I never knew sex could be that good, or could leave me that sore. "What do you think, baby. Have you been thoroughly fucked yet?"

"And then some," I laughed.

"Are you sure? Because I'd hate to think I was depriving you."

"Oh God, please, no more. I'm so sore."

A smile crossed Alec's face. "Just giving you what you asked for." He kissed me on the forehead. "Anything for you, Isabella."

Alec ran a warm bath and helped me in. Part of me was relieved when he decided not to join me. We'd have ended up tangled in the throes of passion and I was certain my body couldn't take any more right now. "Sit down," he said. "The warm water will ease some of the soreness." I didn't argue. There wasn't a muscle in my body that didn't get a workout last night. I made a mental note to choose my words more carefully with him moving forward. He'd taken my half-buzzed demand for sex as a challenge. A challenge he wasn't about to lose.

When I got out of tub some time later I could hear Alec yelling. His voice was the only one I heard, so I guessed he was on the phone. He'd said he was going to order us breakfast, but his clipped tone suggested it wasn't room service he was taking to.

Pulling on one of his shirts, I peeked out of the bedroom to find out what was going on. Alec was pacing around the room, his hands fisted at his sides. What could have him this upset at five in the morning? He'd been in such a good mood when he helped me into the bath. What could've changed in that short amount of time?

"Have Marcus meet me on site. No. I'll be there in a couple hours." Alec reached up and pressed the button on his Bluetooth earpiece then turned his attention to me. "Eat," he said simply, pointing at a tray of food on the table.

I lifted the silver dome off the tray and uncovered two omelets and a selection of fresh cut fruit. Grabbing a handful of grapes, I sat down on the sofa to eat them.

"You're leaving?" I asked after a few minutes.

Alec sat down next to me. "I'm afraid so, baby."

"Take me with you."

"No, Isabella. It isn't safe for you there."

"Nathan is in custody, remember?"

Alec took my hand in his. "It wasn't Nathan," he whispered.

"But I thought you said the police had him on video at your apartment."

"The video shows him placing the package but he

swears he had no idea it contained explosives." Alec squeezed his eyes shut. "And his fingerprints don't match the ones from your house or the hotel."

My head was spinning. What was he saying? Someone else was trying to hurt me? "What about the fingerprints in my room. You said Nathan had been there."

"The fingerprints in the hotel room matched the partial from the alarm system at your house, and when the police discovered that Nathan didn't work at the hotel everyone assumed it was him, including me." Alec cupped my face in his hands, his eyes holding mine in an impassioned plea. "But it wasn't him, Isabella. He's not the one who hurt you."

Wrapping my arms around Alec's waist, I buried my face in his chest. Tears had already started to fall. If it wasn't Nathan, then who was it? "Why, Alec, why is this happening?" I cried. "Why is someone trying to hurt me?"

"That's what I'm going to find out."

Alec held me while I cried, which only made me cry harder. I felt so safe wrapped in his arms, but he was leaving. The thought of being alone frightened me in a way it never had before. Whoever was after me had taken the one thing I never thought I would lose, that part of me that made me who I was—strong, fierce, and unafraid of the world. In a blink of an eye my desperate need for independence was gone. This stranger I'd never known existed inside me was all that was left. All I wanted at that moment was to stay wrapped in Alec's arms forever.

"Take me with you," I cried. "I don't want to be here alone."

"It'll be okay, baby. I'll only be gone for a few hours,

and Frank will be posted right outside your door the entire time I'm gone."

"Please," I whined.

"Let me tuck you in. I'll be back before you even have a chance to miss me." He stood up, pulling me to my feet next to him. Scooping me into his arms he carried me to bed.

• • • • •

I tossed and turned but couldn't sleep after Alec left. I'd wanted to go with him but his insane compulsion to keep me safe kept me here. The beach was full of vacationers enjoying the beautiful Florida weather. I considered hanging out on the beach too, but I hated to drag Frank along. Alec had given him strict orders not to let me out of his sight and he'd given me stricter orders not to ditch security.

Desperate for any distraction I could get I pulled out my laptop to check email. My medical leave was about to expire and I'd be going back to work on Monday, so I should probably get caught up on emails anyway.

Noon came and went and there was still no word from Alec. I'd gotten through all the emails flagged as urgent and was feeling less anxious about being away from work so long. Luckily, Payne Enterprises was the only project I was directly responsible for and, considering Alec was the one who'd insisted I take the leave, I didn't have a whole lot going on.

I called my dad to make sure he made it home safely. He was closing on the ranch so he had to rush back to Colorado. Our conversation was short but they usually were. My dad hated talking on the phone but at least I knew he'd arrived in one piece.

Frank brought me lunch but I wasn't really hungry. Being trapped inside was getting to me. I needed to get my life back to normal, whatever that was. The minutes on the clocked ticked away painfully slow. I needed a distraction.

Val answered on the first ring. "Bella, where are you? I came by the hotel last night and they said you'd checked out." I still hadn't told her about the divorce or the attacks. How was I supposed to explain what was going on? She knew I'd been staying in a hotel, but she hadn't asked me why, and I hadn't offered.

"I needed a change," I said. It wasn't really a lie. I did need a change. "I'm staying at the Sandestin. Where'd you go yesterday?" I asked, quickly changing the subject.

"Sorry about that, Bella. I ran into my ex at the ceremony and I had to get out of there."

"Your ex? Who?"

"Husband number three. He was there with his new girlfriend."

"Oh, Val. I'm sorry. You should've told me."

"You seemed to have your hands full."

"What are you talking about?"

"Alec Payne. I saw the two of you together. He's bad news, Izzy. You should stay away from him. I heard he's a real son-of-a-bitch."

"He's a client, Val. And how do you know him, anyway?"

"I'm serious, Bella, I want you to stay away from him," she snapped, completely ignoring my question. I was beginning to rethink calling her. I'd been looking for a distraction, not a lecture. "How long are you staying in Destin? I want to see you."

"I'm not sure," I answered honestly. "I'll be going

back to work in a couple of days, so probably until then."

"Hey, I'm getting another call. I gotta run now, but I'll let you know if I can make it back down."

"You should try. It'd be good to see you."

"Definitely. Later, Bella." And with that the line went dead. Val had never spoken her third husband's name to me so I had no idea who he was. I had never given him much thought, but hearing he was at graduation had me wondering who he could be. She lived in Chicago. What were the odds her ex-husband would be dating a woman from Ft. Walton Beach?

Staring out at the water from the balcony made me miss my home even more than I already did. Watching the sunset over the water every evening, all those quiet walks on the beach, the sand beneath my feet, the water washing over me, it had been my peaceful sanctuary and now it was gone.

The ringing of my phone brought me back to the here and now. I ran inside to answer it, hoping against hope it was Alec. Only it wasn't. "Hey, Spencer, what's going on?"

"Hi, Bella. I thought you'd want to know Anna called. They made it onboard the ship okay."

It didn't surprise me that Anna had called Spencer. After all, she was a daddy's girl, but I'd hoped she'd call me too. "Thanks."

"Are you okay? You sound upset."

"Yeah, I'm fine. I'm just a little sad about the kids leaving I guess."

"Why don't you come to the house? Cathy is still here. She'd loved to see you." It would be nice to see Cathy. She and Spencer had always been more like brother and sister than cousins. And after we got married she treated me like a sister too, welcoming me into the family with open arms, even when her aunt hadn't. Gladys made no secret of the fact she thought Spencer could do better, but Cathy was always there to reassure me. Even still, there was no way I was going over there.

"Spencer, I can't, even if I wanted to. My car is still at the house." True, my car was still at the house, but Frank would drive me if I really wanted to go. But I didn't. The house was foreign to me now, as was Spencer. What would I do if Cathy started asking questions about the divorce? What had Spencer told her? Plus, he'd been drinking pretty heavily lately and I disliked Drunk Spencer even more than the sober version of him.

"Don't be silly, Izzy. You're practically next door. I'll come get you."

"Actually, I moved to the Sandestin last night. But I'm not feeling up to it anyway."

"I understand. Cathy will too. Feel better, Izzy, and please, call me if you need anything." It was clear Spencer still cared about me, and I him. Nineteen years was a long time to love someone. It wasn't like either of us could just flip a switch and turn it off.

Tears began to fall as soon as we hung up. Nothing was going to stop them this time. My life was in total disarray. My marriage had ended. I'd been forced out of my home, separated from my family, my kids, and even my career. It was all slipping away and I felt powerless to stop it. I'd lost all control. This was not the Izzy James I knew, the Izzy James I used to be. The tears fell faster. I buried my face in a pillow and sobbed, loud, uncontrollable cries.

• • • • •

I was woken by a commotion in the hall. There were several voices, but I couldn't make them out. The door swung open and Alec and Preston rushed in, Frank close behind them. Alec's lips were pressed in a thin, hard line and his eyes were tiny slits on his face. He was mad, really mad. He glared at me, his eyes burning a hole right through me.

"Me?" I breathed. He was mad at me.

"Who did you tell, Isabella?" he shouted. "Who knows you're here?" His voice was gruff. I opened my mouth to answer but closed it, knowing full well he wasn't going to like what I had to say. "Answer me, Isabella! And this is no time for half-truths either."

I took a deep breath to steady my nerves. "My dad," I whispered.

"Is that it?"

"Spencer knows too."

"Damn it, Isabella." He paced back and forth like a caged animal, both hands tugging at his hair. He turned to Preston. "Get me the hotel security video." Preston moved toward the door. "And find out where Spencer James is at."

"I didn't mean to tell him, Alec. It just slipped out."

Alec glared at me, his eyes burning hotter than embers. Pulling a shirt out of the closet, he tossed it to me. "Get dressed," he ordered.

"Alec, what's wrong?"

"You did exactly what I told you not to, Isabella. That's what's wrong." Valerie's warning came rushing through my mind. "He's bad news," she'd said. Shit. Valerie. I forgot to tell him I talked to her, but it could wait. He was already mad as hell and knowing there was someone else I told where we were staying wasn't going to make it any better.

I didn't move, momentarily stunned by his anger. Alec cupped my face in his hands. "Get dressed, Isabella. And don't make me tell you again." His expression on his face had softened a little and his words were like a promise and a threat all rolled into one.

I looked away, trying to hide the grin on my face. "Yes, sir."

"Oh you are going to think 'yes, sir', Isabella." A wicked grin crossed his face, making me blush.

With a smile on my face, I grabbed the shirt he tossed on the bed and made my way into the bathroom to get ready. I hopped in the shower, savoring the feeling of the warm water on my still achy muscles.

Before I could get the conditioner out of my hair the bathroom door flew open. "What the hell are you doing in here, Isabella?"

"I'll be out in a minute," I called through the glass door of the shower.

"Hurry up. We need to go."

I rolled my eyes and reached for a towel. "Go where?"

"I'm taking you home."

Home? As in the house I shared with Spencer? His words were like a punch to the gut. I'd pissed him off and now he was taking me home. Earlier he'd been so freaked out about my safety and just like that his concern had faded. Could he really be that mad that I'd been talking to Spencer?

When I walked out of the bathroom Alec was sitting on the bed, his arms crossed, his foot tapping. "It's about damn time," he snapped.

"Seriously, Alec," I snapped back. "What's your

problem?"

Alec looked up, deep wrinkles lining his forehead. When he noticed me, he looked away but it was too late. I'd already seen the torment in his eyes. "He was here, baby. And he wasn't just here to hurt you either."

"What are you talking about?"

"The security team uncovered a stash of drugs hidden in the stairwell. It contained enough ketamine…" He pulled his hand through his hair. "He was here to kill you."

A shiver ran down my spine. "I'm sorry, Alec. I should've listened to you."

Quickly getting to his feet, Alec pulled me into his arms. "Yes, you should've, but we'll deal with that later. Right now we need to get you out of here."

Chapter Twenty Two

"Where are we going?" I asked when we got to the airport. Alec said he was taking me home but we'd driven to the here instead.

"Oh no, Isabella, I'm not about to trust you with that information right now."

I folded my arms. "I said I was sorry, Alec. I have a right to know where you're taking me."

"Are you pouting, Isabella?"

Shaking my head, I stared out the window. Mr. Control Freak was back in full force now, but was I really about to get on a plane with him without knowing where we were going? Without telling anyone I was even leaving?

Before I had a chance to fully consider what I was doing, Alec was escorting me aboard the plane. A woman with short, black hair was waiting to greet us. She looked surprisingly similar to Ms. Jet Black, but I couldn't be sure it was her. "Welcome aboard," she said in a kind, soft voice, and I knew at that moment that it wasn't her.

"Thank you, Tina. Did you bring the contracts I asked for?"

She handed him a manila envelope. "Yes, sir."

Alec helped me into a seat then sat down beside me. Emptying the contents of the envelope, he quickly flipped through the pages, initialing each one as he went. After signing in a few places, he handed both the packet and envelope back to Tina. "Dinner?"

"As you requested, sir."

"Excellent. That'll be all."

Tina nodded. "Thank you, sir. Have a safe flight." Alec nodded too then Tina moved toward the exit.

"Bye," I called out before she stepped through the exit.

Turning to face Alec, I asked, "Now will you tell me where we're going?"

"Buckle up, Isabella. We're about to take off."

"I want to know where you're taking me first."

He took my hand in his. "You can't always get what you want, Isabella." He was using my words against me yet again. Rolling my eyes, I complained, "*Ugh*! That's not fair! I have a right to know where you're taking me."

Leaning toward me, Alec kissed me on the cheek, a smile on his face. "Did you just roll your eyes at me?" He didn't wait for me to answer before continuing. "I guess I have to punish you now." I bit my lip, nervous and excited all at the same time.

• • • • •

"Would you like another glass of wine, Ms. James?" The flight attendant asked.

Alec shook his head. "No. Bring her a pillow and a blanket."

"Yes, Mr. Payne." She took our dinner plates and disappeared behind the partition.

"But I wanted another glass."

"Later, baby." He kissed me on the forehead. "You should rest now. You're going to need your strength later." My insides began to tingle as I considered what he could possibly have in store for me later.

The flight attendant quickly returned with the pillow and blanket Alec requested. Resigned to his decision, I reclined my seat and closed my eyes, too exhausted to argue with Alec anyway.

My mind began to drift. What am I going to do with you, Isabella? I'll make you think, 'yes sir'. Why do you defy me? What's mine is mine, Bella. You are mine. Pain, there was so much pain. That smell, alcohol, tobacco, and gardenias? I couldn't breathe.

"Wake up, Isabella." My eyes flew open, my heart racing. Alec. He was shaking me gently. "Fasten your seatbelt, baby. We're about to land."

I had no idea how long I'd been asleep or where we were landing but I was beyond thankful that it had only been a dream.

Alec led me off the plane and straight to the waiting car. The airport was unfamiliar and provided no clues to our whereabouts other than the humid air. We were close to the water. The question was where.

When everyone was securely buckled into their seats, Preston pulled the car away from the airport. My heart began to race as the realization set in. I'd put my life in the hands of this man, this man I'd known for such a short time. I let him fly me away to some unknown place. No one even knew where I was. What if he was the psycho that had been trying to hurt me? He said he wanted to punish me. And he was so mad at me when he found out I'd told Spencer where we were. My breathing quickened at that thought.

The warmth of Alec's hand rested on my leg and it made me jump. "Are you okay?"

Forcing a smile, I nodded, but on the inside I was anything but fine. Was I safe? Could I trust him? I'd trusted him so far, and he hadn't let me down, but what if he'd been lying to me this whole time? Spencer lied to me. What if getting me alone was Alec's plan all along? I stared out the window, my body trembling.

The car came to a stop in front of a large iron gate. Preston typed in a code, and slowly but surely, the gate began to open. I rolled down my window to take in the night air as we drove down the long palm tree lined driveway. The sky was dark, making it difficult to see much, but I heard the unmistakable sound of water breaking on the shore. And when I breathed in the salty air I was immediately reminded of home.

Preston pulled around the circle drive, coming to a stop in front of an enormous three story house. Alec helped me out of the car then led me up the stairs to the front door.

"Welcome home," Alec whispered in my ear.

"Home?" I asked, confusion clouding my mind. He'd told me he lived in New York, plus there was the condo in Tampa. Did he own a beach house too?

"You said you missed your beach. So I rented you this house for the summer."

My mouth dropped open. He'd rented me a house on the beach. When? Where? How? The questions spun through my mind, but before I could gather my thoughts enough to ask the front door opened, and a woman I'd never seen before stepped out.

"Good evening, Mr. Payne."

"Mrs. Peters," he replied warmly. "This is Ms. James."

She pulled me into a hug. "It's so nice to finally meet you, Ms. James."

I wondered how long she'd been waiting, and how she even knew who I was, but I didn't ask. I'd been too busy trying to wrap my head around what Alec had just said. *Home?* Not a hotel but a home, a gorgeous house on the beach. "Please, call me Izzy," I said, finally recovering my voice. A silent smile crossed her face.

Alec led me inside, Mrs. Peters close behind. We walked through a huge foyer and into an oversized great room. Three large sofas arranged in a U shape filled the space with a chair on each side of the stone fireplace. Floor-to-ceiling windows on the outside wall offered an amazing view of the moonlight as it danced on top of the waves. I paused to take in all in.

He tugged my arm. "This way, baby."

We came to a stop in the house's state of the art kitchen, all stainless steel and marble. Mrs. Peters wasn't far behind. "Would you like something to eat, sir?"

"No thanks, Kim. We had dinner on the plane."

"Is there anything you need before I turn in then?"

"No, I've got it from here."

"Very good, sir, enjoy your evening." Flashing a smile in my direction, Kim disappeared through a door at the back of the kitchen, leaving us in the room alone.

Alec pulled a bottle of wine from the refrigerator. I recognized the label immediately. It was the Riesling he ordered at Oishi the day we met. When he removed two wine glasses from one of the cabinets, I couldn't help but wonder if he'd been here before. He seemed too comfortable with the surroundings, seemingly knowing where everything was—the kitchen, the wine, the glasses.

Without saying a word, he led me back to the great

room and through a sliding glass door that opened to the pool deck. We walked down a paver covered path, past the pool, and toward the sound of the ocean, stopping just before we reached the water's edge.

"Sit," he commanded, the tone in his voice all business now. I hesitated but only for a quick second. The sand was soft beneath me. It felt like home.

Alec sat beside me and propped the two glasses up in the sand, filling each one with the wine he took out of the refrigerator. He handed me a glass. "Drink," he commanded.

There was no hesitation that time. I lifted the glass and took a long drink, doing my best to calm the anxiety that was building. I'd forgotten how good it tasted, maybe too good. I took another drink, adding just the right amount of courage. "Why did you bring me here?" I asked.

Alec sipped from his glass, his wicked grin slowly returning to his face. "Because you miss your home, because I want you to be happy." He took another sip. "It's the same reason I moved you to the Sandestin, to keep you safe, to protect you." He shook his head as if trying to clear some awful memory. "But you compromised your own safety by disobeying me."

Great. Not that again. I emptied my glass, the liquid courage taking immediate effect. "How many times do I have to apologize for that, Alec? I said I was sorry, and I meant it."

"Well, I said I was going to punish you, and I meant that."

"Oh, you're very funny, Alec Payne."

"That may be, Isabella, but I still intend to spank you."

What? my inner voice snapped. He couldn't be

serious. Could he? Gently, he took the glass out of my hand and set it upright in the sand then lunged toward me. Before I knew what was happening, I was lying in the sand, my arms pinned above my head, Alec's body pressed to mine.

He placed a soft kiss on my lips. "I'm really going to enjoy this, Isabella," he whispered, his breath brushing over my lips. My sex tingled, excitement and fear simultaneously rushing through me.

In one swift move Alec rolled over me and was sitting on the sand with me sprawled across his lap. "I'm going to spank you now, baby." His voice was gruff, not at all the playful Alec of just a few seconds ago. I tried to squirm free, but he held me firmly in place then swatted me on the butt.

"Ouch," I cried out, half laughing. He hit me again, then again. "That hurts," I protested, but truthfully it didn't hurt that bad. He swatted me again. That one really did hurt. "Alec! You're hurting me." Another swat.

"It's a spanking, Isabella. It's supposed to hurt." Again and again he continued. Eventually, I stopped squirming, using all my energy instead to absorb the sensation. Pain mixed with pleasure, an erotic sensation I'd never felt before. When he finally stopped, my breathing was so ragged I could barely move.

"The next time you roll your eyes at me, I'm going to spank you even harder, and not for your pleasure either, Isabella. Do you understand me?"

Still breathless, I couldn't speak. Alec swatted me again. "Answer me."

"Yes," I panted. Another swat. "Yes what?"

"Yes, sir."

He helped me off his lap onto the sand beside him. I winced when my butt hit the ground. "I hope you remember that feeling should you decide to roll your eyes at me again." I sat silently, stunned by what just happened but more so about how turned on I was.

Alec refilled my wine glass and handed it to me. "We're on Siesta Key," he said. "And I expect you to keep that to yourself this time."

We're in Florida. A smile crossed my face. At least I was close to home.

Alec wrapped his arm around my shoulder and tucked me into his side. "Thank you," I whispered.

"You needed a good spanking did you?"

My cheeks heated. "Well, probably, but that's not what I meant." I crossed my arms, feigning insult.

"I'll be happy to put you back over my knee if you want to pout, Isabella."

Quickly, I uncrossed my arms, my butt still stinging. "I meant thank you for this." I waved my hand toward the house, the beach, the ocean. "Thank you for protecting me, for caring about me, for everything you've done for me, for my kids, even for Spencer. Alec, I can't thank you enough."

"I told you, Isabella, anything for you."

We sat in silence for a long while, enjoying the sound of the water as it crashed against the shore and the warmth of Alec's embrace. "I liked spanking you," Alec said out of nowhere. "And I can't wait to do it again."

"So you're expecting me to defy you?"

"No, I expect you to do as I ask, to trust that I'm only looking out for your safety." He kissed me hard on the mouth. "That spanking wasn't because you disobeyed me. It was for rolling your eyes at me, but don't think I've forgotten about you telling Spencer where you were after I specifically told you not to."

The thought of me lying across Alec's lap while he spanked me again made me squirm. What did it say about me that it turned me on?

"It seems like you enjoyed that a little too much. I guess I'll have to do a better job next time."

"You didn't want me to enjoy it?"

"Yes. And no." That wicked grin returned. "I went easy on you this time, but you won't be so lucky the next time." Adrenaline coursed through my veins. I rolled my eyes in an exaggerated fashion, liquid courage hard at work. Alec kissed me hard on the mouth then pulled away. "Keep it up and I'll use a belt to make sure you understand how serious I can be." My whole body stiffened, thoughts of my nightmares, those images, came rushing in faster than the tide that was about to wash over us.

Alec helped me to my feet and we walked hand in hand toward the house. Preston was standing on the edge of the second floor deck. I kept my head down as we walked past him, silently praying he hadn't played witness to my earlier punishment. If he had seen, he kept it hidden well with a simple nod before he went back to staring out at the night sky.

We climbed the two flights of stairs to a third floor bedroom, another room with floor-to-ceiling windows that overlooked the Gulf. A king sized bed and a separate sitting area with a full size couch and chair filled the space. "This is your room, Isabella. All your things are here." *When did he have time to do all this?*

"I'm at the end of the hall if you need me."

Down the hall, my inner voice snapped. "You're not staying in here with me?"

"This is your home, baby. You should have your own space."

"But—"

Alec kissed me gently on the lips then pulled away. "You're not pouting are you?" Reflexively I shook my head quickly, and it brought a smile to his face. "You'll be safe here," he said before closing the door behind me, leaving me standing in this gigantic room alone, a satisfied smile on my face. I'd said I missed my home and he brought me here, to this amazing house with my own private beach.

I slipped off my shoes and found my way to the bathroom. The two person garden tub surrounded by more floor-to-ceiling windows immediately caught my attention. *What was it with Alec and these windows?* My mind quickly filled with thoughts of Alec, and the amazing sex we could have in that tub.

Just like Alec had said, all my things were here. My toiletries were arranged neatly on the Italian marble countertop, my clothes hung in the closet, the pictures from my office in fresh new frames. Alec obviously did this, but how? When? Those were the questions I planned to get answers to after I showered. Thanks to him, I was covered in sand.

The shower had three full size shower heads and a couple smaller ones too. It seemed a bit excessive, but it definitely made rinsing the sand off a lot easier. As I was drying off I caught a glimpse of my reflection in the mirror, the bright red handprint on my ass like a beacon in the darkness. Now I had a whole new reason to find Alec.

Pulling on my robe, I hurried down the hall toward what I hoped was Alec's room. I peeked inside the opened door only to find the room empty. "Alec," I called out as I stepped inside, but he was nowhere to be seen.

A breeze blew in from the balcony door that had been left open. As I moved closer I spotted him standing outside, the breeze blowing through his damp hair. His navy blue pajama pants hung low on his hips, his form fitting t-shirt showing off his muscular build which made me want him even more. "Alec," I called again.

He turned quickly toward my voice, a worried look resting on his face. "Isabella, is everything okay?"

"Everything's fine," I said as I stepped out onto the balcony, feeling somewhat silly for interrupting him and making him worry. "I was just gonna ask about my clothes."

"What about them?"

"Well, how'd they get here for starters?"

"I had them picked up."

"When? How?" I asked, thankful and freaked out all at the same time.

"This is your home now, baby. Your things should be here." He pulled me into his arms. "Now, is there something else you wanted to talk about or did you come all the way down here dressed like that just to ask me about your clothes?" His stern tone left me wondering if he was being playful or serious.

"You mean like the handprint that's on my ass?" There, that should shut him up.

"Maybe I need to leave a better impression." He pulled me close, his eyes are fixed on mine. "From the tone in your voice, I'd say my earlier attempt at punishment didn't get the job done." I still couldn't tell if he was serious, but it didn't matter. My insides were already tingling. Damn my body.

"Are you threatening me, Mr. Payne?"

"I don't make threats, Ms. James." He leaned down

and kissed me hard on the mouth, leaving me wanting more. He took me by the wrist and led me inside. "Get on the bed," he ordered, "on your hands and knees." I quickly did as he asked. I was still swollen from all the sex we had last night, but I couldn't resist. He'd made me feel things I'd never known were possible, and I couldn't wait to feel more.

He lifted my nightgown and slid my panties down. I felt his lips on my skin, kissing the handprint he'd left earlier. The sensation was so hot. I wanted this man more than I'd ever wanted anything. My sex tingled, making me squirm. "Be still," he warned. A swat landed on my butt much harder than the ones before, and I squirmed again. "Be still," he said again, another swat following. I tried hard not to move, but it really hurt. I wanted to cry out, but I didn't dare. I'd practically begged him to spank me again. I'd felt how turned on it made him, and I wanted him to be that turned on again. "I said be still, Isabella." He delivered another swat, each one harder than the last. I wasn't sure how much more of this I could take.

"Alec, please," I cried out, begging him to take me. Another swat. The pain was too much. I collapsed on the bed, unable to handle anymore.

Alec climbed on top of the bed, lying down beside me. "That should leave a better handprint," he whispered in my ear, his breathing ragged too. "Now, let's hope this spanking does the job because my hand is really sore." His admission surprised me and I turned my face toward him. An ear to ear smile rested on his face. He'd enjoyed that, maybe a little too much.

"We better get you in bed," Alec said.

No way was he getting rid of me that easy, not after what I just let him do. My body was on fire, and I wanted him. I *needed* him. Using my foot I shoved my panties the rest of the way off then pushed Alec onto his back and straddled him, my hands working their way under his t-shirt, my hips grinding against his growing erection. My actions were a silent plea.

Snaking one arm around my waist Alec rolled me off of him and onto the bed, the weight of his body holding me in place. "You aren't making this very easy for me, Isabella." Well, I had a news flash for him because he was definitely not making it easy for me. "I kept you up all night. You need to rest."

Sleep was the last thing I needed at that moment. I was wide awake, reenergized after that adrenaline spike, my libido screaming. "But I'm not tired," I whined.

Ignoring my impassioned plea, Alec leaned over and picked up a small remote off the bedside table. After pressing a few buttons, Roberta Flack's *Feel Like Makin' Love* surrounded us. What was he doing to me? I was already on fire, my libido still on high alert, our chemistry palpable.

He climbed off the bed, taking me with him. Placing both hands on my hips he moved me close to him, his erection pressing against my stomach, his firm body pressing up against me, leaving me breathless. I wanted him now more than ever. And he wanted me too.

With my hand in his he started moving to the music, dancing all around his massive room. He could really move, and in his arms I floated with a grace I'd never known before. When the song ended, Alec scooped me into his arms, that wicked grin on his face. My breathing quickened as anticipation built. "We're spending the day out tomorrow. Tonight you need to sleep."

NO! "Alec," I protested, flashing the best pouty face I could manage, but it had no effect. He carried me down the hall, not stopping until we reached my room. I was screaming on the inside and he was all calm and cool Alec once again. I wondered how he managed that, switching from hot to cold in a matter of seconds.

He laid me down on the bed. "Sleep now, Isabella," he said in a stern voice that did nothing to calm my libido. Alec leaned down and kissed me on the forehead, that wicked grin still on his face.

My cheeks heated. "Soon, baby," he said softly, and I knew then it really was a promise and a threat all rolled into one. "Sleep," he said again before sauntering toward the door.

"Goodnight," I called after him.

"Goodnight, Isabella."

My heart was stilling racing long after he left. It took several deep breaths to calm my screaming libido, that and the most luxurious bed I'd ever laid in. As I waited for sleep to find me, my mind started to wonder. It was hard to believe how much my life had changed in such a short time. I'd accepted that Spencer and I were through, but I was still struggling to accept all the other changes in my life, Alec being the hardest of them all. We'd known each other for such a short time, but I had become so attached. It was too soon. I hadn't even taken time for myself after my divorce was finalized.

The closer to sleep I drifted the more I thought of Alec. "Soon, Isabella," he'd said. Those two little words, filled with so much promise.

Chapter Twenty Three

The sun was just beginning to rise when I opened my eyes again. It was a restful night thanks to the amazingly comfortable bed I'd slept in. I was in awe of the view, courtesy of the floor-to-ceiling windows, the light glistening off the water as the sky slowly turned from dark to light. I slipped my robe on and stepped out on the balcony into the early morning air.

As I stared out at the horizon, a sudden urge to be on the beach washed over me, to watch the sun rise with the water washing over my feet, the soft sand beneath. I brushed my teeth then practically ran down the stairs, not even bothering to dress.

The house was quiet and dark, a little spooky even, as I moved quickly toward the glass door, stopping only long enough to slide it open. My feet hit the sand and I felt free, the freest I'd felt in months. I darted toward water's edge. I wanted to touch it, to feel it's warmth wash over me, to let it wash away all the drama that had been overwhelming my life.

A wave washed over my feet, drawing me further in to the water. Another wave crashed against my legs, the water splashing on my robe. Closing my eyes, I let the waves crash into me over and over again. The water ebbed and flowed, the sand burying my feet deeper and deeper with each new wave until I felt firmly rooted where I stood.

When I opened my eyes again the sky was a brilliant red-orange, the hues of blue becoming brighter now. I'd missed that, my home on the beach, watching the sun chase away the dark of night.

"Good morning, Isabella," Alec whispered in my ear, wrapping his arms around me. I had been so lost in the moment I hadn't heard him approach. Dangerous, considering the psycho was still after me, but Alec had made me feel safe.

"Good morning."

Alec kissed me on the cheek, and we stood in silence, watching as the sky changed to day.

When all evidence of night had gone, Alec turned me so I was facing him. "Go get ready. We'll be leaving soon." I was excited by the prospect of going out. When Preston's team uncovered that stash of drugs at the hotel, I was certain I'd never see people again.

Forty-five minutes later I came downstairs, feeling refreshed and ready to go, until the smell of food wafted out of the kitchen, making my stomach rumble.

Alec was sitting on a stool at the breakfast bar when I made it to the kitchen. He smiled when he saw me and patted the seat next to him, motioning for me to sit. "I hope you're hungry because Mrs. Peters has made quite the feast this morning."

"It smells delicious."

Mrs. Peters placed two plates on the counter in front of us: bacon, scrambled eggs and French toast. Just seeing the food made me realize how hungry I really was. And I couldn't wait to dig in.

· · · · ·

Alec and I spent the day in Naples, strolling up and down Third Street South, checking out the local shops, sipping wine in the gardens, and eventually stopping at Campiello's for dinner. I'd been pleasantly surprised when he requested a table on the patio so I could watch the people as they passed. "You said you needed people," he said. It wasn't quite what I'd meant, but the fact that he was trying to make me happy was enough. The day out was just what I needed to take my mind off all the stress I'd been under lately. The wine didn't hurt either.

I'd dozed off on the car ride back to Siesta Key, not waking up until Alec opened my door after we'd gotten back to the house. "Come with me," he said extending his hand, a full mouth smile on his face. "I have a surprise for you." The whole day had been a surprise, an absolutely perfect day. It was exactly what I'd needed, and I couldn't imagine anything more.

I followed Alec through the front door of the house then out the back. My mind flashed back to last night, sprawled across Alec's lap as he spanked me. Alec caught a glimpse of me rubbing my backside and started to laugh. "Don't worry, Isabella. I'm not going to punish you." He kissed me on the mouth. "Not now, anyway."

A soft glow illuminated the beach. Candles, lots and lots of candles, surrounded a blanket that was lying on the beach. I wondered when Alec had time to arrange it all, but I didn't ask. After all I *was* dealing with Alec Payne, the man who knew no boundaries, the man who could undoubtedly make anything happen.

"Amazing," I whispered.

"You like it?"

I threw my arms around his neck. "No, Alec. I love it. I love the surprise."

Alec's smile grew. "I love that about you, Isabella. I love that you can be happy with the simplest of things." He kissed me softly on the lips. "But this isn't the surprise." A wicked grin crossed his face.

Sex on the beach, my inner voice screamed.

Alec sat down on the blanket, taking me with him. He pulled a bottle of wine and two glasses out of the basket that was beside him. After filling then both, he handed one to me then returned the bottle to the basket. When he pulled his hand out again I noticed he was holding a small box that looked suspiciously like a ring box. My heart started to race. It couldn't be what I thought it was. It was too soon. I wasn't ready for that. My divorce was too recent. And we barely knew each other.

He handed me the box. "I saw this today and it reminded me of you."

"What is it?" I whispered.

"It's your surprise."

"Alec," I said nervously.

He kissed me on the lips. "Stop worrying, Isabella. It's just a gift, not a lifelong commitment." His smile disappeared and I immediately felt bad. After everything he'd done for me, the last thing I'd wanted to do was hurt his feelings.

"I'm sorry, Alec. I'm just not used to all of this."

"What? Receiving gifts?"

"Yes. Well, gifts for no reason, anyway."

"It's not for no reason, Isabella. I told you. It reminded me of you, beautiful, precious, and rare." His words made me blush. I took a long drink, gathering the nerve to see what was inside. My mouth dropped open when I saw it. The pareiba tourmaline and diamond ring we'd seen in the window at Cleopatra's Barge earlier.

"Oh, Alec," I gasped. "It's beautiful."

"And so are you." He took the ring out of the box and slid it on the ring finger of my right hand.

"When? How?" It was all I could manage.

"When I see something I want, baby, I always find a way." He pulled me closer and kissed me hard on the mouth, making my insides tingle, again.

I pushed him back on the blanket, spilling the contents of his glass everywhere. Straddling him, I made quick work of his shirt. He'd denied me last night but I wasn't giving him that option tonight. I trailed kisses down his chest to the waistband of his pants.

"What are you doing?"

I looked up at him. "It's a surprise," I said, with a grin of my own. Unbuttoning his pants, I slid his zipper down, reaching inside his boxer briefs to free his growing erection.

His voice was low and throaty. "Isabella," he moaned, anticipating my next move. I ran my tongue down the shaft of his penis, circling the sensitive tip as I caressed his balls. I took him all the way in. His head tilted back, and a moan escaped him.

"Isabella," he moaned again, louder this time. I picked up speed, gently sucking and pulling as I moved up and down. His cock twitched in my mouth, and I knew he was getting close. I ran my tongue under the sensitive ridge and his legs stiffened. His breathing was fast and shallow. "I'm going to come." I ignored him, taking him all the way in, his cock hitting the back of my throat. His hands fisted in my hair and he thrust his hips, the warm liquid of his arousal erupting.

Alec sat up and pushed me back until I was lying flat on the blanket. "That was so hot," he said, his voice breathy.

Before I knew what was happening my skirt was around my waist, my panties had been ripped off, and he was thrusting himself inside me. "Ahhh," I cried out, my insides still swollen from our recent escapades. Alec claimed my mouth with his tongue and pushed deeper inside me. I dug my nails into his skin, and he moved faster. My insides began to quicken and he stopped.

"Alec," I breathed, bucking my hips, begging him to keep moving.

"Not yet, baby. I'm not done with you yet." He kissed me softly, and it only made me want him more. When my body stilled, he started to move once again, slower this time, his eyes fixed on mine as he thrust himself inside me, in and out, in an exquisite rhythm.

Every time my climax threatened Alec would still. It was too much to handle. I arched my back, begging for the release I needed. "Please, Alec," I moaned. "I need to come."

With a renewed sense of purpose, he thrust deep inside me, the head of his cock passing over my pleasure zone before bottoming out. I arched my back further, my breathing becoming so shallow I was practically panting. The world around me began to fade away. "Oh, God, Alec."

"That's it, baby. Let me see you come." He picked up speed, plunging deeper inside me as my body unraveled around him, deeper and faster still until he found his own release.

Alec collapsed on the blanket next to me, a satisfied smile on his face. We stayed that way, lying beneath the stars, talking and laughing and talking some more until the last candle burned out.

I followed Alec upstairs but stopped at the door to my room. I needed a shower, plus, I was way too sore for sex again tonight. Alec's smile faded but he didn't object. "Good night, baby," he said, kissing me on the forehead.

"Goodnight. Thank you for today. And thank you for this beautiful ring."

"Anything for you, Isabella," he whispered then walked away.

It had been a long day and I was more than ready for bed, well, as soon as I could get the sand off me. I hopped in the shower and quickly washed up. I'd need to dry my hair before I got into bed, so I didn't waste any time.

Wrapping my hair in a towel to keep the water from dripping down my back, I slipped on a clean nightshirt and brushed my teeth before beginning my search for the hairdryer. Drawer after drawer I opened without success. My hair was too wet to sleep in, so I was left with two choices; let it air dry or see if Alec had a hairdryer.

Considering how tired I was, air drying wasn't an appealing option. That left me with only one option. I headed for Alec's room, tiptoeing down the hall in case he was already sleeping. His door was ajar, so I peeked inside, only to find him sitting on the sofa, flipping through the pages of some document.

"Hey," I said, feeling guilty about bothering him now. "Sorry to interrupt. It's just, well, I need to dry my hair and I can't seem to find a hairdryer."

"Second drawer on the right," Alec said motioning toward the bathroom. I walked quietly into the bathroom, finding it right where he said it'd be. I collected what I'd come for and walked as quietly as I could back through Alec's room.

"Did you find it?"

"I did. Thanks. I'll bring it back in the morning so I don't bother you again tonight."

"You're not bothering me, baby." Alec put the stack of papers down next to him and walked toward me. "Distracting me, yes, but definitely not bothering me."

Alec leaned down and kissed me softly on the lips. "Let me dry your hair," he said, taking the hairdryer out of my hands.

Without waiting for me to answer, he grabbed a hold of my wrist and pulled me back into the bathroom. "Sit," he said, pulling out the chair that was tucked neatly under the countertop. I wasn't too sure about letting him dry my hair but I sat anyway.

Alec removed the towel that was twisted on top of my head, allowing my hair to fall down my back. He turned on the blow dryer and began running his fingers through my hair, expertly massaging my scalp as he moved the dryer around my head. I closed my eyes, soaking in every second.

"Done," he announced after a while, switching off the dryer. I opened my eyes to find Alec grinning ear to ear, seemingly proud of the work he'd done, and it made me smile too.

"Thanks. You're a pro."

Alec dropped his head, all evidence of his good mood gone. "My mom used to let me dry her hair." The pain in his words tugged at my heart. It was clear how much his mother had meant to him.

"Sleep with me tonight," Alec said, suddenly.

There was no way I could deny him after hearing that confession, no matter how tired I was. I turned so I was facing him. "Sleep?"

"Your appetite for sex is insatiable, Isabella," Alec said, pulling me into his arms.

"No, Alec, I'm serious. I'm exhausted, and way too sore."

He kissed me on the top of the head. "Sleep it is then."

Alec helped me into bed then slid in next to me. Wrapped securely in his arms, I closed my eyes, ready for sleep to find me.

Chapter Twenty Four

We'd been at the beach house for almost a week and I hadn't even explored the house yet. Alec took a few days off work and we'd spent most of our time getting to know each other better. After the third day I was convinced he knew my body better than I did. He could bring me to the edge of ecstasy with a single touch.

Preston and Frank had made themselves scarce the past few days, a fact I'd been pretty happy about. Having a security team constantly watching over me was one thing I didn't think I could ever get used to.

I'd decided to go for a run while Alec made a few phone calls, but the air was so hot and thick I ended up cutting it short. Alec was still on the phone when I got back, and considering all the energy I still had left to burn, I hopped in the pool to finish my workout.

The water was cool to my overly heated skin, so I eased myself into the pool. When I reached the last step, I dove under the surface, moving my arms above my head then pulling down, propelling myself forward, not surfacing until I reached the other end. After a few laps I switched to the backstroke, closing my eyes to block out the sun as I slowly kicked my way to the other end of the pool.

The sky flashed white, followed by the loud crash of thunder in the distance less than a minute later. Startled, I reached for the bottom of the pool, but it wasn't there and I slipped under the surface of the water. When I came up for air I was coughing, spitting up the mouthful of water I'd just swallowed. My eyes were wide open and I realized I was still in the middle of the pool, so I swam to the side to catch my breath.

A shadow moved over the edge of the pool and I looked up to see what it was. "Can you hear the storm that's rolling in, Isabella?" Alec reached down to help me out. I accepted his hand, letting him pull me out of the pool, quickly wrapping a towel around me.

"Thanks," I said, relieved I'd finally stopped coughing. When I looked up at Alec I noticed the disapproving frown that rested on his face. "That storm came out of nowhere," I said quickly, hoping to calm him down.

Alec's expression didn't change. "That was lightening, Isabella."

"I got out as soon as I saw it."

"Didn't you notice the storm clouds before you got in?"

"No, I didn't," I snapped. I had no intention of being scolded like a child, especially not by Mr. Control Freak. I crossed my arms, my look mirroring his.

Alec pulled me close to his, our bodies connecting. "Pouting will only make it worse." His tone made me blush. Why did this man have such an effect on me? He kissed me. A hard, passionate kiss and when he pulled away I was breathless.

"Let's get you out of these wet clothes." He grabbed my hand and pulled me inside, his words so full of promise I could hardly wait. Eagerly, I followed him. Alec stopped at the base of the stairs and swatted me on the butt making me squeal in delight.

"Go change, Isabella. I have work to do."

"Aren't you coming up with me?" I dropped my head, my lower lip protruding in a full blown pout this time.

Alec leaned down and bit my lip gently. "I know what you're doing, baby, and it's not going to work this time. Now go."

"Fine." I turned and stomped up the stairs, expecting Alec to follow me, only he hadn't.

After changing into some dry clothes, I decided to do a little work myself. As long as the storm was on top of us I'd be stuck inside anyway, and Alec clearly wasn't in the mood to play.

I'd promised Chris I'd monitor his account to make sure things were running smoothly, plus, I wanted to check the status of the Ultimate account.

As I waited for my laptop to boot I stared out the window, becoming momentarily lost in the beauty of the storm. The waves had swelled to twice their normal size and were crashing hard against the shore. The rain fell in thick sheets, the wind whipped over the water, the force and power of Mother Nature on full display. Getting lost in the beauty of God's creation was such an easy thing to do. Light flashed, immediately followed by the loud crack of thunder. The storm was right on top of us now. I watched intently as the rain moved closer and closer until it was impossible to see out through the windows.

Eager now for the distraction of work, I double clicked the icon for my email program and waited impatiently as it launched, silently hoping Tim hadn't sent me another meeting request. He'd been pressing me to come to the office for a face-to-face status update on the Payne Enterprises account, but Alec wouldn't hear of it. "That psycho found you twice, Isabella. I'm not taking any chances of you going to your office," he'd said. In all honesty there wasn't much to report anyway, so I hadn't pushed.

Shit. What I was reading was worse than I'd feared. Tim wasn't just asking for a meeting, he was demanding it, and he wasn't taking no for an answer. "Be at the office Monday at nine o'clock for a mandatory meeting," his email read. "Skipping this one isn't an option if you want to keep your job, Izzy." Double Shit! Now what was I supposed to do? Alec would freak if I told him about this email and if I wasn't at the meeting Tim would freak. Pleasing them both would be impossible.

Your career is on the line here, Izzy, my inner voice snapped. And she was right, it was *my* career. And just like that I'd made up my mind. I was going to that meeting. Alec might not like my decision, but he'd have no choice but to accept it. I typed out a quick email to let Tim know I'd be there before I lost my nerve.

I read through the rest of my emails, mostly status updates from department heads who'd forgotten to take me off their distribution list but there was one message that had me worried, a message from Chris flagged as urgent.

Immediately, I opened the email. The night shift supervisor at the Sandestin had been busted renting rooms to underage teens and allowing them to order alcohol from the bar. "I really need your help with this one, Izzy," he'd written. "Our reputation and our liquor license are on the line this time. You have to help." I fired an email to Jonathan asking him to gather all the evidence in the case. I'd need to know exactly what we were dealing with before I could even think about helping. I sent Chris a quick message too so he'd know I was investigating the problem.

There was an email from Valerie that was a couple days old wanting to know if I was still at the Sandestin. Alec would be beyond pissed if he saw that message. He'd be angry I told her where I was staying but knowing I hadn't told him about it would have him seeing red. I shook my head to settle the rattled thoughts. *He can't get mad at you for not remembering,* my inner voice chimed in. And she was right. After everything I'd been through he should just be happy I remembered the call to Spencer.

"I haven't forgotten about you telling Spencer," he'd said that night on the beach after he'd taken me over his knee. A shiver ran down my spine as I considered how he'd react to this bit of information.

Just as I was ready to delete the message I heard him, his harsh tone startling me. "What's the meaning of this, Isabella?" I jumped to my feet, knocking my laptop onto the floor in the process. Alec was waving a piece of paper in the air, an intense look in his eyes.

I swallowed hard. "The meaning of what?"

"Don't play dumb with me."

Had he found out about my call to Val? Surely he couldn't be talking about my decision to go to the office, could he? "I'm not sure what you're talking about, Alec."

"This email from Tim, Isabella, what do you mean telling him you'll be at the office on Monday?"

Great. Tim had emailed Alec before I could tell him myself, and he was even madder than I'd expected. "I have to go. Tim is really mad that I've been ditching him so I need to be there."

"I don't give a damn how mad Tim is. It isn't safe,

and you aren't going."

"Alec, please. Try to understand. The meeting is mandatory. I don't have a choice if I want to keep my job."

"It isn't safe!" he shouted, pulling both hands through his hair. "You're not going. End of story."

End of story? *Really?* Was I really going to give him the final say in my life? "Look, I appreciate everything you've done for me but this is my career. I *have* to go. I AM going." The more I talked about it the angrier I got. "And how the hell do you even know about my meeting?"

"The police recovered prints from a flower vase in your office," he said, completely ignoring my last question. "He's been there, baby. Your office isn't safe."

"You knew he'd been there and you didn't tell me?"

"I was certain Spencer was behind the attacks. I wanted proof before I worried you any more than you already were."

"If Spencer did this—"

"It wasn't him, Isabella. Spencer couldn't have done it. According to the GPS on both his phone and car he hasn't been within ten miles of your office in months. Plus, he was in Chicago the night you were taken to the hospital. Flight records proved that."

"Chicago," I whispered, suddenly remembering the emergency Spencer had to deal with there not long after those pictures arrived. I couldn't help but wonder if *she* lived there.

"Isabella, what is it? You look like you've seen a ghost." I didn't want to tell him about the pictures. I still wasn't ready for that. He pulled me close and kissed me on the top of the head. "What are you keeping from me, baby?"

I wrapped my arms around his waist, squeezing him tight. "I can't live like this forever, Alec. I feel trapped. I need to work. I have to work."

"It won't be forever. Marcus has his best men working on this. We'll figure it out." He pulled me back so he was looking into my eyes. "If working is really that important to you, we'll work that out too."

I sat down on the couch, relieved he finally saw how important my job was to me. Alec reached down and picked my laptop up off the floor, the screen illuminating as he set it down on the coffee table. Shit. My email program was still open with Val's email cued up just waiting for me to hit delete. I took a deep breath, bracing myself for whatever would come next.

He turned toward me, his jaw clenched, his lips pressed in a thin, hard line. "What the hell is this?" he said through gritted teeth. "Please, tell me how you defied me, how you put yourself in danger, and then failed to tell me about it!"

"Alec, I'm sorry. You were so mad at me when I told you about Spencer that I wasn't thinking straight. I just forgot."

"You forgot? That's the best explanation you have. You did exactly what I told you not to do, then you failed to tell me about it, and that's all you have to say."

"Yes, Alec, I forgot."

"Didn't this email spark your memory?" Anger burned hot in his eyes, and nothing I said was going to cool that fire. "Answer me, Isabella!"

"Geez, yes already," I snapped. "Yes, I told her I was at the Sandestin. Yes, I forgot to tell you she called. And yes, when I remembered I'd told her I decided not to tell you because I was afraid you'd freak out, which is exactly what you're doing!"

"Let me get this straight. First you defied me and then you intentionally hid it from me. All because you were afraid of how'd I react?"

"Yes."

Alec pulled me off the couch, into his arms. "Everybody forgets, baby. That's what reminding is for." Without saying another word Alec wrapped his arms around my legs and hoisted me over his shoulder. Although I wasn't sure why, there something about being slung over his shoulder that had me turned on.

He carried me that way down the two flights of stairs and into the study, closing the door behind him. When he finally returned my feet to the ground, he grabbed my wrist and pulled me further into the room, deliberately moving, without hesitation, not stopping until we were standing in front of the large wooden desk.

In one swift motion, everything that had been resting on top of the desk was scattered on the floor. Alec stretched my arms out in front of me, placing my hands over the edge of the desk, forcing me to lean over. "I'm going to spank you now, Isabella. Don't. Let. Go," he said in a clipped tone.

My mind was spinning. Was I really about to let him punish me like this, or at all? That night on the beach he'd be playful, and even though he'd spanked me it didn't feel at all like punishment.

Alec lifted my sundress and slid my panties down to the floor. If I was planning on objecting I was running out of time. But I didn't object, instead I braced myself for what I knew was coming next. Pain shot through me as he delivered three hard blows in rapid succession across my naked butt.

Damn. That really hurt. Two more swats followed. "Ow, Alec, you're hurting me."

"It's a spanking, Isabella, I mean for it to hurt."
Three more swats followed and when he finally stopped
I stood up, glad it was over, but very much turned on.

"Oh, Isabella," Alec said, trailing his long finger
down my cheek. He grabbed my chin and kissed me
hard. "I told you not to let go." In the blink of an eye I
was stretched out across the desk again. "Don't let go
until I tell you to. Do you understand?"

"Yes, sir," I panted.

He pushed my dress up to my back and trailed his
finger over the small of my back. "I'm going to spank
you again, Isabella. And if you're a good girl I'll take you
upstairs and make love to you after. But if you defy me
again I'm going to fuck you right here and it won't be
for your pleasure." His voice was gruff, his breathing
ragged, and incredibly hot.

Without another word I felt the familiar sting. Shit
that hurt. I wanted to rub my skin but I didn't dare let
go. The sound of sex without pleasure wasn't exactly
appealing. I prayed I'd be able to tolerate his
punishment. There was a fine line between pleasure and
pain sometimes and I was definitely walking that line.
Whack, whack, whack, the swats kept coming. It was as if
he was willing me to let go so he could punish me more.
But I didn't. I gripped the edge of the desk tighter, trying
to absorb the pain.

The blows finally stopped, but I didn't dare let go. I
was stretched across his desk, my bare ass in the air,
waiting, wanting. "Good girl, Isabella. You can let go
now." I let go and slowly stood up, relieved I'd been able
to take what he'd needed to give me. Alec spun me
around and scooped me into his arms. "I'm going to
take you upstairs and make love to you now, baby." I
buried my face in his chest to hide the tears in my eyes. I

wanted him to make love to me. I *needed* him to after the punishment I'd just endured without a single objection.

Chapter Twenty Five

I must've dozed off because when I opened my eyes Alec was nowhere to be seen. Scooting toward the edge of the bed I was immediately reminded of my earlier punishment. It hadn't hurt that bad during, but now even the feel of the Egyptian cotton beneath my body was causing discomfort.

My reflection in the bathroom mirror stopped me dead in my tracks. My ass was bright red and Alec's hand print was clearly visible. *You are not the Izzy James you used to be*, my inner voice snapped. I frowned at the thought, suddenly unsure of who I was anymore and what I'd let Alec do to me.

I went back to my room to soak in the tub, hoping the cool water would help soothe the stinging on my butt, enough for me to sit down comfortably so I could work, at least. Now that I'd convinced Alec I had to go to this meeting, I figured I should probably get some work done.

Tim wanted an update on what I'd been doing for Payne Enterprises, but truthfully there wasn't much to report. Not enough to get me out of hot water, that was for sure. Solving the Sandestin issue would be a good distraction for the lack of work I'd done for Payne Enterprises, so I really needed to get on top of that now.

After dressing, I carefully sat down on the couch to get started, the stinging more of an irritation at that point, a distraction of sorts. Maybe that had been Alec's intention all along, to distract me from work. No way was I going to let him win that battle.

Jonathan had already emailed me the information I'd asked for, so I went right to work reviewing it. As hard as I tried to focus on what I was supposed to be doing, my mind kept drifting back to Alec: his passion, his punishment, the amazing sex that followed. It was impossible to concentrate. *Damn you Alec Payne.* He was winning after all.

That familiar ping announcing a new email chimed. Since I wasn't getting very far with the witness statements, I decided a quick check wouldn't hurt. *Wrong.* My mouth hit the floor when I read Tim's message. "You're excused from all staff meetings until further notice." The blood slowly drained from my face as I read it a second time.

"Alec!" I screamed at the top of my lungs. Who in the hell did he think he was screwing with my career? Getting me excused from going to the office wasn't what I'd expected last night when he'd said we'd work something out. I had to put a stop to his interference— immediately. Grabbing my phone, I stormed downstairs, determined to end this ridiculousness once and for all.

After opening the email on my phone, I stormed into Alec's study, not bothering to knock. It was my turn to be pissed. "Did you do this?" I shouted, holding my phone close enough for him to see Tim's message.

He glanced at the phone in my hand then back to me. "No," he said coolly.

I rolled my eyes, knowing full well only Alec could get Tim to change his mind about me coming into the office. He'd been on my case about it for over a week, since before Alec brought me to this fortress on the beach. "So you didn't have Dimarco excuse me from all staff meetings until further notice? Whatever the hell that means!"

"That's not what I said, Isabella. You asked if I did this and the answer is no. You did this. By insisting on going to the office even though I told you it wasn't safe."

"Alec, that's not fair. This is my career and I've worked hard to build it."

"You're right, Isabella, it's not fair. Now, I'm sorry about your career but it's your life I'm working hard to protect. And it certainly isn't fair that you refuse to accept that!" He pounded his fist on his desk; his patience with our conversation clearly running thin.

"Alec, you can't keep me here forever. I need to get out, to see people. I need to work."

"How many times do I have to tell you, Isabella? This is only temporary. It's just until we find the psycho who's trying to hurt you." He wasn't about to budge, but neither was I.

"Fine, cancel my damn meetings if you want, but like it or not I'm going to Pensacola this week. End of story!"

Jumping to his feet, Alec quickly rounded the desk, his jaw clenched, his eyes narrowed. I backed away, but he was moving too fast. Grabbing hold of my arms, he pinned me to the wall, his eyes burning a hole right through me. "That's enough, Isabella!" He pressed his forehead against mine. "I've given you some latitude here because I know how upset you are, but no more.

I've had enough."

"My words exactly!" I pulled out of his grip and tried to push him away, but my efforts were fruitless. He didn't budge.

"You. Are. Pushing. Your. Luck. Isabella."

"I'm not in the mood to play, Alec."

"Good, because I'm not playing. Now let it go before I take you over that desk. And trust me, you won't like it." He wouldn't punish me if I said no, would he? I opened my mouth to speak, but realizing I didn't know the answer to that question I closed it again. Alec kissed the tip of my nose. "Now, stop acting like a child before I put you over my knee." He kissed me again, on the lips this time. The tension in my body melted with his kiss, and I knew I couldn't fight him. Damn it. Why did I give in to him so easily?

"Let's go out," Alec said when he finally broke our kiss. "I could use a change of scenery too." His confession reminded me of his love for the city, of how much he'd given up to be here with me, to keep me safe, and at that moment I resolved to try harder to remember that.

Alec pressed the button on his Bluetooth earpiece. "We're going out," he said simply before pressing the button a second time. Turning his attention back to me he said, "Let's shower."

I squealed in protest as he hoisted me over his shoulder once again, but that didn't slow him down. He swatted me on the butt. "I should spank you again for thinking you can yell at me like that," he said as he carried me up the stairs. I laughed nervously. What happened after he'd punished me was by far one of the best sexual experiences I'd ever had, but I wasn't so sure I could handle that again, not so soon anyway.

My legs were unsteady when Alec finally set me down, the blood rushing from my head back to my body, and I had to hold on to his arm to keep my balance. As I gripped his biceps Alec untied the string holding up my pants, and they fell to the floor. My shirt and bra soon followed, leaving me in nothing but my panties, my wet panties, soaked from my arousal.

Alec ran a finger down my cheek. "You are so beautiful, Isabella," he said, his eyes fixed on mine.

My cheeks heated and I looked away to hide the evidence of my embarrassment.

"Look at me," he said, gently lifting my chin until my eyes met his once more. "You are beautiful, Isabella, and the fact that you don't know it makes you even more beautiful." His lips brushed gently against mine, a sweet, sensual kiss that would've brought me to my knees had I not been holding on to him.

Alec climbed into the shower, and I immediately followed. Moving under one of the many shower heads, I leaned my head back to wet my hair. I squeezed a good amount of shampoo into my palm, rubbing my hands together before adding it to my hair, letting the excess suds slide down my breasts.

"I know what you're doing, Isabella."

"What?" I asked, feigning innocence as I spread the shampoo over my breasts.

"Don't play innocent with me. You know exactly what you're doing." Alec moved closer and kissed my exposed neck.

He squeezed body wash into the palm of his hand. "Turn around," he ordered. I did as he asked, letting him run his soapy hands over my back, my neck, and my arms, the nerve endings standing at attention on each spot the touched, the sensation causing me to squirm. "I like making you squirm," Alec whispered into my ear.

Goosebumps covered my body despite the warmth of the shower. Even this had me turned on. What was he doing to me? Alec squeezed more body wash into his hands and began gently rubbing them over my tender butt and down my legs, between my thighs. When his hand brushed against my sex I let out the breath I hadn't realized I was holding. "Turn around," he said again.

He ran his soapy hands expertly over my body until I couldn't stand it any longer. "Alec, please," I begged. "Take me, here, now."

"No, It's my turn," he said, handing me the bottle of body wash.

My bottom lip protruded in protest. My libido was on fire. I wanted him. I needed him, inside me, making my body unravel around him like only he could.

"Didn't you get enough of me earlier?" he asked.

"No."

Alec kissed me on the lips. "What am I going to do with you, Isabella?"

"I can think of a few things you could do," I mumbled as I worked the body wash into a creamy lather. He didn't respond, and not because he hadn't heard me either. If it was convincing he needed, I could fix that.

Starting with his chest, I rubbed my hands over his body, working my way to his arms, down his sides, to his sex. I pulled his rock hard erection into my hands, gently caressing, my thumb spreading the drop of pre come over the head of his penis, feeling pride that he was just as turned on as I was.

Alec pulled back, freeing himself from my grip. "Finish," he ordered.

I added more body wash to my hands and moved on

to his legs then his feet. When he turned around I ran my hands over his back, his tanned, muscular back and then down his naked body. I was quickly losing my resistance. I had to have him. Impulsively, I sunk my teeth into his bare butt cheek.

"Shit, Isabella." He turned around quickly and pulled me to my feet by my wrists. "Did you just bite me?"

A smile crossed my face. "Yes," I said proudly.

Without saying a word Alec pushed me against the shower wall, pinning my wrists above my head, his mouth finding mine. He released my mouth and playfully bit my chin, my neck, and my breasts. One hand greedily touching me, the other hand kept my arms pinned. His hand was on my sex, his finger circling my clit. The pounding of my heart was the only sound I could hear. And when he slid his finger inside me, my body was begging him to take me.

Alec let go of my wrists. "Turn around, and put your hands against the wall," he ordered, his raspy voice against my ear. Quickly, I did as he said. His hands were my hips, pulling me toward him, spreading my legs apart with his knee. "This is going to be hard and fast, Isabella. Keep your hands on the wall." And just like that he was inside me, slow at first but quickly picking up speed, every thrust plunging deeper and deeper inside me.

"Alec," I cried out, the sensation overwhelming me, my insides still sore and swollen from earlier this morning. My release was rapidly building.

"Come for me, Isabella," he said, with ragged breath.

That's all it took, that one simple command, my body responding in a way I never knew it could. "Yes. Yes. Yes!" I screamed as my inner walls clenched around him, my orgasm washing over me like the tide.

Faster and faster Alec moved until he found his own release. We stood like that for a while. I didn't want to move. I loved the feel of him inside me. But when he pulled out, I finally stood and turned toward him.

Alec pulled me into his arms. "What are you doing to me, Isabella?"

I laid my head on his chest, wondering the same thing.

• • • • •

We took a drive along Midnight Pass with the top down on my car. I'd been so excited when I found out we were going alone. I'd been even more excited when Alec handed me the keys. It felt weird getting behind the wheel after over a month of being driven everywhere I needed to go, but I quickly settled into this recently rediscovered freedom. It was still hard for me to believe that I'd given up so much control to the man sitting next to me. I glanced over at him, his hands pressed against the dash, a sight that made me smile. Alec definitely wasn't used to giving up control.

"Slow down, you're going to kill us both," Alec said when I mashed down on the accelerator.

"Oh, is Mr. Control Freak afraid?" I teased.

"My job is to keep you saaafee—"

I whipped into the other lane to pass a car.

"Don't make me regret my decision to let you drive," Alec snapped.

"Keep your pants on, Alec. I know what I'm doing."

"Keep this up, Isabella, and that's exactly what I'll do."

"Are you threatening me?"

"Remember, baby, I don't make threats. Now slow

down or you can forget about sex for a while!" Yeah, he definitely wasn't used to giving *me* control.

We stopped at Captain Curt's Oyster Bar for lunch. Alec ordered me a Crowne Royal on the rocks when I went to the bathroom. I should've known right then that was his way of getting me out of the driver's seat. The drink went down easily with the oysters and I didn't catch on to his plan until I was halfway through the second one.

"You better let me drive, baby," Alec said, reaching over to take the keys off the table.

I rolled my eyes. "Damn it, Alec. You did that on purpose."

"What do you mean?" he asked, throwing my words back at me now. That man had a memory like a dolphin. I couldn't argue with him though. Between the two drinks and the hormonal spike, courtesy of the oysters, I was in no position to drive. Not that I was complaining though. The time alone with Alec was exactly what I'd needed.

Chapter Twenty Six

There was an empty space beside me when I woke up the next morning. I looked around, searching for Alec, but he wasn't there. He was probably already in his office working, something I should be doing considering Alec had just handed over a project for me to work on. I climbed out of bed and headed back to my room to clean up. I'd spent all but that first night sleeping in Alec's room, but I hadn't bothered to move my clothes. It was a small detail that just seemed so unnecessary.

After I'd showered, I headed downstairs for some coffee. Even though Alec had gotten me excused from the staff meeting tomorrow that didn't change the fact that I wanted to be there. Deep down I knew Tim wanted me to be there too and the last thing I planned to do was jeopardize my career. Sure, Tim drove me crazy most days but that didn't change the fact that he was my boss, the man I reported to, the man who could very easily take away the last part of my old life. The life I was barely clinging to now. If only I could make Alec see how important my job was to me.

I'd already told Alec I was going, insisted even, but still I knew I'd have a fight on my hands this morning.

My last hope of avoiding a major meltdown was to convince him of how safe I'd be. I was prepared to go as far as agreeing to take a whole team of security if necessary, anything to get him to make this one concession.

Alec was on the phone in his study barking orders to someone. I stood quietly outside the door, waiting for the yelling to stop, saying a silent prayer he'd be able to understand how much the trip meant to me.

When the room went quiet I took a deep breath to steady my nerves then opened the door. "Are you busy?"

He looked up from his desk, a smile on his face. "I'm never too busy for you, baby."

I moved closer to him. "What time are we leaving for Pensacola?"

His smile quickly faded and he looked away, turning his attention back to his computer screen. "We're not discussing this again, Isabella. I've already told you, your office isn't safe."

"Alec, I have to be there. I haven't been to the office in weeks. My team needs me. Plus, I really want to go."

"What part of no don't you understand, Isabella?"

He was being completely unreasonable, but I wasn't about to let this go without a fight. Exhaling loudly, I said, "The part where you get to decide. You seem to be forgetting that I'm an adult."

Alec pounded his fist on the desk, standing abruptly. "Enough!" he shouted.

My adrenaline spiked, surprised by his outburst. "My sentiment exactly, Alec. I'm done arguing with you about this. I'm going to this meeting, and there's nothing you can do about it!" That wasn't exactly how I'd imagined the conversation going, but it didn't change the fact that

I wasn't backing down. Not this time.

"I'm tired of reminding you that there's some psycho out there who's trying to hurt you, Isabella. You are NOT going. And that's final!"

He moved quickly around the desk, his hands fisted at his side, his mouth pressed in a thin hard line. I stepped back, but he kept moving. Forward. Back. Forward. Back. I wasn't getting sucked in this time. I was going to Pensacola and there was nothing he could say to change my mind. *Thud*. I hit the wall. Shit. I was out of room.

Alec placed his hands, one on each side of my head, pressing his forehead against mine. Double shit. His breathing was slow, intentionally slow as if trying to contain his mounting emotion. And when he spoke his voice was low and gruff. "Even if I have to tie you up and lock you in your room you are not going. Are we clear on that?"

No. We were absolutely not clear on that. He'd threatened to tie me up, to lock me away, trapped in this house where no one knew where I was. For the first time since meeting him I felt unsafe. "Send a whole team of security if you want to, but I'm going. You can't keep me here either, Alec. Hell, for all I know YOU are the psycho who's been after me!"

He pulled away from the wall, exasperated with my outburst, or maybe my lack of concern over my own safety, and maybe I should have been more worried, but at that moment all I was worried about was my career.

Knowing it could be my opportunity to escape before he made good on his promise to tie me up and lock me in my room, I rushed out of the room and ran as fast as I could up the stairs. I pulled my suitcase from its resting place on one of the many shelves in the giant walk-in closet and filled it with lightning speed, grabbing the bare minimum I'd need to survive until I figured out what my next move was.

Now that the words were out of my mouth I couldn't help but wonder if they could be true. Was Alec trying to hurt me? That seemed unlikely, given the great lengths he'd gone to ensure my safety, but maybe that was all part of some devious plan. Had he staged the break-ins and the attack so he could hide me away? I mean, Frank had been there the night I ended up in the hospital. He'd also been right next door when the psycho broke into my hotel room. I grabbed my laptop bag and headed downstairs, even more determined to leave this time. Before I could change my mind, I tossed my suitcase in my car and sped out of the garage.

By the time I merged onto I-75 the reality of what just happened started to set in. My decision to leave would prove to be either the smartest decision I'd ever made, or the dumbest. Only time would tell.

Turning the music on, I settled in behind the wheel for the seven hour drive that was ahead of me.

• • • • •

The long drive gave me time to consider what I'd said to Alec. There was no way he could be my attacker. My nightmares started before we met. Plus, he was in New York during the attacks. It couldn't possibly be him. The pained look on his face when I said he could be the psycho who was after me would be permanently etched in my mind. He'd been nothing but good to me, and I crushed him. He rented a house on the beach for me, to protect me. I was the one to blame. And to top it off I left without even saying goodbye. Tears began to fall. "What have you done, Izzy?" I cried.

Just outside of Tampa, my phone started to ring. *Alec.* I wanted to answer his call so he wouldn't worry, to tell him I was sorry, but I couldn't. He'd convince me to turn around, and I couldn't go back there. He may not have been trying to hurt me but I knew he'd never understand how important my career was to me. I'd already lost my family and my home. I couldn't bear to lose my job too. Deciding to ignore the call, I cranked up the music to drown out the ringing.

When I got to Tallahassee, I pulled over to refuel both the car and my body. I'd stormed out before breakfast, a fact my stomach was refusing to let me forget. I glanced at my phone before climbing out of the car. Shit. Alec had called three times, plus he'd texted me.

Where R U? Call me!

I sent a quick text so he'd know I was safe. **On my way to Pensacola.**

Alec texted back almost immediately, but I didn't read it. I was emotionally exhausted and still had almost three hours left to drive. What I needed to do was concentrate on the road and push all thoughts of Alec out of my mind. And that's exactly what I tried to do.

The closer to Ft. Walton Beach I got the farther away from home I felt. I'd lived in North Florida for over twenty years, yet it no longer felt like home. Drew was away at college, Anna was traveling with her friends, and my heart was in Siesta Key. Not much tied me to Ft. Walton Beach anymore. There were only memories left now, memories that had been tainted thanks to those horrible pictures.

Every passing second brought me that much closer to the meltdown that threatened. No matter how hard I tried, I couldn't stop thinking about Alec. I needed a distraction. I needed my best friend. Val and I hadn't talked in a few weeks. She'd called several times, even sent a couple emails, but I hadn't called her back. I'd been afraid to call her for fear I'd end up telling her where I was staying. After the way Alec reacted the last time I told anyone my whereabouts I wasn't about to risk it. It didn't really matter anymore though. I was on my way back to Pensacola, not stashed away in Alec's secret hideaway. Besides, I was desperate for a distraction, anything to keep my mind off of Alec and especially that look on his face.

By the time Val and I hung up, I was actually looking forward to being in Pensacola. She decided to fly in on Wednesday so we could finally have that girls' weekend we'd been trying to schedule for months. It'd been so long since we hung out, and I missed her now more than I ever had. I'd finally be able to tell her about Spencer and the attacks and Alec. The call that was supposed to keep my mind off Alec had failed, though, because when it was all said and done all I could think about was what he'd say about me spending the weekend alone on the beach, adding light to the grim reality of what I'd done.

• • • • •

My room at the Crowne Plaza Hotel was considerably smaller than the suite I'd stayed in at the Wyndham, but it was much closer to my office, and it didn't remind me of Alec. It also helped that they had an available room on short notice.

After kicking off my shoes I plopped down on the bed, completely spent from today's events. I sent a quick email to Chris scheduling a meeting for tomorrow.

There was a lot for us to talk about in light of the recent scandal at his hotel, and I figured I might as well make the best of my time here, especially considering what I'd given up to be here.

The unanswered text Alec sent earlier beckoned. I took a deep breath and opened it. **Are you coming back?** it read. He wasn't asking when. He was asking if. It wasn't an invitation either. It was merely a question. My heart sank as I considered what he was asking. Was I going back? He was so controlling but kind and giving too. Did he even want me to come back after what I'd said? My head was spinning with confusion.

I typed out a quick reply. **I made it. And IDK.** I hit send, shutting my phone down immediately after, before Alec had a chance to respond. I needed time to think without the pressure Mr. Control Freak would add.

No matter how tired I was I'd come to accept that sleep just wasn't going to find me. I'd gotten used to sleeping beside Alec, his arm draped over me, the heat of his body lulling me into a deep, restful sleep. The emptiness of the king sized bed left me feeling cold and more alone than I'd ever felt.

After tossing and turning for what seemed like an eternity, I finally gave up and started working on the Payne Enterprises report. Of course, that only made me miss Alec more than I already was. Damn it. I hated what was happening. Six months ago my life had been so simple in comparison to now. We were preparing to send the kids off to college, and Spencer and I were busy making plans for after they left. He'd promised to build me a greenhouse, and we were finally going to take that trip to Europe I'd always wanted. It was going to be an opportunity for us to reconnect, to rekindle some of that passion that had slowly slipped away after nineteen years of marriage and two kids.

But in a blink of an eye it was gone, all our plans, our dreams, our future. It vanished like the dark of night when day breaks. Like the moon and the stars with the rising sun. Like the storm clouds after the rain. Now all Spencer and I had left were the painful memories of his betrayal. Our lives had been forever changed.

Burying my face in the pillow I cried, mourning the loss of who we'd been, of what we'd hoped to be, wondering if I'd ever be able to forgive him. My eyes drifted shut and I prayed then sleep would find me.

Chapter Twenty Seven

Sleep had eluded me most of the night, leaving me sluggish this morning. It had taken every ounce of strength I had just to get through it. Yesterday I'd insisted on going to the office, but as soon as I'd gotten there I couldn't wait to leave. I wanted to call Alec, to tell him I was sorry, that I'd made a huge mistake, but I knew I couldn't. If I backed down after the fit I threw, he'd win, and that just wasn't an option. Not if I wanted to maintain any sort of control over my own life anyway.

Despite wanting to leave the office, the thought of going back to the empty hotel room had been too depressing to deal with, so I stayed until after eight. I'd managed to get through three meetings and get my paperwork caught up, all in an effort to keep my mind off of Alec, whom I hadn't heard from him all day.

By the time I got back to the hotel, I was beyond hungry. Luckily, the hotel restaurant was still open. The first thing I noticed when I walked in was the young couple huddled in the corner, locked in what appeared to be a passionate kiss, and was immediately reminded me of Alec—our dinner at Campiello's, the tourmaline ring he gave me, the amazing sex on the beach that followed. It was more than I could handle at that moment, so I headed straight for the bar.

"What'll be?" the bartender asked as I settled in.

"Captain Morgan on the rocks and your soup du jour."

"Tough day?"

"Something like that." I forced a smile, but I wasn't really in the mood for small talk. As soon as he put the drink down I picked it up, quickly slamming it back, beyond ready to put the day behind me.

The gumbo was just what I needed and the two stiff drinks had gone a long way to helping me unwind. I ordered a third drink, adding a splash of Coke this time, enjoying the smooth sound of jazz that played in the background, thankful for the liquid courage that was getting me through.

• • • • •

I overslept the next morning. An unwelcome side effect of the fourth drink I ended up ordering last night. I grabbed my phone; no missed calls, no text messages. When I opened the email app on my phone, I was disappointed again. Forcing myself out of the bed and into the shower, I wasted no time getting ready. After dressing and zipping through my makeup routine, I stepped back to take one final look in the mirror. My time on the beach had served me well. My skin was tan and healthy looking, and I looked surprisingly well rested, even though I'd barely slept since I'd left the beach house. There was no sign of the Izzy James whose life was in turmoil.

Valerie booked us a ground floor suite with a beach walkout at the Margaritaville on Pensacola Beach. I hadn't thought to bring a swimsuit when I left the beach house, but one good thing about living close to the beach in Florida was the abundance of stores that sold swimwear. It hadn't taken long for me to pick three suits that I liked either. I was really looking forward to seeing Val and wasn't about to be late picking her up. We had so much to catch up on, plus, I really needed a distraction from the fact I hadn't heard from Alec in almost forty eight hours.

She was waiting near the curb when I got to the airport. I pulled into an open spot and hopped out.

"Val!"

"Izzy!"

We locked in a tight embrace, dancing around in a circle, giggling like schoolgirls.

"I'm so glad you came."

"Me too, now let's go to the beach. I could use a drink after that long flight." I wasn't about to argue with that. We climbed into the car and within seconds were speeding toward the beach.

After a series of twists and turns around the heavy summertime traffic we arrived at the hotel. "Get your swimsuit on," Val said as soon as we got checked in. "I want a drink."

Smiling I said, "Bossy as ever, I see."

She flashed me her "do it now" look and I burst out laughing. "Okay, okay," I said, my hands in the air signaling defeat.

Ten minutes later we were lying on the beach, eagerly awaiting the arrival of the Pina Coladas Val ordered. She scanned the beach impatiently. "Where's that damn waiter?" she whined. Val spotted him in the distance as soon as she stood up and began frantically waving her arms.

She spun around in an exaggerated fashion when she noticed all the men staring at her. Valerie loved being the center of attention. Several women were staring by then too. It was hard not to stare at her though, with her long slender legs, her lean body, and those huge breasts courtesy of her first husband. Add her gorgeous blonde hair to her over the top personality and it was easy to see why she drew the attention.

"It's about time," Valerie snapped when the waiter arrived with our drinks. You'd think she was dying of thirst the way she was acting.

I rolled my eyes. "Be nice, Val. He's pretty busy, in case you hadn't noticed."

"Well, I'm on vacation, in case *you* hadn't noticed," she retorted, before taking a long sip through her straw.

A smile crossed my face and I couldn't help the laugh that followed. "Oh, Val, you're too much."

She took another drink then started laughing too.

We talked and drank, and then drank some more. We had a lot of catching up to do. She told me about the divorce with Cody and about her affair. A shiver ran down my spine every time I heard that word. *Affair.*

"At least you don't have kids," I said, thinking of what my own kids had been through.

"Never!" Val snapped. "This body wasn't meant for babies, Izzy." I laughed even though I knew she was serious. Valerie would never be willing to make the kind of sacrifices motherhood required.

"Are you still seeing that guy you had the affair with?"

"No. He broke it off."

"Really?" The news was hard to believe. That made two men who had ended things with her. That was so not Val. "Why? What happened?" I asked, recovering my equilibrium.

"He was married. And before you judge me you should know he was miserable. His wife cared nothing about his needs. He *needed* me."

"Is that why you cheated on Cody? Because you were miserable?"

"Kinda. I was lonely. He worked all the time and, well, you know how I like attention." I wondered if Spencer had been lonely too, if that's why he'd cheated on me. It still wouldn't excuse what he did, but part of me really wanted there to be some simple explanation to why he'd thrown away nineteen years of marriage.

"Why don't you ever talk about your third husband?" My line of questions surprised me but I realized I was just searching for answers, anything that would help me understand what had happened between me and Spencer.

She flashed a pouty look then flagged down the waiter for another round. "I need something stronger. Bring me a Jack and Diet Coke." She batted her long eyelashes at him and he blushed, almost dropping his tray in the process. "And do try to hurry." She was incorrigible at times, but I was prepared to let that go if it meant I'd get the answers I was seeking.

"Yes, ma'am," he said then hurried off toward the bar.

It wasn't long before he returned. She accepted her drink, staring out at the ocean as if looking for something she'd lost there. I took a drink of the Pina Colada he brought for me, strengthening my courage. "Didn't you love him?"

"Who?"

"Husband number three."

"We're back to that?" she snapped. "He didn't love

me. Hell, he didn't even know *me*. Not the real me anyway. He wanted me to be someone I wasn't and it drove us apart." She took a long drink. "Let's talk about something else now, okay?" I could tell there was more to that story, but I let it go. There would be plenty of time to get answers during our week long vacation.

"What do you want to talk about then?"

"Me!" She laughed but I knew she was serious. "I'm putting my life in order, Izzy. Righting a few wrongs if you will." A smile crossed her face and she took another drink. "Whisky makes me want a cigarette, do you mind if I smoke?"

I rolled my eyes. "If you must." I hated the smell of cigarettes, and whisky, and especially the two of them together. A chill ran down my spine as thoughts of my nightmares flashed through my mind.

• • • • •

We closed the tiki bar down before finally calling it a night. Valerie was pretty drunk, but luckily she was still mobile and managed to stay on her feet long enough for me to get her back to our suite. She lunged for the bed, falling face down onto the comforter. I tried to get her back on her feet and out of her sandy suit but she was out cold.

Grabbing my phone off the coffee table, I headed into my room. I'd left it there earlier and was anxious to see if Alec had called. I said a quick prayer then glanced down at the screen. *Nothing*. No texts. No calls. No emails. The sting of disappointment filled my eyes. It was my fault I hadn't heard from him. I left him. And when he asked if I was coming back, I hadn't answered. I had no right to expect anything from him after that.

After showering I climbed into bed, willing myself to sleep so I could finally stop thinking about Alec.

The next morning I woke feeling surprisingly refreshed after crying myself to sleep. I opened the drapes and looked out, past the sea of people, all the way to the emerald green water. It reminded me of the Wyndam and of Alec. I quickly closed the drapes.

We skipped dinner last night, a fact my stomach was reminding me of now. I peeked through the door to Val's bedroom to see if she wanted to get some breakfast, but she was still sleeping, so I ordered room service instead. I was really hungry and who knew how long she'd stay in bed after the amount of alcohol she'd consumed last night.

While waiting for the food to arrive, I changed into a clean swimsuit. I'd resisted the urge to check my messages. I was sure Alec hadn't called, and I didn't think I could take the disappointment of knowing for certain on an empty stomach.

The porter pushed the cart out onto the terrace before disappearing into the hall. I wasted no time digging in. First the French toast then the eggs, stuffing bite after bite into my mouth, trying not to think of Alec or the French toast we ate that first morning at the beach house.

Valerie was still sleeping even after I'd finished eating, so I decided to get some work done, desperate for any distraction I could get at that point. I opened my email program, scrolling through the new messages first, flagging a few for follow up next week, and responding to a few others. There was still nothing from Alec. I considered emailing him, but I didn't, reminding myself of why I hadn't already.

"Hey."

I looked up from the screen. "Well hey. I was beginning to think you were going to sleep all day."

"I'm on vacation, Izzy. You do know what a vacation is, don't you?"

Her sassiness made me giggle. "How are you feeling?"

"Like hell. I can't believe you let me drink so much."

"Let you?" I laughed. There was no way she was blaming me for her drunken state. "There was no stopping you, Val."

"Well, today it's your turn."

"No way, you know I don't like being drunk." The last time I got that drunk was the night Spencer took the three of us to Miami. After that night I promised myself I'd never be that drunk again. "You do remember what happened the last time I got drunk, don't you?" I only remembered bits of pieces of that night, but it was enough to know I never wanted to give up that much control again. We'd all been drunk, without inhibition, given no consideration of tomorrow. It almost cost me my best friend and my relationship with Spencer.

Val bit her lip and grinned, clearly remembering it differently than me. "Okay, so maybe not that drunk, but you are going to loosen up today." There was no point in arguing with her. Telling Val no only made her want it more. She was impossible when she didn't get her way.

"You want some breakfast?"

"No food. I need a Bloody Mary. Get dressed."

"Seriously?"

"Yes, seriously. Vacation, remember?"

I closed down my laptop, did another check of my phone, hoping against hope there was some word from Alec. When I saw there wasn't, I tossed my phone onto the bed, ready to drink away the memory of what I'd done.

Fifteen minutes later we were sitting on a stool at the same tiki bar we closed down last night. "Two Bloody Marys," Val ordered.

"I'm just going to have water for now." If I started drinking that early it would be an early night for sure.

"So order some water, those are for me."

I burst out laughing. I should have known she wasn't ordering for me. "I'll have a bottle of water, please."

"Don't be a party pooper, Bella. Vacation, *remember?*" She exhaled loudly. "Order a damn drink already."

Much to my surprise, I quickly gave in. "Corona, with a lime, too, please."

"Sure thing, ladies."

"Geez, Bella, don't sound so excited about it."

"Cut me some slack, Val. I ordered a drink didn't I?"

We hung out on the beach all afternoon, talking, and laughing, as Valerie ordered drink after drink. I'd wanted to tell her about Spencer's affair but I couldn't bring myself to talk about it. She'd be mad I hadn't told her sooner, and I didn't want to spoil our time together.

"What's going on with you, Bella? Something is clearly bothering you. Now tell me what it is so I can finally enjoy my vacation."

I should just tell her. Maybe it'd even make me feel better to get it off my chest.

"I'm waiting," she snapped.

Liquid courage, that's what I needed. "Let's get another drink. Then we'll talk."

"Now you're speaking my language."

The tiki bar was crowed. Val had worn her bikini to the bar, not bothering to cover up, her gorgeous, sun kissed body glistening in the late day sun, so it hadn't surprised me that she was able to get our drinks quickly. She handed me a metal bucket full of ice and Corona and we made our way back to the beach chairs we'd just left. "You have your drink. Now talk."

Pulling a bottle of beer from the bucket, I took a long drink, the ice cold liquid hitting just the right spot.

"Talk!"

Wow, was she demanding. I took another drink. "Oh, Val, I don't know where to start." I stared out over the water, searching for the right words. "My life is spinning out of control."

"Seriously, Izzy?" she snapped. "You're the most in control person I know."

"Not really." I kept drinking. "I've lost control of everything. My marriage, my home, my career..."

"What? Your marriage? What are you talking about?"

"It's over, Val. Spencer and I got a divorce."

"When did that happen? And why haven't you told me?"

I was drinking faster now. I opened my mouth and the words rushed out. I'd finally said it. The dam had been broken. "I started having nightmares, and then the attacks started, and I lost my home and Alec and maybe my job too." I rambled on and on. I finished the first beer and immediately pulled another one from the bucket.

"Izzy, I can't believe you haven't told me any of this."

"I'm sorry. I just couldn't talk about it. I've been so confused."

"What happened with Spencer?"

"He cheated on me."

"No way! Not Spencer."

"It's true, Val. There are pictures to prove it." The liquid courage was really starting to kick in. I pulled another beer from the bucket.

"Who is she?"

"He wouldn't say."

"What do you mean, he wouldn't say!"

"All he said was she didn't matter, that he'd made a mistake."

"That's bullshit. I can't believe he didn't tell you who he was seeing."

"He's right, Val, it doesn't matter who she was. He cheated. Our marriage is over. That's all I need to know." Her eyes narrowed and her mouth formed into a thin hard line. She chugged the wine in her glass until it was empty and I knew I'd hit a nerve.

"Where are you living?" she asked after a while.

"Well, after we found out the attacks were really attacks, and not just dreams like I'd thought. Alec moved me to this amazing beach house, but we had a fight and I left." I took another drink. "Now I don't know where I'm going to live."

"I don't like him, Izzy. I know he comes across as this charming gentleman but he's controlling and abusive."

"How do you know that?"

"You know he was married before, right?" I nodded, wondering what she was getting at. "Did he tell you why she left?"

"Not really." That wasn't my story to tell, so that was all I was willing to say. "That doesn't answer my question, Val. How do you even know Alec?"

A grin crossed her face. "Let's just say I know Charlee." She pulled a beer from the bucket and took a long drink. "Did you know he used to tie her up and hit her? And he never took no for an answer, especially when it came to sex. You're lucky you got out when you did, Bella."

Her words rolled around my mind and before I knew it, tears had pricked the corner of my eyes.

"Oh, don't cry! You'll ruin my buzz." She took another long drink of beer. "It sounds like we both have fucked up lives." A seemingly satisfactory smile crossed her face as she said it. Sitting back in the lounge chair she stared out at the water. I followed suit, slowly sipping the last beer.

"Drink up," Valerie said after a while. I'll be back with another bucket and I want that gone."

"Val, I've already had too much."

"No, no, no. You're not quitting on me. Now drink."

Reluctantly I took another drink, knowing full well resistance was futile. The more I drank the chattier I became. I told Val how I felt when I saw the pictures. I told her about the divorce, about all the time I'd spent with Alec, and about the amazing sex. She asked me question after question about Spencer, Alec, my job, never once stopping to talk about herself. It was definitely not typical Val. Not typical at all.

Chapter Twenty Eight

My head was pounding when I opened my eyes. A bright light was seeping through the crack in the drapes. The realization of what happened last night slowly sank in. I'd told Val everything—the nightmares, the pictures, *and* the sex with Alec. I shivered at the thought of what else I might've said.

I spotted a carafe of orange juice on the bedside table with a note. My legs were weak and unsteady as I climbed out of bed.

Bella,
Thanks for a great vacation. I had to jet. The room is covered for the rest of the week.
See you soon, Val

"What time is it?" I asked out loud, looking around for my phone, finally finding it on the chair next to my clothes. I unlocked the screen. I couldn't believe my eyes, it was twenty after one. How much did I drink last night?

After a check of my email, and voicemail, and text messages, there was still no word from Alec. I poured myself a glass of juice and drank it down, the tangy liquid instantly quenching my thirst. It didn't do much for the queasy feeling in my stomach, but I hadn't expected it to. Making things right with Alec was the only thing that was going to ease that feeling.

Digging the bottle of Advil out of my bag, I popped four pills into my mouth before sending Val a quick text thanking her for the room. My body was achy and stiff, and a soak in the tub sounded enticing.

After filling the tub I climbed in, the warm water quickly enveloping me. I closed my eyes, doing my best to push the uneasy feeling surrounding last night out of my mind, but it didn't take long for thoughts of Alec to take its place. I wondered if I should call him and tell him where I was staying but quickly reconsidered. It'd been almost a week since I'd heard from him. He'd probably moved on already, something I would need to do soon.

My phone rang, sending me scrambling out of the tub. By the time I reached it the call had rolled to voicemail. Praying it was Alec, I held my breath and scrolled through the call log. *Spencer.* He was the last person I wanted to talk to right now but considering all the break-ins I knew I had to find out what he wanted.

His voicemail didn't provide many clues to the reason for his call. He'd said he wanted to talk, that it was really important. Reluctantly, I dialed his number.

"Izzy, thanks for calling. I was afraid you wouldn't."

"You said it was important. What's up?"

"Are you okay?"

"I'm fine. What makes you ask?"

"No reason really, I just care about you."

I was not in the mood for his considerations. All I wanted was to find out why he called so I could get on with my life. "You said we needed to talk, Spencer. What is it?"

"Getting straight to the point as usual, I see." The tone is his voice changed. "I need to tell you something, Izzy, and I don't want to tell you over the phone. Can we meet somewhere?"

"Spencer, I'm not sure—"

"Please, Izzy. It's really important."

"Alright," I sighed. "I'll be in Pensacola for a few more days." I didn't elaborate beyond that. My life was none of his business anymore.

"Can we meet tonight?"

"Sure. I'm staying at the Margaritaville. Come whenever you want." Alec assured me Spencer had been cleared, so I wasn't worried about telling him where I was staying anymore.

"Thanks, Izzy. I'll be there at five." I glanced at the clock. It was after two and I looked like hell. I'd definitely need to change that before Spencer arrived. The last thing I wanted was for him to know how far out of control my life had become. I quickly dressed and headed to the lobby in search of food.

The tomato soup was just what the doctor ordered. Plus, the saltiness of the crackers seemed to have calmed my stomach. I paid the bill then headed to the hotel gift shop in search of clothes. I'd only packed a few things when I left and most of what I'd brought was being laundered.

They had a small selection of summer attire, mostly touristy t-shirts and stuff, but I managed to find two sundresses I liked. After paying for them both, I hurried back to my room to get ready.

Spencer called from the tiki bar to let me know he'd arrived. I took a deep breath to steady my nerves before heading out to see him. I hadn't laid eyes on him since graduation, and it felt strange to be seeing him now.

My eyes ran from one end of the bar to the next, but I didn't see him.

"Izzy, I'm over here."

"Spencer?" He was almost unrecognizable. He'd lost a lot of weight, not to mention his hair was overgrown and he was sporting a goatee. He opened his arms for a hug. I didn't want to be rude so I moved closer, allowing him to wrap his arms around me. The feeling of him next to me was familiar, maybe a little too familiar, and I pulled back.

"You look great, Izzy."

"You too," I said cautiously, still unsure why he was here.

The waiter approached as soon as I sat down.

"What'll be?" he asked.

"Just a Coke, please."

"Sure thing." He placed a paper coaster in front of me. The Coke quickly followed.

Spencer reached for the glass in front of him. He'd always been a bourbon drinker and I couldn't help but notice the drink in front of him was clear.

"Is that a new drink?"

"Actually, it is," he said, a forced smile crossing his face. "It's called water." His voice was dripping with sarcasm but I wasn't in the mood to deal with one of his tantrums.

"What's going on, Spencer?"

"Izzy, um… I don't know where to start." He stared down at the bar.

"From the beginning." I reached out and touched his shoulder but pulled back almost immediately.

He took a deep breath and exhaled slowly. "I'm an

alcoholic, Izzy." He sat up and looked right at me now. "I made some terrible decisions. I let alcohol control my life. I hurt you. I hurt my family." He looked down at his hands. "I hurt us."

His confession surprised me and I wasn't sure what to say. "Do you have it under control now?" I asked finally.

"I'm working through a program. It's helping." He reached out and touched my hand.

I froze, my whole body tensing at once, but I didn't move. Instead, I sat and listened as he told me about the program, and about how it had taken the divorce to make him realize he had a problem. He admitted that in a small way he was thankful I left because it forced him to re-evaluate his life and take responsibility for what he'd done.

"I'm not happy I hurt you, Izzy. I'm torn apart about that. But I'm happy to be getting my life together." We sat in silence for what felt like an eternity, neither of us saying a word.

"There's more," he said finally.

"Ya know, Spencer, we're already divorced, so you can pretty much tell me anything now." I laughed as I said it, trying to lighten the mood between us. I was touched by his honesty, and thankful he was getting the help he needed. It was at that moment that I realized I'd always love Spencer, just not in the same way as I did before.

"The woman in the pictures, Izzy…" his voice trailed off.

"We don't have to talk about her. You were right, who she is really isn't important."

"No. I have to tell you." He took a deep breath. "Izzy, there's no easy way to say this. The woman in the pictures, the woman I had the affair with… it's Valerie."

I spit Coke all over the bar when her name came out of his mouth. "Valerie who?"

"You know who I'm talking about, Bella."

My head was spinning. Valerie. My best friend Valerie? The Valerie that just left here? It couldn't be her. Could it? The pieces of the puzzle finally came into focus. "You're the man she cheated on Cody with." My voice was weak and my words were barely audible, but I managed to get them out.

The waiter walked by. "I'll have a Corona now please, and a shot of tequila," I said quickly. I couldn't even look at Spencer. I wanted to run away screaming. Why hadn't he told me? Why hadn't she?

When the waiter returned with my order I grabbed the shot glass and slammed it back as fast as I could. A long drink of beer followed.

"Izzy, I'm sorry."

"Don't, Spencer. You cheated on me with my best friend!"

"I didn't mean for it to happen. I ran into her when I was on a business trip. We got drunk and it just happened."

"It just happened. That's the best you've got!" I was drinking faster now.

"What do you want me to say? I screwed up. I know that. Nothing will ever change that." He put his elbows on the bar and buried his face in his hands.

"Why are you telling me this? Why now?"

"Keeping it from you was killing me. Plus, you have a right to know."

"You're concerned about my rights all of a sudden?" I chugged the rest of my beer and ordered another one. "You should've told me earlier if you were that concerned about me," I shouted, the liquid courage getting stronger with every drink. "I feel like such a fool. I just spent the weekend hanging out with the woman who was fucking my husband!"

Grabbing my beer, I stood to leave. I had to get away from him. I couldn't deal with any of this now.

He grabbed my arm. "She was here?"

"Yes, she left this afternoon."

He ran his free hand over his face. "She's bad news, Izzy. You should stay away from her."

"That's the pot calling the kettle black, now isn't it, Spencer." I pulled my arm free and moved away as fast as I could, leaving him to pay my tab. He owed me at least that much after the bomb he just dropped.

Tears started to fall as I hurried down the hall to my room. *My best friend. My husband.* I felt so betrayed.

Collapsing on the bed, I sobbed uncontrollably. My life was crumbling around me, my husband, my home, the psycho, Alec, *and* my best friend. It was too much to handle. "Why, why, why?" I cried into the pillow. "Why is this happening? What have I done to deserve this?" I cried so hard I got sick, barely making it to the bathroom before the contents of my stomach came spewing out.

When the vomiting finally stopped, I climbed into the shower. As I stood under the hot water, I wished it could wash away all the memories of what had happened that year. Replaying the conversation Val and I had about Spencer's affair brought another bout of clarity. She'd acted so surprised, but it was all an act. Her outrage made sense though. Of course she would be mad hearing Spencer had said she didn't matter.

I remembered what she'd said about her lover's wife, about Spencer's wife, about *me*. "His wife cared nothing about his needs. He was miserable." The words cut me to the quick and the tears started falling all over again.

The water ran cold, and reluctantly I climbed out of the shower. I'd slipped on the hotel robe and was wrapping a towel around my head when my phone started to ring. My heart skipped a beat as my breathing stilled. "*Alec*," I gasped, when my breath returned. I prayed it was him calling to take me back, to take away the pain I was feeling at the hands of my *best friend*. Only it wasn't him. It was *her*.

Without giving it a second thought I sent Val's call to voicemail. Nothing she had to say interested me anymore.

Collapsing on the bed, I turned the television on, flipping through the channels, looking for anything that would take my mind off of all that had happened recently. Nothing worked. Everywhere I looked I was reminded of Alec or Valerie or Spencer. I needed to get out of there.

After booking a room at the Crowne Plaza for the night, I called housekeeping to see if they could put a rush on my laundry. When I got off the phone I started packing up the rest of my things, beyond ready to leave the suite I'd shared with Valerie behind.

Housekeeping said they'd deliver my laundry as soon as possible so the knock at the door hadn't surprised me. I swung open the door. "What the hell do you want?" I asked the second I saw her, the cold-hearted bitch who slept with my husband, well, ex-husband.

"I want to talk to you."

"Nothing you have to say interests me. Now leave me alone." I tried to close the door but her foot was in the way.

"I'm sorry, Bella. I wanted to tell you."

"I bet you did, Val. I bet you couldn't wait to tell me all about how you were fucking my husband." I pushed hard on the door but it wouldn't budge. "I bet you're the one who sent me those pictures too."

"You had a right to know."

"And you had an obligation as my friend, my best friend, NOT to sleep with my husband." My outburst surprised us both. She took a step back, and I slammed the door shut.

Val's fists pounded on the door. "Open the door, Izzy."

There was no way I was opening the door for her. Instead, I did a quick check of the sliding glass doors. Locked. They were all locked. Then I pulled the drapes closed.

"Izzy!" She was screaming by then. "Damn it, Bella! Open the door."

Her pounding was relentless, but I picked up the remote, turning the volume up as loud as it would go, doing my best to drown out the sound of her voice.

When she didn't stop, I screamed, "Go away. Just leave me alone."

The hotel phone rang. Shit. Someone must've complained about the noise. I turned the volume on the television down and picked up the phone. "Hello."

"This is the front desk. Is everything okay?"

"Yes, everything's fine."

"We've received some complaints." He paused. "Should I send security?" Double Shit.

"No, the TV, umm... I had it turned up pretty loud. I'll turn it down."

"Thank you, ma'am."

As soon as I heard the click of the call disconnecting, I placed the receiver back in its cradle and walked over to the door. Valerie's screaming had stopped, but she was still pounding.

"Security is on their way," I shouted through the door. The pounding stopped then too. "Security is on their way," I said again.

"Damn it, Bella. This isn't over. I won't be denied this time."

Staring at the door, I silently wondered if she'd gone. I looked out through the peep hole, relieved there wasn't any sign of her. I couldn't wait to get out of there and headed into the bathroom to finish packing.

A noise in the other room caught my attention. I turned to see what it was, but something struck me in the head. Instantly, my eyes closed.

• • • • •

My head felt funny when I opened my eyes. The light from the television was barely visible. Something was covering my face, my silk nightshirt maybe. My arms, they wouldn't move. My heart started to race so fast I could barely breathe. I looked to the right, to the left, there were only shadows. The shadow moved. No! It couldn't be him. How had he found me?

He moved closer. I opened my mouth to scream, but my voice failed. My eyes were too heavy, and I couldn't hold them open any longer.

Muffled sounds surround me. Someone was touching my leg, warmth radiating from his body to mine. I tried to pull away, but my legs wouldn't move either. I was tied up. When I forced my eyes open again he was standing next to me. I twisted and turned, pulling on my restraints, desperately wanting to escape.

"I like it when you fight." That voice. I knew that

voice.

"You take and you take, Bella."

Take what. What did I take? I wanted to ask but it was no use. His hand was on my cheek. I turned my head to move away but he grabbed my chin, effectively holding me in place. Ripping the covering off my face he squeezed my chin tight, pulling my bottom lip down, claiming my mouth with his. Something tickled my face. I strained to see what it was. *Hair, long, blonde hair.*

When he released my face his hands moved around my neck, squeezing tight, his nails digging in my skin. *Nails. Sharp nails.* My eyes closed.

"Stay with me, Bella. I'm not done with you yet!" His hand connected hard with my cheek. "I do matter, Bella."

My eyes flew open as I started to cough. He moved toward my feet, trailing his sharp nail down my leg. I could see his hand, his nails. Something wasn't right. They were long, and red. He moved closer to my feet and I could finally see him, his blonde hair, his long legs, his tiny waist. My eyes moved quickly up his body. *Breasts.* It wasn't a man. It was a woman. A woman? But who? She was wearing a mask. Her voice was gruff. Her movements were familiar but my head was too fuzzy to even attempt to figure out why.

There was a sudden stinging pain on my leg. "I matter, Bella!" I felt the pain again and again. "You always defy me."

The blows were coming faster, harder. "Stop," I finally managed to say, my voice barely above a whisper. "Please. Stop."

"You took him from me, Bella." She hit me again and again. Climbing on top off me she ran the instrument she was holding in front of my face. The brown leather paddle reconciling the pain I was feeling in my mind. She lifted it up and brought it down hard against my breast before lifting it again. Over and over she repeated the process.

"NO!" I screamed out, my voice louder now.

"Hush." Her voice was harsh, gruff. She hit me again. I bucked my hips and pulled at my restraints when she turned her wrath to my other breast.

"Stop!" I screamed now, my voice having returned. "Stop! Why are you doing this?"

"It was my life, Bella." She leaned closer, her face inches from mine. My senses were starting to return. She smelled of whisky and cigarettes. "You can't keep me from what's rightfully mine," she growled in my face.

Her mouth was on mine. I pulled away but she grabbed ahold of my hair, keeping me in place. She kissed me again, forcing her tongue deep inside my mouth this time. I twisted and turned, pulling as hard as I could on the restraints.

"Fight me, Bella. I like it when you fight." She ran her mouth over my chin, my neck, my ear.

"Please. Stop." Tears were streaming down my face.

"You stole him with your sex." She punched me in the stomach, stealing my breath. "So I will punish you with mine." She punched me again. Her mouth was on my breast, biting.

"Stop!" I screamed when my breath returned.

She sat up, straddling me now. Her hands moved quickly around my neck. "I said HUSH." Squeezing tight, she continued yelling. "Why do you insist on defying me?" I was seconds from passing out when she released my neck and slapped me across the face.

"HELP! SOMEBODY! HELP ME!"

She slapped me again.

"Help," I screamed again, but the sound was muffled by the pillow she was holding over my face, making it hard to breathe.

There was a loud knock at the door. She let go of the pillow, but it was still covering my face. I felt a sharp pinch. My head was spinning.

The knocking was getting louder. "Security," the deep voice called out. "We heard screams, ma'am. We're coming in."

Yes. Come in. Hurry. My eyes were too heavy to open.

· · · · ·

"Oh my God, Izzy. Quick, call 911! Get an ambulance here now." I couldn't see. I opened my mouth to speak, but my words failed me now.

"There's an ambulance on the way. Stay with us, ma'am."

My chest hurt. Too much pressure. "Hurry up. We're losing her."

"We need to start and IV, ma'am. You'll feel a little pinch," a softer voice said. He was touching my arm, it was free.

Something was covering my face. I reached up to move it. "That's an oxygen mask, Ms. James." He put the mask back over my mouth and nose.

My eyes finally opened. "Welcome back," he said. "I'm a paramedic. The name's Max. We're taking you to the hospital."

The hospital? Wait, the attack. I remembered. I couldn't hold my eyes open any longer, and they slowly closed.

• • • • •

"Get a CBC and a tox screen, STAT."

The hospital. I'd made it.

"Ms. James, can you hear me?" The voice was familiar, but who? My mind was too foggy to place it. A bright light flooded into my eye. "Can you hear me, Ms. James?"

"Dr. Jensen?" I tried to speak but I couldn't. It was so hard to breathe. My chest was tight.

"There was another attack, Izzy. You were drugged." Something cold touched my chest. "Can you hear me?"

"She did this," I whispered.

"A woman did this?"

"Yes," I breathed. It was all I could manage. I couldn't hold my eyes open any longer. Muffled voices surrounded me. There was a loud beeping sound. Pressure filled my chest. I was so sleepy.

"Clear."

I opened my eyes, coughing, feeling as though I'd been kicked in the chest. Someone was standing over me, something in his hands. Shiny. Silver. My eyes closed again.

"Stay with us, Izzy." The tightness in my chest stole my breath.

"Clear!"

Chapter Twenty Nine

"Code Blue. Code Blue. ICU. Code Blue." A disembodied voice was saying.

A woman stood next to me. "Stay with us, Ms. James," she was saying. Who was she? She was injecting something into my IV. I couldn't breathe. "You're in the hospital, ma'am. You're safe now."

Safe. I was safe. I closed my eyes. The voices were getting farther and farther away.

"She's in V-tach."

"Clear."

There was that kick again. Damn that hurt.

"Again."

"Clear."

My eyes opened wide. "We have sinus rhythm."

"Thank God!" Dr. Leonard. She was there too, standing beside me, staring at me. "We had another scare, Izzy." Another scare, another attack! My heart rate increased.

"She was here?" I froze, paralyzed by fear that she had found me here.

"No, Izzy. You're safe." She touched my arm as she said it. "Please, try to relax. We need to keep your heart rate stable." I took a breath, doing my best to stay calm but I was stopped by the enormous pressure in my chest.

I exhaled loudly. "My chest. What happened?"

"You developed a dangerous rhythm and we had to shock your heart to stabilize it." Her normally all business persona had softened. "You have a high dose of ketamine in your system."

I scrunched my nose, not at all sure what she was talking about. "It's a dissociative drug," Dr. Jensen offered. "It's what your attacker used to subdue you. In high doses it can cause dangerous heart rhythms like the one you've experienced."

My eyelids were heavy. I couldn't hold them open any longer.

Voices. Lots of voices.

"Can I touch her?"

"Yes, of course, just be careful of her IVs."

"Oh, Mom, I'm sorry I wasn't there to protect you." Drew. He was holding my hand in his. I wanted to squeeze it, but my fingers wouldn't move. My arm wouldn't move either. Something was holding my legs. I was tied.

"NO," I tried to scream but there was no sound.

My chest hurt. So much pressure.

Alarms sounded all around me. "Push two units of lidocaine, STAT."

"Mom, it's okay. You're going to be okay." He squeezed my hand tighter. "She will be okay, won't she?"

Who was he talking to?

"Wake up, Mom, please. We're here. You're safe now. Everything is going to be okay." I wanted to open my eyes but I couldn't. They were too heavy. "Please wake up," he whispered over and over again.

"She hears you, Drew. Keep talking to her," Dr. Leonard was saying.

Why can't I wake up?

"I love you, Mom. We all love you." I focused on Drew's voice but was drifting fast, drifting, drifting.

"Mom, please! Just wake up." Anna. She was there too. "When is she going to wake up, Drew? Why won't she wake up?"

I want to wake up, sweetheart, but I'm so sleepy.

"Stay strong, Sis. We have to have faith. She'll wake up soon."

Wake up, Izzy.

"Open your eyes, Mom. It's time to wake up now," Anna cried.

No, don't cry. I'm here. I'm okay. Why can't she hear me? Why won't my eyes open?

"Shouldn't the effects of the ketamine have worn off by now?" Another voice. Who was that? Why couldn't I open my eyes?

"Unfortunately there's no way to predict exactly how long it will take," Dr. Leonard said, but who was she talking to? "Try to be patient, Alec. I know this can't be easy."

Alec? Did she say Alec? My heart started to race. My breathing quickened.

"We're here, Mom. You're safe. We're all here." Drew held my hand again. My breathing slowed. The voices were getting farther away.

"Isabella. Oh, baby, please wake up." I felt a soft kiss on my hand. Alec. He was really here.

"Excuse me, Mr. Payne."

Alec let go of my hand. "Detective Rux, any news?" No, don't let go, please stay with me.

"The FBI was able to match the print. Does the

name Stephanie Sanders mean anything to you, sir?"

Who? What's he saying?

"What? A woman did this to her?"

Yes, Alec. It was a woman. She has long blonde hair. And red nails.

"We found DNA at the scene, so we'll know for sure very soon.

Now, does that name sound familiar or not, Mr. Payne?"

"No."

The pain in his voice tugged on my heart. No, Alec, this wasn't your fault. I wanted to tell him, but I couldn't. Why couldn't I open my eyes?

My heart started to race. I couldn't breathe. A loud beeping sound surround me. It was so loud. Too loud.

My chest. Something was crushing my chest. I wanted to open my eyes, but I couldn't.

People. Lots of people.

People everywhere.

"Code Blue. Code Blue. ICU. Code Blue." The disembodied voice said again.

"She's in V-tach."

"Isabella!"

"Move away, Mr. Payne," a voice I didn't recognize yelled.

No. Alec. Stay with me.

"Everybody. Clear."

"Again."

"Clear."

There was so much pressure.

"Push two more units of lidocaine."

"Clear."

Damn. That pain. My chest.

• • • • •

"Izzy, can you hear me?" Dr. Leonard asked.

A wave of relief washed over me when my eyelids finally responded. "Yes," I whispered. My voice was weak, but I could speak.

"Isabella," Alec moved between me and Dr. Leonard and picked up my hand. "Thank you, God. Thank you for bringing her back to me." He kissed my hand over and over again.

"Alec?"

"Yes, Isabella, I'm here."

My heart was beating faster. How did he know? When did he get here? I had so many questions.

"Mom." Anna bent down and held on to me. "I was so worried about you." She squeezed me tight.

Drew moved closer and hugged me too.

My head was pounding, but at least it was clear. I looked around the room, the tiny room. "Where am I?"

"You're in the ICU. There was another attack."

The hotel. Her hair, her long blonde hair. Her red nails. My heart started racing. That beeping sound coming back again.

A nurse pressed a button on the large monitor next to me and a blood pressure cuff squeezed my arm. "Try to stay calm, Ms. James. You've been through a lot these past few days."

Did she say few days? "What day is it?"

"Today is Wednesday."

"Wednesday," I repeated, trying to process what she'd just said. "How long have I been here?"

"Five days," Alec said quietly, "five excruciatingly long days."

"Five days?" I repeated, struggling to wrap my mind

around what they were saying. My job. Chris. I was supposed to call him on Monday. "Does Tim know I'm here?"

"Don't worry about that right now, baby. You're in the hospital. In ICU. We almost lost you." He pulled his hand through his hair. "I'm so sorry, Isabella. I should've been there. I was supposed to protect you."

"Alec, no, this isn't your fault. I should've listened to you. I should've stayed."

He sat on the edge of the bed and took my hand in his. "And I should've come after you."

"You're both right," Drew interjected. "You should've listened to Alec. You should've stayed where you were safe." He looked from me to Alec. "And you shouldn't have let her go. But what's done is done." Drew leaned down and kissed me on the cheek. "You're gonna be okay, and that's all that matters now."

"Please don't ditch your security again, Mom," Anna added. "I was so scared." Her voice caught in her throat.

"Excuse me," Dr. Leonard said from the foot of the bed.

Alec turned so he could see her, not letting go of my hand this time.

"Your labs look much better tonight, Izzy. I feel confident saying the worst is behind us now." She looked from Drew to Anna and back again. "Go home and get some rest. Your mom is doing much better. The hospital will call you if anything changes." Dr. Leonard looked at me again. "I want to monitor your heart here tonight, and if everything goes well we'll get you moved to a regular room tomorrow."

I nodded. "Can I get out of bed?"

"That should be fine. But let me get the nurse in here to remove that Foley first."

What? I looked under the sheet, appalled by what I was seeing. When did they put that in? My face was burning from embarrassment.

"Try to sleep tonight, Izzy. I'll see you in the morning."

I moved the bed forward until I was sitting. "She's right, guys. You should go. You should all go." I didn't want any of them there after seeing that tube inside me. I just wanted to pull the covers over my head and pretend it was all just a bad dream.

"I don't want to leave," Anna sulked.

"That's enough, Anna," Alec scolded. "Both of you need to get some sleep. Preston will drive you to the hotel tonight and you can come back in the morning."

He reached up and touched the Bluetooth that seemed to be permanently attached to his ear. "Drew and Anna need a ride to the hotel. No, I'm staying here," he said, then pressed the button again.

"Alec, you don't need to stay."

"I'm not leaving you, Isabella." His voice was soft but stern, and I knew he wasn't taking no for an answer.

After I kissed the kids goodbye, they disappeared through the glass door.

Fortunately, it was only a short while later when the nurse came in to remove that stupid tube. "I need a few minutes alone with Ms. James," she said looking right at Alec.

"Do what you have to do. I'm not leaving her."

"Alec, please, this is embarrassing enough."

He started to object but the look on my face must have made him reconsider, and he finally agreed to step out into the hall. It was bad enough knowing he'd seen me like this, weak, vulnerable, unable to care for myself.

I wasn't about to let him watch as they pulled out the catheter.

In a matter of seconds it was gone. The nurse helped me to my feet so I could use the tiny bathroom inside the ICU room. My legs were wobbly and weak, the effects of spending five days in bed. The bathroom wasn't exactly private either, but it was definitely better than the alternative.

Alec returned as soon as the nurse left. Sitting on the edge of the bed once more he took my hand in his. "I'm so sorry, Isabella." A single tear rolled down his cheek. "I don't know what I'd do…"

"Don't do this, Alec." I reached up and wiped away the tear. "Stop torturing yourself. This isn't your fault." What happened to his family hadn't been his fault either but that hadn't stopped him from blaming himself, and I didn't want him blaming himself for what happened to me. If anything it was my fault. I was the one who left, who'd made the decision security wasn't necessary any longer. "I'm just so thankful you're here, especially after the horrible things I said to you."

He wrapped his arms around me. "Anything for you, baby," he whispered.

I buried my face in his chest, more than thankful he was here with me.

•   •   •   •   •

It was dark. I couldn't see. My arms were tied. My legs too. Long blonde hair, red nails, that leather paddle. Pain. There was so much pain. Voices. Voices all around me. That smell. Her nails. Cigarettes. Whisky. Sharp red nails. Blonde hair. I couldn't breathe. My heart was racing. "NO," I screamed. "HELP ME! PLEASE!

SOMEBODY HELP ME!

"Isabella, wake up. You're dreaming, baby. It's just a bad dream. You're safe now."

Alec was sitting beside me when my eyes opened. The nurse was injecting something into my IV. "It was only a dream," he said again.

My eyes were heavy. I couldn't hold them open.

· · · · ·

I jolted upright in bed, my head pounding. Light flooded the room and I knew it must be morning. I looked around, wondering where I was. This wasn't the same ICU room I'd been in last night. It was bigger, much bigger. And everywhere I looked I saw flowers, lots and lots of flowers, and Alec. He was asleep in the chair near the bed, looking so peaceful, not at all the control freak I stormed out on almost two weeks earlier.

"Good morning, Izzy," Dr. Leonard said as she walked through the door. "How are you feeling today?"

"Better, except my head is pounding."

She nodded but continued to remove the stethoscope from around her neck. "Do you think you can you sit up so I can listen to your heart?"

I raised the back of the bed, my eyes fixed on Alec as he stirred. "Nice and strong," Dr. Leonard said.

"Does that mean I can go home?"

"I think we can manage that in a day or two."

I frowned when the words were out of her mouth. I hated hospitals and the thought of staying even one more day was depressing.

"Don't pout, Isabella," Alec said, kissing me on the forehead. "This is for your own safety."

I rolled my eyes, silently wondering how many times

he planned to use that against me.

"I saw that," he whispered, that wicked grin making a brief appearance, but it was enough to make me blush.

"I'll leave you two to work this out," Dr. Leonard said, laughing. "I'll have the nurse bring you something for your headache." She patted me gently on the shoulder before leaving the room.

"I've missed that," Alec said.

"Missed what?"

"Your feisty attitude, those crimson cheeks, your shy smile." Alec kissed me softly on the lips.

Oh how I'd missed that kiss.

A loud knock against the door cut into the private moment we were sharing. "Come in," Alec said sharply.

"Excuse the interruption, but I heard Ms. James was awake."

"Can't this wait, Detective? Isabella is still pretty weak."

"It won't take long, Mr. Payne. We have some new evidence we'd like Ms. James to look at if she's feeling up to it."

"What new evidence?" I asked.

"We've isolated an image from the hotel's security video." He pulled a picture from the manila folder he was carrying. "Does the name Stephanie Sanders mean anything to you?"

Stephanie Sanders? Why did that sound familiar? Unable to place it, I shook my head.

He moved closer to the bed. "That's likely an alias anyway. Take a look at this picture and see if you recognize the woman."

Alec stepped in between us, effectively blocking my reach. "Isabella, you don't have to do this now if you're not up to it."

"I need to do this, Alec. I want this psycho bitch caught."

Without another word, he stepped out of the way, and I took the picture the detective was holding. The picture was grainy, and she wasn't looking at the camera, but I recognized her immediately. *Valerie.* Tears filled my eyes. I dropped my head into my hands, the picture falling to the floor.

"Baby, what's wrong?"

I was frozen; unable to move, unable to speak. Alec bent down and picked up the picture.

"Do you know who that is, Ms. James?"

"Charlee!" Alec shouted. "Her name is Charlee Barnes."

Charlee Barnes? Valerie was Charlee Barnes? Alec was husband number three. My heart began to race, and I couldn't breathe. Spencer and Valerie and Alec. Tears fell in a steady stream. Valerie? She did this? My head was spinning.

I swung my legs over the edge of the bed. "I'm going to be sick," I cried.

Alec held the trash can in front of me. My stomach contracted and that was all it took. My emotions came flooding out of me like water through a broken dam.

"We're done here, Detective," Alec snapped.

A nurse rushed through the door and quickly injected something into my IV. "Your heart rate is dangerously high, Ms. James. I've given you an injection of Lidocaine to slow it down. We can't risk another episode." She turned toward the detective. "I'm going to have to ask you to leave now. Ms. James' medical condition is still pretty fragile."

"Wait, that's not her name," I cried. "Her real name is Valerie Russell. She lives in Chicago."

"Are you sure about that, Ms. James?"

"Positive."

"Thank you. I'll be in touch." The detective took the picture from Alec's hand and showed himself to the door.

Alec wrapped me up in his arms. The medicine the nurse gave me had already started to take effect, and I leaned against his chest. "Valerie said she knew Charlee. I had no idea this is what she meant."

"Let's not talk about that right now, baby. You need to try and stay calm."

"It was Valerie, the pictures, Spencer's affair," I continued, my voice beginning to fade. I was so tired. My eyes closed.

Valerie…Charlee…husband number three.

Chapter Thirty

Drew and Anna stopped by for a visit the following afternoon. While I'd been dreading having to tell them about Valerie, I was more than happy for the distraction from the awkwardness that had fallen between me and Alec. Learning he was husband number three had proven harder to accept than Spencer having an affair with Val. Looking back, it all made sense with Val and Spencer. The way she laughed at everything he said, how she always had her hands on him, small, subtle touches that had seemed so innocent at the time. Actually, I couldn't believe I hadn't seen how she felt about him sooner.

Alec, on the other hand, now that was completely unexpected. Granted, Val could certainly turned heads, I just hadn't expected she'd ever turn *Alec's*. Certainly not the Alec I knew, anyway. Even though their relationship only lasted six weeks, I was still having a hard time wrapping my head around the idea that Val had managed to keep her true self hidden for so long, and that was where the awkwardness came in. Had he known who she *really* was and married her anyway? Was that the type of woman he was interested in spending the rest of his life with?

Anna brought me a magazine to help occupy my time, and Drew brought chocolate. Not just any chocolate either, but Ferrero Rocher, my favorite. It was supposed to lessen the sting of him leaving, but it hadn't helped much. I knew he had to get back.

Summer session was only eight weeks long and he'd already missed an entire week being at the hospital with me. But even knowing that hadn't made the fact he was leaving any easier. To make matters worse, Anna was leaving too. She planned on spending the next few weeks getting acclimated to Gainesville before fall semester began. Summer was slipping away so fast. My life seemed to be moving at warp speed, and there was nothing I could do to slow it down.

I needed to tell Drew and Anna that Val was the one responsible for the attacks, but I was stalling. Anna adored her Aunt Val, and I knew telling her was going to split her heart wide open. The very thought made me frown.

"Mom, what is it? What's wrong?" Drew asked.

I exhaled slowly. Time was up. "I need to tell you guys something." I looked over at Alec. He nodded, encouraging me to continue. "Come, sit, both of you." They sat beside me, one on each side. "I don't know how to tell you this—"

"Just tell us already," Anna interrupted.

I took a deep breath. "Aunt Val—"

"Oh my gosh. No! She's not hurt too, is she? Tell me she's okay, Mom. Tell me." Anna's voice quivered as she spoke.

"No, Anna, it's nothing like that."

"Then what is it?" Tears had filled her eyes. She was on the brink of a meltdown, and what I was about to tell her would surely push her over.

"Aunt Valerie did this. She's the one who attacked me."

"Aunt Valerie?" Drew and Anna said simultaneously. Unable to take the pain on their innocent faces, I closed my eyes and nodded.

Anna jumped up from the bed, her sudden departure jolting my eyes open. "I don't believe you. Aunt Val wouldn't do this!" Pacing back and forth next to the bed, she added, "There must be some mistake."

"I didn't want to believe it either, but it's true."

Drew finally spoke. "How do they know it was her?"

"There's a surveillance video from the hotel. It was definitely her."

"Why would she want to hurt you, Mom? It doesn't make sense."

"None of this makes sense," Anna cried.

Tears were rolling down her cheeks in a steady stream, the pain on her face ripped at my heart. "Anna, I'm sorry, sweetheart, but we have to face the facts here. She did this."

Drew moved closer and pulled her into his arms. "I'm sorry too, Anna."

"But Drew," she cried, even louder. "It's not fair. Aunt Val said I was like a daughter to her. Why would she want to hurt us?"

"I don't know, Anna. I just don't know." She unraveled in his arms, hysterically sobbing. He rocked her gently back and forth, comforting his baby sister, his twin.

Tears filled my eyes again as I played witness to this bittersweet moment. They'd been through so much— the divorce, the attacks, and now this. Discovering your beloved aunt was trying to kill your mother was enough to rock anyone to their core.

"If she contacts you I need to know about it," Alec said after a while, "any calls, texts, emails, and especially if you see her. Are we clear on that?"

Drew spoke first. "Yes, of course," he said.

"She took me shopping this morning," Anna said through her tears. "I'm meeting her for dinner later."

As soon as the words left Anna's mouth, Alec asked, "Where?"

"Um." Anna hesitated before answering. "I can't tell you. I wasn't even supposed to tell you I'd seen her."

Adrenaline coursed through my veins at the mere thought of my baby girl having dinner with the crazy bitch who'd almost killed me. *Aunt Val,* yeah, her pseudo title meant nothing to me anymore. I didn't want her anywhere near my family. "You're not having dinner with her, Anna."

"Mom's right. What if she tries to hurt you too?"

"Look, there has to be a mistake. Aunt Val didn't do this. She would never hurt mom. And she definitely wouldn't hurt me!" Anna's voice quivered as she spoke. "Plus, I promised her I wouldn't tell."

"Well, I never thought she'd hurt Mom either, but look where we are." Drew motioned around the hospital room. "Now, I don't give a shit what you promised her, tell us where you're supposed to meet!" Drew's patience with his sister was waning, his voice raising several octaves when he spoke.

Anna folded her arms across her chest, her head shaking. An act of stubborn defiance I'd seen countless times over the years.

"Sweetheart, please," I begged. "Promise me you won't have dinner with her. Not today. Not ever."

"Mom, she wouldn't hurt me. And even if she *wanted*

to, she couldn't do anything in a public place. But she doesn't even want to. She loves me!" Her tears began falling once again.

"This isn't a game, Anna," Alec barked, standing abruptly. "Now tell me where you're supposed to meet her!"

Anna's face turned white as the color slowly drained from her cheeks. She wasn't used to having someone yell at her. Spencer was always so gentle, never wanting to upset his princess. "Five Sisters. It's on West Belmont," she finally answered, her voice barely a whisper.

Alec stepped out into the hall, Drew close behind.

Anna sat back down on the edge of the bed. Her face buried in her hands. "This can't be true. Not Aunt Val," she cried.

I wrapped my arms around her, pulling her close to me. "I'm so sorry, Anna. I wish it weren't true. But you have to accept the facts here, and I need you to promise me you won't see her."

She sat up and wiped the tears off her face. "Are you sure? I mean *really* sure she did this?"

I nodded, my silent answer to her pleading question. Breaking her heart was killing me. Anna threw her arms around my waist and burst into tears once more.

Time stood still as I held my baby girl in my arms, doing whatever I could to comfort her, rubbing her back, kissing her forehead, telling her how much I loved her. It could have been minutes or even hours. None of that mattered. My Anna, her heart was broken.

When the door finally opened, it was Drew who came into the room. "We have to go," he said as he crossed the small room to my bed. "I'll be back in a few weeks though."

Anna wiped the tears from her eyes. "I'll be back

too," she said.

Reluctantly, I climbed out of bed to get one final hug before they left. Drew kissed my cheek. "I love you, Mom."

Anna kissed the other cheek. "Me too. I love you too."

The most convincing smile I could manage crossed my face. "I love you both so much. Be safe." I took one of their hands in each of mine and squeezed. "Call me. Often."

Anna walked out into the hall first. I heard her talking to Alec, but I couldn't hear what they were saying. Drew kissed me one final time then followed his sister, closing the door behind him. I buried my head in my hands, my heart aching for the pain they were feeling, trying not to cry but failing miserably.

• • • • •

Alec hadn't come back into the room since hearing Anna was supposed to meet Valerie for dinner. The sun had set over an hour ago, and I was starting to get antsy being stuck in the room by myself. I'd wanted to go for a walk, but the security team posted outside the door wouldn't allow it.

I'd already finished the magazine Anna brought me and most of the candy. Nothing interested me on the television, but I flipped through the channels anyway, for the third time. I closed my eyes, hoping to relax for a while, but images of the attack quickly flooded my mind—her long red nails, the leather paddle, her hands around my neck, the hatred in her masked stare. Valerie. My friend, my *best friend*, was responsible for all that.

The door swung open, pulling me out of the half

fitful sleep I'd fallen into. Detective Rux walked through the door, Alec close behind. "What can we do for you, Detective?" Alec asked.

"The Chicago police have finished searching Ms. Russell's home." I sat quietly, eagerly awaiting the news. He looked at me then Alec then me again.

"Well?" Alec snapped, his patience wearing thin.

He exhaled loudly. "They found her journals. And they also found some disturbing pictures…"

My heart beat faster, and I prayed he wasn't talking about the pictures of her and Spencer. "What kind of pictures?" I whispered.

"We believe they're pictures from the attacks." An uneasy feeling started to wrap its ugly arm around me. Not pictures of Spencer. Pictures of *me*. The thought of someone seeing me tied up, defenseless, had my stomach turning flips.

"And it looks like there were several we didn't know about," Detective Rux continued. That news didn't come as a total surprise. My nightmares started months before the attack that sent me to the hospital. I'd figured the broken ribs and fractured forearm had been the result of an attack I didn't remember. But were there others? Were all of my nightmares real?

"How many?" I asked, finally deciding I needed to know.

Detective Rux shook his head. "It's hard to say, Ms. James. The pictures could be from a few attacks, or from several. Her journals haven't supplied many clues to that question."

Annoyance was starting to set in. I wanted answers, and my patience was in short supply. "Well, did her journals give you any clues about why she wants to hurt me?"

"We're still sorting through them, along with all the other evidence the Chicago PD collected, but I can tell you her hatred for you is deep seated. She blames you for taking Mr. James from her."

Memories from the last attack flashed through my mind. She'd said I stole him with my sex. It didn't make sense. Valerie didn't even meet Spencer until after he and I started dating.

Detective Rux opened his tiny notebook and flipped through the pages. "Yes. Here it is. She refers to him over and over again as her 'one true love'." He looked up at me again. "Her hatred toward you grew with each milestone in your relationship with Mr. James: your engagement, the wedding, the birth of your kids."

I searched my memory, looking for clues of my own. The trip to Miami, her reaction when I told her Spencer had proposed. It all made sense. She had been in love with him.

"When Spencer broke off the affair and you began dating her former husband it was more than her psyche could handle and her hatred turned dark."

"I didn't have anything to do with Spencer ending the affair. And Alec and I aren't dating, Detective." The words tasted bitter coming out of my mouth. As much as I wanted to believe I meant more to Alec than a quest for control, he'd never made mention of it. If we had been dating, surely he would have come after me when I left the beach house, or at least asked me to come back. Only he didn't do either of those things. No, all Alec asked was *if* I was coming back, and that certainly wasn't a question you'd ask someone you were in a relationship with.

"That may be all well and true, but her perception is what led her to escalate the attacks, and until she's caught, I'm afraid it's her perception that matters."

The detective turned toward Alec. "I'm afraid she's after you too, Mr. Payne."

"Why would she be after me?"

The detective turned a page in his notebook. "According to her journal, she wants you dead because you betrayed her."

"That's ridiculous, Detective. Charlee, I mean Ms. Russell, ran off with my finance manager soon after we were married. If anything, she betrayed me."

"Look, I'm not saying anything she's written is true. But it's how she sees it." He closed his notebook. "Did you know she's broken into your office three times already?"

Alec nodded. He nodded! My head was starting to spin, the words around me suddenly making no sense. He knew Val was behind the break-ins and he hadn't bothered to share that with me? I shook my head, trying to still the thoughts that were racing through my mind.

"And I'm afraid we found evidence of bomb material at her house," Detective Rux said. "Add that to her mention of having you killed in the parking garage of your Manhattan apartment and that's enough evidence for some serious jail time."

"Well, what are you doing to find her then?" Alec snapped, finally ending that unpleasant trip down memory lane.

"We've issued an arrest warrant and put out an APB for her car. We've also notified the airlines and Port Authority. If she tries to board a plane or train, we'll know about it." He shook his head slowly. It made me wonder if there was something else he wasn't telling me. "We consider her extremely dangerous," he said finally.

"Anna!" I shouted, suddenly. "She was supposed to

meet Valerie for dinner. I begged her not to go, but she wouldn't promise me."

"You knew Ms. Russell was here and you didn't call me?" It was Detective Rux's turn to be mad now. "Where are they supposed to meet?"

Alec answered for me. "Five Sisters. I already have a team in place in case she shows."

"What if she lied about where they're meeting?" I asked.

Alec tilted his head to one side. "Anna wouldn't lie to you, would she?"

"She certainly wouldn't be the first teenager to lie to her parents, now would she?" Detective Rux said sarcastically before bolting out of the room.

Alec pulled his hands through his hair. It was as if he hadn't even considered the possibility Anna wasn't telling the truth. He tapped the Bluetooth earpiece, "Anna, its Alec. Where are you? Call me."

He touched the button again. "I want to know where Anna is. Now. Find her." He touched the button one more time then turned toward me, his stare so intense it felt as though I would burst into flames any second.

"If anything happens to my daughter, Alec…" I dropped my head in my hands. "Please, you have to find her." In that moment nothing mattered but the safety of my daughter. Not Valerie, not Alec keeping things from me. Only Anna.

He sat beside me on the bed and pulled me back into the safety of his arms. "Don't cry, baby. She's going to be okay. We'll find her." He leaned back on the bed, his arms wrapped tightly around me as I tried to stop the flow of tears.

After a while, Alec spoke again. "Why did you tell Detective Rux we aren't dating?"

"Are we?" I asked, confused by his question.

"Are you in the habit of casual sex, Isabella?"

"No. Of course not."

He kissed me on the top of the head. "Well, neither am I."

I wrapped my arms tighter around him. Dating. Not casual sex. Not his latest fling, but his *girlfriend*. I was in a relationship with Mr. Control Freak, with Alec Payne. But did I still want to be after everything I'd learned recently?

"Payne," he said sharply and I knew he was no longer talking to me. He sat up quickly, bringing me with him. "Good work, Marcus. Yes. Go. Text the address to Detective Rux."

"You found her?"

"Yes. Marcus tracked the GPS in her car."

"Detective," Alec called out. Detective Rux rushed through the door. "We have an address. My head of security is sending it to you now."

"Is Ms. Russell with her?"

"I don't know yet. My team is on their way now."

"You better leave the police work to us, Mr. Payne. Ms. Russell is very dangerous. There's no telling what she'll do if she feels cornered." He looked down at his vibrating phone then raced toward the door.

Chapter Thirty One

"You can't be too mad at her, Isabella."

"And why not?" I folded my arms in protest. "I told her it wasn't safe. I asked her not to see Valerie, but she went anyway."

A smile crossed his face. "Like mother, like daughter, huh?"

"What's that supposed to mean?"

"Doesn't this sound even vaguely familiar?" His smile widened, but I didn't find humor in what he was saying. "I remember telling you it was too dangerous, asking you not to go to." He leaned forward and kissed me on the forehead. "She's just as stubborn as you are, baby."

I opened my mouth to object but closed it again. He was right. Anna was a lot like me. She insisted she'd be fine. I bet she even thought I was being too controlling. I frowned, my lower lip protruding, which Alec instantly bit.

"You're not pouting again, are you?" he said with a smile.

Under normal circumstances that might have made me smile too, but I wasn't in the mood for him right now. He'd kept information about the break-ins from me, and now that I knew Anna was safe I had to find out why. "If you knew Valerie was behind the break-ins at your office, why didn't tell me?"

His smile quickly faded. "I had no idea Valerie was involved, Isabella. Until yesterday I thought Charlee and Valerie were two different people."

"Why didn't you tell me *after* you found out you had been married to my best friend? Didn't you think I'd want to know that she was trying to hurt you too?"

"As far as I knew she wasn't trying to hurt me, Isabella. Do you know what she stole from my office?" he snapped.

"Information."

"Yes, that's right. She stole information. About you! The background check Marcus ran on you. Your client list. Even your credit report. Every detail I'd collected. She knew where to find you because of me. The mistakes of my past had come back to hurt you. How do you think that made me feel, Isabella? I failed, just like I had with my family. I was supposed to protect you but she got to you *because* of me!"

Silent tears rolled down my cheeks. The torment in Alec's eyes was too much to take. I hadn't even considered what Alec could be feeling about his unlikely connection. He had to know none of it was his fault. Didn't he?

I reached out to touch his arm, but he pulled out of my reach. "You didn't do this, Alec."

He didn't look at me, his hands still fisted in his hair, out of my reach.

"Valerie knew where I lived. And after thirteen years with the same company she even knew most of my clients. None of this is your fault, Alec. Not even the attacks. Those started long before I met you."

"You heard the detective. The attacks didn't escalate until after you met me. If only I'd left you alone."

"A couple of hours ago you were calling me your girlfriend. Now you're saying you wish you'd just left me alone. Is that what you want, Alec? You want me out of your life?"

"No, Isabella. God, no, that's not at all what I want." He sat down on the edge of the bed again, holding both my hands in his. "I was miserable when you left. There's something about you, this feeling deep inside, this need I have for you, it confuses me." A pained look crossed his face and he closed his eyes. "I was confused about why you left, about what I should do about it, about how it made me feel." He closed his eyes and took a deep breath. When he opened them again he continued. "I was mad, Isabella. Mad at you for leaving. Mad at myself for not going after you. And when Drew called and told me what happened…" He pulled me closer to him. "I was so afraid I'd never see you again. Afraid I'd never get to tell you how much you mean to me."

Abruptly, he released me and stood up, running his hands through his hair. "I love you, Isabella. I've loved you since the first time we met. I've tried to deny my feelings, to convince myself they aren't real, but when you left I couldn't deny it any longer." He sat back down and wrapped his arms around me. "I love you," he said again.

My mouth dropped open. I didn't know what to say. *Well, say something*, my inner voice pleaded. *Tell him you love him too*. I shook her off. I loved spending time with him and was definitely attracted to him. But did I love him? Did I even believe in love after all that had happened?

"I don't want to lose you again," Alec whispered.

I took a deep breath to steady my nerves, saying a silent prayer I could make him understand my feelings without hurting him anymore than I already had. I leaned in, placing a soft kiss on his lips. "I love being with you, Alec, but I'm afraid." The tension in his body had me wishing I could tell him what he wanted to hear, what I was incapable of saying, no matter how much I thought it could be true. "What I mean is, well, I loved Spencer with all my heart, and I thought he loved me too, but look how that ended."

"I'm not Spencer, Isabella. I'd never do that to you. I've been afraid to love again too after what happened to my parents and Hope, and then with Charlee." He shook his head, a pained look in his eyes. "But when I met you I realized how good life can be when you have someone to share it with."

"Alec, I'm scared."

"I'm scared too, baby."

"I need time."

He kissed me on the mouth. A hard, passionate kiss that spoke volumes about the torment I was putting him through, and it made my heart ache even more. "Take all the time you need. Just don't leave me again. Everyone I love leaves me." He pulled me close and wrapped his arms around me.

"I'm sorry, Alec. I shouldn't have left like I did. I promise I won't do that again."

He squeezed me tighter. "That'll do for now, baby." He kissed me again, only this time his kiss was soft.

My head was spinning from all that had happened the past couple of days, but most of all from the bomb Alec had just dropped. *Holy shit*. He loved me. He'd not only said it, he'd said it first. When I left the beach house and realized how much I missed him, how my heart ached for him, I thought maybe, just maybe it could be love. But I was too scared to tell him. It nearly killed me when I found out about Spencer's affair. Would I ever be able to put myself in the position to be hurt like that again?

• • • • •

Preston walked through the door of my hospital room, Anna in tow. "I want to speak with you," Alec said sharply, looking right at Anna. He grabbed ahold of her arm and pulled her out into the hall before she could say a word. The door closed behind them, and all I could hear was him yelling. A couple hours ago he'd told me I couldn't be too mad at her and all the while he was ready to explode. How did he do that? How had he managed to stay so calm and collected on the outside when he was anything but on the inside?

"Did you find Valerie?" I asked Preston, trying to take my mind off what was going on in the hall.

He shook his head. "I'm afraid not. She slipped out the back before we could reach her." Preston stared out the window, neither of us saying another word, the look on his face saying it all. She'd gotten away. Our lives were still in danger and he blamed himself. It saddened me to know he felt responsible too. None of it was his fault, either.

Alec walked back into the room with Anna by his side, his hand still firmly grasping her arm, her tear stained face red and blotchy. "I'm sorry, Mom," she whispered. "I shouldn't have lied to you. It was wrong. I put myself in danger and that was wrong too." Alec let go of her arm and she ran to my side. "I didn't believe she could do this, Mom, especially not to you." She buried her face against my shoulder. "But she just laughed about it. She said you deserved to die for what you'd done." I wrapped my arms around her, holding her as tight as I could, my heart breaking for my baby girl.

After Anna had finally calmed down, Alec insisted Preston drive her back to the hotel. "Don't let her out of your sight," he'd said before they left. He was so upset with her for lying to him, I thought his head was going to start spinning, but in reality he was more worried than mad. Valerie had managed to slip out the back door of the restaurant before the police could reach her. There was more to that story, something he was keeping from me, but it wasn't the time for probing, not about that anyway.

What I could ask him about was his conversation with Anna. I'd never seen her so subdued. Every time he looked at her, tears sprung to her eyes and she looked away, clinging to me as if her life depended on it. "What'd you say to Anna?" I finally asked.

Alec kissed me on the top of the head. "That's between me and Anna."

"You made her cry."

He shook his head. "I didn't hit her if that's what you're worried about."

"No, of course not." I reached up and touch his cheek. "It's just, well, don't you think you were pretty hard on her?"

"Not even a little. If she was my daughter, I'd have done a lot more than just yell at her. She lied to me. She lied to you. And she knowingly jeopardized her safety. That's just not acceptable. It's as simple as that." He kissed me again, on the cheek that time. "Now drop it before I take *you* over my knee."

I smiled, relieved his sense of humor had returned, even if it was only for a moment.

• • • • •

"Knock, knock," Dr. Leonard called out from the doorway.

"Shhh," I whispered, pointing at Alec. He hadn't gotten much sleep last night. Every time I moved he opened his eyes to check on me. I'd tried to convince him to go to the hotel with Anna and Preston, but he wouldn't hear of it. Not even with the new security team posted outside my door. He'd been spooked ever since he saw that picture from the hotel. "I'm not letting you out of my sight," he'd said. "Not until Charlee is off the streets."

"It's okay, baby. I'm awake."

Dr. Leonard smiled. "How about we get you two out of here?"

"Hell yes!"

"Tell me how you really feel, Izzy." Dr. Leonard laughed. "Seriously though, your labs and vitals look good, so I feel comfortable sending you home."

"Thank you, thank you, thank you," I said enthusiastically. She laughed again, knowing full well how much I hated hospitals.

"Is it safe for her to fly?"

"I'd much rather she take the short flight than the long car ride."

Shit. Dr. Leonard knew where we were staying. I just hoped I wasn't the one who told her. Nervously, I glanced at Alec, but he didn't seem the slightest bit phased by what she'd said. Good. It hadn't been me.

He climbed out of the bed. "Thanks for everything," he said extending his hand.

"Anytime, Alec, although I hope we don't have to do *this* again." She listened to my heart one final time and then hugged me goodbye.

Soon after I'd dressed the nurse was back to remove my IV's, discharge instructions in hand. I was lucky that Valerie had been interrupted before I sustained any real injury, other than the massive drug overdose that sent my heart into hyper drive. The nurse cautioned me about over stimulating my heart then sent me on my way. I was free and more than ready to go.

By the time we made it outside, storm clouds were threatening, a typical summer afternoon in Florida really, but I didn't care as the humidity was soothing to my overly dry skin. I took a deep breath, soaking it all in, my lungs expanding as the salty air passed through my nose. It was the familiar smell of home. I was excited to be going to the beach house, even with Alec and all his controlling tendencies. "Let's go home, baby," Alec whispered in my ear. And I couldn't help the smile that followed.

The flight was crowded with all six members of the security team aboard. "I'm not taking any chances," Alec said when he saw the frown on my face. I'd thought they were undercover police officers. I hadn't even considered that they worked for Alec. That was just what I needed, a constant reminder of how stupid my decision to leave the beach house had been. Somehow the near death experience seemed reminder enough.

Shortly after takeoff, I fell asleep, not waking until the wheels touched down in Sarasota. Preston and Marcus searched the airport, looking for any signs of danger before Alec let me get off the plane. As soon as he got the all clear from his staff, he escorted me down the ramp toward the waiting car, the rest of the security team close behind.

Alec helped me into the car, sliding in right behind me. Preston took his place behind the wheel and soon we were pulling away from the plane. I caught a glimpse of the security team as they filled the two black Escalades that were parked on the tarmac. One SUV sped ahead of the X6 Preston was driving, the other fell in behind us. Never in a million years had I imagined needing an entourage.

Chapter Thirty Two

The house seemed bigger somehow as we pulled around the fountain in the middle of the driveway. The ground was wet, evidence of a recent rain that had cleared, and a cool breeze was left in its wake. It passed over my legs, sending a shiver through me.

Alec put his arm around my waist. "Welcome home, baby," he said then kissed me on the lips. A soft, gentle kiss that made my knees buckle. He scooped me up and carried me through the front door.

The windows were open and the sound of the ocean surrounded me, that familiar sound of home. Being on the beach was all I could think about at that moment. "Let's go for a walk on the beach," I said suddenly.

Alec tilted his head to one side.

"Please, Alec. I've been cooped up for so long. I really need some fresh air."

"Okay, but I'm coming with you."

A half smile half smirk crossed my face. I was expecting a lecture on safety or something after just getting out of the hospital, so his answer surprised me.

He pulled me into his chest. "Is that a problem for you, Isabella?" He kissed me hard on the mouth.

My eyes widened, my heart rate increasing. There was no hiding my crimson cheeks then and I nervously bit my lip.

"We won't make it to the beach if you keep looking at me like that, baby."

I looked away, rolling my eyes as I did. Alec bent down and wrapped his arms around my legs, lifting me over his shoulder. "Alec!" He smacked me playfully on the butt. "Put me down!" I tried to sound annoyed but only ended up laughing.

"Am I amusing you?"

"Yes!" It was funny how much I'd missed his controlling ways. Even as much as I resisted them, there was something comforting in knowing Alec was in control.

Alec carried me all the way to the kitchen where Mrs. Peters was busy preparing dinner. "Don't mind us, Kim. I'm just getting some wine."

He pulled the bottle from the refrigerator, and when he turned around I could see the grin on Kim's face. I was so embarrassed. I wanted to object, to insist Alec put me down, but I didn't. The last thing I wanted right then was to make this any worse than it already was.

When we reached the patio, Alec finally put me down. Holding on to his shirt, I waited as the blood slowly returned to my body. Alec poured two glasses of wine, handing one to me, and then clasped his hand around mine. "Come with me."

"Where are we going?"

"You'll see." That wicked grin crossed his face, and suddenly I didn't care where he was taking me. He led me to the water's edge where we walked quietly along the shoreline, slowly sipping our wine, until I was totally lost in the sound of the ocean as the waves broke on the shore.

We started back toward the house and I noticed two chairs sitting near the waterline which hadn't been there an hour earlier. I paused, looking up at Alec, silently wondering when they'd gotten there. I'd given up asking how months ago.

"I thought you'd like to watch the sunset," Alec said, answering my unspoken question.

A smile crossed my face. He knew me so well. I threw my arms around his neck. "Oh, Alec, thank you."

He kissed the top of my head. "I love you, Isabella. I'd do anything for you."

After refilling my wine glass, Alec motioned for me to sit in one of the chairs. I shook my head. I'd been trapped in that hospital bed for days and was enjoying the feeling of the sand beneath my feet.

"Isabella, sit down," he said, his voice stern.

My cheeks heated and instinctively I looked away so he couldn't see the effect he had on me.

Alec grabbed my chin and tilted my head back until I was looking right at him. "Don't hide from me, baby."

I took a deep breath, his smell intoxicating me. My breathing increased, my insides started to tingle. He kissed me hard on the lips.

My knees giving out, I stumbled, spilling wine all down my shirt. "Shit!"

"Here, let me help you with that," Alec said. I could hear the humor in his tone. I shot him a dirty look, but that only made him laugh.

"My shirt. It's all wet."

"That's what you get," he admonished, as he took the glass out of my hand, preventing me from spilling the rest of it. "You should have sat down when I told you to."

Two towels rested on the back of one of the chairs. I snatched one off the chair in a mock huff before sitting down in it, doing my best to dry my shirt. When I'd finally given up, Alec handed me my glass, still laughing.

I took a long drink, draining what was left in the glass. "Are you laughing at me?"

"Yes. That's not problem for you, is it?"

"It's not a problem for me, Mr. Payne." I set the glass down in the sand. "But it might be for you."

Jumping up from where I was sitting, I moved quickly toward his chair. Climbing on his lap, one leg on each side of him, I grabbed his shirt and pulled him toward me, kissing him hard on the lips. He dropped his glass and ran his hands up my back, kissing me too, a deep, passionate kiss.

In one swift move, Alec lifted me off his lap, depositing me gently on the sand, my arms pinned above my head. "What were you saying about a problem?"

Pulling on my arms and kicking my legs, I tried to wiggle free but he tightened his grip, kissing me on the forehead, the nose, the chin. "Because this is definitely not a problem for me," he whispered against my lips.

I raised my head to kiss him but he moved just out of my reach. My insides were on fire, I needed to touch him. "Alec, let go." Tugging against his grip, I simultaneously bucked my hips trying to push him off me.

He let go of my wrists and straddled me, his knees buried in the sand. "Let's get this wet shirt off you." Sliding my cardigan over my shoulders he lifted my shirt over my head, dropping both in the sand. His eyes were fixed on mine, his stare intensifying as I squirmed beneath him. Pulling his shirt off, he dropped it next to me, too. His chiseled chest glistened in the fading sun.

I reached up to touch him, but he caught my hands, pinning my arms back onto the sand, kissing me in the process.

"Don't move," he warned as he took his hands off my wrists. Instinctively, I pulled my arms to my side.

With narrowed eyes Alec lifted my arms back above my head. "Don't. Move," he said again.

Alec ran a finger from my temple, down the side of my face, to my chin, slowly down my neck, between my breasts, circling my bellybutton as he moved toward the waistband of my pants.

Arching my back I moaned as I did my best to absorb the pleasure. My insides quickened as Alec trailed kisses along the same path his finger just took making me moan even louder. Bucking my hips, my sex rubbed against his growing erection.

"You're moving, Isabella."

"Stop teasing me."

"Oh, baby, I'm not teasing." He arched his eyebrows then leapt to his feet, dropping his pants in the sand.

Kneeling between my legs Alec ran his thumbs under the waistband of my pants and pulled, sliding my pants past my ankles, tossing them to the side, straddling me once more.

I moved my hands to the waistband of his boxer briefs and ran my finger along the edge as he'd just done.

Pulling my hand toward his mouth, he slid my middle finger inside, his tongue circling my long digit. "Do you ever do what you're told, Isabella?"

After two weeks away from Alec, his touch was like fire burning me up inside. I closed my eyes, arching my back, absorbing every ounce of pleasure. "Alec," I panted, my insides quickening.

Slow down, Izzy, he hasn't even touched you yet, my inner voice snapped. I took a deep breath, doing my best to calm my screaming libido.

"You are so sexy, baby. I'm going to take you. Right here, right now." In one swift move, he was lying on top of me, spreading my legs with his. Poking his thumb through the lace in my panties he ripped them off, tossing the useless fabric onto the sand with the rest of my clothes before freeing his erection from his boxer briefs.

He slid a finger inside me. "Ahhh," I moaned loudly.

Pulling his finger out he said, "You are so wet, baby." *No,* my libido screamed. *Don't stop.*

Alec rubbed the head of his erection against my sex, pushing the tip inside me. I moved my hips to meet him, but he pulled back. Leaning down, he kissed me, a deep passionate kiss, his tongue finding mine, twisting, turning, leaving me breathless when he pulled away.

His hands moved between my breasts along the fabric of my bra, pulling it down until they popped out. I arched my back, moaning even louder still. My nipples hardened as he rolled them between his finger and thumb, taking one in his mouth then the other, gently tugging with his teeth.

"Alec! Please. I need to feel you inside me."

"Not until you come, baby."

I bucked my hips, begging him to touch me again. Alec flicked my nipple with this tongue, trailing his finger on my inner thigh, back toward my sex, before slipping it back inside me again.

"Ahhh!" I screamed, my insides quickening as my release hit, unable to resist any longer.

Passion burned in Alec's eyes. He rubbed the tip of his erection against my sex again, only this time he entered me, moving slowly at first as I adjusted to his fullness. Picking up speed, he quickly found his rhythm. I moved my hips to meet his, wanting him more than I ever imagined I could. I dug my nails into his flesh as he buried himself deep inside me, hitting that special spot over and over again until I was begging for release a second time.

"Come for me, Isabella. Come for me again."

His words were my undoing. My insides quickened as my body unraveled around him, his release soon following.

Kissing me softly on the lips, Alec eased himself out of me, collapsing beside me on the sand, his arm draped around my waist.

"Alec, that was incredible." I turned my head so I could see his face. He was propped up on his elbow, his head resting in his hand, an ear to ear grin on his face.

Leaning forward he kissed me again. "Yes. It was."

After tucking himself back inside his underwear, Alec grabbed our clothes. "Put this on," he said handing me his shirt before sliding his pants back on. I lay still, not wanting to take my eyes off him for even a second. "Isabella, put it on." His eyes moved from me to the shirt I was holding then back again.

Reluctantly, I sat up and adjusted my bra then dusted the sand off my body before pulling his shirt on. Alec helped me to my feet so I could put my pants back on too. I tightened the string around my waist, and when I looked up Alec was standing in front of me, beads of sweat still covering his chest.

I reached up and touch his toned muscles and Alec wrapped his arm around my waist, pulling me in to him. His husky voice sent an unexpected wave of pleasure through me. "I love you, baby."

I looked down at his feet, his sexy, sand covered feet, but Alec wasn't having it. He grabbed my chin, lifting my face as he'd done before then kissed me softly on the lips. "You, Isabella. I. Love. You."

Finally, Alec sat down on the sand taking me with him. The clouds had completely cleared, revealing an amazing red-orange sunset. We sat side by side, his arm around my shoulders, my arms around his waist, silently watching as the sun faded below the water. I leaned against him, realizing how much I loved being next to him.

"I love you, Isabella," he said again then kissed me softly on the lips. "And I want to spend the rest of my life proving it to you."

Closing my eyes, I snuggled up next to him, feeling safe and happy and confused by how much he meant to me after such a short time. As I sat there, wrapped in his arms, I realized how much I loved this man. Mr. Control Freak, my control freak.

"I love you too, Alec Payne."

Contact HD Kelley at:

Email: **me@authorhdkelley.com**

Website: **www.authorhdkelley.com**

Facebook: **www.facebook.com/AuthorHDKelley**

OTHER BOOKS BY HD KELLEY

Betrayed by Love Series
Shattered Dreams
Broken Promises (Winter 2016)

USF College Series (Coming Soon)

www.greenwaypublishing.com